My Name Is Ben

Karl Bullock

For Amy
She always believed I should write a book.
Thank you for over forty years of love, encouragement, and support!

Prologue

The room had been made small and as bland as it could be. The walls were painted an off-white, the single door was plain, constructed of unfinished wood as was the floor, with no paint or varnish. The only lights in the room were two candles on opposite walls. In the center were two benches also of unfinished wood, made simply as one could be and still be called a bench, and between them and off to the side a bit sat a simple small end table. That was it. No pictures, no other furniture - nothing. The entire room was the epitome of the term "nondescript".

The benches faced each other about five feet apart. On one bench sat Thomas Reed. He was dressed much like the room – nondescript. Dark woolen pants, simple black belt, a white cotton shirt, and black semi-dress shoes with black socks. The only other thing he had on him was his wallet in his right back pocket – no pen, no jewelry, no watch – nothing else. Tom had planned this moment for years, so he was understandably nervous and was picking at a place on one of his fingers that he notoriously chewed on when he was thinking. He just sat there waiting.

After about five minutes, he heard five loud beeps on the other side of the door, and he sat up straight with both hands in his lap. Seconds later there was a man standing before him, holding a small walking stick, and looked to be right in the middle of a sentence when the realization set in, then a slow look of bewilderment appeared on his face, and he looked at Tom with shock.

"What has just transpired?"

"Please, sir, sit down," Tom said as calmly as he could, "and I will gladly explain it to you. The first thing you need to know is that you are not in any danger."

The man paused, looked around for a second, then sat down slowly, with an understandable look of concern and yes, fear, but he sat and again said, "Please, I pray you….tell me what has transpired".

"Sir, my name is Tom. Again, you are safe, so try not to be concerned until I have explained the situation to you. First, what is your name?"

The man sighed, folded his hands in his lap and said, "My name is Ben."

The hairs on the back of Tom's neck stood up…..

Chapter 1

Star Trek. It only ran for three seasons, and was actually canceled because of low ratings. But the iconic characters it produced, and the futuristic visions contained in its story lines became very popular once in syndication, even though the story lines were campy and the acting was almost satirical. The movies, additional television series in syndication, and of course the merchandising dollars that it spawned made it one of the most successful entertainment franchises in history. Even now, fifty years later, the name Star Trek produces immediate images of Captain Kirk, Mr. Spock, "Bones", Sulu, and the rest of the gang that are immediately recognizable, along with such catchphrases as "I need more time, Captain", and the inevitable "Beam me up, Scotty", even though that exact phrase was never really said in the series. But, it was this last phrase that has fascinated me since I first saw one of the movies when I was young.

Now, the notion of teleportation is not just fascinating, it's filled with sticky issues. The method portrayed in the series shows a character disappearing, molecule by molecule, only to reappear on some nearby planet arriving, again, molecule by molecule until, voilà, teleportation. Here's the problem: The only real way to transfer an organism is to copy it, then reassemble it, bit by bit, at the destination without needing to tear apart the original. You then have both the copy at the destination, and the original at the origin. Now, you can't just have two people of completely identical DNA walking around because after, well, any number of "copies", it tends to get real messy. Not only that, they become immediately different because the experiences at the time of the transfer diverge. Just watch the movie "Muliplicity" and you might begin to get the idea. Suffice it to say, the problems quickly dwarf the convenience.

So, the only way for this to feasibly occur, is to transfer the duplicate to the destination, then destroy the original. Funny how they don't address this in the TV series! Assume you want to "teleport" to another location. You step in the transporter knowing you're about to die, but you'll still live on - memories, bad breath, body odor and all - at the destination. If you design the destruction mechanism so you simply go to sleep quickly, it's painless. Now come the legal problems. You, the transporter operator, just killed a man! The lawyers would all get rich, and you'd quickly get poor, not to mention most likely incarcerated. Scratch that idea. I hate lawyers.

There was, however, one episode of Star Trek that was also fascinating. In the movie "The Voyage Home", the crew travels back in time from the twenty-third century to 1986 in order to pick up a whale to save the earth. Don't ask – it was humorous, but also pretty cheesy. They did so by traveling faster than the speed of light, which supposedly changes how time operates allowing them to travel backwards in time. Einstein would have a big problem with this. But, there's another theory that, by taking advantage of wormholes and black holes, one might be able to, at a minimum, peer back in time, and possibly move back in time. Copying something from back in time to the present would then become possible by applying both "Star Trek" methods. If you could "look back" in time, you should certainly be able to copy something from there to here. Putting something back there, however, would be really problematic, especially when you take into account the enormous effects that would have on changing history. Theoretically, then, one way teleportation through time is the only practical way to "travel" through time, and I could see how it might be possible.

This is where I spent the last thirty or so years of my life. So, now here I am in my almost-ready-to-retire years, I'm playing around with this method, and guess what? I've done it – I think....

Chapter 2

When I was twelve years old my Mom bought a complete set of World Book Encyclopedias. Kids in the present day don't know what it was like to explore the pages and pages of glossy photographs and articles about everything under the sun. I spent several days going through each one, many times sitting cross-legged on the floor by the shelves Mom had chosen to store these treasures, fascinated by some of the articles, bypassing others which didn't hold my interest. Sometimes I'd just pick a random volume and thumb through the articles. As I said, I spent several days going through these until one afternoon I picked up the "Q-R-S" volume and began to thumb through it. About a third of the way through there was an article on 'Radio'. It was somewhat interesting, because it showed the inside of a radio station, which I'd never seen, and went on to describe how radio broadcasting worked. In those days, radio was king. TV was around, of course, but kids my age had a radio because nobody in my neighborhood could afford to have more than one TV in the house, so if we wanted our own entertainment, radio was the best option. Now, as I said, the article was somewhat interesting, so I spent a little time reading it, but then went on to the next article. The title of that article was "Radio, Amateur"

Now, I'd never heard of that, and my first thought was '*I can have my own radio station?*' The short answer was "yes", but I quickly found out that one thing that was forbidden was broadcasting. What? Then what good was it? But, there was a picture of Joe America sitting beside an array of equipment with a microphone in his hand and a telegraph key on the table, and after spending a few minutes reading, I found out it was person-to-person communications and that the other person could be literally anywhere in the world.

Intrigued, the article mentioned a national organization, the American Radio Relay League, where one could hopefully obtain more information, so I wrote to these folks in Connecticut and got a list of resources, none of which I could afford (my allowance was $1.50 per week, so it would take a couple of weeks to afford even the cheapest book). But, as it turned out, many of these were available in libraries. On our next trip to town I had Mom drop me by the library while she shopped, which, as a library science major she was happy to do, and I found and proceeded to check out several of these books that someone had donated. Loaded with arms full of reading material, for the next several days I devoured all the info I could until it was time to return these materials, and I grabbed another arm full for the next two weeks. Back and forth I'd go each week, returning one set of books, and grabbing another set, then starting over with the first set again. Eventually, my name was the only one on the check-out cards, but it wasn't like anyone else was waiting on them.

To get "on the air", you had to obtain a license from the Federal Communications Commission, which meant you had to learn Morse Code and pass a test of sending and receiving one minute of text at a speed of five words per minute (the examiner would send five minutes of text and you had to have one continuous minute of perfect copy), then pass a written test on elementary radio theory and rules and regulations. The trouble was, I didn't know how to get tested. So, I bugged my Dad enough that he went ahead and bought me a shortwave receiver so I could at least listen in to what the guys were doing and saying. Two years later, we moved to another town where I found someone who already had his radio license and could give me the test. The first thing he did was test me on Morse Code, which I passed. Then, he ordered the written test materials from the FCC, and loaned me a book to study until they came in. When they arrived, he filled out the papers, had me sign a bunch of stuff, then proceeded to administer the written test. About six weeks later I came in from school one day and noticed the cork bulletin board my Mom used to put notes, reminders, schedules, etc. It was completely cleared off except for a small form she'd pinned to the center. It was my license! I, Thomas Reed, was a Ham Radio Operator – sort of. You see, the problem was, I could only listen. I had a receiving set, but no transmitter. So, again, I bugged my Dad, complained to my friends, and basically moaned and groaned until one day, my friend, the one who'd given me the test, told me he was going to Nashville that weekend and said he'd find me something to transmit with. Sunday he came back with a small transmitter, and the whole world had to watch out, because "Tom" was on the air!

Now, the relevance of this is that interest in one form of technology will naturally spawn interest in other forms of related technology. As a Ham Radio operator, obviously electronics was in the picture. I was interested in stories, movies, and I was a voracious reader, so my new interest in technology naturally meant that science fiction would soon appear on my radar. In those days technology was all about the space program, so when I discovered Star Trek, it became permanent on my watch list. But it wasn't until much later on, when the movie "The Voyage Home" came on that something clicked in my mind. "Hmmm...", I thought. "Is time travel possible?". As a result of this 'perfect storm' of interests, engineering seemed a logical pursuit, so that's the direction I headed when college came around. I had set my sights on working in the space program, so off to the University I went to study electrical engineering and computers. But, one semester, I took a course in physics, and part of that course touched on Einstein's theories about time and space, and suddenly the Star Trek movie came back into the forefront of my inquisitiveness. I remember the day I

5

re-played that movie. When the movie was over, it was time to go to the college library and do some investigating.

So, here I am one day, sitting in my college counselor's office, changing my major from electrical engineering to physics. He was telling me how difficult a degree in physics was, making sure that I knew what I was getting into, until I reminded him that the dropout rate in engineering was eighty percent, and that I was not leaving because I couldn't handle the curriculum, but because my interests had changed. Besides, NASA's budget had been cut, the Apollo program was gone and they used up all the parts for a sort-of space station, the Shuttle program was going, but it looked like it was near-space only and suddenly the space exploration program was turning into something I wasn't sure I wanted to be a part of, so there. I kept working on my minor in computer science, but began working on my master's degree in physics studying the latest theories of space, time, particles – the whole enchilada. I never really forgot about my time travel idea, but it got put on the back shelf behind the other work. Then, one day, it came right back up front!

Chapter 3

It all started with a conversation I was having with a representative of The Defense Advance Research Products Administration, or DARPA, I met who was visiting the campus. I was in the pre-pre-selection stages of my Master's thesis in Physics and was really having trouble coming up with a project. I wanted something of substance, but at the same time something that might not have been done before. After all, either go big or go home, right? Anyway, this guy from DARPA, Tony, was on campus looking at promising students to recruit into the program, and I was one of a group of five students he took to dinner one night at an upscale restaurant near the campus. As I found out later, he was picking our minds about what we wanted to do with our lives, and he casually mentioned that he understood I was a fan of Star Trek.

"Well," I told him, "Not sure you'd call me a 'fan', but apart from the sometimes questionable plots, there was some really interesting science the series writers came up with," and I proceeded to give him my thumbnail sketch of how the transporter would work.

"You really think something like that's possible?" he asked.

"Transporting something, or someone, from point to point?" I said. "It's really sticky. The real problem transferring living organisms is in needing to destroy the original. Plus, copies of a living organism? There's all kinds of problems there. Now, inanimate objects – sure – maybe. It's just an interesting thought experiment".

I thought that was the end of it because he went on to ask questions of the others, and we had a pretty lively discussion about some of their ideas and the possibility/probability of theirs, and the ramifications, or even the point, of a couple of them. It was all very interesting, but all very theoretical. But, as we were leaving, he asked me if I had a few minutes. I said '*sure*' and he offered to drive me back to my apartment (since I'd come with a friend). So we bade the others goodnight, and when we got in his car he started peppering me with questions about how something like a transporter might work.

After about an hour, Tony suggested we meet the next day. Since it was Friday night and thus no classes the next day, I said '*sure, no problem*'. When he came by my apartment to pick me up the next day, he told me to pack for a couple of days overnight stay and that he was flying me to Washington to talk to a colleague who was interested in something similar. Wait, really! Well. Color me curious. He promised to pay all expenses, have me back in plenty of time for classes Monday, and even give me a private tour of the DARPA lab. How could I resist?!

The next thing I know, I'm in the 'inner sanctum' with Tony, three of their top scientists and a gentleman who didn't say much, but was clearly above all their pay grades. After I explained my crazy ideas and answered a lot of 'what if' questions, Mr. Secret (not his real name) suddenly took over. He asked if I would be interested in pursuing the project.

"What, you mean for real?" I asked.

"Yes. With our backing, including the paying off of your student debts if the project has possibilities".

"Well", I said, "how will you know what the odds of success are?"

"Aren't you looking for a thesis project?"

"Why, yes, I am. How did...."

"We have already talked to your professors," he said. "They also think you have promise and have agreed, if we sanction this project, that your thesis will not only cover this possibility, but we'll donate a sizable amount to their department's equipment budget. The caveat is that your thesis, if it has merit, will be classified, and you will lose the ability to publish it."

Now my head was really spinning. "What will I do after I graduate with no publication to point to?"

"You'll come to work for us. We'll start you off at $45,000 per year with an expense account, and your student debts will be paid."

I thought about that for a minute. "What if the thesis makes no sense, or if I decide I just can't do it, or if I want to just do something else?"

"You have the perfect right to change your mind. But if you do, all the incentives disappear. In reality, you'll be no worse off than you are now. But, and this is important, you'll have to sign a letter of intent, a non-disclosure agreement, and a transfer of intellectual property on any idea that has to do with this project. As long as you don't proceed with this project for a period of ten years after graduation, you'll be free to do anything you want if you do something else for whatever reason."

I was stunned. This had all been a fun intellectual exercise until just this morning, but now these guys were talking to me as if this were actually possible and they wanted me to show them how.

"So, that's it?" I asked. "I write the thesis, you evaluate it, and if it succeeds everyone wins. If not, I go on as if nothing happened?

"That's it," he said. "The only real danger is that if it's not feasible, it might not qualify as your college thesis, so you may have to take a chance and do double work, but that's your decision."

"OK," I said. "Let's say I do this and all these things fall in place. You accept my thesis and give me a job here. What would I be doing?"

"Well, obviously, you'd primarily be tasked with actually making this thing work."

"And, if I fail at that?"

"Then we'll call it a wash. The project will still be classified, but you'll have your time here at DARPA as a resumé item. That'll help you anywhere you go. But, even with current technology, we know this is going to be a long term project, so we're willing to go the distance."

I sat back in my chair and did one of those quiet whistles as I exhaled. I know this is the government talking to me, and that scared me. I had heard many stories of how people were shafted by government agencies, or how things just didn't pan out like they thought it would, so my antennae were up looking for a loophole. Then, I asked the only question I knew to ask.

"Will all these stipulations be on paper? In other words, is this a voice agreement, or a contractual agreement? Can I have an attorney look at any agreement?"

He looked at the rest of the group and quipped, "This kid's good!" Then back at me. "You find an attorney you like. We'll vet him to see if he can keep a secret, then we'll prepare a contract for him to review. If we work out the details, it'll be a contractual agreement between you and DARPA."

"Including the funds for the Physics department at the college?"

"Of course," he said.

"And I can back out any time?"

"Yes."

"How much time do I have?"

"Take the week," he said. "Your college advisor is aware of our proposal, and he can help you with the construct of your thesis if you wish, though we don't want you divulging any technical specifics of how the project would work. He won't be able to read your thesis, but has agreed that if we approve the end product, it will result in an 'A' on your thesis."

"This all sounds too good to be true," I said, "and you know what they say about that!"

"Yes," he said. "But sometimes they're wrong." He leaned forward and looked me straight in the eye, and said, "Mr. Reed, Don't pass up a great opportunity. The worst case is you end up proving it can't be done and it'll cost you a few extra months to come up with another thesis. Your advisor's good with that outcome as well. Mr. Reed, this is one of those once in a lifetime offers. So, do yourself a favor. Give it a serious chance. Here's a number where you and your attorney can reach me. Have your attorney give me a call to get the process started. Call me if you have any questions, and I'll contact you at five p.m. your time a week from Friday for your answer."

He handed me a card with a telephone number on it, then stood up and the rest of the group stood as well. He shook my hand and said, "Thank you for coming. Tony here will see you out." and he and the others left.

I walked out of the building in a daze, got in the vehicle with Tony, and we didn't say much for a few minutes. I was lost in thought, my mind reeling on what had just happened. Tony knew exactly what was going on.

"Look, Tom. You have a lot to think about. You have two weeks to decide, so just let it go for now. Let's go get a bite to eat. We have a couple of hours before the flight back, so just put it in the back of your mind for now. You'll figure it out."

I looked at him. "You guys really think I can do this?"

"We don't know," he said. "But we're willing to take a chance."

So we went to Pizza Hut.

Then I flew home.

Chapter 4

The next few days I did what I do best. Research. I started with an attorney. My family had one that Dad had used for his will, but I'd never really had a need for one. But, it was a starting place, so I called my Dad's attorney and gave him the gist of what I was looking to do. Government. Can't talk much about it. Absolute secrecy. You know, was he willing/capable? He basically passed, but he knew a friend of his from law school that was in Virginia that had handled government contracts before, and had once been in the military in the JAG Corps, so he gave me his contact.

I had a pre-law buddy of mine look him up and I was sufficiently impressed to give him a call. Since DARPA had agreed to pay the legal fees, should I decide to go forward, I gave him the contact at DARPA, then I went on to other research.

I looked up Mr. Secret at DARPA and, as expected, there wasn't much on him. My buddy looked him up for any legal problems and, once again, nothing. Tony, on the other hand, had been around. Like my attorney, he'd been in the military, Air Force, and had done a lot of work in scientific circles. He wasn't famous or anything, and I got the impression that was on purpose. I guessed that in his own world he was fairly well known, but not so much publicly. Again – no red flags.

Then, DARPA itself. It was an impressive organization. I once again had my friend do some legal research on DARPA and, apart from the normal legal entanglements any large organization might have, and the usual suspects who didn't like anything government (yeah, I get that!), they didn't appear to have any issues where they'd nailed anyone to the wall, though I had to keep in mind that everything was done on a non-disclosure basis. I checked in with some of the USENET groups beginning to appear online, and I dropped into to a physics online bulletin board and just dropped a couple of questions like "anybody every have any dealings with DARPA?" and "Anybody ever shafted by the guys at DARPA?". The responses I got had to do primarily with personnel and anti-government/anti-military issues rather than '*they told me a bunch of lies and took my intellectual property*' type stuff, and a couple of the responses I got were worded in such a way that I could see why they didn't work there any more. But, again, nothing that set off any major red flags.

On Thursday my attorney called and told me he had a document for me to look over. I had him express mail it to me and a couple of days later I was looking at an annotated contract he'd prepared. He'd explained all the legalese and underlined a couple of clauses that were pretty specific about penalties. Also attached was DARPA's non-disclosure agreement, which was filled with '*you better not, or else*' language. I took the night and read it, then called him back the next day. After a few minutes of discussion, I just asked "What's your advice?"

"Well, I can't decide for you if you can actually pull this off, but from what I've determined, if you can't, or won't, as long as you don't talk out of school, it's a pretty good deal. Also, if you decide to bail after signing you won't be able to do anything on this project or one similar for ten years, so if you think it'll actually work, you either turn this down and do it yourself, or you go with DARPA."

"One thing that keeps popping up in my head," I said, "is my Dad telling me that something appears too good to be true, it likely is. This looks too good to be true."

"Let me say this," he said. "I've seen some government contracts that were too good to be true, and there are red flags all over those kind of deals, but people are so blinded by what they perceive the upside to be they ignore them and are sorry later. This is not one of those deals. If this thing you're working on has military applications, there's no telling what it will be worth to the government. Here's the second part of that. If you do it on your own, and it has military applications, particularly something they consider to be too valuable to let the rest of the world in on, they'll simply classify it and you'll be out in the cold anyway. Do what you want, Tom, but on paper this looks like a solid deal, and I'm not aware of anything like this where DARPA has '*shafted*', as you say, anyone before. Their reputation, for a government agency, is not that bad."

"I see," I said. "So what you're saying is that if I think this will work, this is a good deal".

"I'm saying that I don't know what you're doing, but they're bankrolling the project and paying you a premium to develop it. I'm guessing you'd be hard pressed to find that kind of support anywhere else, and since they were first in, they'd probably block any military contractors from doing it for you. I have no legal problems with what they're proposing. So, at this point, it's a personal decision for you."

I thanked him, told him to prepare the final document and express it to me, and send me the bill. I thought about it all weekend, and on Tuesday I received the paperwork from the attorney. I looked it all over, decided I didn't have any more questions, so I just waited for Friday. Sure enough, Mr. Secret called, I said 'Y*es*', and expressed the contract, the NDA, and the attorney's bill to him, and he disappeared. What I did get a few days later was a check for $3,000.00 as a 'signing bonus', something we'd never talked about. So, my friends and I had a pizza party that night, and I paid off both my telephone and cable TV bills for the first time in two years!

Now. What in the Wide, Wide World of Sports am I going to put in that thesis?

Chapter 5

DARPA

Eighteen months later, research done, paper sent to DARPA, and all my classes finished, I'm sitting in my apartment one afternoon when who shows up at my door but Tony - completely unannounced with instructions to "Pack your stuff, you're headed to Arlington."

For the next couple of days I closed out my business on campus. The Dean had already received the call from DARPA, and the last grade necessary from my Masters was in place – a nice "A" in the thesis, subject undisclosed. The only down side was that I would not be going to graduation. I'd be working. The diploma would be mailed, but for all intents and purposes, I now had a master's degree in Applied Physics, with a minor in Computer Science, and instant employment at one of the top research labs in the world. DARPA paid a moving company to pack up my stuff (there wasn't really much – they got it all in a 14 foot trailer) and hauled it to Virginia. The real surprise was that we flew back to DC on the DARPA private jet. Man, was that nice! Suddenly I felt two different extremes: I felt really important because these guys were rolling out the red carpet. But, at the same time, I was deathly afraid of failure. That's not a nice roller coaster to be on, but the nice flying accommodations didn't hurt!

On arrival they gave me two weeks to get settled in, so I found an apartment not far from the facility, called the moving company and had them bring all my stuff over, then called my parents, told them I was coming, and spent the rest of the two weeks at home. While it was disappointing I couldn't tell them all I'd be working on, they were thrilled that their 'boy' had graduated with honors and scored a cushy job in a government research lab. And while I would like to have told tell them what I was doing, it was OK, they were just proud, and that was enough.

Then, back at Arlington - my first days. It was intimidating. There was lots of paperwork to be filled out, and some really intimidating orientations on security and access, and then I was told I was to head the research project but had no real authority, meaning I could complain about somebody's performance but couldn't hire or fire. That was OK, I didn't really want the personnel headaches anyway. But, a few days later they brought in candidates for evaluation, and they were all smarter than me, or at least I thought so. How was I going to lead this bunch?

We finally selected a small but brilliant group. Then there was the initial lab setup. Based on my thesis, they'd estimated what lab resources I would need and stocked it very well. The computer system assigned to us was similar to the one at college, so I set that up myself, all within their security guidelines, of course.

Finally, after getting everyone settled in a few days later, we had our first official meeting. I was, by far, the most nervous one in the room, but the people I was working with were super nice and helpful so it didn't take long for us to develop a rapport and we were quickly able to get down to business. Everyone had the same security level, so nothing was off limits as far as what we could discuss and which direction the project could head in. So the first discussion began and it was lively. I was feeling better.

There was a design criteria. The military wanted to be able to send objects anywhere in the world. Imagine, for instance, you needed to bomb a building in Iran. Instead of sending aircraft on an hours long journey where they might be shot out of the sky, or have equipment problems, you just transport an explosive device into the building and blow it up. Or, suppose you needed to have video of an event in North Korea. Just transport a miniature satellite-enabled camera to the top of some building or the ceiling corner of some room and watch it in living color. This was going to be a daunting task, and it would not come easy or soon. But, I had been given assurances by the powers at DARPA that they were willing to go the distance.

But, the really big question everyone wanted to know was, "Can we send a human being"? I had discussed this with Tony in our first meeting, as well as in the DARPA meeting where I was courted, but apparently they still wanted to know if it could be done. So, we would start with inanimate objects. How could we do that?

Our first job was to find a way to scan in the molecular structure of an object and store that information so we could later recreate it at another location.

A lot of research went in molecular scanners, and as it turned out DARPA was already doing research on this idea, so we aligned ourselves with that group. Around 2011 information about the ability to identify a single molecule out of billions was leaked to the trade press. That ability, which we had been using for years to do rudimentary molecule mapping of a substance, had led to the real innovation when that technology was eventually married to a supercomputer with the ability to scan and store enormous amounts of information in a relatively short period of time. Suddenly, the leap in technology we'd needed to do all the computing necessary was in place. Then, the team was able to book some time on the molecular scanning research project and we scanned in the molecular makeup of a pencil. It's a rather complicated item, though seemingly simple. It contains lead, wood, metal, rubber, ink, paint – all differing items that would have to be recreated to produce a duplicate. A separate team was initiated to do further development on molecular scanners for our purposes, and we went on to focus on the next item.

Once we have the makeup of an item, how do we reproduce it? The Law of Conservation of Matter states that matter can neither be created nor destroyed, but merely changes states. Liquid to ice, back to liquid, to vapor and back, etc. But, what if we want to get more involved? The first thing you need is matter. It can literally be anything, but it would have to be 'reassembled' into a different configuration. I recalled how in Genesis 2:7 the Bible stated that "God formed man from the dust of the ground". How about that? Molecular reorganization and assembly! So, that's the tact we took.

By this time work had also been done on a way to build things at the molecular level, so we obviously wanted to get a bit deeper than that. The goal was to take, literally, a pile of dirt and turn it into something else. Kind of a modern day alchemy process, only really expensive and with supercomputers. The team DARPA had formed just to bring up a molecular re-assembler into being had made significant progress.

Marrying the two projects up, scanning and re-assembly, interfacing them with the supercomputer DARPA had provided, making the technology work, all took many long days, nights and weekends, until in one night we did the unimaginable. We replicated a pencil, complete with tooth marks on the wood, and a small missing piece of the eraser. It wrote perfectly.

All of this was highly classified, as you might imagine. If we succeeded in making the project larger, the implications were enormous. A year later we finished a crash project in enlarging the capabilities of both the imager and the assembler to the point that by the first of the following year we could reproduce larger, more complex items. That done, DARPA rolled further development into a different team composed of the two teams we'd brought on board, and tasked us with replicating biologics. That was a whole other story!

The problem with replicating a biologic is that a living organism is never completely still. A pencil will just sit there until you move it. But, a biologic always has moving parts – blood, heart, lungs (or gills, depending), not to mention a myriad of other juices in constant flow. The first few attempts we made were, shall we say, very disappointing. Visions of "The Fly" came into mind, but much more disturbing! We just couldn't see any way to make that work until I hit on an idea I got from reading about the CERN Supercollider and theories about how it might be able to open up a worm hole. What if, then, we could open a worm hole to a point in the past? How would that help? Well, not much, unless you could open it for a microsecond, then re-open it at the same point in time and just put that whole open/close, open/close process in a loop so that the object was perfectly still locked in a single microsecond. If you could then scan that object as you observed it, and then replicate in a similar time just a few seconds later, the object would just 'appear'.

With all the 'moving parts' to this project, we were managing the different parts simultaneously. A few years ago there was a news item about how the Large Hadron Collider, the CERN Supercollider, had a 'magnet quench' that placed it down for repairs for a year. That article is true. The only part they didn't tell, was that I was the one who caused it. The U.S. Government had leased time on the LHC for the purpose of determining if a small worm hole could be opened up at a point in the recent past, then immediately shut back down. There was....a small glitch....

Anyway, after our first attempt, and the repairs to the LHC were completed, we took another bite at the apple. After a complete rewrite of the software that controlled the process, early one January we were able to do just that – open then immediately close a worm hole into the recent past. That opening of the worm hole allowed us to peer into that time for just that instant, and while it was all very exciting, it wasn't something you could actually look at. It was only detectable on our instruments, but it was there. A month later, we opened the hole, and produced a one-second loop of that period in the past where we were able to photograph a wristwatch that was off by two minutes – the length of the time we'd gone in the past. Over the next several weeks, we married our supercomputer to the interfaces at CERN via a dedicated highly-secure data link and began, when we could book time safely, experimenting on opening and closing the loops at a time and location of our choice. We still had a couple of glitches, including one we never really understood, but at least we didn't crash the LHC again!

We finally got the software to a point where we were confident that it was working properly. The folks at CERN couldn't see what we were doing, but essentially we had that worm hole opened up at our research facility in the countryside outside Arlington, and the results were spectacular. Once we could do that on a regular basis, we brought in the molecular scanner and scanned that same pencil, only twenty minutes in the past. Then we fed it into the Assembler. We knew reassembling the pencil took about five minutes, so we opened a portal five minutes and five seconds in the past, and instructed the Assembler to replicate it through the portal. Five seconds later, as the Assembler was still working, the pencil appeared in front of us!

NOW. We took everyone's favorite biologic – a cockroach – and once we had the issues worked out, we did the same procedure, only this time the process took about twelve minutes. As soon as we started the assembly, the cockroach appeared in front of us. Over the next weeks, we progressed from cockroach to mouse, rabbit, dog, even a chimp, as we learned how to manipulate the process.

But, here was the problem. Now we had two of everything! While quantum physics postulates matter can exist two places at the same time, we were not going to find out what happened if that actually occurred in these instances, so we were careful to keep each of the two specimens completely separate, until someone realized it wasn't actually the same matter, but a duplicate of existing matter! But, going forward, if we kept replicating biologics, that could get messy. So, we abandoned further replications until we pondered the implications.

After many meetings, arguments, discussions, and research, it was determined that replicating humans, or even other biologics, from anywhere on earth to anywhere else on earth was just too dangerous and had too many involved implications to be feasible. But, and this was a big one, it might be possible to transfer someone from an earlier time to present day, particularly if we only chose individuals who were deceased. The problem with that is that the further back in time you go, the less control you have over the wormhole "window", meaning that one would have to know exactly when and where an individual was, and even then, precisely timing the transfer would be problematic. In the end, it was decided the only way to do this would be to load the identity of an individual, along with all the specific time/place information we could get into a database, and write the software to look through those parameters in order to "lock on" to the individual you wanted. Even then, it would take multiple passes through the time/place window to find one of the times the software could actually perform the transfer with any degree of accuracy. But, in the end, none of this fit the parameters of the project as desired by DARPA.

So we arranged a demonstration for the military and the DARPA brass. We had them construct a small explosive device in a warehouse in Colorado and give us the physical parameters of it as well as the exact location. Then we issued a command to the LHC to copy the device and replicate it to the test area where we were in rural Virginia. Once it appeared, we notified the folks in Colorado and they disabled the device on their end. I then pressed a button on a remote control and was rewarded with an impressive explosion just a few hundred feet from where all the military brass was sitting. After a few minutes of phone calls where they checked with their sources on the other end, I received many hearty handshakes and congratulations. So, we turned the project over to DARPA as an inanimate-object-only project, and kept the biologic worm hole software and its associated scanning and reproduction classified. I received a bonus and a big raise. However, I just couldn't get this possibility out of my mind, and began compiling a list of historical figures that would be interesting to meet in the twenty-first century.

It was during my time at DARPA that I met my wife-to-be, Kathy. She was a staff manager working on another project, and our initial meeting was arranged by a colleague who was working on the transfer project with me. Kathy, at five seven, was two inches shorter than me with brown shoulder-length hair and a cute nose that I kidded her about. She was beautiful, and it didn't take us long. Very early on we both knew that we'd each found our life partner, and a little over a year later we tied the knot and she moved into my apartment with me. Her effect on me was more than just as a partner. Her strong faith led me in a direction that I wish I'd gone years earlier. I became a believer in and a disciple of Christ and we became active in a local Church, something that thrilled my parents to no end!

Throughout the time the transfer project was winding down, I kept thinking about the historical-transfer aspect that we had decided not to go forward with. Many times Kathy and I would sit at home and toss around names of individuals we might be interested in, and even developed a list where we ranked them from the most "desirable" to the "least", though anyone on this list would be a great candidate. But, it was nothing more than an idea that was looking for a purpose. Neither of us thought anything like this would ever go anywhere, but it was fun to dream. Slowly, it kind of took a back seat to the other projects we were both working on.

Then, one day I was complaining to a member of our team about that having missed that possibility, and we were laughing about how much time Kathy and I had invested in something that could never be. At some point he stopped and said, "You know, wait a minute. I have an idea. Don't tell anyone else about this. There might be a possibility".

"You're nuts," I said, but he got semi-serious. He suggested that maybe DARPA wasn't the place for this, but he might know of a place where we could at least pitch the idea.

"Well, that's too bad," I said. "The whole project's classified, so where else could it possible go?"

"Let me talk to a guy I know upstairs," he said, "and I'll get back to you."

A few days went by and I thought nothing about it since we were still busy with further refinements on the replication process, until I got a phone call one afternoon from the Legal Affairs department asking me to attend a meeting the next morning. I was more than a little concerned. But, when I showed up for the meeting, there was my colleague, a couple of Agency attorneys, along with who else but Mr. Secret.

The gist of the meeting was that a contact they had at the National Science Foundation was interested in talking about the project. This contact had once worked at DARPA, and still had his security credentials, so he was kind of a go-between for DARPA and NSF when crossover projects might come up. I was asked if I would be interested in talking to them.

"Sure," I said. "How would this work?"

Mr. Secret spoke up. "Much the same as our original proposal. DARPA would 'loan you out' indefinitely to NSF. They would establish a facility, stock it with the necessary equipment, provide you with staff and security, and you and your staff would work on making your theory become reality."

"How would that affect me personally?"

"Well, the same security conditions would be in place. Your salary, at an increase I might add, would be paid through NSF's budget. The rest of the provisions of your contract with us would remain the same. You would just work at the new facility until further notice."

19

I thought about that for a minute. "Is there a new contract?"

"It would be an addendum to your existing contract that could be sunset at any time, depending on circumstances. You original agreement would remain in force."

"I would be able to have my attorney review it, just like last time?"

"Of course."

"I see," I said. "I have to say I'm intrigued. Where is their facility?"

"Philadelphia."

PART 1

ARRIVAL

Chapter 6

Thursday - First Week

The look on Ben's face said it all. He was apprehensive, frightened, bewildered, with a small measure of anger, and I was really surprised that he didn't appear angrier than he already was. But, he seemed to be a cool customer, though he needed to be put at ease. I certainly didn't want the shock of what had just happened to cause a heart attack or something.

But, I'm guessing he was also observing the look on my face, and to be honest with you, I might have been susceptible to a heart attack myself. For, sitting before me was an elderly gentleman, who looked to be in his late seventies, dressed in what can only be described as late eighteenth century attire, at least from what I'd seen in pictures. But it was his eyewear that had made the hair stand up on the back of my neck. Since we'd programmed the software with an algorithm to pick an individual from the past from my list, from a place and time where one could be fairly certain that person would physically be at the time of the transfer, it was entirely possible that I'd end up with anyone on my list, all the way from the top to the bottom. But, the man that showed up was near the top, which put this possibility beyond my wildest dreams – or at least that's what was going through my head.

"Please, sir, before we go any farther, will you allow me a couple of questions?" I asked.

Ben hesitated, then sighed and said, "I shall consent to answer your questions. What would you like to know?"

"Well," I said, "the first thing I'd like to know is your full name".

I braced for what I knew was coming next, but it still hit me like a ton of bricks when he straightened up, and pulled his shoulders back.

"My full name is Benjamin Franklin of Philadelphia, Pennsylvania."

Now I would like to have seen my own face. It really might be time to be concerned about my own coronary. Of all the people from the past I could have chosen, Ben Franklin was, as I said, near the top of my list. I had known the instant he said 'Ben' that the last name would be Franklin, but there was a large part of me that thought it was just too fantastic to have guessed. Yet, here he was, in all his glory, sitting right in front of me. For some reason the title of a movie instantly crossed my mind: *'The Gods Must Be Crazy'*. I don't know how long I sat and just stared at him, but it was he who broke the ice.

"What else would you like to know, Sir?"

"I'm sorry..." I said, shaking my head as I came out from under my trance. "Other than the obvious concern you have right now, are you in pain anywhere? Do you feel alright?"

"Sir, I am certainly concerned, and more than a little confused, but I am in relatively good health today. I pray, sir, will you please explain what you have done to me, and where exactly am I?"

"Of course, sir," I said. I had practiced this little speech a hundred times, but I instantly knew it was not going to go at all according to script.

"First, you are still in Pennsylvania, not a very long distance from where you were a few moments ago." That was another amazing thing. The building Benjamin would likely have been coming out of in the eighteenth century when he was transformed was just a few miles from our offices. I reminded myself to check and make sure no one had fiddled with the software. I don't believe in coincidences, and this one was going to take the cake.

"I know your next question is how did you get here. Before I answer that question, there are several things I need to explain. You see, I know something about you, Mr. Franklin, but I am sure that is not unusual. You are, of course, a well known individual. But, I know much more about you than most people. I have studied your life and followed it since you're apprenticeship on your brother's newspaper and your publication of the Silence Dogood letters."

I must give Ben credit for his calmness. Had someone snatched me up and plunked me in a blank room with a stranger, I don't think I would be nearly as calm as he was right now. But, I've not led the adventurous life Ben Franklin did, so maybe that had a lot to do with it.

"Don't bother searching your memory for me, because you have never seen nor heard of me."

Now it was time for the really hard part. "You see, sir, you are now part of a phenomenal experiment that I dare say will change your life irrevocably. You are a scientist, and as such you understand much about time and space, am I correct?"

"Yes," Ben said, "I suppose I do. How does that apply to my current situation?"

"Well, sir, while I said a few moments ago you were in Philadelphia, one important fact has changed. Answer me this one last question. What day is today – specifically the date and time?"

Ben frowned, then sighed and said, "Well, sir, It is 17 September, 1787, in the late afternoon, I'd say half past five o'clock."

Here we go. "I would like to correct that for you. You are currently sitting in that chair, in this room, at a date much further in the future."

I opened a drawer in the small table to my left and pulled out a newspaper.

"Sir, it is currently half past eleven in the morning, and this is today's newspaper."

I handed the newspaper to him with today's date circled in ink. He took it, read the date at the top, then glanced over his glasses back up to me, then back at the newspaper. Then he did the last thing I expected. Ben stared at me for a second, then a wide smile crawled across his face and he began to laugh.

Chapter 7

Day One

"Why, that is the most preposterous thing I have heard in a fortnight," laughed Ben. "I suppose the time of day is possible because you may have most certainly used some form of potion on me to bring me here, but just look at me!" as he extended his arms and examined his hands in front of him. "I am most certainly not a young man, but do I really look to be 300 years old to you?"

"Sir, you are exactly the same age as you were a few moments ago," I said. "You are somewhat correct, though, that we did do something to transport you here. But that 'something' we did is the part you are going to find the most difficult to believe. But, I assure you, sir, the proof I will give you will be as indisputable as it will be incredible."

Ben sat back, gave me a stern look, and said, "Alright, sir. Make your case." and he sat back and folded his arms.

This part I had practiced. I rose from my chair and went over to the wall behind me just beside the door. On the wall was a hidden light switch. I simply pressed the switch which turned on the LED lighting in the ceiling. The glow of the light enveloped the room. I then went and extinguished both the candles that had been providing the light until this point. Ben reacted immediately by unfolding his arms and staring at the ceiling. I let him sit there for a few moments, then I pressed the switch again, plunging the room into complete darkness. Two seconds later, I pressed the switch again, turning the lights on, then returned to my seat.

Next, from a pocket in the back of my chair I retrieved a copy of the King James version of the Bible, opened it to a verse I had bookmarked and underlined, Luke Chapter 1 Verse 79. I handed the Bible to Ben and pointed to that verse.

"Read that to me, sir," I said.

Ben looked at the Bible, then at me, then back to the Bible and softly read, *"To give light to them that sit in darkness and in the shadow of death, to guide our feet into the way of peace."*

"Look at the publish date inside the front cover"

Ben did so, then, he closed the Bible, while at the same time examining the leather cover and the binding of the Book. Then he looked back up at me and said, "I must give you credit, sir. That is an interesting demonstration," and he looked back up at the ceiling lights, then back at me, "but that is not convincing evidence of anything you have said." and he handed me the Bible back, and I placed it on the table between us and sat back down.

"Oh, sir," I said. "This is just the beginning. The things I wish to show you will be so overwhelming that I must be careful in how I present them so as not to cause you more stress than I already have. But, before we continue, would you like something to eat or drink? I'm not sure we'll have much of what you are accustomed to eating and drinking, but I believe you will like it anyway."

Ben thought for a second, then sat back in his chair and said, "I am not really hungry at this point, but a beverage would help."

"How about we start with a glass of cool water?" I asked.

"That would be fine," he said.

I rose, went to the door, opened it and whispered to the man guarding the door, "Hand me that pitcher of ice water and those two glasses, please".

He grabbed a tray from across the hall and brought it over. I took the tray with a pitcher of ice water and a couple of glasses, and placed them on the table beside the Bible and poured us both a drink. I handed Ben his glass and he took a pensive sip, clicked his tongue a couple of times and said, "My, that is very refreshing. How do you keep it so cold?"

I pointed to the pitcher and said, "Ice cubes."

Chapter 8

Thursday - First Week

I had always known the process would be slow, and the "new guest" skeptical, and I was even prepared for him to become violent at such a gross violation of his personal being, but Ben was amazingly calm. It was one of the reasons I had him near the top of my selection list, because I perceived him to be a thoughtful man who might think before acting, but in my mind when I placed myself in his situation, I don't know that I would have been that calm.

"Ice cubes," he said as he leaned forward and examined the pitcher of water. "Amazing".

"Dr. Franklin, this is just the beginning of things that will amaze you. In the last 230 years, science and technology has increased at an alarming rate to the point that the entire economy is now based on it. But, I don't want to get ahead of myself here, because you have, literally, a long way to go."

He straightened back up in his chair and said, "Well, get started then sir! I have things to do and I would like to get back."

This was the part I dreaded. So, I punted. "Fine. The first thing I want to do is begin with a couple of things that you might be able to relate to in your own time."

"That's another thing I am curious about," he said. "You have not yet convinced me that anything has changed other than where I am sitting, and possibly the time of day. I would ask you, sir, to provide some evidence that I am in a different time."

"Well, that's fair," I said. "Let me retrieve something else."

I got up and went back to the door, opened it, and whispered to the attendant, "Bring me the first package."

He went over to a table and picked up a small woven basket with a cloth covering its contents and handed it to me. I had chosen a woven basket because a pasteboard box would have been something from too far in the future, and I wanted to make this easy, at least at first.

I took the basket back over, sat down, and retrieved something from under the cloth.

"Pardon me, sir, but do you have a timepiece?" I asked.

He reached into a small pocket on his vest and retrieved a shining gold pocket watch and showed it to me. I opened my hand and displayed a simple traditional mechanical wristwatch with a leather band and handed it to him. He paused as he looked at it, then at me, then he replaced his pocket watch and examined the wristwatch.

"So small a time piece." he mused. "Does it keep accurate time?"

"Better than your Wagstaff," I replied.

He looked up at me. "How did you know mine was a Wagstaff?" he inquired. "I didn't even open it up."

"I told you. I know a lot about you, sir," I said.

He returned to examining the wristwatch. When he looked on the back, he saw the manufacturer's name, but I had purposely chosen one with no dates on it.

"I've never heard of this 'Elgin' company."

"Of course not," I said. "They weren't established until 1863."

He gave me one of those 'don't kid a kidder' looks, and handed it back to me. "Interesting, but still not proof," he said.

I took it, replaced it in the basket, and pulled out another watch.

"Take a look at this one, then."

He took the watch from me, but when he looked at the display his eyebrows rose. It was a Casio digital, and the seconds were ticking off one at a time.

"This was my wristwatch when I was in school. I have kept it all these years, not realizing it might come in handy to show someone like yourself."

He just kept staring at the watch as the time clicked away. Then, slowly he looked up at me with a perplexed look on his face. "I must say, I have never dreamed of a device like this. How is it done?"

"Well," I said, "as it turns out, you had something to do with this."

His eyebrows rose again. "In what possible way?"

"Do you remember your experiment with the kite and the lightning where you discovered the properties of electricity?"

"Why yes, of course."

I leaned forward in my chair, as I explained, "As it turns out, even two centuries later, the properties of positive and negative forces are still referred to in that way since you were the first to declare them. This device operates on a small electrical charge that will allow it to operate for years without any outside assistance. These days we use a similar term called 'electronics'. It is the same basic physical properties of electricity that you discovered, but with vast applications that we cannot even begin to go into here. Suffice it to say that this small device is but a scratch on the surface of things you will see as we progress."

Ben glanced back down at the digital watch again, examined it front and back, then without looking up said, "How do you make the internals so tiny?"

That, sir," I said, "is a much larger discussion. How do you feel about my assertion that you are no longer in the eighteenth century now?"

He looked up at me, back down at the watch, then back up and said, "Well, I must say – this is certainly hard to explain." Then he handed the watch back to me and smugly said, "Show me something else."

I replaced the watch into the basket, then took out the last item. It was a small, thin, rectangular object with some buttons on the face of the front. "This is something called an MP3 player." I pressed one of the buttons and it began playing a song. "This song was written and performed by a group of young men who were the most influential force on music in the twentieth century. Two of these members are now dead, and the gentleman singing this song is now nearly eighty years old. This song was written and performed when he was thirty-three."

He looked up to me in amazement as I handed the player to him, and his eyes grew large as he listened to the song play. The look on his face when he looked back up at me was absolutely priceless.

I continued, "We have the ability to record live events and play them back any time we choose. This particular player has over 1000 performances recorded on it, and I can select from that list any performance any time I desire, and play it over and over again. Do you have anything like this in 1787?"

As he slowly stared intently at the player, his head slowly shook from side to side as the sound of Sir Paul McCartney singing "Blackbird" came out of the internal speakers on the player.

Chapter 9

Thursday

"Dr. Franklin, I cannot begin to understand what might be going through your mind at this point," I said as he looked up from the music playing in his hand. "I know this is a lot to take in, but believe me, there is so much more. I am trying to bring you up to date, literally, in as careful a way as I can."

He paused for a moment, looked back down at the MP3 player as 'Blackbird' continued to play, then he handed it back to me and said, "I wish to know your intentions, sir."

This was the moment I had put off as long as I could. I took the player, stopped the recording, replaced it in the basket, and looked into his eyes for a long second before continuing.

"Sir, there are now two Dr. Benjamin Franklins. One was left in Philadelphia in or near what we now call Independence Hall. The other is sitting in front of me. In the twenty-first century, we have discovered methods of replicating biological life from times in the past into the present day and place. The good news is that all the things that you accomplished in your life are unchanged, and indeed, the Dr. Franklin in 1787 is completely unaware of what we have done. The other news, which is both good and bad, is that, and I'm sorry there is no easy way to say this, you are now permanently in the present day with no way of reversing the procedure."

I half expected him to pass out. Instead, the expression on his face did not change, and in fact, didn't even flinch.

"Now, sir," I said. "You can take this as good news – an opportunity to see the country you were so instrumental in creating and all the progress of humanity since your time, or you can take this as bad news, in which case our proceeding from here will be much more difficult. In either event, I would like to sincerely apologize to you for upending your life as I have done, and this is my doing and mine alone."

"But, you see," I continued, "scientific progress has always left consequences in its wake, and while that is no excuse, you still have much to give to the world. You have so much knowledge that has been lost both to us physically as well as intellectually, particularly in understanding the origins of our country and the things you in your time knew of which we are no longer aware."

He sat back in his chair, and rubbed his chin as I could see the wheels turning in his mind.

I continued, "I can only try to put myself in your place and hope that if I were given such an opportunity, I would embrace it, secure in the knowledge that my former self still accomplished everything history recorded. But, sir, that is your prerogative, and I will honor your intentions, even if they include seeing me as one of the greatest pariahs in history, which may well turn out to be the case anyway."

He looked around the room in contemplation, leaned forward, the palms of his hands on his knees as he stared at the floor for a few moments, then looked up at me and said, "You earlier mentioned something about food?"

I paused, then smiled for a second, then said, "Oh, sir, you have no idea."

Ben Franklin sat back up, with raised eyebrows, and softly said, "Then I suggest you enlighten me."

I smiled at him again and said, "When I was in college I lived in a small apartment with another roommate, and neither of us was very skilled at preparing food. In fact, you could say we were terrible at it. On weekends, we would ask some of our female counterparts from our home county to come over and prepare a meal for all of us. We would purchase the food, and they would cook for us. But, during the week, we had to make other arrangements. There was one food that was a staple for us, and to this day I could probably still eat that same food most days of the week. Would you like to try that?"

He smirked a bit, then said, "Yes, let us eat your college 'staple' then."

I cleared the basket and other items off the table to the side, placed the table between us, then went over to the door and said a few words to the man in the hallway. He nodded and left for a moment, then came back with a box and some beverages in glasses on a small tray and handed them to me. I returned and placed the tray on the table. Ben leaned forward and stared at the box for a moment, then said, "What is a 'Pizza Hut'?"

"Well, sir," I said. "I read somewhere that you have an affinity for Parmesan cheese, because a letter you wrote in the mid 1700s extolling its virtues has survived to this day."

"You mean to say you have been reading my private correspondence?" he exclaimed, as he sat upright. It took a moment to recognize his horror was only half real, and half mockery.

"Well, you must remember, you are no longer living at this point, and your effects have been preserved for history. That is why I am careful what I commit to paper," I said with a wry smile.

He smiled and said, "Well, then, you are correct. Continue."

"In the late 1800s," I began, "the Italians created a type of 'pie' from flat bread and other ingredients, one of which is Parmesan cheese. This creation became known as 'pizza'. There are several variations, but the one I prefer has a thin crust, with melted mozzarella cheese, and a topping that is a type of salami meat known as 'pepperoni'. When hot, just before eating, you sprinkle Parmesan cheese on it. Now, I love it, but I would like to get your opinion."

"Fine, sir," he said. "This pizza is made in a 'hut'?"

"Well," I said, "not exactly – that's just the name of the establishment that made this one. I have a suggestion, sir. Why don't we eat and I will extol to you the virtues of pizza. However, there is another surprise as well. Something you had nothing like in your time." I took one of the glasses and handed it to him. "This is something called 'Mountain Dew'," I said. "In my college days you simply would not consume pizza without Mountain Dew. I will tell you that the name has virtually nothing to do with the ingredients. It is not from the 'mountain', and it is not made from 'dew', other than the fact that 'dew' is water. We call these 'soft drinks', because they contain no alcohol, though there is a soft 'bite' to them. They are made from carbonated water and other ingredients, and I have had to reduce my consumption of it simply because, as the Bible tells us, we should be moderate in all things."

He took the glass, smelled of the liquid, gave me a quick look, and took a sip. He swallowed, looked at the glass, then took a larger gulp, then clicked his tongue and said, "Yes, that is in interesting taste. It is also cool as well. I see you have an affinity for this cubed ice in your day."

I laughed. "Yes, you could say that." I opened the box, and inside was a medium double-pepperoni thin crust pizza, and the staff had placed some small napkins and a shaker that contained some Parmesan cheese. I took the shaker and shook the Parmesan liberally on the pizza.

"You want to add the Parmesan just before you eat it." I reminded him, as I finished. Then, I took out a slice of pizza and placed it in one of the napkins and handed it to him. "Just eat it directly without utensils," I said. He took a bite, swallowed, and again clicked his tongue.

"I can see why this might have been a staple for a young college man," he said. "This is quite tasty!"

"If you like that, wait until you see what we have tomorrow."

Chapter 10

Thursday - First Week

As we ate, the silence between us began to be uncomfortable, so I thought now might be the right time to start Ben's "education" process. After all, over 200 years had occurred since that day Philadelphia, and knowing the curiosity and intelligence of the man, I knew he would soon begin asking anyway, so we might as well get started.

"Dr. Franklin," I started. He stopped for an instant and sat back in his chair as he continued to chew on the pizza. "First, I would like to know if you are accepting yourself in the twenty-first Century yet, or you still believe you're in 1787?"

"Well, sir," he said when he swallowed, "I still find the prospect of traveling or, how did you put it, being 'replicated', through time a fascinating concept, but nonetheless near impossible to believe." He looked at the basket I had set on the floor, the MP3 player beside it, the pizza box, at the partially eaten piece of pizza in his hand and the Mountain Dew on the table in front of him, and continued.

"But, you have shown me strange things I cannot readily explain, and I must say this 'pizza', as you call it, is not something I have tasted before, and I have traveled much in this world. Let us say I am willing to entertain more evidence, but I am also curious," and he leaned forward in his chair. "Why, under the assumption anything you say is true, would you choose me? There are so many other interesting individuals from history that, if I may say, I would like to meet that would be much more entertaining than myself".

I leaned forward. "Well, it is like this: To be able to replicate another organism I must be able to know exactly when and where someone would be, both physically and in time, to perform the replication. After much research, I made a list of possible people from history where I could identify, with varying degrees of accuracy, their place and time. Then I arranged these names in order from the most desirable to the least, and used that list as a tool for making the choice."

"You mean that, in all of history, I was your first choice?" he asked incredulously.

I chuckled and said, "Well, not exactly. You were very high on the list, though. The choice was made based on that list and the ability to actually perform the replication. If individuals higher on the list were not, shall we say, 'available', the next name on the list was tried until one could be successfully replicated."

"My!" he said. "How long did it take to get to me, then?"

"Well, sir, the details to that answer I am afraid will have to wait. Not because I do not want you to know, but because at this stage, the answer would make no sense to you."

He sat back in his chair. "So, what is necessary for it to 'make sense'?"

"That, sir, is the question. To get you to that point, I need to help you build a background – an intellectual history, if you will – of information for you to draw from. Once you have enough of this information, I will gladly show you how it was accomplished, and I assure you, it will be one of the most interesting things you will have ever encountered."

He took another bite out of his pizza and another drink of Dew as he pondered the process.

"If you are ready, continue your meal, and let me retrieve the next item I have prepared." I got up and went to the door and asked the man on the other side to bring the next item. He left for a few minutes as I waited. When he returned he had a wooden table with small wheels. On the table was an old telegraph key an electromagnetic 'receiver', and old 'B' battery. I wheeled it over beside Ben's chair.

I pointed to the battery. "This is something called a 'battery'. It is similar to the Leyden jar which you may be familiar with, but with increased capacity to store electrical energy." I then pointed to the receiver. "This is a coil of wire around a piece of ferrous metal. When electricity of a sufficient level is sent through these wires it causes the ferrous metal to become magnetic, which then attracts this bar and causes it to snap down creating an audible 'click'." I pointed to the key. "This is called a 'key'. It turns the electricity on and off, like this.."

I pressed the key and the metal tab immediately snapped down with an audible 'click'.

"When I release the key, the tab returns to its previous position." then I released the key. "In the early 1830s a man by the name of Samuel F. B. Morse created a code that one could use to signal letters of the alphabet, numbers, and punctuation over distances like this."

I sent the letter 'A' by closing and releasing the key, then closing it again and holding a half second longer then releasing it. "That was what is termed 'one dot and one dash'. A 'dot' is a short click and release, and a 'dash' is a longer click and release, roughly three times as long as a dot. In Morse's alphabet, that is the letter 'A'. Someone who has memorized these patterns and is skilled enough to recognize dots and dashes and translate the code, can send and receive written material over long distances. For instance, this is your first name, B-E-N."

I slowly sent the three letters, Dash-Dot-Dot-Dot, Dot, Dash-Dot. "That was at a speed of about five words per minute," I said. Those skilled in this method can send and translate to paper by hand nearly thirty-five words per minute. This system is called the 'telegraph', and is also known as 'telegraphy'. This system was the primary method used to send messages quickly from one place to another for over one hundred years."

Franklin looked at the telegraph, reached out his hand and said, "Do you mind?"

"Of course not."

He pressed the key several times, the resulting dots and dashes making no sense whatsoever, then sat back. "Well, that's novel. Do you not use the post any more?"

"Oh yes, we use the postal system you created even today. In fact, millions of pieces of mail, packages, and cards are sent and received every day."

"Millions?" he asked with a raised eyebrow.

I stood back and said, "Dr. Franklin, you have no idea how the nation you helped to create following the Revolution and the signing of the Constitution has fared. We are now a nation of fifty states from the coast of the Atlantic Ocean to the coast of the Pacific, from Mexico to Canada, and includes a number of territories in both oceans, as well as the Caribbean. In fact, two states are not even contiguous to the United States. The forth-ninth state was Alaska in the far northwest, and the fiftieth the Hawaiian Islands in the Pacific. Our – your – nation now consists of over 350 million citizens."

That fact was the first time I had seen Ben's jaw lock open. As that information began to sink in, I closed the pizza box, moved the soft drinks to a lower shelf on the table, reached back into the drawer in the side of the wooden table and retrieved a topographical U.S. map with state boundaries (no highways shown – too soon for that!), unfolded it, and placed it on top of the pizza box.

"This is your country, sir."

He glared at the map for a moment, looked up at me, then back at the map. He picked it up and examined it through his trademark spectacles for several minutes. I could see that the first thing he looked at were the original thirteen colonies, though he most certainly recognized Florida and some of the other areas that were adjacent to them. As he was doing that, I also pulled another item out of the drawer in the wooden table.

"This, Dr. Franklin, is the Flag of the United States of America," I said as I unfurled it.

Chapter 11

Thursday - First Week

Over the next several hours, after we had finished the pizza and soft drinks, I regaled Ben Franklin with a quick historical overview of the nation he had, just moments before being copied and replicated, been instrumental in establishing. He was pleased with the Bill of Rights, and the establishment of the District of Columbia, and I even told him how the city had grown in the intervening years. He was not too surprised at the War of 1812, as he told me, "I never really believed we were done with Britain after the Revolution". He was particularly enthralled about the story of the burning of the White House, and the First Lady (I was careful not to mention names of any of the Presidents besides Washington at this point – I wanted to ease him into that discussion) fleeing with the portrait of George Washington just before the British showed up.

He was severely disturbed by the story of the Civil War and how the country had almost destroyed itself over an issue they had struggled with in the first Continental Congress. "If only we had done our jobs better!" he had exclaimed as he shook his head.

Then came the War to End All Wars, followed by the even more violent World War II. I told him of a terrible weapon the United States had developed that finally ended the war without going into any details, and how that war had cemented our place as the greatest nation on earth, now termed a "Superpower". Then came Korea, Vietnam, and finally terrorism and radical Islam.

By the time we had finished our discussion, the afternoon was leaving us and soon nighttime would come on. There were some things he needed to be aware of before we left the room we were in and sat down to the evening meal.

"Dr. Franklin, I need to prepare you for some things you will see in a few minutes. You see, there is a reason we have not yet left this room. I had purposely designed this room for this reason. I made it as plain and bland as I could with none of our modern conveniences, save for the things I've already showed you. But when we go through that door, the reality of the changes that have occurred since the eighteenth century will become more apparent and in increasing visibility. I just want you to be prepared for some things that will most certainly be strange, and maybe even shocking to you."

Franklin nodded his head. "I understand, sir. I am more and more over the last several hours becoming aware that you are either telling me the truth about my current whereabouts and, I don't know if there is a term for it, but shall we say my 'when-abouts'; or you have duped me on a grander scale than anyone since the Greeks surprised the Trojans at Troy," and he sat back and laughed at his own joke.

"But tell me this, sir," he said, and I leaned forward, "I do not see a privy here. How does one in your time relieve oneself?"

I smiled and said, "Well, I apologize sir. I should have asked you about that before now, but you have to know this is as much an event for me as it is for you. But to answer your question, in our time we refer to these places as the 'restroom', or the more the colloquial "bath room", since most 'privies' now are also places where one bathes. On the other side of the door is a restroom, and I'll give you a quick lesson in the operation of the facilities."

"My," he said, "I thought I had learned that when I was a small lad. I didn't realize there were more lessons in that area!"

"Well, obviously your body operates the same as it did. It's just what you do with the products that has changed," I said as I smiled. "Quickly, let me tell you a couple of things. First, you already have seen the light in the ceiling that is operated by that device by the door. These lights will be ubiquitous from this point on, and the light switch will be visible on a wall in every room. You will also see more modern clothing on the other individuals that work with me here, and we will help you choose some clothing that fits your personality and comfort when you are ready for that. Finally, once you're finished with your restroom experiences, we will adjourn to a dining room for a, hopefully for you, sumptuous evening meal."

I rose, stepped aside and waved my hand towards the door and said, "If you are ready, Dr. Franklin."

He arose and I proceeded to the door and opened it. On the other side of the door, William Simpson, who had been doing my bidding since Ben had showed up was waiting. I went through the door and held it open for Dr. Franklin to come through.

"Dr. Franklin, I would like you to meet William Simpson who has been a good friend and has worked for us here in various functions for some time now. Bill, this is Dr. Benjamin Franklin."

Bill extended his hand and said, "It is a pleasure to meet you, Dr. Franklin."

Ben shook his hand, and I must say, he took it much calmer than I would have guessed. Bill was ex-Navy and had been a Navy Seal, much of which he couldn't really talk about. Just over six feet tall and obviously fit, he could be physically intimidating if he needed to be, but he was also easy going and a genuinely nice guy. Bill's security clearances allowed us to immediately plug him in as our chief of security, so he'd been in the loop on our project since his joining us several years ago. I doubted, though, anything he'd been through would top this one for telling his grandchildren, if he was ever allowed to.

"Sir," said Ben as he bowed slightly. Bill wasn't sure what to do, so he just nodded and smiled, which seemed appropriate both to me and, apparently, to Ben.

"Dr. Franklin, if you'll follow me I'll show you how to use the facilities," and I walked down the hall to the first door on the right, opened it, and turned on the light. Franklin followed me into the room and his eyes widened as he inspected the sink and vanity, and gave a quizzical look at the toilet, then the shower in the corner. As he walked further into the room, he saw his reflection in the mirror behind the vanity, and stopped for an instant.

"I say, sir, this mirror is exquisite. I have never seen one so polished and clear."

I smiled. "Every home in the nation has at least one of these, and many have several. This one is actually quite ordinary, and can be obtained almost anywhere that household goods are sold."

Then he saw the faucets, and looked at me as he pointed to them.

"Ah yes," I said. "Every building nowadays has running hot and cold water on demand. The handle on the left controls the hot water. It will run cold for a few seconds, but then will become quite hot. The handle on the right controls the cold water. Here, let me show you."

He stepped aside as I turned each faucet on then off again. "See, simple. Give it a try".

He did, then just shook his head. "I am beginning to believe this is not subterfuge!"

I smiled and said, "Well, progress then! Let me show you how to use the toilet."

I proceeded to show him the toilet and how to flush once he was finished. He was particularly interested in the toilet tissue on the roll, especially when told he could just discard it into the toilet and, when flushed, it would disappear with the rest of the waste. It was not lost on me how much we take for granted in even the simplest of tasks.

"So, I'll leave you in private, sir. If you require assistance, please just call me – I'll be on the other side of the door. Take your time, and if you wish to wash up before the meal there are towels and facecloths here."

"Thank you sir," he said. "I...should be fine".

I left the room and closed the door. Bill was now standing across the hall from the restroom, and I looked at him, laughed quietly, and said, "His first bathroom break!"

Bill snickered, as we had talked about this very thing before, and I'm sure some of the bathroom humor we'd engaged in was on his mind. "How is he doing?" he asked.

"Well, I have to say, he's taken it pretty much in stride. If someone had snatched me up and carried me over 200 years in the future, you'd probably hear me screaming back here in the twenty-first century. But, as someone with almost boundless curiosity, I'm hoping that will carry him through. It was one of the criteria that moved his name near the top of the list in the first place. If we get through the next few hours and through the night, I think he'll be fine. Still, it's a lot for anyone, no matter who they are, to take in."

Bill nodded. "Well, dinner should be ready. Miriam came down the hallway shortly before you came out and asked if we were on schedule, and I told her I thought we were, but with the insulation we had built into some of the walls here, I couldn't hear anything that was going on. But, as it turns out, I was right. Dinner should be hot and ready to eat."

"Good. I'm hungry, and I'm guessing he is as well," I said as a made a nodding gesture towards the bathroom door.

I heard the faint sound of a toilet flush, then the water running in the sink. Actually, the water came on, then went off, then came on again, about four times before it ran long enough for him to wash up. Then it went off for the last time, and in a few seconds the door opened and I asked, "Any problems?"

"Hot and cold running water!" he said. "Is this commonplace?"

"It is in every building in the land," I said. "I told you the changes would come more swiftly. Are you ready for the evening meal?" I said, and motioned back down the hall.

"After you, sir!" he said, and we returned down the hall, rounded the corner, and I opened the first door on the right which opened into the conference room that doubled as our dining room.

The table was already set. There was a pitcher of iced tea, some dinner rolls, a bowl of green beans, some mashed potatoes, and a large roast beef on a platter in the center of the table. I motioned for Dr. Franklin to take the seat at the head of the table, and to Bill to take the seat on the other side of the table.

"Dr. Franklin, would you like some soft music while we dine?" I asked.

He looked around, then said, "That might be nice."

"Do you remember the small device I placed in your hand that played music?"

"How could I forget?" he said.

I walked over to the wall where there was a round knob adjacent to the light switch, and I turned it to the right just a bit. Some light classical music began playing through the speakers in the ceiling.

"How is that?" I asked.

Ben looked for a minute to see where the music was coming from, but then said, "Very good!" and sat down. I sat in the chair opposite Bill, and said, "In my home it is customary to pray before our meals. Is that acceptable to you?"

"Well, of course!" Ben exclaimed. "It is comforting to know the Almighty is still listening!"

I laughed and said, "Well, some things haven't changed, even in 230 years."

I bowed my head and offered a short prayer of thanks for the meal, then at the 'Amen', asked Ben if he'd like for me to slice the roast. He was definitely ready for that!

As I sliced the roast and put a generous portion on Ben's plate, Bill poured us each a glass of iced tea from the pitcher. When he was finished, Ben took his glass and looked at it and said, "Am I to presume this is tea?"

"Yes," said Bill. "I know you are used to hot tea, but over the years in our country, iced tea has become the beverage of choice on many dinner tables. Tom and I are both from the Southern United States, and we prefer our tea with sweetener, but if you had rather it be unsweetened, we can get that for you".

He took a quick taste, then smiled and said, "No. This is acceptable. I am guessing there are many things I will need to acclimate myself to, and this is likely not the worst of the lot."

"Well," said Bill, "that is generally the case, but following dinner, if you wish, we can have a pot of hot coffee ready. That is a custom in many homes."

Ben nodded his head. "Yes, I would like that, I think."

Bill called for Miriam, and when she came through the door, Ben noticed her with raised eyebrows. "Miriam," said Bill, "will you prepare a pot of coffee for after the meal?"

"Glad to", she said.

"Oh, Miriam," I said. "I apologize. I should have introduced you."

She came around to my side of the table and both Ben and I stood as she approached.

"Dr. Franklin, I would like to introduce Miriam Wilson. She is, among other things, our primary researcher and office manager, and she's been keeping us all in line around here for the last few years, as well as her three children which, I know at some point, she would be delighted to tell you about. Miriam, meet Dr. Benjamin Franklin."

Miriam's eyes virtually glowed as she extended her hand to Ben. Ben took her hand, which Miriam had expected him to shake, and bowed and kissed the back of her hand. Miriam, not sure what to do, did a very awkward curtsy, and said, "Nice to meet you, Dr. Franklin. This is indeed a pleasure."

Ben replied, "The pleasure is all mine, madame, and I would be delighted to hear of your children as well."

"Thanks, Miriam," I said. "Would you like to join us?"

"Of course – thanks. You gentlemen go ahead and start, and I'll be back in in a few minutes." With that she smiled at Ben, then turned and went back into the kitchen. Ben waited until she had left the room, then we both returned to our seats, and Ben paused for a moment before saying, "Well, sir, you told me there would be some differences, but I had not expected to see a woman wearing pants!"

"Yes," I said. "In the intervening years, much has changed between the sexes, and I want to save that shock for you for much later. Suffice it to say that most women in the twenty-first century no longer wear dresses, but pants and blouses."

"Well," he said, "that will certainly take some getting accustomed to."

Bill and I smiled at each other with knowing looks as we began our meal.

Chapter 12

Thursday - First Week

During the meal, Ben began asking questions. We had covered a lot of territory already today, and this was just the basics. His questions ranged from the history of the United States and the world, to technological changes since the eighteenth century. It was history, though, that had the most land mines. I tried to soft-pedal as much of it as I could, but since we had already covered the basics of the wars that had occurred since his time, it was natural that he would want to understand the forces and underpinnings of these wars, as well as how society was faring. He was particularly interested in the Civil War, since he understood the issue of slavery more than the issues surrounding most of the others, and since that issue had been at the core of their problems in producing our Constitution. But, there were other things that fascinated him as well.

"If I am to understand the causes of the Civil War, then, they were as much about regional jealousies as they were the issue of slavery?" he asked.

"Yes. But do not let that minimize the issue of slavery, because we are still struggling with racial tensions today. The Southern states resented the Northern states telling them how to handle their internal issues, and the Northern states were insistent that all humans had worth, and black Americans were no less God's children than white Americans. But, it was that jealousy of the South, and the arrogant insistence of the North that provided the fuel that would erupt in Charleston at Fort Sumter. From there it just spiraled out of control and the resulting five year war left nearly one million of our citizens dead. It is still the largest number of U.S. citizens killed in any conflict, since the dead and wounded on both sides *were* citizens. The effects are still felt today in the jealousies between North and South – Yankees and Rebels. It even permeates our sports. There are two sports teams that can trace their roots back to the Civil War – The New York Yankees and the Ole Miss Rebels, among others."

"New York I am, of course familiar with, but Ole Miss?" he asked?

"Yes. It's a college in the southern state of Mississippi and the name of their sports teams are the Rebels".

"What manner of sports do they engage in?" he asked.

I smiled. "Well, that's a whole different discussion, and I'm afraid that sports is such a major part of our society today that even beginning that discussion would preclude us from getting any sleep tonight, so let's save that for an afternoon when we have more time. When the time comes, I'll gladly take you to some of these events for you to see yourself."

"Speaking of which," he said, and paused a moment and looked down at his lap before looking up at me and asking, "Am I a prisoner here?"

I had been waiting on this question as well. "Well, sir, to be frank, I am not sure how you would be classified. According to our laws, if I were to prevent you from leaving, I could be charged and tried for a felony offense. But since you were essentially 'copied' from your former self, I'm afraid the issue would be, or rather is, very complicated legally. Suffice it to say that if you insist, I would have to allow you to leave. But, in this current time, that might be dangerous for you, given all the changes that have taken place. I would much rather you allow me to prepare you for that eventuality, which will come as quickly as we can make sure you will be safe. That is not to say that there will be those who will immediately wish to cause you harm, but as you will see when we've had a bit more time to bring you up to date, so to speak, on how to make your way in the very much changed world in which you find yourself."

He nodded, and I continued. "That is not to say that you are inept, by any means. But I dare say that if I were to transport myself 200 years into the future, I would have much the same problem."

He pondered that for a moment, then said, "I am still struggling to believe that I am, as you assert, no longer in 1787, and that if I were to venture outside I wouldn't see the same world I was in just this morning."

"I understand that, Dr. Franklin. I have tried to bring you carefully into that realization, and I have an idea that I was saving for later in the process, but I believe it may be necessary to finish convincing you. Would you be prepared to see something that is absolutely not possible in 1787, or even one hundred years later than that?"

I glanced over at both Miriam and Bill, and the expression of their faces was one of those '*just what is he going to pull now*' looks.

I looked at Dr. Franklin, and he said, "Well. If you can show me absolute proof, then let us get to it!"

"Fine," I said. I looked over at Miriam and said, "Miriam, you might as well join us and witness this as well. I'll help with the clean up later".

"I appreciate that!" she said with a smile.

"Well, with that, would you all follow me, please," and I rose. "This way, Dr. Franklin," and I waved my hand towards the door.

As he rose I went through the door and into the hallway and as he approached I led him to the first door on the left further down the hall, opened the door, switched on the light, and allowed him, Miriam, and Bill to enter. I closed the door and asked them all to take a seat. In the room was a leather couch, three leather chairs, a coffee table in the center, and a cabinet on one wall.

"Dr. Franklin, if you would please take this seat." and had him sit in one of the chairs, which was a recliner directly opposite the cabinet. "Miriam, if you would take the couch, and Bill this chair," and I pointed to the chair on the right, leaving the chair between Ben and Miriam open for me.

"There are actually two things I want to show you, Dr. Franklin, and they are related, as you will see," I said as they took their seats. I went over to the cabinet and opened a door at the bottom and pulled out a large book. I took it over to my chair and placed the book on the coffee table.

"One of the great inventions of the nineteenth century was a way of preserving still life permanently. In your time there were many portraits, and indeed many of them, including portraits of yourself, still exist even today. The problem with that was that you must sit for an artist to paint the portrait, and as you know that can take some time. What if there were another way to save a moment in time that was much quicker?"

Ben nodded and said, "Well, that would certainly save some time. Continue.."

I took a breath. "In the early 1800s inventors began experimenting with chemical compounds and different types of paper and eventually were able to produce a chemically-treated paper that was sensitive to light. By exposing this paper to an image, then treating the paper with other chemicals, that image could be reproduced permanently on the paper. The process became known as photography, and the image, a photograph – or colloquially called a 'picture' or 'photo'. Originally these photographs were only in black and white, and the shades of gray in between. However, over the years this process was perfected, and eventually these photographs could be produced in full color. In addition, inventors were able to create something called 'film', which would allow one to take one photograph and reproduce it many more times."

"I know something about this," I said, "because my daughter is a photographer and she takes photographs of events like school functions, weddings and birth announcements, family photographs and so forth." I pointed to the book on the table. "This book contains a number of photographs I had her prepare for me. There is nothing special about them – they are just ordinary people at school events, weddings, and there are a couple of newborn infant pictures here."

I took the book, and opened it up. I handed it to Ben and placed it in his lap. He looked at the first set of photographs, then back up at me, then back down to the book. As he examined them, he began the turn the leaf over to the next set, then the next.

"Amazing!" he said. "The clarity of these portraits is extraordinary!"

As he continued through the album, I said, "Each of these photographs took only moments to create and they can be reproduced over and over again since the film can be used over and over again."

Then came my first zinger.

"Would you like for me to take your photograph?"

Ben looked up from the book, peering over his spectacles, and said, "That....would be interesting!"

"First, let me tell you how this works. The device I will use to do this is now several decades old, and the whole process occurs over the space of about one minute. No one actually uses this process any more because there are even more amazing ways to preserve images, but I chose this because it shows you the whole process from beginning to end right before your eyes."

I went back over to the cabinet, opened the other door, and retrieved a Polaroid camera. "Now, Dr. Franklin, this device is called a 'camera'. It will produce the photograph. I want to warn you, though, when I press this button on the camera, there will be a flash of light. It is necessary to expose the film, so don't be alarmed. It only flashes for an instant, thought it will be quite bright. Just prepare the expression on your face as you would for a portrait, and look directly at this part here." and I pointed at the lens on the camera. "I will count to three before I press it, so please remain still, and don't blink your eyes, until after the flash."

I could only wonder what was going through Ben's mind at this point, but he said, "I will try, sir. Proceed."

I took the Polaroid, aimed the camera at Ben, then counted to three and pressed the button. The camera flashed, and the undeveloped picture came out the front of the camera. I took it over to Ben, and placed it in the center of the page he had open in the photo album and said, "Watch this. The picture will develop before your very eyes".

As we watched, the picture began to take shape, slowly but surely becoming recognizable. Ben's eyebrows raised as he watched the process and the picture become clearer and clearer. After about a minute there was a nice photograph of Benjamin Franklin, sitting in the leather chair with a photo album in his lap and a very Franklin-like look on his face.

"Sir!" I said, "You make a very good photograph!"

Ben took the picture, brought it up to his face and examined it, front and back, then looked back up at me.

"Well, sir, I have seen many portraits in my time, but I have never seen anything like this!" He looked over at the camera and said, "All those chemicals in that little box?"

"Actually," I said, "there are no chemicals in the box. All the chemicals were on the paper and the camera just spread them across the photo as it exited the box which started the developing process."

He examined the picture again, and said, "Yes, I can smell some of the chemicals now. I assume that smell will go away once these chemicals dry?"

"Absolutely," I said. "I will also say that we have performed another historical event today of some significance. This is the first photograph ever taken of Dr. Benjamin Franklin! I expect this will be displayed in some of the world's elite museums over the next several years. Do you mind if I save this photograph for posterity?"

He raised his eyebrows and said, "Well, I am glad I didn't have a quizzical look on my face, but I assure that beneath, it was so!" and he handed the photo to me. I laughed and said, "I imagine it certainly was!" and then gave it to Bill and said, "Bill, would you take care of this, if you don't mind".

Bill nodded and took the photo, and I turned to Dr. Franklin and said, "Now, would you now like to see the definitive proof I spoke of?"

Franklin's face lit up in surprise. "You mean this wasn't the proof you were going to show me? This was amazing enough, even though I have seen many portraits. Show me this 'definitive' proof!"

"Certainly!" I said. I got up again and went over to the cabinet one more time. As Ben put the book and portrait on the coffee table, I opened the two doors at the top of the cabinet and reached in a grabbed a small black object, a small book, then brought it back over to my chair.

"Of the other inventions over the years," I said, "many have changed the course of human events, and the way our societies interact with each other. Few have had the effect of this device, though. You have now seen still pictures. A gentleman named Thomas Edison born in the mid nineteenth century was a prolific inventor, and in the coming days you will hear his name associated with many inventions. One of the things he did was take the inventions of others that had produced these photographs and invented photographic film, and devised a way to make motion pictures. By quickly viewing many photographs that are similar but with small differences, you can have the *illusion* of motion."

I took the small book and showed it to him. "This is something called a flip book." and I opened it up. On the pages were just some stick figures. "These are simple drawings that any small child could draw, but they were drawn slightly differently on each page, then these pages arranged so when you flip through the pages quickly, you get this." and I flipped through the pages. The stick figure appeared to be walking.

Franklin's expression changed to one of wonder and a small smile crept across his face. "Well, this is ingenious!" he said. "We could certainly have done that in my time, but no one has ever thought of it".

"Well," I said, "This is a very very rudimentary version of what we now call 'motion pictures'. Imagine if I could take pictures just like the one I just took of you, except take them in rapid succession as you walked across the room, then arranged them in a similar fashion as this book. That is exactly what happened when Edison invented the Kinetoscope, what we now call the 'motion picture projector'. Except instead of flipping the images like a book, he was able to devise a way to project these images on a wall using a light behind the images. These are called 'motion pictures', or the more colloquial 'Movies'."

"I would very much like to see one of these 'movies'!" he said with raised eyebrows.

"Well, sir," I said, "I want to take that a step further. In the early twentieth century an Italian inventor named 'Marconi' was credited with an invention that allowed communications to be sent from place to place without wires. Do you recall the 'telegraph' I showed you earlier this evening?"

"Yes," he said, "But it had wires".

"Marconi discovered a way to use electromagnetic waves to send those same signals through the air over great distances without wires. That method is now called 'radio'. In fact, this 'radio' is something I use on a regular basis as a pastime. I enjoy communicating with friends I have made all over the world using wireless radio, and people like me that do this are called 'Amateur Radio Operators'. There's even a nickname for us - "Hams", but that's not what I want to show you. Shortly after the invention of radio telegraphy, other inventors were able to convert sound and send them via these 'wireless' signals, and in the early twentieth century, others invented ways to send these motion pictures through the air as well."

Franklin just stared at me in disbelief. "How is this possible?" he asked.

"I assure you, sir, it is not only possible, but I will explain it more detail later and I can provide you with all the documents they produced explaining in excruciating detail how this happens. This method of sending motion pictures through the air is called 'television', and the device used to view these images is called a 'television set', or 'TV', for short." I pointed at the top of the cabinet and said, "What you see in that cabinet is a TV set with a forth-two inch viewing screen manufactured by a company named 'Samsung'."

"Now, I was once told by a colleague of mine that when demonstrating something new that you should only say the words 'watch this', so whatever happened you could pretend like that's what you intended to happen," and I chuckled at my own joke. "So, without further delay, Dr. Franklin. Watch This!" and I aimed the remote in my hand at the TV and pressed the 'on' button.

Now, I had prepared for this moment, but had planned to doing some setup beforehand it at a time when I knew what programming would be on. I had no idea what channel had been watched last, so the 'watch this' comment was real! I was prepared for the worst, but to my absolute delight, when the picture came on, the sound was perfect, the picture was high-definition clear, and what was on was the MLB network, and the Atlanta Braves were playing the St. Louis Cardinals. As the picture came on, the pitcher went through his wind-up and threw a strike to the batter who took a swing and hit a home run to the left field bleachers. The score at the bottom of the screen showed the game tied at five runs in the bottom of the ninth inning in Atlanta, and this was the game-winning home run. The crowd went wild. I could not have scheduled it any better.

I looked over at Ben and the look on his face was total shock. We just sat there for a minute as the announcers began shouting over the crowd that the Braves had just won in a walk-off homer as the crowd behind them continued to rock the stadium.

Bill and Miriam were smiling from ear to ear, and as we all exchanged looks and grins, I looked back over at Ben and said, "So, Dr. Franklin. What do you think now?"

Chapter 13

Thursday - First Week

Ben just sat there watching the end of the game, eyes wide, mouth open, utter astonishment on his face. Bill, Miriam, and I looked at him, then at each other, then back at him. He was mesmerized!

"Dr. Franklin?" I said.

Ben's head slowly turned towards me, still in astonishment, and said, "Well, sir. I do believe you have convinced me. I am not sure what to say, and I am a man who is seldom at a loss for words. But, this..." and he pointed back at the TV, "is something that in my time might have been grounds for witchcraft. I am, at this point, not entirely convinced that you are not a participant in the dark crafts!"

I shifted in my seat, turning a little more towards him, and leaned forward with my palms on my knees. "We are aware of the Salem trials and the suspicions that may even still exist in your time, but believe me, sir, when I tell you that there is no sorcery involved. This is pure science, and as I said a few moments ago, I can provide you with all the scientific documents, from your time until ours, that explain how this came into being."

I paused for a few moments while that sank in, then sat back up. "Sir, I was afraid I was bringing all this new information to you a bit too quick, but with your intellect and experience in all your scientific endeavors, I believed you could handle the shock. As I said earlier, I might have these same problems were I to experience the same change you have."

Franklin nodded slowly. "I will not say I can 'handle' the shock, as you say, but I must admit I am very curious. Shocked, yes, but also curious."

"I was hoping that's how you would be once we got to this point," I said. "Now comes the real issue. I again must apologize for what I have done to you, but in my defense, I hope I would jump at the chance for the same to happen to me." I paused for a moment before continuing. "My original plan was to bring you up to date on all that has occurred since your time, hopefully gain some knowledge that has been lost to history and time, and hopefully find some way you could contribute once again, as you have so prolifically in the past. Given that this is a one-way trip for you, does this plan sound acceptable to you?"

He sat and pondered quietly for a moment. Then he looked over at Miriam, then back over to his right to Bill, then back to me. He stroked his chin, looked over his spectacles to me and said, "Well, I do not see a choice, but I may have a problem depending on how you see us proceeding."

"Let me guess," I said. "Who is in control of the life of Dr. Benjamin Franklin?"

"Precisely!" he said. "Not to be blunt, but you did bring me, or at least some form of me, a concept I still struggle to understand – maybe even believe – against my will, so what kind of slavery do you place me under?"

This is the part I expected. He was right. I had, without his knowledge or permission, basically kidnapped him from his place and time to a place and time not of his choosing, and I had done it in a way that was, at least in the current state, impossible to correct. He really was my prisoner. I almost winced at the 'slavery' reference, but I could see his point. He could really have been my slave. Who was he to contact, and what would he tell any authorities? If he went to the police and told them that he had been kidnapped, the first thing they would want to know is who he is and where he lived. What is he going to say at that point? *'I live in Philadelphia, and it's 1787'*? They would put him in the loony bin. I guess in one respect, he really was my slave. He would, at least for the time being, be completely dependent on me for everything, a stranger unable to live in a world that was as foreign to him as Pluto would be to me. Of course, that was not my intention, but I could certainly see his point.

"Dr. Franklin. It is not fair, at least in the short term, what I have done to you. Part of this experiment is to determine if this method is at all useful, or if it is completely detrimental, and your use of the word 'slavery', certainly points to the latter. So, let me tell you my intentions."

He sat back in his chair as I continued.

"You will certainly be completely dependent on me, us, for the near term. But my intention is to bring you to the point where you can come and go as you wish. In fact, we will prepare identities for you, all the legal documents necessary to be a citizen in the United States in the twenty-first century. We will even have a place that will be your permanent residence as long as you wish, and we have set aside an endowment for you so you will not have to seek employment to live your life comfortably. In the near term, I must ask, though, that you stay here, but only until we can acclimate you to the current living conditions. You will have your own apartment here, and you can come and go most places in this building, and we even have a yard in the back that is fenced in and hidden from others that might pass by our facility where you can get sunshine, some exercise, and enjoy nature that, hopefully, you won't find much different than your time."

I paused. "Once you have acquired enough information to safely live in a society that has a much faster pace than your own, you can transition to being a private citizen, with all the rights and privileges of any other citizen in the United

States of America, at which time we would hope you would continue to consult with us on all things scientific, historical, governmental, and cultural. Does that meet with your approval?"

He sat there for a minute, then said, "What documents do I need to be a citizen in this day and age?"

"Well," I said, "That is a very good question. I would, again, like to defer until some more historical information has been presented, but it is essentially minimal. I must confess, though, that we will be breaking some twentieth century laws to make this happen, but all things considered, I think that will be a minor thing when you consider that you are a man from another time, born over 300 years ago."

"Interesting," he said. He placed his fingers together and placed them under his chin as he thought for a moment, then said, "Well, sir. Seeing that I have little choice, and cannot return to my own home and time, I suppose I must make the best of the situation. However, I must tell you that the only reason I am being so agreeable is that I am very curious as to the changes in our country, and especially in the scientific advances." He pointed to the TV, still going in the background. "This....thing....if this is just the beginning, I must admit my curiosity has seized me such that I wish to know more. There is one thing I do need, though, before we continue."

"Certainly!" I said. "What would that be?"

"While I am certain I will have difficulty, with the turmoil of the last few hours, I am tired and would like to sleep, if that can be arranged."

I smiled. "I know you have seen a lot, and I don't know how many actual hours you have been awake today, but we already have your apartment ready, the bed is turned down and ready for you whenever you are ready."

"Well, since we signed the Constitution today, I rose early this morning, and I must confess, it has been a most tumultuous day."

I sat back in astonishment for the first time since he'd appeared before me this morning. "Dr. Franklin, it had entirely slipped my mind of the significance of the day you were having before we intervened. I apologize again. That single event gave us the government we have had for the last 230 plus years, and now I have heaped all this change on you in addition to your duties earlier today. I suppose you are tired. If you are ready, I'll gladly accompany you to your apartment."

I rose, as did the other three in the room, as we prepared to go. I reached down, took the remote, and turned off the TV. Franklin looked at the blank screen and said, "Amazing. I truly wish to know how such magic has come to be."

I laughed, "Well, it certainly seems like magic sometimes."

I turned to Miriam, "If you would clear the conference room, I'll take care of the rest after Bill and I take Dr. Franklin to his quarters."

Miriam looked at Ben and said, "Dr. Franklin, if you have need of anything I can help you with, please do not hesitate to ask."

"I will, madam – thank you!" he said.

I walked over and opened the door and held it while Miriam went into the hallway and back to the kitchen. "This way, Dr. Franklin. Your apartment is to the right at the end of the hall."

He walked ahead of me, and Bill and I followed him through the hall. "Bill," I said, "would you mind going to see if Phillip is here. If so, bring him to the apartment. If not, come on back and we'll work out the shift changes."

"Sure," he said, and turned and went back down the hallway.

When we reached the door at the end of the hall, Ben turned the handle and went inside the room. There were some empty offices in the building that had been vacated when recent employees had moved on after their part of the project was completed, and we had taken one and converted it into a simple one-bedroom, one bath apartment with a desk, a comfortable chair and a lamp between the two. At the side of the bed was a nightstand with two drawers and a lamp that was built into the back of the top. In the corner on the same wall as the door was an open closet, and below it a large drawer.

"The bathroom is similar to the one you used earlier this evening. There is paper and writing utensils in the drawer of the desk." I went over and took out a piece of paper and a ballpoint pen. "This is called a 'pen'. It is different from the quills you used in your time in that the ink is built into the pen. All you need to is put it on the paper and write, thusly." and I wrote my name at the top of the paper.

"There are other means of recording important information, but we will talk about that later on. The lamp on the table is operated by touch. All you need do is touch the base of the lamp to turn it off, then touch it again to turn it on." I went over to the nightstand and demonstrated the lamp.

"Let's talk about your attire," I said. I went over to the open closet. "Obviously you have only the clothes on your back. For the time being, we have some clothing that Miriam placed in here earlier this evening that should fit you. In the drawer below are some modern undergarments." I opened the drawer and pulled out a set of boxers and held them up. I looked at them and said, "They're self-explanatory, so you shouldn't have any problem with them. The pants in the closet are button up, since you have never seen zippers – an invention I'll show you tomorrow, at which time we will have a tailor come by and outfit you with a suitable wardrobe. You can, of course, keep the clothing you have."

Ben came over and inspected the boxers and said, "I think I can work these." then handed them back to me with a wry smile.

I chuckled. "Yes, I think you can, as well. But, just in case," and I pointed at the fly, "this is the front." and I smiled. He gave me a bit of a smirk, and I put them back in the drawer, closed it, and went over to the bathroom. Ben followed, and I said, "The toilet is the same as in the other bathroom, as is the sink. In the drawers are facecloths, and as you see, there are towels in the rack above the toilet." Ben nodded.

"Now," I said, "about bathing. How often did you bathe in your day?"

"Well sir," he said, "I am a practitioner of 'air baths', and I take them frequently. However, I usually like these in the presence of a nice breeze, but I see there are no windows in this structure."

"Ah, yes," I said. "I remember reading about your air baths. I would not recommend them here! Our Miriam might object. Besides, we have a much improved way of taking baths."

I went over to the shower which was adjacent to the toilet opposite the lavatory. It was an open shower, meaning there was no shower curtain, just an opening in which to step. I pointed through the opening.

"This is a shower. The term comes, literally, from the water falling on one just like it would if you were outdoors during a rain-shower. On the wall here are two controls, just like the one on the sink. To start, turn on the hot water control until the water is warmed completely, then turn on the cold until it is warm, just short of being hot, to the touch. Then simply enter, wash in the shower water, then turn both controls at the same time to turn off the water. There is a bar of soap here above the controls, and the floor of the shower is non-slip so you shouldn't fall down while showering, but be careful anyway. This throw rug on the floor outside the shower will prevent your slipping until you're dry. When you finish, you can wear this robe until you're ready to dress. I believe you will find the process refreshing. I know I do."

Franklin asked, "How often do people nowadays 'shower'?"

"Most people shower daily, and some even shower more than once, particularly after a long hot day. You will find the soap is lightly scented as well with a, shall we say, manly scent – at least for our time. We can talk about shaving and other personal care later."

"Impressive," said Ben. "I will certainly try this 'shower' in the morning."

"Fine," I said. "Do you have any questions, or is there anything else I can do for you?"

"I think not, at least at this time," he said.

"Superb!" I said. "I will leave you for the evening, then. In the morning, when you're ready, come back to the dining room, and we'll prepare the morning meal for you."

There was a knock at the door, and Bill and Phillip entered.

We went back into the apartment, and I said, "Good. Phillip, I would like you to meet Dr. Benjamin Franklin. Dr. Franklin," I said as I turned, "This is Phillip Moore. He will be here during the night. He's our night security for the facility here, and will be down the hall. If you have any needs during the night, just ask Phillip, and he'll be glad to help you".

Phillip was a Marine (as he continued to remind me, you are never an ex-Marine), and he had that look. He wasn't as tall as Bill, though he had that stout look to him and could be tough if he needed to, but also like Bill, his demeanor fit right in with our little group here. Phillip walked over and offered his hand and said, "It's an honor to meet you sir!"

Franklin shook his hand and said, "The pleasure is mine, sir. Did I understand that you are the 'night security'? What exactly does that entail?"

"Well," said Phillip, "As you might imagine there is a lot of expensive and sensitive equipment here, and it is my job to make sure that no one comes in that isn't supposed to be here".

"I see," said Ben. "Does your job also entail making certain that individuals that are not supposed to leave stay in the building?"

Phillip looked at me with a '*help me with this one*' look on his face, so I answered, "Well, Dr. Franklin. As we discussed, I would very much prefer that you do stay inside, at least for the first day or so, until we can prepare you for an excursion outside."

Franklin looked at me with a small smirk and said, "I see." he said. "I suppose I can assent to incarceration for the night".

"Let's call it 'protective custody', sir. And I assure it, that is entirely what it is," I said.

"Then," he said, "I believe I shall retire."

"Fine," I said. "I hope you have a pleasant night's sleep. I believe you will find the bed to your liking, but again, if you have need of anything, please let Phillip know. I am going to my home, but I'll be back early in the morning, and we'll begin the process of Ben Franklin in the twenty-first century."

I almost did it like Daffy Duck in the "Duck Dodgers" cartoon, but I was afraid the laughter that might entail would only confuse Ben, so we said our good nights, and left. However, Phillip, Bill, and I did have a chuckle in the kitchen when I told them how I almost said it.

Chapter 14

Thursday - First Week

Home was only about a ten minute drive or so, depending on traffic, and by the time I had finished some paperwork and notes in my office, the traffic was light. As I was driving I thought about how Ben's brain would have exploded if I'd simply loaded him in my SUV and driven him to my house that night. No, there was just too much information to absorb before I could introduce him to the 'real world', which of course would seem like a fantasy world to him.

Kathy was waiting for me when I got home, as I expected she would be. As my bride of thirty-five years, she had not only been in on what I was doing at work, she had been my right hand when we had first started. But, with the kids growing up, she had stepped back to raise our two daughters, and was now in the process of completely spoiling our grandchildren – a role she relished almost as much as sitting in on meetings about time transference and the mine fields that would open up. What she didn't know were two things: Had it worked, and who did the algorithm retrieve?

With the secrecy of the project we had agreed to not discuss details over the phone, and I would always store my phone away from the living area so if it was compromised, nobody would be able to hear our conversations. Additionally, our house was regularly swept for listening devices. Early on we had told our girls the nice men who came so often were from pest control. Though they had been told not to talk about things that went on in our house to their friends, I expect at some time the words "pest control guys were over again" came out of their mouths, leaving their friends wondering what kind of infestations we had. Unless someone asked, I wasn't too worried about that kind of rumor. If it did come up, I would simply tell people we previously had a bad infestation, but we were in 'maintenance' mode now. The only real lie to that statement was that, other than the fact that all cellphones are essentially listening devices for marketing companies, we'd never really had an "infestation" problem. Once, though, I did toy with the idea of releasing some actual cockroaches, then having the "pest control guys" come over, but I just didn't want those little critters in my house. So, I justified the small lie. The guilt was not overwhelming.

As they grew older, I gradually let them in on some of the work I was doing, but not on the 'best' parts. They knew I was working on a transportation system, but they didn't know it would transfer matter (which it actually doesn't), or the more serious through-time part. It wasn't that I didn't trust them, but in the interest of sanity on everyone's part, I just didn't want to burden them with that kind of knowledge that could, under no circumstances, be divulged. Since they were now grown and out on their own, with families of their own, the regular visits for security sweeps were no longer a real issue, and Kathy had a pretty good handle on when one of the kids might show up, so she could re-schedule for the next day, or even later in the same day if anyone from the extended family was coming over. I had scheduled a sweep especially for earlier in the day today, though, because I knew this subject would most certainly come up, and I wanted to be able to talk about it freely when I got home.

As expected, she was waiting for me at the door. We already had a 'code' of sorts we could use upon arrival before I would place my phone in the secure container.

"How was your day?" she asked, with an very impatient look on her face. I gave her my best 'wait until you hear this' look on mine, but simply replied, "Oh, just another red-letter day at the factory."

The words 'red letter', even when said in jest, was code for 'something big happened today'. She knew it was going to, but even so I put my best 'can't wait' look on.

"Well," she said, "Why don't you put your things away and then you can tell me all about it."

I went into the bedroom, put my laptop case/briefcase on the trunk at the end of the bed and put my cellphone in its charger. Then took off my shoes, since my feet were killing me, and went back into the dining room. She had some hot cocoa waiting for me, and we sat down at the table.

"All OK?" she said – another code for 'are we secure?'.

"Yep," I said. "You just ain't gonna believe today!"

"Well tell me! I've been sitting on pins and needles all day waiting to see if it worked," Kathy said as she sat down to her own cup of cocoa.

"It was spectacular!" I began. "The software worked perfectly, and as hoped, we got someone from the top of the list. I didn't get my first choice, but I think in retrospect the person I got was exactly the one we needed."

"Well, don't hold me in suspense!" she said. "Who'd you get?"

"Let me put it this way, and I'll let you guess," I said. "I don't think you'll have a hard time."

"Oh, you're mean!" she said as she punched my shoulder.

"OW!" I said in mock pain. "How hard do you want me to make this?"

"OK, Mr. Smartypants – just give me the first clue".

I smiled. "Alright. I heard the countdown beeps in the hallway, and when it hit zero, he just appeared – just like the test specimens had. No sound, no flash, just a top-to bottom quick-drawn fully-clothed and breathing human. Of course he was surprised and frightened, so I had to calm him down even before he'd fully settled in. Bill was right outside the door ready to burst in if needed, but as it turns out, our new friend was relatively calm. That was my first clue that we had the right guy. As soon as I was sure he wasn't going to bolt, or worse, attack me – and while that last part had always been a concern, when you hear who this was, you'll understand I wasn't as concerned. Anyway, he's relatively calm, lucid, but appropriately apprehensive, so I said, 'Sir, My name is Tom. What is your name?' His answer, from his appearance, was exactly what I had hoped he would say. He simply said, 'My name is Ben'"

Kathy's eyebrows rose, and she sat back in her chair. Then her eyes got wide and she half-said/half-whispered, "Are you telling my you have Ben Franklin?"

"Yep. Benjamin Franklin originally from Boston, Massachusetts, now living in Philadelphia."

"Oh my gosh...Oh. My. Gosh!" she said, almost breathlessly.

"But, Kathy, that's not even the most astonishing part. Later, after I had calmed him down, given him some basic information about what had happened and, as a matter of fact, not too long before we wound the day up, I simply commented that I knew he'd had a long day, and a lot to think about, and he might want to get some rest before we continued. He said, '*Well, since we signed the Constitution today, I rose early this morning*'."

She did a double-take.

"Kathy! We grabbed Ben Franklin on the afternoon of September 17, 1787 as he was leaving Independence Hall after having signed the Constitution of the United States!"

Kathy's jaw dropped, she leaned forward and put both her palms on the table, almost knocking her cocoa over, and said, "Please tell me you're serious!"

"Yep. As serious as the 300 year old man sleeping in the apartment at the office."

She sat back in her chair, folded her arms, and said, "Boy, is he in for some surprises!"

"Oh, he has no idea. But, that's just the beginning of surprises". I pulled out a small plastic bag and showed it to her.

"What is that?", she asked.

"Hair of Franklin," I said.

She screwed up her face, then went into full surprise when she saw a few gray hairs in the bag.

"Whatever are you going to do with this?", she asked.

"Well," I said. "turns out we have a daughter who works in a bio lab. She's not going to know whose this is, but she's going to do the first ever DNA test on Benjamin Franklin, so I can compare it to known descendants DNA as confirmation for the folks at NSF."

"You're kidding?"

"Nope. Gonna see her first thing in the morning and lie to her."

"You can't tell her whose it is, can you?"

"No. She's unfortunately not cleared. I'll just tell her it's part of a project we're working on and I just need some independent data."

"If she ever finds out, she'll kill us both."

"Well, she'll get the insurance settlement then, won't she?"

I laughed. Suddenly she leaned forward and grabbed my arm. "Tom – when can I meet him???"

Chapter 15

Friday - First Week

I awoke the next morning surprised somewhat that I had slept well all night – at least what was left of it. I know the fact that I had spent long hours the previous day both in preparation and in execution of the transference had much to do with it, but the knowledge of who we'd ended up with, and his demeanor throughout the entire ordeal gave me a peace of mind that kept me from obsessing over it, and sleeping instead. On top of that, I hoped that no call from Phillip overnight meant Ben had slept well also. I know he'd had a long day, but if he also didn't obsess over it all night, this might turn out better than I'd hoped for. But, I had risen early in anticipation of Ben's doing the same – after all, Ben's day began at five a.m. most days, though with no windows, and my specifically leaving no alarm mechanism, I had hoped he would sleep later than that since the evening before had lasted longer than he was traditionally accustomed to.

Kathy had breakfast ready as I came in from showering, shaving, and getting dressed. It had just turned five-thirty when I finished wolfing down the eggs, sausage, toast, and gulping down my morning juice, and I was in a hurry to leave. Kathy walked me to the door.

"You want to come down later today?" I asked.

Her eyes lit up. "Of course!! I *really* want to meet your new 'guest'!"

"How about you come and eat lunch with us. I'm going to serve Ben something he's never seen, but I'm guessing he'll enjoy very much."

"Well," she said. "I know you've already served the pizza, so let me guess. Burgers and fries?"

"See you at lunch," I said, kissed her goodbye, and left.

It was a nice day for late April. Normally this time of year there'd be plenty of showers and still a bit cool, but 'The Almighty', as Ben referred to Him, had seen fit to give us upper seventy degree weather with a nice sunshine, and the forecast for the weekend was more of the same, maybe even creeping up into the low eighties. Unseasonably warm weather would come in handy, but I was under no illusions that the rains were gone. Earlier in the month it had rained especially hard, so those 'May flowers' that April showers were supposed to bring didn't have to worry about dehydration.

I went by my youngest daughter's house on the way and conned her into a DNA test on the sly, spent a few minutes catching up, then told her I had to get to work and she promised to email the DNA info to me in a couple of days. I wanted to compare her results to the ones Dr. Ken would be doing. If I was going to present Dr. Benjamin Franklin from 1787, I wanted plenty of evidence!

Arriving at the office, I pulled into my parking space, grabbed my laptop/briefcase, and as I got out of the SUV, Bill pulled up along side me, a bit early for his shift.

"So, you want to see how our 'friend' fared last night as much as I do, I see," I said has he shut the door to his H2. He had never really been too concerned about gas mileage. He just really liked the look of a baby Hummer.

"OK, I admit it. I'm intrigued. Who wouldn't be?"

"Yeah, when I told Kathy who we had, she almost knocked me out of my chair asking when she could come down," I said. "So, I'm taking a point of personal privilege today and I asked her to come down and eat lunch with us. Whatcha wanna bet she shows up at eleven?"

"Well, do you blame her?" he said as we walked up to the door. He punched in his passcode on the entry keypad, opened it and held it for me to go in. When you enter our building, there's a small reception area just on the right adjacent to a door that leads to a hallway the extends down the length of the building. If you follow the hallway all the way around, you'll end up back at the front door, making a square around the center conference/dining room. Going straight puts you in the room where Ben first appeared just past the communal restroom. My office is adjacent to the "arrival" room and adjacent to Ben's apartment, but I normally take the longer route to the right. Bill's office is at the end of that hallway, so I would be walking with him towards his office.

I punched in my passcode to the right hand hallway entry door and opened it for both of us. As I passed by the kitchenette, Miriam was also already there. "My, aren't we all punctual this morning?" I said.

I got an ugly look in return. "You may be punctual, but you know I had to be here early. Not that I'm complaining, you understand."

Phillip was standing at the door on the other side of the kitchenette drinking a cup of coffee. "Any news from our guest this morning yet, Phillip?" I asked.

"Nope. Quiet as a church mouse so far, skipper. I kept an eye on him all night, and he slept pretty good, once he got used to the bed. I don't know what he's used to, but he seemed to acclimate himself pretty well. When I came in here a few minutes ago, it was all still snores in his apartment."

What Ben didn't know was that we had cameras in every room except the restrooms. We even considered putting them in his bathroom and in the ceiling of his shower. I know that sounds creepy, and the point was not to be voyeuristic. But since we would have someone completely unfamiliar with our facilities, particularly in the bathroom, we needed to make sure he wouldn't end up harming himself, accidentally or on purpose. We were not worried at all about the latter, based on how the previous day had gone, but I didn't want to lose Ben Franklin because he slipped in the shower. The "*I've fallen and I can't get up*" excuse just would not go over well. But, in the end, the creepy factor overwhelmed safety issues.

"Well, that's how I'd hoped it would go for him," I said. "Since the walls are very well insulated, nothing we can do, short of setting off an explosion or getting in a gunfight should wake him, so let's let him sleep a bit longer as we get today's game plan together."

Bill said, "I agree. Phillip, if you want to go on, you can. I can take over from here."

"No way," he said. "Losing a little sleep today won't be a problem for me tomorrow. Besides, being the bachelor of the bunch, I don't have anyone to answer to like you slaves do."

With that he gave us a pity look, and came across the kitchenette and went past us headed for the security office.

"Think you're smart, huh?" I said. "I'll remember that next time I want to go somewhere with Kathy and need someone to keep a watch on things."

"Yeah – shoulda kept my mouth shut," he said as he went around the corner.

We all laughed, and just as I turned to head to my office I stopped, looked back in the kitchenette, and said, "Oh, by the way, Miriam. When you make the lunch run, buy an extra one for Kathy. She brow-beat me last night into seeing Ben, so I told her to join us for lunch. And since I run the place here, I get to let her. Might come in handy next time I need something from her."

OK," she said, chuckling. "I gotcha covered."

"Tell you what," I said, "how about we all meet in the conference room in twenty minutes and get the game plan together for today."

"Will do," she said.

"Sounds good," said Bill.

Down the hall I heard, "I'll be there too. Thanks for the invite…."

I went towards my office, and as I passed by Phil's office, I said, "Feeling lonely there, single guy?"

In my wake I heard him say, "Everybody's a comedian..."

I settled in, pulled out the laptop, and began checking my email. There wasn't too much. My schedule for the day was published on our internal site – which all those involved in any way in our project had access to – and it indicated we were doing maintenance on our systems today, and would be closed for all but emergency or priority issues, so I had not expected much. I flipped on the radio set behind my desk, and spun the dial around twenty meters quickly to see what condition the bands were in today, and was gratified to see it was open to Europe and the Atlantic. I intended at some point to show Ben how real instant worldwide communications was, and thought how great it would be if someone from the U.K. was on the air. I wondered how he'd react to hearing the voice of someone from the country they'd just defeated coming from this little box on my desk. I reached up to the rotor control and made sure the Yagi antenna at the top of the seventy foot tower behind the building was pointed towards western Europe, and hoped there'd still be someone on there later today. NSF had allowed me some personal liberties with the facility, and I didn't feel guilty at all about it!

I did a quick look at my news aggregation sites to see what was popping in the world, then closed the laptop, and picked it up and went into the conference room. Shortly after I sat down, Bill and Miriam came in, followed by Phillip. Phillip and Bill both had their tablets with all the camera feeds so we could keep a watch on things while we talked.

I started the briefing. "I have scheduled Dr. Ken Matthews to come by at eleven, and we're going to give Ben his first ever full physical. I'll prepare him for the inoculations the doctor and I had agreed upon, and hopefully we won't find anything to be concerned about. He's going to draw some blood, do a DNA test – that should have some interesting results – and check out his basic physical condition. I fully expect he'll put Ben on some maintenance medications, and if he doesn't find anything else terribly wrong, maybe that'll be it."

"I read last night," said Bill, "that his mobility was impaired, probably because of his gout condition."

"Yes," I said, "Ken is fully aware of his conditions. I updated him on the way home last night, and texted him some historical websites to review so he'd know what to look for. The new gout treatments should fix that problem. I'm more concerned about any other physical issues he may have that we don't know about. We know from history that he died a little over two and a half years after signing the Constitution from pleurisy. Ken should have something to preemptively address that condition, and hopefully we can prolong his life a few years longer. At any rate, I'll begin preparing him for that as he's eating breakfast."

They all nodded, so I went on. "Next, I want to start familiarizing him with modern speech use – idioms, aphorisms, colloquialisms, slang, and alternate word uses. There's no way I can get all that in before eleven, but I still want to cover as much of that ground as I can. I would very much like you all," and I looked over at Phillip, and sarcastically added, "including you, Phil," (at which he gave me a sour look as I went on), "if you want, to help me come up with language we use in everyday conversation that would be unfamiliar or confusing to someone from 200 years ago. For instance, as I had warned you before we began yesterday, anyone from a time earlier than the twentieth century would not understand the term 'OK'. So, we've avoided using that until we had time to do some explaining."

Miriam perked up and said, "That might be fun. Actually, I guess the question is, How much fun are we allowed to have."

"Well," I said, "Ben is already wary of women who wear pants, so you might want to watch yourself there, young lady!" That got me a sour look.

"Anyway," I continued, "we'll do that until Ken shows up. Now, after lunch I have a tailor that does some work for the FBI coming over. He's signed an iron-clad non-disclosure, so we won't have to be too careful around him, but let's not divulge any more information than we have to. His job will be to get Ben's measurements and acquire whatever clothing we – and Ben – feel he might need for the next several days or weeks. Hopefully he'll have some of that ready by the end of the day, and that should get us to the weekend."

Bill spoke up, "How are we going to handle the weekend?"

"Well," I said, "I plan on keeping a week-day schedule this weekend. I know you're coming over tomorrow, and we'll have Phillip here again tonight, and I hope that, by Sunday, we'll have him dressed, acclimated to his immediate surroundings, and ready for his first venture into the unknown outside."

Miriam spoke up, "I'll gladly keep the same type of schedule, if you want. I'm really intrigued about how all this is going to play out."

Phillip spoke up next. "Don't count me out! I'll gladly be on duty all weekend as well. As far as I'm concerned, I can go back to the regular schedule next weekend and be fine."

The other two nodded and both agreed to the same.

"I appreciate that, thanks!" I said. "Kathy is coming for lunch, and I'll bet my house she'll want to stay. I'm guessing she'll help out with the language issues as well. I am a little afraid she'll tell Ben too much about me, but I guess that's what you put up with when you agree to that 'better or worse' deal. So, I guess we're all set."

I looked down at my watch. "Has he stirred at all?"

Both Phillip and Bill looked at their tablets for a moment. Bill spoke up, "Yeah, just a little bit."

"OK," I said. "How about I go get him up, and let's get this show on the road!!"

Chapter 16

Friday - First Week

I checked the monitors in the security office before entering Ben's room. I watched him for a minute or so, and when I saw a leg move, that seemed as good a time as any to go in. I went to the door of his apartment, knocked on it, waited a second, then eased the door open.

"Dr. Franklin, do you feel like getting a start on the day?" I asked. He rolled over on his back, raised his head and said, "Yes, I suppose. What time is it?"

"It's almost seven a.m., and breakfast will be ready in the dining room when you're dressed."

"Good heavens!" he said. "I have wasted away the morning."

I chuckled and said, "Oh, sir, there is plenty of day left. Remember, we have all these lights now that let us work way into the evening. Did you sleep well?"

Ben rolled out and sat up on the edge of his bed. He was not, shall we say 'wearing pajamas'! I looked behind me to make sure Miriam wasn't in sight.

"I must say," he said, "this bed is as comfortable as some of the best in Paris. You must have spent a fortune getting it here."

"Actually," I said as I made certain the door was closed, "I was afraid we should have spent more. The bed I sleep on at home is much more expensive than this one. My daughters both have more expensive beds. Apparently, Ben Franklin is much easier to accommodate than both of them."

Ben was in the middle of a stretch when I told him that last part, and he looked over and gave me a wry smile, then asked, "Does everyone have such a restful bed these days?"

"Well, I suppose there are some that don't have as good a one as this, but for the most part, yes. Do you need anything before I leave you to get prepared for the day? I highly recommend the shower I showed you last night. It feels wonderful first thing in the morning."

"Yes," he said, "I think I shall try this 'shower'."

"Good!", I said. "Pick whatever clothing you need from the closet area over here, and come to the dining room when you're dressed and ready to begin. We have a bit of a schedule today, and I'll get your permission for what I have planned when you get there."

"I shall be along presently," he said.

"Wonderful," I said. "Call for us if you need anything," and with that I closed the door and went into the security office and picked up a tablet so I could monitor him as he dressed. The last thing I wanted was one of his 'air baths' down the hallway! I went into the kitchenette and told Miriam that Ben was up and in the shower, and she said she'd bring his breakfast out when she heard him come out of his apartment

True to his word, Ben tried out the shower, and it was a bit comical hearing him play with the faucets. About a half hour later, after he'd looked at virtually every item in the closet and in the drawers, he'd selected suitable attire and, yes, even underwear, and headed for the door. I quickly shut off the tablet and put it in a drawer in the side table by the door.

As Ben came through the door, Miriam entered from the kitchenette with a tray containing a plate of eggs, sausage, bacon, toast, and two glasses of orange juice, and placed Ben's meal in front of his chair, then placed the second glass of juice in front of me. Ben looked at the meal, then bowed slightly to Miriam and said, "Thank you, madam. I must confess I am quite famished."

"You are most welcome, Dr. Franklin. If you need anything, please ask," she said and turned to go back to the kitchenette.

"I had a similar meal at home early this morning, Dr. Franklin, so I'll just drink a glass of juice while you eat, if you don't mind."

"Of course," he said, and sat down to his meal.

"I like my eggs slightly salted and peppered, and we have a shaker of each if you wish," I said as I pointed to the shakers. "I'm sure you're acquainted with sausage and bacon, and later we'll have a discussion of the types of foods you are accustomed to and Miriam will be glad to help you with meal planning. We want your time here to be as pleasant as we can make it."

Ben took a bite of the eggs, then grabbed the salt shaker and salted the eggs lightly. As he did, I picked up my glass of juice and said, "I suppose you didn't have orange juice in 1787, but you must have encountered oranges somewhere along the way." and I pointed to a bowl of oranges in the center of the table. "This is the juice squeezed and prepared from these oranges, and is found on many breakfast tables. While it is primarily a breakfast beverage I, like many, also enjoy it at other times of the day."

Ben took his glass and took a taste sip. As he swallowed, he raised the glass up a bit and looked a it. "Well, I must say, you have provided me with yet another tasty beverage." Then he put the glass back down, sliced off a piece of sausage and said, "Exactly how many types of beverages do you have in this day?"

"Thousands!" I said. "There is an entire industry of hundreds of beverage companies of all types and flavors. I know in your day, beers, ales, and other like beverages were the preferred drink, and while those are most certainly prevalent, the non-alcoholic beverage industry is huge as well, and people like me prefer that to alcohol because we can drink as much as we want without the diminished mental capacity that occurs with alcohol, but we obviously will work all that out for you."

He dove into the meal as Bill and Phillip both came in with cups of coffee. "These two," I said, pointing to the pair, "are coffee drinkers. My wife is also a coffee fanatic, but I've never developed the taste for it. You already know my affinity for Mountain Dew..."

He interrupted and said, "Yes, I enjoy the 'Dew' as well!"

"Great! Another convert!" and they laughed.

Bill and Phillip asked about Kathy, and that gave me the opportunity to say, "Oh yes. Dr. Franklin, my wife, Kathy, will be joining us for the noontime meal, and she is anxious to meet you as well."

Ben nodded his head. "I would love to meet your good wife, so I too look forward to that meeting! You said something earlier about a schedule for today?"

"Ah yes," I said, and retrieved my notebook from the side table behind me. "First, with your permission, I have a physician coming at eleven. We want to have him give you a physical examination, just to make sure we haven't aggravated anything. I know, for example, that gout has been a problem for you, and I noticed you favoring one foot over the other, so there's good news for you in that regard. We have very effective treatments for that, as recently there have been discoveries that effectively treat gout and almost completely eliminate the pain and other symptoms, which should allow you much more mobility."

He stopped and looked over at me. "A physician? I would certainly like to meet this gentleman. And if he has something to ease my gout I may even want to befriend such a man!"

We all chuckled, and I continued, "Well, Dr. Ken Matthews is a good friend and a fine gentleman, and I'm guessing you will both become friends as well. He's a very learned man, and we may even use his expertise to bring you up to date on all the medical advancements in the last 200 or so years. Today, however, we will probably only have time for the exam."

"I shall look forward to that, then," he said.

As he continued his meal, I resumed. "First, though, everyone else here will sit down with you for a discussion on language. As you might imagine, everyday conversational English has changed significantly since your time, and if you're to be able to communicate with others effectively, we want to acquaint you with those changes, and perhaps give you some historical context on them. I will start off with an idiom we regularly use but have avoided because it's use began some years after your time. It will alleviate our having to be careful of the words we use, and acquaint you with how the rest of the population talks."

"As you apparently already know," Ben said, "Language is a pastime of mine, and I anticipate learning some new uses for my tongue!"

"Well, we can certainly accommodate that!" I said with a smile. "That should take us up to when Dr. Ken shows up, and after the noon meal, I have a tailor coming to talk to you about the types of clothing we have available, and look at getting some styles you would be comfortable with. He will take your measurements, present some examples, then return later in the day with purchases he has made to get you started. Anything that needs to be altered or created he will do and bring that to you at a later date."

Ben looked down at the clothes he was wearing and said, "Well, these are most comfortable. I find the undergarment very easy on the skin as well." As he went back to the last of his meal he said, "I, of course, am not acquainted with clothing styles in this time – and you may have noticed I have accepted your premise that I am now in a different time than I was yesterday morning – so this encounter with your tailor will be enlightening as well, I believe."

"Sir, you don't know how relieved I am that you have finally believed where, or more appropriately, 'when' you are. Did you come to this belief last night or this morning?"

"Well I must say the demonstration of the Tee-Vee set last night was hard to refute. As I was settling in that nice bed last night, I had no other option than to accept what you had been telling me, and I suppose that's when I finally surrendered the past."

He finished the last bite, wiped his face with the napkin, and took the last drink of juice, then sat back in his chair.

"What I struggle with most is whether, or maybe how much, to be angry that you snatched me from my place and time without my permission."

I hung my head, and things got real quiet around the table.

After an uncomfortable pause, though, Ben continued. "However, two things temper that anger. The first is knowing that I accomplished all that I would in my own time. I assume you have some historical documents to back that claim up, so I will hold you to that proof. The second is, as you had already guessed, that my curiosity has seized the best of me. The things you have shown me are simply amazing, and would be impossible to believe had I not seen them for myself. From our conversations thus far I surmise there is much more to follow, so I must relent and give myself over to my wonder and curiosity. To that end, I shall not hold anger towards you or your associates, so long as this proof you say you have is forthcoming."

I looked straight into the eyes of Dr. Benjamin Franklin, and said, "Sir. First that removes a load of dread off my shoulders, so I thank you for that. Secondly, your experiencing these other changes, just as you did yesterday, will be the only way for you to believe what life in the twenty-first century is like. And I will be most honored and privileged to be among the ones to show you these things."

"Fine, sir," he said. "Then, if you are ready, I would like to get to this talk about changes in language. I am most curious to see what time hath wrought!"

"Funny you should use that term, sir. Because the first words sent over that telegraph you saw yesterday were "What Hath God Wrought!"

Chapter 17

Friday - First Week

I grabbed Ben's plate and asked him if he wanted anything else to drink before we started. He declined, so I put all the plates and glasses on the tray and carried them into the kitchenette. Miriam had just finished cleaning up the cookware, so she took the plate and other items and put them in the dishwasher, closed the door, and started it up. It was a very silent model, so its running would not disturb our conversation in the next room. We both came back into the room and Miriam sat down next to me at the table.

"First, as I said earlier, Dr. Franklin," I began as I came through the door, "there is one term that almost everyone in the country uses on a regular basis, and as I said earlier, we have avoided it's use until now." I sat down. "That term is 'OK'."

"O K?" he asked with a wrinkled brow.

"Yes," I said, and I looked down at my notes. "Like the term for television last night were the letters 'T' and 'V', it is just the letters 'O' and K'. Miriam here is a history major, so I asked her to help out with some of the historical perspective on some of these terms. Miriam?"

"Yes, Dr. Franklin." she began. "The term first appeared in the early 1800s, likely as a humorous misspelling of the words 'orl korrekt' with a 'k' which meant 'all correct', and was said to have been written on documents after they had been checked for accuracy and spelling. But, it was popularized during a presidential election. Martin Van Buren, born in Kinderhook New York, was the eighth President of the United States, and in 1840 he was again a candidate for President. His supporters began referring to him as 'Old Kinderhook' and would flash a symbol with their fingers..."

She flashed Ben the 'OK' gesture with her hand.

"... and say something like 'Van Buren is OK with me', or words to that effect. The term stuck, and even though Van Buren lost the election of 1840, even today when you ask someone if something is agreeable with them, they will often reply, 'That's OK with me'. In print, you may see just the two letters OK, both capitalized, or you may see the word o-k-a-y, either capitalized, partially capitalized, or all lower case. It doesn't seem to matter, people are OK with it either way," and I chuckled at her joke.

Ben nodded, and said, "OK? That's it? That's the term you have been so carefully avoiding around me?"

"Sounds infantile when you put it that way," I said, "but yes. We all use it so much that we knew if we used it without explanation, this is the discussion we would have. So, is it OK if we continue?"

Ben smiled, and said, "O K – proceed."

Everyone at the table laughed, and we lit into the litany of modern terms we had all collected just for today's session. There were plenty of laughs and lots of questions, historical etymologies, and sometimes even outright horror at how the language had changed – some for the better, some obviously for the worst, and Ben enjoyed himself immensely through the discussion and was very animated the deeper and weirder things became. And by the way, he already knew the word 'weird' - just not all the ways it was used in modern conversation.

There was a huge discussion on the way some words were used to mean just their opposite, such as the word 'bad', how it could mean something evil, or it could mean something unique. The word 'cool' was another one, and there were many others. Ben was both aghast and amused at the ways the English language had been maligned and misappropriated over the years.

For two hours this conversation went on, and we finally had reached the end of all our lists. I knew other items would appear down the road, and told Ben that as they came up if he would make mental notes, I'd gladly explain anything to him later, unless it was something that required immediate explanation.

Finally, I said, "Well, we've been at this for a while. How about a break?"

"Yes," said Ben. "I would like to stretch my legs."

"Great!" I said. "As I told you earlier, we have a nice lawn behind the building. Would you like to go outside and stretch your legs there?"

"Yes! I would very much like to do so!" said Ben. "I won't be able to stretch them for long because of the gout, as you pointed out earlier, but if your physician has something to relieve the symptoms, I won't mind the discomfort much longer."

"Fine, so let's go then," and I rose, along with everyone else at the table. "You folks can come if you wish, though someone needs to be here in case Ken shows up early, or if someone else comes in. You can draw straws, cast lots, or just fight it out, I don't care." and smiled.

Phillip said, "I'll stay in. I'll let you know if anything pops."

"Good man," I said.

"Pops?" said Ben.

"Yes – missed one," I said as I laughed. "If something 'pops' It's slang for 'If something happens.'"

"My, I fear even the slang may be the death of me," laughed Ben.

We all exited and I led Ben down the hall towards his apartment to the exit door. It was locked and required a special key card, which we all had, to exit the building, because I didn't want Ben wandering out on his own just yet. Since we hadn't discussed computerized devices yet, I blocked what I was doing with my body as I unlocked the door and held it open for Ben and the other two to pass through, then locked it in the open position. Outside was a patio, patio table with an umbrella, and four chairs. The temperature was in the low seventies and it was turning into a beautiful day. I had worried that we might need jackets, but the wind wasn't blowing, and our long sleeve shirts were plenty sufficient.

Ben surveyed the yard and the manicured lawn and hedges that defined the fenced in area. "How do you keep the grass at this height?", he asked.

"Well, we have something called 'lawn mowers'. It consists of a long piece of metal sharpened on the sides, like a double-sided blade, and a mounting hole in the middle. It bolts to a shaft which rotates at a great speed causing the mower to cut the grass at a uniform height. This entire lawn can be 'mowed' in about thirty minutes. We employ a company that does nothing but lawn maintenance, and they come by every couple of weeks or so during the warm months and maintain this look for us."

"Interesting," Said Ben. "Do you have one of these 'lawn mowers' on the premises?"

"Not right now," I said, "but I can arrange to bring one by for you to see."

"Yes, I would like that," said Ben. He wandered further out into the yard. We had underground telephone and power service, so I didn't have to explain that, but after a minute or so in the yard he noticed two things: The HVAC outdoor unit near the end of the building, and the radio tower with the seven-element Yagi antenna adjacent to it.

"What in heaven's name are those?" he asked.

"Ah!" I said. "Well, first the unit on the ground. Have you noticed that our building has no windows?"

"Yes!" said Ben. "I have been meaning to inquire about that!"

"Well, there are reasons for that. The primary is that we do some sensitive work here, so the building was constructed so as to control entry. In other words, the two doors are the only way in and out of the building. But, that also means we need some method of heating and cooling."

"Indeed!" said Franklin. "The State House was quite hot, as we also required some privacy in which to work. But I have noticed that is not the case here, especially without windows!"

"Yes," I said. "That's because of an invention by a man named Lewis Carrier in, I believe, the early twentieth century. He discovered that some gases, when maintained under pressure, turned quite cold, and by passing air over pipes containing these gases, the surrounding air could be cooled. We call it 'air conditioning', and the entire building is cooled through ducts which transport air from that unit over there throughout the building. Also, in winter time, we use a hydrocarbon gas to heat the building much the same way. Both functions are performed in that unit."

"Remarkable!" he said. "And how does this tall appendage contribute to that process?"

I chuckled a bit. "It doesn't. That's something different entirely. Do you remember me telling you I am an amateur radio operator?" I asked.

"Oh, yes. Is this part of your 'radio'?"

"You could say that," I said. "This is called an 'antenna', or 'aerial'. It's purpose is to create electromagnetic waves when I send messages out, and to detect similar waves when I receive messages. It is directional. If you'll notice, some of the horizontal elements are shorter than others. The longest one is called the 'reflector', and the shorter ones are called the 'directors', and those terms are literal. They actually reflect and direct those waves in a particular direction. Currently, the entire antenna is pointed in a northeastern direction towards Europe."

Ben looked back at me with a bewildered look on his face. "You mean to say you can send messages to Europe through that contraption?"

"Dr. Franklin, when the conditions in the earth's upper atmosphere are correct, I can send messages directly to the other side of the earth. The term is 'sky wave', and in reality what happens is that those invisible waves leaving that antenna bounce off a charged band of particles above the earth called the 'ionosphere'. Those particles are charged from energy coming from the Sun, and when sufficiently charged, they reflect these waves which can then be detected on the other side of the world. Literally, they bounce off this charged band at or above the horizon in that direction, and come down all over Europe. I have a radio in my office, and earlier this morning I heard some other amateurs in Europe. When we're through here, we'll stop by my office and see if they're still there."

"Will we have time before your Doctor friend shows up?" He asked.

"Sure. We'll make time," I said.

"So, one can sit in a room with no windows, not be too hot or too cold, and radio with amateurs in Europe?"

I laughed again. "Yes, I know. Sounds strange even when I say that, but yes, that's pretty much the truth!"

Ben laughed, nodded and walked over to the fence and examined the hedges, which were thick enough he couldn't see anything on the other side. There was little noise back here so I wasn't worried about traffic sounds, but at the same time I was a bit concerned a plane might fly over, and we hadn't even thought about getting to Orville and Wilbur yet!

After a few minutes Ben came over and sat down at the table and leaned down and rubbed his foot. "Gout, again?" I asked.

"Well, that and the fact that I've had these same legs for over eight decades now, and I do believe they are telling me to give them more time off," he laughed. While he was sitting there, he looked at the exterior wall of the building. "I know some masons," he said, "and this is fine work!"

"Well, the art has been refined over the years, as well as the materials," I said. "One thing I look forward to doing is taking you to a home supply store and showing you all the types of building materials available to the public today. Hopefully it won't take us long to get to that point. Bill, here, is a craftsman. He's very skilled in woodworking, and does that for a pastime in the basement of his home."

Ben looked over at Bill and said, "What sorts of things do you build?"

Bill perked up and said, "Well, right now I'm working on an end table for my living room. My wife just redecorated and wants to replace some of the older furniture we have, so I'm working on those items for her. When you go into Tom's office, have him show you a couple of items I made for him".

"I will! And you, madam," and he looked at Miriam, "what do you do for a pastime?"

"Well, I am very active in my Church, so I suppose you could say that is my pastime. I help with the children and youth activities, and serve on the Hospitality Committee. I have two sons, both in their teens now, so they take up a good space in my life as well."

"What does your husband do?" he asked.

"He is an attorney. In fact, he handles some of the legal issues with our group here. We've been married twenty five years this October."

"I would like to meet both your spouses when the time comes," said Franklin.

"Oh, you will," I said. "In fact, when the time is right we will bring in other members of our families so you can begin the process of getting out into the world."

"Well, then, I look very much forward to that!" he said as he straightened up and smiled. He pulled his pocket watch out and looked at it, then said, "I see our good Doctor should be here within the hour. Would it be 'OK' to see that radio contraption now?" and grinned at me.

"Of course. Let's go back in," I said. "How about one of those 'Dews', Dr. Franklin? I'll not tell the good Doctor if you won't. He looks down on my addiction to them."

Franklin rose and said, "Yes. Let's, especially now that I am assured I won't bake in this house with no windows!"

We all laughed, and Ben and Miriam got up as well, and as she did Miriam said, "I'll bring the drinks in to you."

"Thank you, kind lady!" said Ben and we all went in. Bill went towards his office, saying, "Gotta make a couple of calls."

"Fine," I said. "This way, Dr. Franklin".

We followed Ben down the hall to my office door and went in. I had a chair against the wall beside my desk and I motioned for Ben to take his seat while I pulled my chair up to the radio desk. As in the other rooms, I had 'safed' the room so no technologies we had not as yet discussed would be visible.

Ben said, "What did William mean when he said 'a couple of calls'?"

"Oops," I thought. "Well, let's just say he will make contact with a couple of people here locally. I'll explain what he means by 'calls', later this afternoon, if you don't mind."

"So many things to have explained," he said, shaking his head.

"Yes, I know it is a bit frustrating, but as I said earlier, much has changed," I said as I pulled down the cover on the desk that doubled as a writing surface and a lid to the radio equipment. It was already powered up, and the backlit panel showed a signal strength meter moving about halfway up the scale and back, as well as several other backlit controls on the front panel, and in the middle was a digital display that showed a number of parameters, the largest being the frequency the radio was tuned to: 14.285.

Miriam came in with the drinks and put them on the end of my desk. I took a quick sip, but as I did I looked back over at Ben and his eyes were wide as he surveyed the panel and all the other items adjacent to the radio. "This is the radio itself," I said as I pointed to the transceiver. This," and I pointed to the rotator box, "controls the direction of the antenna you saw outside. This device," I pointed to the microphone, "converts my voice into electrical impulses which the radio turns into electromagnetic waves that emanate from that outside antenna."

"When I press this little bar," and I pointed at the red bar at the base of the microphone, "the radio begins that process. When I release the bar, as it is now, the radio reverses that procedure and turns waves picked up by the antenna into audible sound that comes out of this." and I pointed to the speaker beside the radio. "This is called the speaker – oddly descriptive – and I'll explain how it works later on. There is a lot that goes on inside that little box, and it's even been said it's indistinguishable from magic, but, again, it is pure science."

Ben took a gulp from his glass and said, "Amazing! Could you demonstrate for me?"

"Gladly!" I said. "I spend hours in front of this and one like it I have at home. Let's see if anything is coming in today." I took another sip, put the glass down, then pulled my chair up to the radio.

I turned up the volume and could hear some muffled signals off to the side of the frequency I was tuned to. I turned the tuning knob to the right a bit and the muffled noise became a voice. "...and I was on that boat for nearly four hours before we finally figured out all that was wrong was the spark plug was fouled. I took it off, blew it out, put it back in, and merrily on we went. No fish for the day, but another story to tell at the pub."

'God must be smiling on me', I thought. The voice from the speaker was heavily British.

"Anyway, that's my little adventure weekend last. We're planning another excursion soon, but I'm afraid my Sally wants me home this weekend. So, that's that, I suppose. How copy on your end. Whiskey Four Alpha Foxtrot Echo, Golf Four Sierra Tango."

I pressed the transmit button quickly and said, "Whiskey Three Tango Tango."

"Hold on, lad," said the Brit. "I think we have a breaking station. Whiskey Three Tango Tango, G Four Sierra Tango. Copy you five-by-nine old man. How copy?"

"G4 Sierra Tango, W3 Tango Tango, solid five nine here as well. Name's Tom, and I'm in Philadelphia. Don't want to break up the conversation, but I'm demonstrating the rig to a new friend. His name's Ben. So, back to you. G4ST, W3 Tango Tango."

"Well, hi to your friend Ben, there Tom, and welcome to the world of Amateur Radio. Name here is William, and the QTH is Bexley, just southeast of Merry Old London. Rig here is a Kenwood TS-2000 feeding a three-element Yagi up eighteen meters. I work in marketing here, which keeps me quite busy. What do you do in Philadelphia? Over."

"Well, I work for a laboratory that does some contract for the government. Nothing serious, just transportation mostly, but it pays the bills. Well, like I said, just wanted to do a quick demo for my new friend Ben here, so I won't disrupt your QSO any longer. Thanks for the quick contact. QSL information's online if you wish, and hopefully catch you later some time and we'll resume where we left off. Golf Four Sierra Tango, Whiskey Three Tango Tango. Seventy-three from the Cradle of Liberty."

"Yeah, you Yanks just can't keep from rubbin' it in. Seventy-three to you Tom, and to your friend Ben. OK, Smiley, where were we? Whiskey Four Alpha Foxtrot Echo, G4ST."

I turned down the volume and turned to face Ben. I can't describe the look on his face. I grabbed my glass and took another drink. "There is so much to ask." he said. "Did I understand him to say he was outside London?"

"That's right, though I've never heard of Bexley. I'll have to look that up later," I said as I wrote the contact in my log book. "We amateurs use a lot of shorthand and code words that have developed over the years. For instance, you heard both of us use the term 'Seventy Three'. You know, I'm not really sure where that originated, but back in the days when all that we could do was send Morse code – like I told you about yesterday – to keep from having to spell out in code frequently use words, they developed these shortcuts. Seventy-three is the equivalent of 'best wishes', or what would be a parting handshake if you were in person. 'QSO', is short for a contact, or a conversation over the radio. 'QTH' means your location, and all the 'Tangos' and 'Whiskeys' were ways of sending individual characters of the alphabet over sometimes noisy conditions. 'Tango' simply means the letter 'T', 'Whiskey' the letter 'W', and so forth.

What we were sending were our identifying 'call signs'. Each amateur over the world has a unique one, and W three T T is mine.

Ben just sat there, then said, "So they call us 'Yanks' still over there?" he asked.

I laughed. "Yes, but it's a term in jest these days." I paused and took the last drink of my Dew and put the glass back on the desk. "Remember when I told you about World War Two yesterday?"

"Yes", he said.

"The United States and Great Britain were staunch allies in that war, and still are today. As a matter of fact, our two greatest allies outside our own continent are Great Britain and Israel." Instantly I knew I'd stepped in it.

Ben's eyebrows shot up. "ISRAEL?" he asked.

I will forever be in debt to Bill. About that time he stepped in and said, "Ken's here."

Saved by the good Doctor.

"Tell you what, Ben. Let's get this exam over, and we'll go from there. The Israel story is a long one."

"Israel," he said, shaking his head as we both rose and went towards the conference room.

Chapter 18

Friday - First Week

Dr. Kenneth Matthews, or 'Dr. Ken', as we called him, had been my family physician for years. He was a tall, distinguished gentleman who had a very good bedside manner, and was the kind of doctor you always wanted. He would sit and listen (actually listen – not just 'pretend listen') to your complaints and take your opinions into consideration when responding, and when you were misinformed about something, he would take the time to explain, in layman's terms, what reality was and how it applied to your particular situation. It had taken Kathy and me a while to find him after we had 'interviewed' numerous other physicians, and we had always felt comfortable with him. Not only that, if something was outside his knowledge base or his area of expertise, he would readily say so, and seek other expertise. I think highly of Dr. Ken, so he was the obvious choice for Ben's first examination. He had been a doctor in the Navy, and I asked him to select someone who also had some service experience to accompany him. They had both signed the appropriate paperwork to insure their ability to maintain secrecy, and we had read them in on what we were doing. To say Ken was anxious to help out would be an understatement.

One of Miriam's tasks in all this was to keep the appropriate people appraised of not only who our guest was, but where we were in the 'education' process, so I wasn't surprised when we walked into the room and Ken was looking at a large dossier that, as I discovered, contained everything he could find on the historical Ben Franklin. Ken was accompanied by his chosen nurse, Emily, who stood slightly behind Ken.

"Hi, Ken, good to see you, and thanks for coming," I said as we shook hands.

"I wouldn't miss this for the world," he said. "Thanks again for thinking of me."

"My pleasure," I said as I half turned back towards the door where Ben was. "Dr. Kenneth Matthews, I'd like to introduce you to Dr. Benjamin Franklin of Philadelphia and Boston. Dr. Franklin, this is my friend and personal physician Dr. Ken Matthews".

Ben stepped forward and extended his hand. As they shook, Ken said, "This is an extraordinary pleasure, Dr. Franklin. I will remember this day for the rest of my life, I assure you".

"Sir," said Ben, "The pleasure is mine. I presume you are the one to examine me and repair all my ailments, correct?"

"Well, we will try, Sir," said Ken. He turned towards Emily and said, "Dr. Franklin, this is my nurse, Emily Warner."

Emily stepped forward and said, "Dr. Franklin. I am so pleased to meet you," and extended her hand. As before, Ben took her hand, and simply bowed before her saying, "My pleasure, madam". The look on Emily's face was priceless. I'm guessing not many people had bowed to her before.

"Well, shall we get started?" asked Ken. "We'll start with the basics. If you would, Dr. Franklin, please step over this way and let's get your weight. I know you are familiar with scales for determining weights", and he motioned to the bathroom scales he'd brought with him. "These are common household scales. They are not as accurate as the one in my office, but I just need to get a preliminary idea of what we call your 'body mass index', and your weight is a primary measurement. If you would, just step on the scales and hold there until the indicator stops."

Ben did as instructed. "235 pounds," said Emily as she read the numbers, then wrote them on the form she had on a clipboard in her hand. "You may step down now, Dr. Franklin," she said. She produced a long wooden measuring rod that extended to about seven feet tall with a sliding bar that had a small protrusion at the top. "If you would stand as straight as you could, sir, let me get your height." Ben did so, and Emily slid the bar until the protrusion was even with the top of Ben's head and then said, "Five Feet, nine and a half inches." and wrote that number down.

"Now, sir, if you would please have a seat in this chair, let me check your blood pressure," she said motioning to one of the chairs they'd positioned to the side of the table.

As Ben sat down, he said, "Blood pressure?"

"Yes," said Ken. "I'm not entirely versed on the history of blood pressure measurements. In your time it may have been referred to as arterial pressure, but it is one of the primary factors in our determining potential issues with a person's cardiovascular system – the heart and it's associated circulation system in your body. We have a simple device that will tell us maximum pressure of your blood during one heartbeat – that's called the 'systolic', and the minimum pressure during one heartbeat, the 'diastolic'."

"I see...." said Ben.

"This measurement, along with other measurements we take, help us to determine if there are any issues that might need addressing to prevent problems later," said Ken.

Emily stepped up and showed Ben the measuring device. "This device has a rather long name," she said, "but it's use is simple. I will put this cuff around the upper part of your arm. Then, I will inflate it with this bulb. When I do, you will feel some pressure on your arm. It won't be very uncomfortable. As I deflate it, I will listen with this device, called a 'stethoscope', to the blood as it flows through your arm. The sound changes that I will hear will indicate both the systolic and diastolic. It's really simple, and only takes a few seconds. Does that sound OK to you?"

Ben chuckled and looked up at me and said, "You were correct about your use of the term 'OK'. Apparently everyone is in on this little historical word." Then he looked back at Emily. "Yes, that sounds 'OK' to me".

Emily looked up at me and I laughed. "It's going to take him a while to get all the lingo down."

Emily smiled, and turned back to Ben. "Fine, then," and she smiled at Ben, as she wrapped the cuff around his arm. "I'll inflate the cuff now, so just relax while I take these measurements." She inflated the cuff, and placed the stethoscope just beneath it and listened as she released the pressure until she had both numbers.

"130 over 85," she said as she removed the cuff, then wrote the numbers on her form.

"Well, that was interesting," said Ben. "I assume you understand what those numbers mean?"

"Yes," said Ken. "That is a bit high from what we know to be the normal of 120 over 80, but that's to be expected at your age, weight, and particularly with whatever amount of stress you have undergone the last couple of days. As a matter of fact, I'm a bit surprised it isn't higher."

"Yes," I said, "That's one thing I like about Dr. Franklin. He has taken this very much in stride, and I suspect no one else in this room would be this calm after what we've put him through."

"I find this entire experience has been most mystifying," Ben said, "But I must confess that my curiosity has overcome all my other emotions, and perhaps that is why this 'calm', as you say, has taken place. May I ask," he said as he looked at Ken, "about the meaning of those two measurements, the '130' and the '85'? What do they actually measure?"

Ken responded, "Great question, Dr. Franklin. In the early days of measuring blood pressure, the devices used were mercury-filled tubes to determine this pressure, and these numbers are in relation to the surrounding atmospheric pressure. The first number is the 'systolic' and the 130 means 130 millimeters of mercury above the standard atmospheric pressure. The lower number is the 'diastolic' and the 85 is 85 millimeters of mercury above the standard pressure. Now, the device Emily used is calibrated to measure that pressure, and as she said, she can detect when both systolic and diastolic have been determined."

"Most enlightening!" said Ben. "What is the next of my measurements to be determined?"

Emily said, "Well, two things we'll do at the same time. First," and she held up a small white device, "this will fit on the end of your finger. It uses small pulses of light to determine the oxygen level in your blood. Normal is between 95 percent and 100 percent, so the point is to determine if your blood is receiving enough oxygen from its flow through your lungs. While that is working, I will put this device under your tongue to determine your body temperature. Both are painless, and only take a few seconds."

"Interesting!" said Ben. "Please proceed!"

Emily put the clip on Ben's finger, then placed a disposable sleeve over the temperature probe and placed it under Ben's tongue. About five seconds later the attached meter beeped, and she said, "Ninety Eight point eight degrees – very good!" Then she removed the clip and read the tiny meter on it. "Ninety Six percent. Not too low, but near the bottom, so it's fine as well".

"Fit as a fiddle!" said Ben. We all laughed.

"Well, just two or three more things for today's examination," said Ken. He pulled up a chair and placed it opposite from Ben, then sat down. "I know you literally invented bi-focal spectacles like the ones you are wearing, but in the intervening years, significant advances in care of one's vision have been made, so I'd like to do a cursory eye exam to get an idea as to your current abilities. Emily has placed on that wall an eye chart." and Ken pointed to the wall behind him. "What I'd like you to do is remove your spectacles, cover your right eye, and read aloud to me all the letters you can read."

Ben did as told, and got part-way down the list, and Emily noted this on his chart.

"Now, do the same with your other eye." and Ben did as asked, Emily recording the progress

"Now, please put your spectacles back on and do the same with each eye". Ben repeated the procedure, and Emily noted the results.

"Well, I am no optometrist, a doctor who specializes in eye care, but I think we may be able to improve your vision somewhat. I have a friend who has a clinic here in town who could perform a detailed eye exam and have some lenses custom made for your eyes. If you want, I can schedule you an appointment."

I said, "Ben, you might want to at least get your eyes checked. As you can see, I wear eyeglasses, and you might be interested in how that's done these days. It's totally painless."

"Yes, I'd be interested in seeing that, as it were." quipped Ben.

We both laughed at his pun, and Ken said, "Good. I'll set that up and let you know. Dr. Franklin, from the history of your life we know that you may have suffered from gout and possibly kidney stones...."

"Kidney stones?" I asked. "I guess I missed that tidbit. That would have been nice to know."

Ken gave me a suspicious look and said, "Why?"

I looked down at the floor and said, "Well, his first meal was pizza and Mountain Dew."

Ken put his hand on my shoulder and said, "You gave a man with kidney stones a soft drink? I'll deal with you later, but yes, that would have been nice to know."

Then he looked back at Ben and said, "I think Tom here may have done you a bit of a disservice with his favorite beverage since its contents can aggravate kidney stones, if that's what you indeed suffer from. Do you have any abdominal pain right now?"

"Not today," said Ben. "It was rather disturbing a few days ago, but not today."

"That's good," said Ken. "Maybe we can address that in a few minutes. Next, let me check your legs. We have found over the years that some ailments present symptoms in the lower leg, and I already know from your history that you have gout. So, I'd like to check your legs and feet, if you don't mind."

"Surely. The gout has been especially severe the last few days. I am told you have treatments for that now."

"Yes, we do," said Ken, "But right now, just sit back as I take a look." and he sat down and pulled off Ben's shoes and socks. Ben's big toe was red and swelled, and I was surprised he was walking at all. "Yes, I'd say that is a pretty bad case," said Ken. Then he replaced his socks and rolled up the cuff of his pants and examined the calves above his feet.

"Have you have any problems with your legs when walking"? Ken asked.

"Other than the fact they have a large number of years holding me up, I believe they are still serving me well." smiled Ben.

"Very good," said Ken. "I don't see any indications of diabetes disease or any other problems, but we will, at a later date, do a much more thorough exam at my office."

Ken replaced Ben's shoes, then stood up and said, "Next, if we could adjourn to some place where you can lie down, I'd like to check your breathing and see if we can find out about your abdominal pain."

"Yes," I said, "we can go to Ben's temporary apartment here for that. If you'd follow me".

We all went down the hall to Ben's room, and Ken had Ben lie down flat on the bed and unbutton his shirt.

"Dr. Franklin," Ken said, "I am going to use something called an 'ultrasound' device on your abdomen. It uses sound to peer inside without us having to perform any surgery to give us an idea of what's causing your pain. If it's what I hope it is, we can certainly help you with that."

"Sound?" asked Ben.

"Yes, it's all very scientific, and to be honest I'm not entirely sure how it works. But I do know that if I apply this device to your stomach," and he showed him the transducer, "an image will appear on this device in my hand and help me to determine how to proceed. It's entirely painless, I assure you."

Ben looked up at me, so I said, "Just another piece of modern day technology we haven't talked about. Don't worry about it, we can discuss how it works later, but right now let's see if Dr. Ken can help with finding out the source of your abdominal pain you've been having."

Ben looked at Ken and said, "Very well, proceed then, sir." and he unbuttoned his shirt and laid on the bed.

"First," said Emily, "I'll apply a lubricant to keep this sound device from irritating your skin. It might be a bit cold, but it's entirely harmless, and we'll clean if off once we're finished."

She took a tube and applied a generous amount of lubricant, Ben watching what she was doing with interest. When she was done, Ken turned on the portable ultrasound device and placed the probe on Ben's abdomen. As he did an image appeared on the screen. I have to say that, even though I'd seen this done before, I was fascinated at what this thing could do. Ben's eyes were glued to the screen, and Emily held up the screen so we could all see it.

After a few seconds Ken said, "Yes – just as I suspected. It's a bit hard to see if you don't know what you're looking for, but these are your kidneys. Inside are these hard deposits, generally calcium, that not only are hard but sometimes have little barbs on them that can really irritate. As you probably already know, the pain can become intense sometimes."

"Yes, indeed it can!" said Ben. "You can see that inside me from out here?"

"Well," said Ken, "it's just a picture made from the reflection of the sound waves, but it's accurate enough for me to tell. I've seen hundreds of these before."

Ken removed the transducer and handed it to Emily, who turned off the ultrasound and placed it at the foot of the bed. Then she took a moist disinfectant cloth and cleaned the lubricant off Ben's abdomen.

"Fortunately," continued Ken, "we have very effective treatments for kidney stones today. The first thing I want to do is have you take some pain medication which should ease your discomfort." and he shot me a dirty look. "Then I want you to take some medicine that will both soften the calcium deposits, and shrink them so they'll pass through your urine. When they do pass, there may be one last bit of discomfort, but many times, particularly if you continue taking the pain medication, you may not even know the stone has passed."

"I am sufficiently humbled by your expertise, Dr." said Ben. "If you can rid me of this pain from my kidneys, and relive my gout, I shall be forever in your debt."

"Oh, don't worry about that," said Ken. "Tom here is picking up the bill. Besides, how many people these days can say they helped cure Benjamin Franklin?"

Ben got a chuckle out of that as did we all.

"Next," said Ken, "and there will be a small bit of pain with this test, we want to draw some of your blood."

"Oh, I've had blood let many times before," said Ben.

"Well, this is not a 'blood letting' as you are accustomed to. We want to draw a sample which we will send to a laboratory where they'll perform some chemical tests to see if there are any indications of further items we may need to address."

Ben nodded. "Well, take what you require!"

Emily stepped up, and Ken said, "Emily is very good at this. You shouldn't feel much at all."

"Gratifying!" said Ben.

Emily took a cotton ball, put some alcohol on it, and rubbed Ben's arm. Ben was following every move she made. Then, she took a syringe and pulled the protective plastic cover off the needle, then took her gloved finger and thumped the area on Ben's arm she'd just sterilized, causing the vein to appear, as well as cause the nerves there to go partially numb for a second, then deftly inserted the needle, immediately finding the vein, and drew the appropriate measure of blood. When finished, she put the cotton ball over the entry area, withdrew the syringe, then told Ben to draw up his arm.

"Just hold it there for a minute until the blood clots, and we're done!" she said.

Ben looked at her, then to Ken. "You were correct, Doctor. She is very good at this. I felt nothing!"

"Emily was a medic in the Army, and she's been in combat areas attending wounded soldiers. Not causing pain has been a goal of hers since then."

"I am in awe of you, then madam!" he said. "So much experience from someone so young and attractive! I see our militia is in good hands!"

Emily, slightly embarrassed, smiled and simply said, "Thank you, Dr. Franklin!"

Ken then said, "Finally, if you would, Dr. Franklin, please sit up, and I want to use this stethoscope to listen to your breathing and heartbeat," and he pointed to the stethoscope hanging around his neck.

"On one condition, sir," said Ben.

"Sure," said Ken. "Name it".

"May I listen as well?"

Ken chuckled, looked over at Emily, who smiled, and said, "I told you. I win". Then he looked back at Ben and said, "Absolutely, Dr. Franklin. Let me do my part first, and then I'll let you listen as well. Emily bet me five dollars on the way over that you would want to listen."

Ben nodded once, and sat up on the side of the bed. As he did so, he looked up at me and said, "Am I to understand the currency is still being measured in dollars?"

I looked at Ken and smiled, then said, "Yes. And that is a discussion I relish. As a matter of fact, we'll talk a bit about currency in a few minutes." Then I looked back at Ken and winked.

Ken did his exam, then sat back down in the chair and handed the stethoscope over to Ben, and showed him how to position it in his ear. Then Ken unbuttoned his own shirt and said, "Listen to my heart. That way the blood flowing through the veins in your head won't interfere." Ben mimicked the way he'd just watched Ken use the device and listened for a few seconds to Ken's heart.

When he'd finished, he said, "Most interesting! I may wish to obtain one of these devices myself!"

Ken said, "Hear anything in my lungs that gave you pause?"

Ben looked up with a sheepish grin and said, "Sir, as I am not trained in its use, I would not know what to listen for!"

Ken laughed and put the scope back around his neck. "I guess we can both button up now," he said.

Then he came over to me, opened the folder in his hand and showed me the email he'd received from Miriam the night before. There was a sentence in it he'd underlined. He pointed to it and said, "Well?" The sentence said, "*One thing Tom wants you to be prepared to do is inform Dr. Franklin of the cause of his ultimate death, and begin now treating the possible causes. If you have an issue with this, please let Tom know before saying anything to Dr. Franklin.*"

I looked up at Ken. "Don't you think that's the best course?"

Ken paused, and said, "Yes. It's better to address it now rather than later."

"Are you OK with it?" I asked.

"It's part of my job," he said. Then he took the second chair, and placed it so he would be facing Ben, then sat down. "Dr. Franklin, overall your health is pretty good for a man at your age, and I know the life expectancy in your time was an age much younger than yourself, so you've done a pretty good job taking care of yourself."

Ben looked pleased and said, "I have had several things to say about taking care of one's self over the years, and it is gratifying to have those activities validated, so I thank you, sir."

"Yes," said Ken, "I have read much of what you had to say, and I thank you for clearing a good path, so to speak, for those of us who came after you. Now, there is something serious I do need to discuss with you."

Ben's face got a bit more serious, and he said, "Well, just speak your mind, sir".

Ken paused, then looked Ben in the eye and said, "At the time you were – what is the term Tom used, Replicated?" and he looked up at me, and I nodded. He looked back at Ben, "Replicated, then. That was the year 1787, as I understand. Dr. Franklin, you were already much past the life expectancy of the day. You lived to experience more than most of your time, and of course, now *this you* is experiencing something no other human being has before. However," and Ken's voice softened a bit, "the Ben Franklin that you left in Philadelphia that mid September lived another two years and seven months, and finally succumbed to pleurisy in April 1790."

He paused to let that sink in. Ben sat back in his chair, keeping his eyes on Ken.

Ken continued, a bit more upbeat. "The good news, though, is that we know how *that* Ben Franklin passed away, and thus we know what to look for. When I listened to your lungs a few moments ago, your breathing was relatively clear, but I did detect some very light congestion, that you probably are as yet unaware. Knowing what we know now, we can begin treating that congestion so that it doesn't develop into the pleurisy that took the Ben Franklin in 1790, and hopefully extend and improve the quality of your life."

Ben's eyebrows raised. He said, "Well, I certainly knew, based on what I've been told, that the man that was standing outside in Philadelphia went on unchanged, and that I was 'copied' and placed here. So I knew that 'me' was long passed, but when you tell me what my future was in those terms, it changes the way I see myself to a large degree."

"I understand that," said Ken, "and that is fully what I expected. But, let me add some context to that thought. By taking you, or a copy of you, and bringing you here, fully the same man that was on that street, and placing you in twenty-first century Philadelphia, Tom and his associates here may well have saved and extended your life. Now, you can take all this information however you wish, but I would hope you would take that simple fact into consideration, and celebrate the life you have here and now, taking advantage of all there is to offer in this time. I read that you once advised people that '*To succeed, jump as quickly at opportunities as you do at conclusions*'. I submit to you, sir, that you have a golden opportunity right in front of you."

Ben pondered that for a few moments, then slapped his legs with his hands, sat forward, and said, "Great advice from a great man!" and laughed – we all did.

"Wonderful!" I said. "Ken, is there anything else you need to do?"

"No," said Ken. "Until we're ready for a more thorough exam," then he looked back at Ben and handed him a small pill bottle, "I have some medicine for your gout. The instructions are on the label. Basically, take one of these tablets each day, at noontime would be a good time, with your meal, and in a few days you should see the symptoms of your gout began to subside." He produced another pill bottle. "This one is for your kidney stones. Take one of these at each meal, three times a day. Then he produced another bottle, "these are for pain. Take them as needed, but no more than four per day. I'd suggest one at each meal, then one just before bed at night for the first couple of days, then only as needed until there is no further need. Wait at least two hours between each one. If your pain gets worse, have Tom let me know and we'll increase the dosage if we need to. I'll check back on you in a week and see how you're doing. I'll also set up that eye exam for you and let Tom know when that is so he can get you there. Finally, this," and he produced a final pill container, "is to combat that chest congestion. Take one of these once a day at meal time. You can take it at noon with your other medications, or at the evening meal – entirely your choice."

Ben took the pill bottles looked at each one as if he were examining moon rocks.

"The top of this bottle twists off," said Emily, taking one of the bottles from Ben, "Like this. You press down on this tab, then twist to the left until the top comes off. Then simply replace it the same way until you hear or feel this little tab click back into place, and the tablets will be kept dry and safe until the next time. This top is designed to keep small children from getting hold of these tablets."

"Yes," I said, "That came from horrible episodes in the past, so we've built in many safety features when it comes to things like this."

She handed the bottle back to Ben, and he examined it for a moment, then placed it in his pocket.

Ken said, "Well, I believe we'll be going now..."

"Just a minute," I said. "I believe there was a wager to be paid here."

"Oh yes!" said Emily. "Where's my five dollars?"

Ken gave me a sour look, then pulled out his wallet and handed Emily a five.

"Thank you!" she said with a grin.

Ben witnessed the exchange, then said, "May I see that?"

Emily looked over at me, and I nodded, so she handed it to Ben. He took it and examined it carefully. "You know, I have actually printed currency before, and this is really detailed work!" he said. "Who is this gentleman pictured on the front?"

"Do you remember when we briefly discussed the wars the United States had been in, and how the Civil War was the bloodiest?"

"Yes," said Ben.

"Well, that is Abraham Lincoln, the sixteenth President of the United States, and one of our most revered Presidents. He served as our President during the Civil war."

"Do you have pictures on all your currency?" Ben asked.

I looked over at Ken, and smiled. "As a matter of fact we do." I took my wallet and took out a one dollar bill and showed it to Ben. "Do you recognize this gentleman?"

Ben's eyes shot up. "General Washington!" he exclaimed.

"Yes, and our first President. He is revered and famous for refusing to serve more than two terms. But, let's not get into that just as yet, we'll talk U.S. history later this weekend in detail."

Ben examined the front and back of the bill. As he did, I said, "You know, these bills have some designs in them to prevent counterfeiting. I read somewhere that you had done some work in counterfeit prevention."

Ben shot me a glance. "Yes, but not in such detail as these. I'm very much intrigued by the process that creates such intricacy."

"Well," I said, "We'll get into all that," and I took back the dollar. "Now, Ken, as a physician and a man of renown, I suspect you might have a larger bill in your wallet."

Ken paused for a second, then his eyes lit up. "Of course!" he said, and he reached in and pulled out a one-hundred-dollar bill and handed it to me. I straightened it out and handed it to Ben and said, "Tell me, Dr. Franklin. Do you recognize this man?"

Words cannot describe the look on Ben's face.

Chapter 19

Friday - First Week

It took a few moments for the realization to set in. Ben examined the bill, his mouth open and his eyes wide. He looked up at me and asked, "How many of these exist?"

"It has been a while," I said, "but the last time I looked, around thirteen billion.

"How is that possible?" Ben asked. "How many printing presses are printing these?"

"I don't think I know that," I said. "I know they are printed in two different locations, but I don't know how many actual presses there are. However, modern printing presses can print many hundreds of pages in the time it would take you to print one or two, so the number of bills in circulation are not as hard to print as you might imagine."

"But, why my picture, and why on a bill of such a large denomination?" Ben asked.

Ken took up the answer to that one. "Dr. Franklin, perhaps it hasn't been impressed upon you just how famous you are to this day. As you've seen, George Washington is on the most circulated bill, as you would expect as our first President, and many other of the Founders of our country are as well. Alexander Hamilton is on the ten dollar bill, James Madison is on, I believe, the five-thousand dollar note, and many Presidents since Washington are also on some of our currency. In fact, Washington is also on our five-cent coin. Here, I think I have one." and he reached in his pocket, pulled out some change, and handed a nickel to Ben.

"Well, of course I've seen some minted coins similar to this," Ben said, "not of this quality, though," as he turned the coin over in his hand.

"Would you do me a favor?" asked Ken.

"What favor would you like, Doctor?" said Ben.

Ken took the pen out of his pocket and handed it to Franklin. "Would you please sign this bill for me. Having a bill signed by the man whose picture is on the front will be something none of my friends have, though I'll have to wait until you and Tom decide to make this public, if you ever do, but it would sure be a nice keepsake."

Ben took the pen and signed the front of the bill right under his picture. "Are you sure you want to keep this amount of money around without being able to spend it?"

"That's no problem." smiled Ken. "I'll just add that amount to Tom's bill, so it's really his problem".

"Thanks a lot," I said.

"Mr. Franklin," said Emily, "Would you sign your chart for me as well? I can simply copy this information onto another one, and I won't even have this added to Tom's bill."

Ben smiled and said, "Of course!" and he took the clipboard and signed the form across the middle. As he looked at the form he said, "Such precise printing here as well, all these boxes and characters. I would very much like to see the printing press that produces these!"

I spoke up before Emily could say anything. "That's part of the process we haven't discussed yet, Dr. Franklin, but you will most certainly see one of those 'presses'," and I winked at Emily as Ben handed the form back.

"With that," said Ken, "we really need to get back to the clinic."

"We are about to fetch lunch, Ken. Would you and Emily like to join us?" I asked.

Ken looked over at Emily, then back to me and said, "If you don't mind, I think we need to take a rain check on that. As much as we'd both like to stay, as you know I don't do house calls, and unfortunately with the latest outbreaks, I have an office full of patients. If you don't mind, I'll have my secretary call and arrange another time when we can all sit down to a nice meal with you and Dr. Franklin".

"I understand," I said. "I appreciate your taking the time, both of you, to come over. Please say hi to your lovely bride, and yes, have your secretary call and we'll set something up."

"Thanks, Tom. And, Dr. Franklin, it is a huge honor for me to meet you. We'll see you again in a few days when Tom brings you over for a more thorough exam, and I promise you that will be interesting."

"I shall look forward to that visit!" said Ben. He shook Ken's hand, bowed again to Emily, which she took a bit more in stride this time, and they both exited.

"That was most interesting," said Ben. "It seems every few moments you have yet another surprise for me. I am not sure how to assemble all this new knowledge. How much more is there to learn?"

"I'm afraid there is a great deal," I said, rubbing my chin. "But, don't worry about putting all the pieces of this puzzle together. There are ways to organize such information, and once we pass a certain point in your, shall we call it, orientation, I'll start providing you with written documents in an organized fashion that will help you."

"Earlier, you mentioned Israel. Am I to understand such a place exists now?" he asked.

"Let's go back in my office, and I'll tell you a most amazing story. First, let me make sure about our noon meal." and I walked over to the kitchen door. Miriam was just on the other side. "Is lunch on the way?" I asked.

"I am going to get it in about fifteen minutes. What time is Kathy going to be here?" she asked.

"Actually, I'm surprised she isn't already here. When she comes, have her wait in here until Dr. Franklin and I are through in the office, and tell Bill in case she comes while you're out."

"Will do," she said.

I walked back over to Ben and said, "Let's adjourn to the office," and we walked back out into the hall and to the office. As we sat down, I opened a drawer in my desk and pulled out a world map. Ben sat down, and I placed the map on my desk and opened it up.

"First, we are somewhat casual in this office. It makes for a more relaxed working atmosphere, so don't hesitate to use our first names when addressing us. Miriam, Bill, and Phillip all answer to their first names, and mine, of course, is Tom. Even when greeting new individuals of equal or lesser public stature than yourself in a non-formal environment, first names are generally acceptable."

"I understand," said Ben. "Then, if you wish, you may call me 'Ben' or 'Benjamin'"

"I appreciate that," I said, "even though you are of a much larger historical stature than I, so forgive me if it comes out a bit awkward at first, or if I continue to mix 'Dr. Franklin' in as well."

"I will answer to either," he said. "Now, this looks like a map, though is appears more detailed than the ones I'm accustomed to."

"It is," I said. "This is a relatively recent map of the world. As you see, here's America, with all the current countries both North and South. As I told you earlier, our nation encompasses the majority of land in North America between the Atlantic and Pacific oceans. Here is the state of Alaska, and way out here in the Pacific is Hawaii, our fiftieth state. It was admitted as a state around sixty or so years ago in, I believe, in the 1950s, and the story of Israel sort of begins here."

"Here? On this island?"

"In a manner. We have a naval base there, one of the largest in the world. Before admittance as a state, Hawaii was a territory of the United States. We had first established a military base there at the turn of the twentieth century, and as time went on, and probably as a result of the First World War that we spoke of yesterday, the base grew. On December 7, 1941, our island was attacked by surprise and much of our Navy was damaged or destroyed. This event is what led us into the Second World War. My father was in the Army during that war and was injured in the Pacific."

"You say a 'World War'," said Ben. "How many countries were involved?"

I swept my hand across the map and said, "Well practically every country was affected in some way or another, but the primary combatants were The United States, Great Britain, and Russia on one side, with Germany, Italy, and Japan on the other. It was Japan that attacked us on what our President, Roosevelt, termed the 'Day of Infamy'. That day is still remembered today as a dark moment in our history."

I paused. "But, I don't want to get too deep into the discussion of that war, because there is a wealth of information, and we should save that for a topic unto itself. The reason this matters, is because of something that happened at the end of the First World War, and a most tragic time in history that happened during the Second. So, for the discussion of Israel, I'd like to focus on those two events, and we'll cover the war in much more detail later, or probably even just provide you with the written history for you to read at your convenience."

"I understand," he said. "More and more information, but proceed anyway, Tom."

I smiled. "Great. Here is what led to what I believe was one of the most significant events in all of human history."

For the next several minutes I explained how issues in the Middle East, particularly in Palestine dovetailed with changing attitudes towards the Jews and those who were termed Zionists, who supported re-establishment of a Jewish state, and how all that led to the 1917 Balfour Declaration – so named for one of its principle authors Arthur Balfour - in which Great Britain called for the establishment of a national home for the Jewish people in Palestine. That conversation languished until the end of World War II, when the public became aware of the atrocities committed by the Nazis in Germany, specifically the attempted genocide of six million Jews. That culminating event, and the outpouring of support that followed, completed the conversation, and in 1948 the British Mandate demanded the creation of a Jewish State. Then in May that year, the Jews formed a government and declared independence as the Nation of Israel, with their capitol in Tel Aviv on the Mediterranean coast.

Ben sat enthralled as I recounted the story of Israel and it's history. I know it was a lot of history to grapple with in a short span of time, but this was going to be his lot for the next several days, so maybe this would serve as practice for the both of us.

"Those like myself who read and believe the Bible, particularly in the book of Revelation, understood that at some point in time the nation of Israel would have to exist again, because it was prominent in Biblical prophecy," I said. "For the last 2000 years, people had difficulty understanding how it would be possible for the nation that had been destroyed by Titus and his Roman legions in A.D. 70, since the Jews had been scattered across the globe. But here it was, in the middle of the twentieth century. As you might imagine, Israel's detractors were not pleased, and indeed three times in just her recent history, Israel has fought major conflicts to repel those who want to, once again, destroy her. The first war was the war that won their independence in 1949. The second was what's called the Six Day War in June 1967 that, literally, lasted only six days. Finally, the Yom Kippur War in 1973, where even though Israel was caught completely by surprise, they were able to prevail. In the last two major engagements Israel not only prevailed, but gained more territory, and there's a fascinating story of the Yom Kippur War where they thought all was lost, only to turn it around in literally one small battle."

"Finally," I said, finishing up, "when all the wars were completed, the Jews were not only back in their Holy Land, but in control of Jerusalem, and all the ancient lands promised by Jehovah to Abraham. Now, I don't know about you, but in my lifetime, I have seen Biblical prophecy literally fulfilled. In 2017, the President of the United States, in a unilateral move, declared the capitol of Israel to be Jerusalem, and moved our foreign embassy there. The promise was complete. Had the United States not been attacked in 1941, we likely would have delayed our entry into the war, and the events that followed would have turned out much differently."

I sat back in my chair, as did Ben. He had hung on every word. "I have so many questions," he said.

"I know," I said. "That is a lot of information in just a few minutes, and there are so many parts. But here's the salient point: Without the murder of six million Jews by a madman and his henchmen, Israel would likely still not exist today. It is one of those times in history when all one can say is 'I don't understand it all, but I can say that God is most certainly in control'."

"All this happened within the last 120 years," Ben stated. "and this is just the story of the Jewish reestablishment?"

"Yes," I said. "There are many many other stories, just surrounding the two world wars. In fact, when the time is right, there is one story that will eclipse almost everything you've seen thus far. But, there is more background before that and..."

Phillip stuck his head in the door. "Excuse me," he said, "but Miriam has returned with lunch."

"Wonderful!" said Ben. "I'm interested to see what is on today's meal plate!"

"Oh," I said. "you're gonna love it!", and with that I rose and said, "Let's eat! Is Kathy here, Phillip?"

"Oh yeah. She's been here a few minutes and I think she's on pins and needles."

"Are we speaking of your wife, Tom?" Ben asked.

"Yes we are, and she'd very much like to meet you," and I motioned him towards the door.

When we entered the dining/conference room, Kathy was standing just a few feet inside the door. I walked over and gave her a peck on the cheek, then with my arm on her shoulder, turned back towards Ben and said, "Ben, I would like you to meet the love of my life, Kathy. Kathy, Dr. Benjamin Franklin."

Kathy was literally beaming as she held out her hand. As before, Ben took it, kissed her hand as he bowed, and said, "This is indeed a distinct pleasure, Kathy," and he looked back at me with a 'Did I do it right' look. I smiled and nodded.

Kathy blushed a bit, then said, "Dr. Franklin, I have been waiting a long time to meet you!" Ben released her hand, smiled a bit, did another short bow and said, "Well, I hope I meet your expectations. I must say, I am truly a stranger in a strange land!"

"I suppose you are," she said as she gave me a glance. "I know Tom and his friends will do all they can to make you feel like one of the family."

"They certainly have," said Ben, "and I've been informed that the use of one's first name in conversation is more normal than in my time, something I'll have to get accustomed to, so please, and all of you," he said, as he glanced around the room, then back to Kathy, "Please call me Ben. I have a feeling we will all be spending a great deal of time together."

"That we will, Ben, and let's start by sitting down and having a meal."

"Excellent!" he said. I motioned for Ben to take his usual place at the head of the table, and for Kathy to sit beside me on his left. Phillip and Bill sat opposite us, and Miriam brought in a rolling table with everyone's meal.

"Before we pass lunch around, let's bow for thanks." and I proceeded to issue a small prayer of thanks for the meal. "Now, Ben, today we eat light. In this country we have something called fast food. I know Dr. Ken would probably disapprove because, like you, he keeps an eye on the foods he consumes and warns the rest of us, but I'm not really that concerned about one meal."

"You'll have to explain the meaning of 'fast food'," said Ben.

"I will, but let's not let it get cold"! At that Miriam placed beverages in front of each of us, then a plate containing the day's lunch. "This is something called 'Burgers and Fries'," I said as I picked up my burger. "The 'burger' is actually a hamburger. It's two pieces of bread with cooked beef between them, as well as mayonnaise, which is made from eggs; ketchup, which is made from tomatoes; and dill pickles. Some like theirs with onions as well, but not knowing which you would prefer, I had yours placed separately so you can try it if you want."

Ben eyed his plate. "Beside that," I said, "are French Fries. In England they're called 'Chips', and though they're called 'French' fries, nobody's really sure who came up with them, though France and Belgium both make that claim. It's simply cut potatoes fried in oil, then lightly salted. This particular cut is what I call 'crinkle fries'. As you see, they are cut with these waves in them which, I believe, gives them a crunch straight fries might not have. Some prefer theirs just plain, and much of the time that's how I like them. Kathy prefers ketchup with hers, but I can take it either way. To each his own, I suppose. If you'd like some ketchup, there's some in this container," and I took the ketchup bottle and squeezed a bit on my plate.

"You just eat by hand, and there are some paper towels here if you get some on your fingers," I said as I pointed to the paper towels Miriam had placed between us all on the table. "Finally, we all have our beverages of choice. I know from your comments yesterday you like the Mountain Dew, but after Dr. Ken took me to task today, and since I don't want to aggravate your kidney stones, you and I will stick to iced tea. Kathy also likes iced tea with hers, and what's that you have there, Bill, Coke?"

"Yep," said Bill.

"It's Dr. Pepper for me," said Phillip.

"I'm with Kathy on this one," said Miriam, as she sat down beside her.

"Eat up, and I'd be interested to see if you like this All American meal."

Ben took one of the fries and took a small bite. "Yes, I taste the salt. I think I like these fries not from France!"

We all laughed. "Try dipping it in some ketchup and see how you like that." I said as I squirted out a small bit on his plate. Ben dipped the fry into the ketchup and took another bite.

"Yes! That's tasty as well. I may be like you, Tom. Unable to make up my mind."

I laughed. "Well it's all up to you. Try the burger. Careful, because the condiments that add flavor to the beef sometimes make it a bit slippery on the inside."

He picked it up and took a medium bite, and the burger held together well. As he chewed the bite, he examined the burger, peeling back the top bun to see the inside. "Yes, I believe I like this as well!"

"Wonderful!" I said. I took a bite of my burger, as we settled down to the meal. Ben wasn't kidding. I could tell he really enjoyed his burger and fries, but I knew that later on wiser heads would prevail, and we'd all return to meals with slightly more nourishment and less calories.

"You termed this 'fast food' moments ago. Please explain," said Ben.

"Well, our society is much more hectic than the one you have been used to," I said, "and many times between work, family, outside activities, and entertainments such as sports, finding time to prepare and savor a large meal becomes more difficult. So since World War II, after all the men came home from the war and started families, small eateries and cafes began appearing and people soon found that eating out was much easier than preparing your own food. As our society began to get busier, finding places where food could be obtained more quickly became popular, and so entrepreneurs soon discovered a market for places that could prepare a meal in literally minutes. Eventually, as these became popular, some of these entrepreneurs opened multiple such places across the nations, and the term 'fast food chains' was born. Now, virtually every community of any size at all has at least one of these fast food chain establishments, as well as smaller single-owner versions as well. There's a term for where we bought these burgers. It's called a 'burger joint'. 'Burger' is obviously enough, but the term 'joint' is a slang word for what was once a, shall we say, less savory, establishment. The term was co-opted for those who made fun of fast food restaurants, most of which served burgers and fries, so the name stuck. Welcome to your first meal from a burger joint, Ben!"

Ben chuckled as he was finishing off a bite. "Tom, I must say, you have a vast knowledge of how things came to be. Did you study all this history just for me?"

I laughed. "Well, yes and no. I am a fan of history, particularly strange history, plus I like trivia. I like knowing little things that add some spice to life, and it is sometimes just to know something no one else does. Plus, they are all great little stories, don't you think?"

"Indeed I do. One thing that has put me at ease is your taking the time to explain all these new concepts and contraptions to me. Do you know, Kathy," Ben said as he looked at my wife, "that Tom here actually spoke to a man just outside London on his 'radio' box this morning? I still believe he may have some of the devil's own craft somehow, but he assures me it is all very scientific. Can you assure me I am in no danger of losing my soul for his crafts?"

Kathy laughed out loud and said, "Well, Ben. If you are in danger, then I am done for. When we first met one of the first things he did was show me his 'radio' box. I was just as amazed. His interest was so infectious that he's even enticed me into that world, so I guess we are both guilty of the 'devil's craft', as you put it. However, don't worry about your soul. I'm assured by the Almighty that I'm safe in that department."

Ben laughed. "I will take you at your word, then, and no longer concern myself that he may 'drag me' into sorcery!"

We all laughed as we finished our meal. Miriam said, "Dr. Franklin, if you have room left after your burger and fries, I have some banana pudding. Would you like some?"

"I sure would!", I said.

"I was talking to Ben, if you don't mind, Tom."

I held up my hands in mock surrender. "OK OK, just save me some!"

Ben said, "Well, since that term OK has appeared yet again, I will say OK as well, though I'm not exactly sure what a banana pudding is."

"Oh, trust me, Ben," I said. "You'll love it!"

"I'll take some", said Bill.

"Me, too," said Phillip.

Kathy said, "Well, Miriam, looks like we're waitresses today. I'll help you." and she rose and went into the kitchen. In a few minutes they came back out with bowls of pudding for each and we all dug in. Turns out I was right – Ben loves banana pudding!

As we finished, Ben turned to me and asked, "So, Tom, what is the schedule for today?"

"Well," I said, "shortly, Henry Latimore is coming over to talk to you about your wardrobe. We want to outfit you with everything you will need for everyday living, as well as some formal attire when you might need it, for all seasons, and that will be entirely up to you and Henry. Now, Henry works for the Federal Bureau of Investigation. As the name sounds, it's an arm of the Federal Government that investigates and brings charges on those who break the federal laws, as well as those who participate in crimes across state boundaries. He will not be here, obviously, to investigate, but in his capacity as an agent of the FBI, he assists other agents with their wardrobe when they might need to remain anonymous in their pursuits of justice. His family owns a number of clothing stores where he worked growing up, so he seemed to be the perfect man to take on the outfitting of an individual in your situation. Obviously right now we don't want word getting out of what we're up to here until you are ready, so not only does he have the knowledge needed to suggest your clothing, but his family has the items in their stores, and he knows how to keep things quiet while we get you assimilated."

"I see," said Ben. "How much clothing will I require?"

"Well," I said, "you'll need at least one set for each day. Some days you may want to change into another set of clothes for whatever reason – change in season, you may get the set you're wearing to dirty too wear, or you may have a function that requires a different set. I will leave that entirely up to you and Henry. In fact, it will be strictly you and him, while I take care of some items I need to finish up this week."

"I look forward to his visit as well," said Ben. "What of the remainder of the day?"

"Well, I've thought about this for a long time, and since you have already seen what has been done with full motion pictures, how would you like to see a motion picture story tonight?"

"What kind of story?" Ben asked as he leaned forward.

"Well, there are literally thousands to choose from, but to save having to explain some things you haven't been exposed to yet, I wanted to choose a story of something that might have occurred from your own time."

"How exactly is this story told?" Ben asked.

"Well, in your time, I am sure you have seen a number of performances played out on a theater stage," I said.

"Of course. Many times," said Ben.

"I thought so. Imagine that same play, but performed, preserved, and played back on the Television you saw last night. In essence, that's what it is. A performance in moving pictures."

"I see," said Ben. "What types of plays might one see?"

"That was my problem," I said. "As I said there are literally thousands of movies spanning all genres, but I wanted something that might have some historical significance to it. We have something these days called a 'docudrama', a more-or-less true account of an historical event, but with certain elements chosen for content intended to entertain as well as inform. But, I also wanted something that would capture one's imagination, and maybe even tug at one's emotions. Additionally, I wanted to get your critique of the accuracy, or in this case the likely inaccuracy, of an event. Does that make sense?"

"Some," he said. "Have you made a choice of these 'thousands' you say are available?"

"Yes, I think so," I said. "A number of years ago, a performer originally from Australia became well known here, and eventually moved to the States, and one of his performances was concerning the American Revolution. The story is an amalgamation of characters, some of which represent real people, some of which represent a combination of characters, some you may even recognize."

"Does this play have a name?"

"Yes," I replied. "The performer's name is Mel Gibson, and the name of the movie is 'The Patriot'."

"And you want me to critique this performance?" he asked.

"Yes, in a manner," I replied. "These types of performances are primarily to entertain, and those that produced it use the history as a backdrop to tell a, hopefully, entertaining story. My point is that I want you to enjoy the movie, but when it's finished, I would love to hear from someone like you who actually lived through those times."

"I will gladly provide my perspective, and I'm anxious to see how this 'movie' storytelling works."

"Wonderful!" I said. "While we're watching the movie, you can think of a beverage you might like to enjoy, and I also thought I'd introduce you to a snack food, something I don't think you had in abundance in 1787."

"And what might that be?" asked Ben.

"Popcorn!" I said.

Chapter 20

Friday - First Week

I was a bit concerned about how bad an influence I was becoming on him. First, pizza and soft drinks, then burgers and fries, and tonight, popcorn and a movie. I consoled myself, though, that as time went on Ben's better instincts would kick in, and after he'd discovered all the junk food, he'd discover things that were healthier, so maybe the short term corruption wouldn't be too bad. Not only that, I was sure Dr. Ken would put the kibosh on the junk food, so perhaps I was actually doing a good thing here. He might as well have as much fun as he could before reality set back in.

As we finished up the pudding, Ben regaled us with stories of his youth, and the famous incident with the Silence Dogood letters I had mentioned to him the previous day. One thing was for sure, Ben was a great storyteller, so it is easy to imagine him holding court in a pub or at a social gathering, and he got quite animated when he told his stories. I could have listened all afternoon, but partway through one of his stories, Henry showed up with his fabric samples, catalogs, and tape measure, and as I made the introductions Ben mentioned something about wanting to learn more of this 'FBI' I had told him about.

Henry looked at me and said, "Well, I see you haven't lost any time while Dr. Franklin's been here, Tom." He look around the room and before he could say anything, I beat him to the punch.

"Don't worry, Henry. Everyone here is under the exact same NDA as you, so you weren't singled out!"

Henry had taken a bit of offense when I insisted he sign an NDA before working on a project with me. With anyone else he would have probably told them to go 'pound sand', since he was unaware of the government ties our little enterprise had, but when I assured him that, once he'd learned what we were up to, the NDA would only be a minor irritation. Seeing my wife there probably didn't help, but he knew she had worked for me before. Either way, once he realized he wasn't singled out, he seemed to relax and get back to the project at hand.

"What is this 'NDA' term?" asked Ben. "Is it anything like 'TV' or 'OK'? People seem to like abbreviations in this day!"

I chuckled. "'NDA' stands for non-disclosure agreement. It's a legal document that requires one to keep any information learned about our little enterprise here a secret unless we give him written permission to disclose it, or unless a judge orders its disclosure. Since Henry works for the FBI, he originally thought an NDA to be redundant, but I think he's OK with it now, right Henry?"

"Do I have a choice?" he said with a grin. "Yeah, I'm OK with it. I do have to say, though, that when I was informed of who your guest here was, that kind of took the sting out of signing it."

He turned back to Ben and said, "Dr. Franklin. Would you like to talk haberdashery?"

"Yes," said Ben. "I am most interested to see the fashions of this twenty-first century."

"Fine," I said. "Ben, I will leave you and Henry to it. If the rest of you would give them some room, I'm pretty sure we have some other things to do around here. Kathy?" I said as I turned to her. "Want to come on into the office while they work out their haberdashery details?"

Kathy nodded and said, "Sure."

"Give a yelp if you need anything Hank," I said as we left.

For the next hour, Ben and Henry went over the types of clothing and the different looks Ben might want to have. He took Ben's measurements, and they talked about shoes, neckties, formal versus informal wear, the definition of 'business casual', and they looked at a number of fabric samples. Ben was very interested in the catalog, and the models and quality of the pictures. Thankfully, and I had already gone over this with Henry, there were no items in the pictures (cars, planes, trains, etc.) that I would have to explain, so Henry had done a good job putting his 'catalog' together.

Kathy and I retired to the office where we talked about Ben and I filled her in on all that had happened since we last spoke. When we got to the subject of the movie I'd picked out, she admitted she was a bit concerned.

"Do you think that might me just a little too violent for his first movie?" she asked.

"I don't think so. I'm sure Ben has seen some pretty serious stuff in his time, since they had just finished with the Revolutionary War and he was, after all, a newspaperman. I figure he's seem some things that would make us queasy."

"I suppose so," she said. "Still, couldn't you have eased him into it?"

"Well," I explained, "I really wanted a period piece, something with which he would be familiar, and might be able to better critique when it was over. I know the Gibson piece is historical fiction mixed with historical fact, but I know from reading his comments on the picture that some characters were amalgamations of two or more individuals, and some of the events were altered to tell the story, or were combinations of actual events. I think if I explain these things to him before the film, he'll be OK with it. I really want to see his reaction to the story once it's over. I feel like it might spur some actual stories that may have been lost to history."

"I hope you're right," she said. "Shoot, you've already corrupted him with pizza and burgers and fries so why stop there? What are you going to do with the rest of the afternoon?"

"He's already seen the TV and my radio," I said, as I pondered the afternoon. "For now I thought we might cover communications, maybe get into computers, and I was thinking of introducing him to the United States Government. After all, he's just been examined by the FBI, so I might as well peel back more layers of the onion for him. What do you think?"

"That's a pretty big question for one afternoon," she said. "Do you have a game plan?"

"Only an outline in my head. Since I wasn't sure who would appear yesterday morning, I'm having to design all this on the fly. So far there's no gray matter on the walls, so maybe it's going well enough."

I paused. "What do you think about taking him to Church Sunday?"

"Church?" she said with raised eyebrows. "Do you think that's too soon?"

"I'll know more tomorrow afternoon, so I'm not going to bring it up until I see how things are progressing, I was thinking of taking him for a ride in the SUV. So, how do you also feel about a short visit to the house?"

"Man!" she said. "I'm glad you said something. If you'd waited until tonight to spring that on me, I'd have beat you with your own baseball bat. What do you mean when you say 'short'?"

"Well, I thought we'd take him for a ride around the block this afternoon, and then bring him over to the house for a few minutes later today. I was thinking a half hour at the most. Maybe serve him a piece of pie or something. Just give him an opportunity to see some stuff outside this building."

She thought for a second. "I have some peach pie in the refrigerator. How about that and some authentic hot tea?"

"I think he would love that," I said. "As for Church Sunday, I though we'd just skip Sunday School – I can have Tish sub for me – and we'll just show up for the service and leave as soon as it's over. If we park on the north side, we can avoid most of the crowd as we leave."

"That might work." she agreed.

"OK, it's a plan, unless a monkey wrench gets thrown into the mix."

I had a few letters to look at, and Kathy went into the kitchen to chat with Miriam. After a while, Miriam stuck her head in the door and told me they were finishing up. I got up and went back to the conference room as Henry was finishing his notes.

"How did it go?" I asked.

"Excellent!" said Ben. "Fashions have definitely changed in the last 200 years. Henry was showing me this 'zipper' device that one uses to facilitate the opening of one's fly. I can think of a few times when that would have been handy in my day!"

"Ben has excellent taste," said Henry. "Much of what he has chosen I can readily supply. The everyday wear should present no problem. Formal wear may take a bit of tailoring, but again, not much of a problem. I'll have him a change of clothing this afternoon so he can start dressing like the locals."

"Great!" I said. "If you don't mind, give Miriam a call when they're ready, and I'll have them picked up. I do have a special request, though. Can you make sure at least one outfit is 'business casual', just in case?"

"Sure. No problem," he said. "With that, let me get to it. Ben," he said, "I am honored to know you. I'm sure everyone you've met thus far has said this, but if I can be of assistance at any time, please let me know."

"Indeed, the honor is mine," said Ben as they shook hands. "And thank you for the lesson about your Federal Bureau of Investigation. It is most interesting!"

"Again, my pleasure," said Henry. He shot me a look and said, "See you later Tom."

"Thanks, Henry. Take care," I said as he turned to leave.

"So, Ben. Soon you'll be indistinguishable from the average man on the street – except, of course, that you're Ben Franklin, and they are not!"

Ben laughed. "I suppose that could be said of anyone"

Miriam and Kathy came into the room, and Kathy walked up and stood beside me. "I think I'll be going," she said. "I have a lot to do before tomorrow. Don't be too late." She then turned to Ben and said, "I have very much enjoyed the afternoon. Dr. Franklin. I look forward to more."

Ben bowed, and said, "My pleasure, madam. And please, since you are now a friend, call me Ben. I have been instructed that this is the custom now".

"It is, but it will take some getting used to, Ben," she said. "Bye Miriam," and she turned back to me. "See you at home," and gave me a peck on the cheek, then waved and exited.

"Miriam," I said, "When Henry calls with Ben's clothing, you, Bill and Phillip fight it out to see who goes and picks it up".

"No problem," she said. "Ben, would you like anything from the kitchen?"

"Yes. I do believe I would like to have some of that iced water that is so delicious. If I could bring one thing back to my time, it would be ice cubes!"

We all laughed, and Miriam said, "Right away."

"Just bring it into the office," I said, "if that's OK with you, Ben".

"OK with me!" Ben said with still-obvious amusement at the term.

We walked down the hall and back into my office. Miriam followed with two glasses of iced water and set one on my desk, and the other on the end table beside Ben's chair.

"Thanks," I said.

"Sure," she said and exited.

As we sat down, Ben asked, "When you told Henry and Miriam about a 'call', are you referring to someone yelling at a distance, or are you using one of those 'radio' contraptions?"

"Good question. Actually, do you remember our discussion about telegraph, and how wires carried those messages that were sent in Morse Code?"

"Yes. Most fascinating!" he said.

"In the late nineteenth century a gentleman by the name of Alexander Graham Bell, another prolific inventor, who did a lot of work with the deaf, began experimenting with sound. He was able to create a way, working with a helper by the name of Mr. Watson, to send sound over those same wires. He succeeded, and the first words spoken over wires were '*Mr. Watson, come here – I want to see you*'. Watson, who was in the other room heard his voice clearly over the device in his room and came running. In the ensuing months, Bell was able to demonstrate his device to interested investors, and since there were already wires in place for the telegraph, he was able to convert many of these to use for sending voice. The device was called a 'telephone'. Now, everyone, almost without exception, has a 'telephone' available to them, and there are telephone companies all across the world. In fact, I could pick up a telephone right now and call London, much the same as I talked to them this morning, in fact, even clearer. Just as clear as you and I sitting here."

Ben just looked in amazement. "I was so enthralled with the telegraph and your radio this morning that it didn't even occur to me the possibility of wires transporting voices. Do you have such a 'telephone' here?"

"Actually, we have several!" I opened the top right hand drawer of my desk and pulled my phone out and set it in its usual place on my desk. "I had this hidden until I could explain it to you. Would you like to see its use?"

"But of course!" exclaimed Ben.

"Let me tell the others that this particular subterfuge is finished," I laughed as I stepped into the hall and shouted Miriam's name. She stuck her head around the corner and I said, "Telephones are back in order. Put yours back out, and I'm going to give you a call. Ben wants to see it work."

"Will do!" she said as she scurried back around the corner.

I returned to my desk and picked up the handset. I punched in three numbers, then punched the 'speaker' button, and laid the handset back down. Miriam picked up on her end.

"Yes?" she said in a bit of a sing-song voice.

"Oh, cute!" I said. "Say something to Ben."

"Hello, Ben. Can you hear me?"

"Why yes!" said Ben with raised eyebrows. "I hear you very clearly."

"Well, this is telephone!" she said. "I am certainly glad to have it back. There are some calls I need to make!"

I laughed. "Tell Bill and Phillip that we're back in the twenty-first and go ahead and put the other phones back in place."

"Gladly!" she said, and I pressed the button hanging up the call.

"What do you think?" I asked.

Ben sat back. "Let me think. Thus far you have showed me the telegraph," and he began counting them on his fingers, "the TV, the radio, and now the 'telephone'. How much communicating do people do these days?"

"Quite a lot, and there are many more advances we're going to talk about. Let's start with the next logical advance – where we marry telephone and radio."

Ben sat up straight as I reached into my desk drawer and pulled out a simple flip phone. I held it up and showed it to Ben.

"This is something called a 'cellphone'," I said. "It is a small radio with a much shorter range than my radio over there," and I pointed to the Ham rig. "But it communicates with something called 'cells'. These are actually miniature radio stations peppered all across the country that can handle dozens of calls at the same time. Each telephone, whether it's connected by wires, or if it's one of these cellphones, has its own unique telephone number. If I know someone's number, I can simply use this little pad here to call it, and if the person on the other end is nearby, they will answer just as Miriam did."

"Shocking!" said Ben. "Could you demonstrate this as well."

"That's my plan!" I said. "A few moments ago Kathy left to go home. I happen to know she'll go by the post office – the very postal service you created – to drop off some packages, so she hasn't had time to get home yet."

I punched in her number and pressed the 'call' button. Just before the second ring, Kathy picked up.

"Well, I wasn't expecting to hear from you. Anything wrong?"

"Nope," I said. "Remember that I told you Ben and I would be discussing communications this afternoon?"

"Yeah.."

"Well, we made it to cellphones. Would you like to talk to him?"

"Yet another dumb question, Tom. Of course I would!"

I handed the phone to Ben and said, "Just put this part up to your ear, then talk in a normal voice just like I did."

He did, and said a tentative '*Hello*'. I watched him listen as Kathy spoke, then he said, "Well, I can tell you that if General Washington had access to something like this, we could have won the war in a fortnight!"

Kathy said a few more words, then Ben said, "Certainly. I am told there is much more to come, but at this point, I am a bit overwhelmed. Therefore, I shall hand this back to your husband."

I took the phone back, and deadpanned to Kathy, "Congratulations. The first ever phone call from Ben Franklin. Your mother would be proud."

I'll not repeat what Kathy said back, but I hung up on her. Suffice it to say she questioned my IQ level and family lineage.

I looked down at the desk phone, and all three outgoing lines were in use. I pointed them out to Ben and said, "Looks like my colleagues are getting caught up on their calls. Each light is a call in progress."

"I can see why this would be useful," said Ben.

"Oh, it's more than useful," I said. "In fact it can be addictive. When my oldest daughter was young, we would punish her by taking away her telephone privileges. Her gossiping with her friends would come to a halt and she would promise anything to get those privileges restored. It is not unusual for people, particularly young people, to spend hours talking to their friends on the phone. For most of the last one hundred years, most business in the world has been done over the phone."

"So when you told Henry to 'call' when he had the clothing ready, this is what you were referring to?"

"Absolutely. If I tell someone to call me, the telephone is implied."

"Simply amazing!" he said as he raised his hands to his chin. Then he sat up, took the glass of water sitting on the table beside him, and took a drink. "I might have to change my mind about the one thing I would take back with me," he said. "This telephone would be most useful. I could even use it when taking my air-baths!"

Chapter 21

Friday - First Week

So now I was officially freaked out by the mental picture of Franklin sitting *au naturel* in front of a window in his home talking on the cellphone. Some mental pictures you can't erase no matter how hard you try. Sometimes the only thing you can do is heap more stuff in there hoping to cover it up. Time for a subject change.

"Ben, I want to talk to you about government and how it's faring, but before we can even begin that conversation, there are some other developments you need to be aware of – things you and your contemporaries could never have imagined – that shaped the nature of how this government you established interacts with the rest of the world. If you don't mind delaying the conversation about government just a bit longer, let's talk about those other factors first."

Ben sat back in his chair and said, "Yes, I am most curious about our little experiment, but I will accede to your plan. So, please proceed. What are these 'factors'?"

I took a deep breath. "First, you have already seen how the changes in technology have changed the way and speed in which we communicate with each other, so that is certainly one factor."

"Yes," he said. "I can imagine that it has!"

"I read that you had actually seen what was called a steam powered fire extinguishing device invented by someone in Great Britain," I said.

"Yes, I did!" said Ben. "It was a most interesting way of extinguishing fires. In fact, it started me thinking about a way to attach such a device to a fire engine, but it was just too large to do so."

"Well you will be gratified to know that a few years after that, someone actually did invent a steam engine for use in putting out fires, and that today, any history of firefighting always includes a reference to you and your creation of the first fire department."

Ben smiled with a bit of pride. "Always gratifying to find something you had a hand in was found useful!" he said.

"It was more than useful" I said. "But, that's just one of the things steam engines were used for. What you may not be acquainted with is rail cars –

wagons that ride on metal rails – two rails side-by-side four to five feet apart. These were being invented about the time you signed the Constitution. The Scotsman James Watt, the inventor of the steam engine, had refined it to the point that it could be fitted onto one of these rail cars, providing power for the car to move on its own on the rails."

Ben said, "I am not surprised. I supposed that many uses could be found for such an engine. Is this still in use today?"

"Not exactly," I said. "Once a method of self propelling something had been developed, as you can imagine, others began improving on it. In fact, in the United States, the government began promoting, through land grants and other methods, installation of these rails for these engines to ride upon. The engines were improved over and over again, and by the time of the Civil War in 1860, they were a primary method of transporting goods, and people, over long distances."

Ben nodded. "That would be expected," he said. "Once a method is shown, there are usually those who can improve on it and ultimately make it useful to others. How much of the country has use of these rail cars?"

"After the end of the Civil War, much progress was made in building railways in the U.S., and just a few years after the end of the war, a railway from the Atlantic to the Pacific was completed. Following that, railways were built across much of the United States, and today hardly a community of any size doesn't have a railway, or what came to be called a 'railroad', going through it. It was this expansion of railroads that led to the requirement for faster communications. Because of the railroads, the telegraph became necessary. Railroad companies needed some way to keep the trains running efficiently, so telegraph lines were built along the railroads, and suddenly you have coast-to-coast railroads and communications."

Ben's eyes brightened as I continued.

"If you wanted to go from New York to California on the Pacific coast, you could ride, in comfort, regardless of weather, in a rail car and the entire trip would take just a few days. But, that's really only the beginning of the story."

Ben's expression changed to one of thought. "If I understand you, sir, horses were no longer needed?"

"Oh, horses were still around, even during the height of the expansion of the railways," I said. "You still needed to go into town to purchase supplies, ride the range, plow fields, or just ride to go see friends and neighbors, but for long distance travel it was hard to surpass the railroad," I said, and I went on to explain tickets, stations, etc. When I mentioned delivery of the mail, Ben perked up.

"So, there was a more efficient method of delivery of the mail, then? Gratifying!" he said.

"Yes, for a while there was a service, particularly out west, called the 'Pony Express', where horse riders were hired to carry the mail across long distances, but the railroad quickly replaced them. However, to this day their legend lives on."

"How long does it take for a letter to travel from New York to, say, Charleston?" he asked.

"Before I answer that question, there are still more advances you need to know. Let's just say mail delivery is much faster than you can imagine," I said.

"More, then? Proceed!" said Ben.

"Take what I've already told you about the steam engine, and add another dimension to it. One of the things I read about you was that you had created one of the first electric motors, something you called an 'electric wheel'."

"I did!" he exclaimed. "It was most fascinating to see the forces of electricity actually move objects, but it was simply an oddity, as it was too weak to be of much other use".

"It turns out you were very close, though," I said. "Just like the steam engine, several advances were made to the electrically powered motor such that modern train engines run on electrically powered motors. But, before we even consider how these electric motors get their power, there is another advance that has totally changed how people live. A Frenchman and a German were instrumental in creating something called an 'internal combustion engine'. These engines are powered by refined oil that is pumped from beneath the earth's surface, and as it turns out the amount of oil to be found is massive – upwards of many billions of gallons – and we are still drilling for and discovering new oil reserves today."

"Of course I know about oil," said Ben. "since we use them in our lamps. But can this oil be used as a fuel for an engine?"

"Yes, but only after it is refined and turned into something extremely combustible we call 'gasoline'. I believe the first refinement produced a fuel called 'kerosene', which is still used for other purposes today. Then further refinements yielded two other fuels – Diesel and gasoline – both of which are used today. Let me show you how it works".

For the next few minutes I made some rudimentary drawings of the internals of a gas-powered engine and we discussed how it worked, and how oil was still used, but as a lubricant rather than the fuel. Ben was most fascinated by the process, particularly when I told him of the precision necessary to make these devices work without friction destroying them in short order. Then, I pulled out the 'coup de grâce'. I reached into my desk drawer and pulled out a three-ring binder of photographs, and showed them to Ben.

The first photograph was of the first steam-powered railroad engine. Then I showed him later versions of the steam engine. Then came the bicycle and a quick discussion of its part in the evolution of personal transportation. Next, I showed him a steam-powered car, complete with a mustached rider and passenger.

"This was called a 'horseless-carriage,'" I said. "At the turn of the twentieth century, these were more a novelty than anything else, but as with everything else we've discussed today, there were more advances to be made." Then, I flipped the page and Ben leaned closer and looked at the picture.

"This is a vehicle called the Ford Model T. It brought an entirely new class of vehicles called the automobile, or the more common 'car'. It was the first vehicle that captured the imagination of the public, and people, particularly in more urban areas, abandoned horses for the Model T," I explained. "A man named Henry Ford perfected a process of mass producing these vehicles such that each one was identical to the one before it and, more importantly, the parts were interchangeable. So, if a part of the internal combustion engine, or the 'motor', were to wear out or break, that part could be replaced with an exact duplicate, rather than the need to replace the entire engine. Moreover, it was designed for the common man, because the effectiveness of mass production put the cost of this vehicle with the range of any person or family above the poverty level."

Then I turned the page to the Model A. "This was another of Ford's vehicles – the Model A. While the Model T was built for price, the Model A was built with more features and styles, making the price higher. It was a step up in features and styling for those who could afford it."

"How many people own one of these?", Ben asked.

"I don't know what the exact numbers are," I said, "But these were first produced in the early twentieth century, and even today, with many different models since, it is I believe, still the largest selling model in automobile history. But, this was actually just the beginning. Let me show you a series of advancements since the Model T and the Model A."

For the next few minutes, I flipped through the binder, one page at a time. Fords, Chevrolets, Buicks, a smattering of foreign cars, all the way up to the Volkswagen. As I explained the evolution of each model, I also pointed out the advancements in braking, starting, lighting, steering, fuel consumption and usage, as well as safety features. I showed him cars, trucks, buses, taxi cabs (which brought on a whole other conversation on mass transit), and even limousines. The last vehicle I showed him was the postal delivery vehicle, at which he was delighted.

"As you might imagine," I said, "many of these vehicles, though no longer manufactured, still are on the road today. As a matter of fact, there is an entire culture built around the preservation of older models called 'vintage cars'. The older and more rare they are, the higher the acquisition price."

Then I turned the page.

"These are some of the models currently sold today. These are owned by everyday people. From single individuals wishing a car with a bit of flair," and I showed him a couple of sporty-type cars, "to those just beginning a family." Time for the Volvo. "Then there are vehicles for those with a bit more money to spend, such as this Lincoln, named for Abraham Lincoln for some reason. Finally, there's a whole class of vehicles called 'Sport Utility Vehicles', or

'SUVs'. This is one of the vehicles I own," and I showed him a picture of Kathy and me standing beside our Lincoln Navigator."

Ben looked up and said, "One of the vehicles? How many vehicles do you own?"

"We have two," I said. "One for Kathy, and one for me. Mine is something called a Tahoe, which is an Indian word, but also the name of a resort area in the state of California." Then I flipped the page. "This is mine," and there I was standing beside my vehicle.

"Are you a wealthy man, if you don't mind my asking?" said Ben.

"Not really," I said. "Vehicles are priced so that anyone with any means at all can own their own personal car, truck, or SUV, depending on their means. I am what might be considered upper-middle income class, meaning I'm well above the poverty level, but beneath the range that someone in this nation might call 'wealthy'. Of course, there are very impoverished places on earth that would consider even our poor to be wealthy, but that has always been so."

Ben sat back in his chair. "Sir, I must say this is most overwhelming. You have, in the last couple of hours, taken me from a world where people either had to walk somewhere, or they had a horse or horse-drawn buggy or carriage, to a world where such vehicles as these," and he motioned to the book, "have completely replaced everything I am accustomed to. And all this to the point that I can scarce believe such advancements could be made."

"Yes," I said. "I understand that. It is a lot to take in. There is one more very large advancement to tell you about, but before we even begin that discussion, would you like to see my 'horseless carriage'?"

Ben's eyes lit up. "Yes, very much so!"

I punched the intercom and said, "Bill, can you come to my office for a second".

Bill said, "Be right there".

Ben said, "All this, and I'm still amazed by voices coming out of that little box!" and I chuckled.

In a few seconds, Bill stepped in the room.

"Bill, is Phillip still here?"

"Yes, he's just catching up on some...uh..mail." (He'd almost said 'email', but caught himself at the last second). "What do you have in mind?"

"Have him mind the store," and I looked back at Ben, "another colloquialism," then back to Bill, "while you and I take Ben on a little trip".

"Trip, huh. Where are we going?"

"Oh, I thought I'd show him the neighborhood....in my Tahoe."

Bill's eyebrows went up. "Oh, so we're up to vehicles now, huh?" and he looked at Ben the back at me.

"Sure. Let me tell Phillip. Give me a couple of minutes and I'll come back by and get you."

"That'll work," I said. Bill left and I thought of one other thing to tell Ben.

"Ben, when we leave, you're going to notice the streets are not dirt or gravel. They are paved with a substance called 'asphalt'. It is a hard surface that takes the bumps and shakes out of traveling, particularly at the speed we'll be going."

"Oh?" he said. "Exactly how fast will we be going?"

"Not very fast relatively, today, since we're just going to drive locally. But, on open highways, particularly between cities, speeds can go over seventy miles per hour."

"Miles per hour?" Ben said in amazement. "Does that mean you can go seventy miles in just one hour?"

"That's exactly what that means," I said. "Our maximum will be about thirty. However, I realize that even this speed is very fast for you, but I have been driving cars since I was fifteen years old, as has everyone else in the vehicles you will see today. Even though we'll be passing very close to them as they go the opposite direction, or as we travel in traffic with other vehicles, the number of times vehicles bump or hit each other is very small. However, even with that, there are some safety procedures every vehicle operator on the road uses, but you'll see those when we go outside."

About that time Bill came back in and said, "Ready?"

"I am," I said. "Ben, are you ready for your first ride in a 'horseless carriage'?"

"Indeed!" said Franklin, "on the condition you don't bump or hit another horseless carriage."

"That is the plan!" I said.

Chapter 22

Friday - First Week

As we made our way to the front door, I gave my keys to Bill and told him to unlock the SUV and Ben and I would be right out. When we got to the front, and through the security door (which Bill had opened, so I didn't have to get out my security key card), I paused at the front door as Bill went on out.

"Ben," I said, "You will see many things we may not have talked about. If something just has to be explained right then, let me know. I'll do a bit of narration as we travel, but take mental notes of things you want to discuss when we return. This will be your first excursion into the world of the twenty-first century outside this building, but it will most certainly not be your last, and each time you go out you'll find something new. Is that agreeable?"

"Of course," said Ben. "I was already under the assumption there were many other items for us to discuss, so I am most anxious to see what 200 years has brought!"

We both smiled, and I said, "OK, so here we go!"

As we walked through the door, Ben said, "OK," and chuckled a bit.

It was another nice day. The sun was shining, and the temperatures were about the same as the day before. Our parking lot is on a side street which is about two blocks from any traffic, and with the hedges and trees around our lot, there wasn't much to see until you exited the parking lot. Ben followed me out to the SUV where Bill was waiting.

"Are we ready?" asked Bill.

"Ready," I said. "Just had a last minute thought. I'll drive, since it's my vehicle, and Ben, Bill will show you to the passenger side of the vehicle. Bill, you can choose whatever seat is left," I said with a grin.

"I figured as much," he said. "This way Dr. Franklin, and I'll help you in. It's a bit of a step, but don't worry, I've got you."

Ben followed Bill to the other side of the Tahoe where Bill opened the door and helped Ben navigate the step, then slide into the passenger seat.

"Of the vehicles you showed me earlier, this one seems very large," said Ben as he surveyed the inside of the Tahoe.

"Yes," I said, "I like to have plenty of space for my stuff. Plus, I feel a bit cramped in smaller vehicles. Kathy feels the same way, so we both have somewhat larger vehicles. Most people here have smaller cars for fuel efficiency and ease of parking, but I guess I'm a bit strange. Let's get you buckled up. It's for safety, and there is a state law that requires all occupants of motorized vehicles to use the seatbelt."

Bill grabbed the seatbelt, handed it over to me, and I clicked it into the lock.

"Now, Dr. Franklin. You're safely strapped in. To exit the seatbelt, you just press this red tab here," and I showed him mine, "and the belt will release."

"I understand," said Ben, obviously in brain overload with all the gadgets displayed on the console, but at least I had anticipated today's excursion, so I had constructed a cover – essentially a piece of cardboard – over the navigation/radio display in the center of the console. I didn't want to have to explain computerized devices yet. If you didn't know about the LCD display behind the cardboard, you wouldn't know it was covered. I had done a pretty good job on the cover, if I say so myself! Bill got in, buckled, and we were ready.

Bill handed me the keys, and I put them in the ignition, but before I turned it, I said, "Now, when I start up the motor, lots of lights are going to come on here on the dashboard," and I made a waving motion with my hand across the dash. "For now, just pay them no attention, as we'll talk about all that later. What I want you to do is just enjoy the experience and see some of the changes."

I started the motor, and Ben's eyebrows went up and he shot me a wide grin as he heard the purr of the motor.

"Our office is actually somewhat north of Philadelphia near the Hatboro, Westbury and Willow Grove area. Philadelphia is actually about fourteen miles away, but we won't go there today because of the traffic. With people starting to get off work in a few minutes, everyone will be trying to get home. We'll save that trip for later. I'm just going to drive a few blocks and show you some of the local sites. That should be enough to get you started."

"How long does one take to get to Philadelphia?" Ben asked.

"Normally, in the middle of the day, we could be there in a half hour. Today, though, at this time, it would take over an hour. Let's save that trip for a less busy time."

"I look very much forward to that," said Ben, "But I suppose I understand your reasoning. Show me then these local sites!"

With that, I said, "All right, then. Here we go."

I put the gear in reverse, backed out of my parking space, then shifted again and headed out of the lot. I took a right, then headed to the next street and took a left. That headed us out of the cul-de-sac and towards the highway just a few hundred feet away that led to the business area. As we drove, I kept the speed relatively low. We passed several houses and small subdivisions on the way.

"I like the styles of some of these homes," said Ben, "but there seem to be an awful lot of poles and cables on this street."

"Yes, and it's that way most places," I explained. "The longer you're here, the less you tend to notice them. Our office has all these facilities brought underground, so that's why you didn't see any there. It's more expensive to do it that way, but more aesthetically pleasing."

We began passing some businesses, including a small shopping center and a gas station. I pointed to the gas station and said, "This is one of the places where I buy fuel for my vehicle. They sell four different types of fuel, depending on the requirements of your particular vehicle."

Ben's head was on a swivel as more businesses came into view. We came to a red light and stopped. Ben looked over at me with a quizzical look, so I explained as I pointed to the light.

"This is a traffic light. The three colors tell drivers what they're expected to do to keep from crashing into each other at this intersection. Red means stop and wait. Green, on the bottom, means it's safe to go, because the vehicles in the intersecting roads have the red light. Then there's a yellow light in the middle that comes on for a second or two as the light transitions from green to red. It simply is a warning that the light is about to turn red, so proceed with caution, or just go ahead and stop. If you continue when the light is red, you risk crashing your vehicle into another and causing damage or injury. There are constables on patrol, the local police in this case, who will pull you over and give you a citation if you do. The fine for running a red light is moderately severe, plus, if you get more than three, your license to drive is revoked for a period of time, and you're either dependent on someone else to transport you, or you're back in the nineteenth century," and I laughed as the light changed from red to green.

"Safe to proceed now, then?" asked Ben.

"Yes, it is," I said as I accelerated. As we proceeded I saw something coming up on the right.

"Do you remember that pizza you had yesterday – your first 'meal' here?"

"Yes!" said Ben. "Most delicious!"

There's the place where they make it.

"Ah yes!" exclaimed Ben. "It even somewhat resembles a hut."

"That was the general idea, I think," I said.

I pointed out several other types of businesses, primarily those that had functions he might be somewhat familiar with, but also many that we would end up discussing when we got back.

As we drove, Ben said, "This ride in this vehicle is certainly much more smooth that in my buckboard across some of the roadways in my time. I have noticed some worn areas and cracks in the road that, when we crossed them, did not shake my teeth like my buckboard would."

"Well, the wheels on this vehicle are outfitted with tires made from a substance called rubber, which is both flexible and extremely tough. This rubber tire is then filled with air, so we don't feel every little bump in the road. Also, each vehicle is outfitted with springs that further absorb any vibrations, particularly when we hit a small hole, which people call 'potholes', in the road. Still, on many roads, it can still get a bit bumpy, especially after a hard winter has slightly altered the bed the road is built upon."

"Interesting. I would like to hear more about this 'rubber'," said Ben.

"We'll examine the tires when we get back," I said, as I made another turn to start heading back towards the office. As I pulled up at a stop sign, I explained the difference between a stoplight and a stop sign. After we turned, a patrol car passed us going the other way, and I pointed to it.

"That was one of the local police officers," I said. "If the lights on top of his vehicle start flashing, someone is in trouble! Just glad it wasn't me today!"

"The side of his vehicle said 'To Protect And Serve'," said Ben. "I like the sound of that!"

"Well, I hope we got some things right in the last 230 years," I said.

In a few minutes, after a few turns, we ended back up at the office. Bill exited the vehicle first, and I helped Ben get out of his seatbelt and Bill helped him out.

"I expect entering and exiting this vehicle requires a bit of practice," He said.

"Yes, but it doesn't take long. When you've done it thousands of times as I have, it just becomes something you automatically do," I said. I pointed to the front wheel and said, "This black area is the tire made from rubber. As you can see if you press on it, it seems quite hard. But, there's about thirty two pounds per square inch of pressurized air inside, so when it finds a bump or hole in the road, it flexes enough to take much of the shock."

"You say these are extremely tough," said Ben. "I can see how that might be true. Do they ever need replacing?"

"Oh yes. You see these ridges on the outer surface? As these wear down after use, the tire gets near the end of its useful life. Without these ridges, not only would the tire lose some of its ability to grip the road, but in wet weather the water would form a thin barrier that would make the vehicle slide over the road. I've had these about six months, and they will last nearly sixty thousand miles."

"That much!" said Ben. "Are these made locally?"

"I don't think there's a manufacturing facility here, but I'm not sure. They are, however, sold many places – including a couple of places we passed today. Next time we're out, I'll show you one of those places."

"Agreed!" said Ben. "We did pass many places about which I have questions. Shall we discuss these while they are still fresh in memory?"

"Sure," I said, as I motioned him back towards the building. Bill went ahead to open the security door, and as we went inside the front door, Ben said, "One of those places I would like to know about is a place that had a sign outside that said 'Computers'. What are 'computers'?"

"That, my dear sir, is a huge topic of discussion, and let's save that one for later this afternoon, if you don't mind. As a matter of fact, I suggest we go straight to my office, and you write down as many of these topics as you'd like and we'll see what we can get through before the evening meal."

"A capital idea!" said Ben. "First, I need to visit the room where one both disposes of waste, and bathes. The 'bathroom', is that correct?"

"Yes, and I forgot one of the first things I still have to remind my family when we get ready to go somewhere. 'Does anybody need to use the bathroom'! I apologize, but since the trip was short, it just didn't occur to me. Go ahead to your private bathroom, and come back to the office when you're finished, and we'll go from there."

"Thank you, Sir," said Ben. "I shan't be but a few moments, as you have certainly simplified this whole process!"

Chapter 23

Friday - First Week

Well, I knew this was going to be fun. If ever there was a mind from before the twentieth century who would eat up technology, it was Ben Franklin. As I prepared to introduce him to the world of computers, I knew that when this part was over, much of the modern world would begin to come together. And, while there were many, many other things he would have to learn, there were only two big pieces left: Computers and air travel. But, since the day was waning, Orville and Wilbur would have to wait until the morning. Plus, I was really looking forward to a trip to the airport!

In a few minutes, Ben came back into the room.

"I must say, had we the conveniences you have today in my day, I might have had more time for my investigations!" said Ben. "But, I suppose someone 200 years my junior would say the same. So," he said as he sat down and slapped his legs again. "With what are you to dazzle me this afternoon?"

"Computers," I said. "Probably the biggest advance in technology since the ability to drive. Plus, I thought I'd also bring you up to date on publishing, since as it turns out, the two are intertwined these days."

"Oh?" said Franklin. "Do tell!"

"Let's start with some pictures," I said, reaching back into my drawer for yet another binder.

Ben brought his chair closer to my desk and leaned forward in anticipation. I opened the book to a picture of something he was familiar with.

"Oh, of course I recognize this!" exclaimed Ben. "I use these printing presses myself! I don't suppose you are going to tell me this has changed?"

"You are right on that account," I said. "but, this is a likely starting place. From here, we go to the rotary press." and I turned the page. "This greatly sped up the printing process, making it possible to print one copy after another seconds apart."

"Yes, I can see that," said Ben. "Then what?"

"There was a need for a method of doing small printing for offices and individuals, so numerous inventors over several years, through incremental inventions, eventually developed a method of printing directly to paper using fixed type." I turned the page to an early typewriter.

"This is a typewriter," I said. "When I was growing up, every office had one, and many people had them at home as well. The paper would fit around this round spool called a 'platen', and an inked fabric would put the inked impression of each metal type directly onto the page. Each of these keys caused a different arm with a character at the end to strike the fabric and transfer the character to the paper. As each key was pressed, the entire platen assembly would move from right to left, and the inked fabric would move the width of one character so it was ready for the next one. When one neared the edge of the paper, you would reach up and pull the assembly back to the left with this handle, which would also advance the paper to the next line."

"Ingenious!" said Franklin. "These were available to anyone?"

"Yes, anyone who could afford them, and as time went on, obviously, they became better and cheaper. This is the model I learned to type on." and I turned the page to an Underwood model. "They also applied small electric motors to both the movement of the platen, and the movement of the type." I turned the page to an IBM Selectric. "This model had a spinning ball that contained all the printable characters and all these movements of paper, type, platen, and even the return, would be accomplished by these motors each time one of these keys was pressed. With this model, I could type nearly one hundred words per minute"

"You are that skilled?" he asked.

"The others in my typing class thought I was showing off, but since I played a musical instrument, my fingers were just more nimble. But, yes, I guess it was a skill. However, there were many just as skilled, if not more so, particularly those who were in the newspaper business!"

Ben smiled at that reference. "So how does one print newspapers today?"

"That brings us back to printing. The next development was something called 'offset printing'. The printing is transferred to a rubber blanket, which is then used to print the images on paper. This is one primary method used today. This is an early offset printing press. But, that has progressed to the modern day offset press that is electrically operated and can print hundreds of thousands of complete newspapers in one night."

I turned the page to show a current printing press. "This is the printing room of the New York Times," I said. "They print as many as one million complete editions of their daily newspaper, and each copy could contain hundreds of pages. The entire printing and assembling of each edition is done by these presses in one night, in time for early morning delivery. The New York Times is the nation's largest newspaper."

Ben's eyes were wide in amazement as he contemplated the enormity of what I had just said. So, I demonstrated. I opened the bottom door of the table behind me and retrieved the Times from the last weekend.

"Now, I will let you read this paper when we've completed a few more updates, but this is the Sunday edition from this last weekend." and I just held it up flat so he could see the thickness without seeing any of the stories.

"This is one paper of a million printed in one night?" Ben asked incredulously.

"Yes, and they print a somewhat smaller edition each day."

Ben looked at me and said, "I would never have conceived of such a large process occurring in such a short span of time!"

"Well," I said as I replaced the paper in the table and shut the door "this is just the beginning. Now for the next item – the one you asked about. Computers."

I returned to the book and turned the page to a picture of an abacus. "I assume you are familiar with this," I said.

"Yes, yes. I have one of these myself. Several are in the Philadelphia area"

"Good. The need to perform more calculations in a shorter period of time became necessary as businesses increased in size and volume, so the next leap was something invented by Charles Babbage in London in the early 1930s, called an Analytical Engine." and I turned the page.

"This machine was a great leap forward in computations. It had the ability to be 'programmed', or set up to perform different calculations, depending upon your requirements. This is the basis for modern day machines that we call computers. The next step was to reduce the size and increase the capacity, and that led to a number of smaller computing machines, primarily adding machines that accountants, merchants, schools and many other places used to add and subtract, as well as multiply and divide numbers quickly."

I turned the page to a desktop adding machine. "My Dad had one of these on his desk, and I used to play with it – at least when he wasn't looking."

Ben was hanging on every word. "Then came World War Two. It was necessary to have a device that could do massive amounts of calculations in a short period of time. The Axis powers, the nickname for those against which we were fighting, were communicating via radio, but they were encoding their messages, much like Washington did during the Revolution."

"Yes!" said Ben. "I had a conversation with General Washington about that very thing. Very ingenious!"

"Well, the Germans took that to the next level. They had a machine that would encode their messages for them." and I turned the page to display an Enigma machine. "As the key was pressed, these wheels would cause an electrical circuit to display a light under a character at the top of the machine. Pressing an 'A', for example, might light up a 'Z', or an 'S', and the ingenious thing was, that if you continually pressed the 'A', a different letter would light up each time. It was all controlled by these wheels, which moved each time a letter was pressed, and these cords in the back would be plugged in the same way on both sides of the communication to determine how the circuit was completed.

The possible combinations were virtually endless. Without the right settings of the wheels and these cords, it was almost impossible to decode the message"

"But," said Franklin. "I'm guessing a way was deduced to do so?"

"Yes," I said, "But it was all because of a design flaw in the machine, and because human beings do not like to change. For one thing, a letter could never be used to encode itself. In other words, if you wanted to send an "A", the machine was set up so it would never be an "A". It would always be another letter. Secondly, they were supposed to change the combinations each night, but many times they just wouldn't. Next, if the messages sent the same greeting, or contained the same information, such as the beginning of a weather report, one could begin guessing what the settings would be using these 'cribs', as they were called. Still, that was a lot of computing to do, so a young mathematician in England built a machine to do just that. His name was Alan Turing, and his invention was called the Turing Machine. It was the first electronic computer."

I turned the page to a picture of one of Turing's 'bombes'. "This machine would go through combination after combination until the 'crib' was decoded, and it would stop. When the machine stopped, all one had to do was make a note of the settings, then go set up their version of the Enigma machine, and decode that day's messages. The design was improved by another Brit named Gordon Welchman to the point it became so efficient that the allies on our side were reading the messages before the commanders on the other side did. It shortened the war by years!"

Ben sat back and looked at me for a moment. "This is so much to absorb!" he said.

"Yes it is!" I said. "And there is much more to tell, so since you've had an eventful day already, how about we check on supper, and return to this subject tomorrow morning. Besides, I want you to view a movie with me tonight, if you feel up to it."

"Why, yes. I think we might do that." He pulled out his watch, then said, "Ten past five. If the meal takes less than an hour, then that would put us at six o'clock. Would it be acceptable for me to rest for a few moments and settle my thoughts before we continue with your 'movie'?"

"Of course, of course! You have had a very full two days, and I suppose the muscles in your brain need a rest. Let's check on supper and see where we are."

"Very well!", he said. With that we rose and went into the dining/conference room. Bill and Phillip were sitting there, and Kathy had come back to eat with us.

"Mrs. Reed!" said Ben. "So nice to see you again. Will you be dining with us tonight?"

"Yes. I thought I'd surprise you two. Are you learning much?"

"Too much, I'm afraid," said Ben. "I just told Tom here that I must take a few minutes after the meal and let my brain rest. He took me for a short ride in his 'S-U-V' this afternoon. That was quite an awakening, but for the last little while he has regaled me with the history of something that is very familiar to me – printing. He was just getting into this thing called 'computers' when he mercifully gave me a break. I assume you came over in your, what was it, 'Navigator'?" and he chuckled.

"Why yes, I did! It's parked outside. I see he's told you quite a lot. Are you absorbing it all?"

"Oh, not nearly all," he laughed. "I may require some refreshing once we're finished, but I'm told there is plenty of reading material, so I suppose I should be busy for quite a while!"

Bill said, "I think Miriam just about has the meal ready. She went to Outback and brought home some steaks."

"Great!" I said. "Ben, how do you feel about a nice grilled beef steak with, I'm guessing, mashed potatoes, green beans, maybe a salad?"

"That sounds delicious!" said Ben.

"Great! Let me check on Miriam, and we'll get ready to eat!"

As they sat down, I went towards the kitchen. I heard Ben ask Kathy, "Tell me. Does this contraption you drive really do all the navigating for you?"

Kathy laughed and said, "Tell you what. When you finish your lesson on computers, I'll take you for a ride in my SUV, and show you."

Ben's eyebrows shot up and he said, "I can scarcely bear to wait!"

Chapter 24

Friday - First Week

As we sat down for supper, Ben was quite animated with his recap and commentary on the day, and it was quite apparent the short ride through the edge of town made a big impression on him. He commented on the architecture in the homes and businesses he saw as we drove, but he was most impressed that one could drive such a large vehicle down paved roads with such ease, passing within mere inches of other vehicles as we rode. He had paid much more attention to the mechanics of driving than I had noticed, and had several questions about the operation of a motorized vehicle. What amazed him most, though, was when I told him that people begin driving cars and trucks at the age of fifteen.

"I was once fifteen years of age myself!" he exclaimed to everyone's laughter. "I scarcely think, though, that even with my age and experience, I would be able to accomplish such a feat."

"Well," said Phillip, "you must understand that all of us grew up with all these inventions already in place and were passengers in cars from the time we were born. After a while, it just begins to rub off on you, and you're not so much concerned with how you drive, as you are anxious to get your turn. As a teenager, driving a vehicle by myself was a huge status symbol."

"I should see how that would be!" said Ben. "Were you allowed to actually own your personal vehicle?"

"Not at first," I said, "But by the time I was a senior in high school Mom and Dad bought me my own vehicle, and that was a very big deal! Not only that, but if you go to a school you can tell the teachers' vehicles from the students'. The teachers' vehicles are usually older with a bit more wear, and with less shall we say, flash, than the students.'"

"That seems backwards," said Ben, "but I suppose I understand how parents still want the best for their children."

"Some things never change," said Kathy. "I know I would walk through fire for my daughters, even today".

"We both would," I said. "I expect that is something that has also always been so."

"Here here!" said Ben. Then his demeanor changed a bit. After a small pause, and as he looked at what was left on his plate, he said, "I lost my Francis at four years old from the Pox. I could have saved his life had he been inoculated, and to this day I still feel that failure."

The silence around the table was palatable. All either had lost either a family member, or at a minimum someone close, and this statement instantly brought the pictures of each of those individuals to the minds of all of us seated there. Thankfully, the feeling didn't last but for a few moments.

"Tell me, Tom," said Ben. "You used 'high school' a few moments ago. I have some idea as to its definition, but please explain the term more specifically."

"Yes," I said. "some terms we just take for granted – just another example of how the use of language has changed in the last 200 years. Originally, as you know, parents were primarily responsible for educating their children, and if they desired to further that education, parents had to, in many cases, pay a tuition for that privilege. Then, of course, came higher learning institutions like Harvard and Yale, among others. Though many of these institutions were geared primarily towards the education of ministers. Not long after the Revolution, most states had established tax-subsidized elementary schools, and by the late nineteenth Century, the U.S. population had the highest literacy rate in the world."

"Impressive!" said Franklin, nodding his head.

I continued. "By the turn of the twentieth century most states had compulsory laws requiring attendance at least through age fourteen. A man named Thomas Dewey was instrumental in starting the 'progressive education' movement that emphasized pragmatism as a primary method of teaching and learning. Over the years, the modern education system was divided into four areas of study. Elementary School, the first six years, or 'grades' of study, taught the basics of reading, writing and arithmetic with basic history and science. Middle School, or Junior High, comprising the next three grades expanded on history, science, and mathematics, and replaced basic reading and writing with literature and creative writing, as well as adding social studies, government, and world, U.S., and state history. High school, grades nine through twelve, completed all areas of secondary school study and culminated in the awarding of a diploma for graduating all twelve grades of study. Following that, one could attend a two year trade school and obtain a completion certificate, or a four-year college that would result in a college degree. If one wished to go to a 'graduate school', one could obtain a Master's degree, or a Doctorate in any number of areas of expertise."

"Is this the standard through the country now?" Ben asked.

"It's the standard throughout the world," I replied. "The United States still leads the world in education, though there are areas of the world where certain studies may exceed us. But for an overall education, and in many areas of expertise, the United States is where the world comes to. I mentioned Harvard and Yale, which you are, of course familiar with, and Oxford and Cambridge in England are highly sought after institutions, but the greatest collection of prestigious Colleges and Universities are here in the United States."

"So, Harvard and Yale have progressed over the years?" asked Ben.

"Yes, but they are no longer institutions for the training of ministers. Those functions have been largely discarded in the nations institutions of higher learning, and moved primarily into private colleges and seminaries either funded privately, or through attendance fees, or operated by religious denominations."

Ben frowned. "So religious instruction is no longer practiced in public institutions?"

"For the most part, that is correct," I said. "In fact, due to some decisions handed down by the Supreme Court, participation in any religious activity by institutions supported by government funds is now forbidden."

Ben sat back, stunned for a moment. "Oh, dear!" he said. "Do your citizens not realize that this was the very reason we sought independence from England – to allow the freedom to read, study, discuss, and yes, even worship, wherever one wanted to?"

"Well, that's a discussion we need to have when we have a longer time than we do now, but the short answer is 'no', they don't. But, before we can even have that discussion, we need to talk about Madison's proposed Amendments and how that fared, as well as the interpretations and modifications down through the years. If you don't mind, let's just leave that on the table for now. We'll pick a time when we can go through the entire history of Constitutional government, and come back to how that affects not only our institutions of learning, but modern day life. Suffice it to say that as citizens, we are still free to follow our own consciences and beliefs when it comes to religion."

"I see," said Ben. "I very much look forward to that discussion".

I paused, looked at Kathy, then said, "I tell you what, Dr. Franklin. Since your wardrobe will be ready, for the most part, by tomorrow, how would you like to attend worship services at our Church day after tomorrow?"

Ben's eyebrows went up and he said, "I would very much like that! Where is your Church...what is its name?"

Kathy spoke up on this one. "We attend the Northside Baptist Church, about a fifteen minute drive from here. Tom teaches a Sunday School class, as do I, but this Sunday is the fifth Sunday of the month, and in our Church, the substitute teacher always teaches the class on the fifth Sunday – both to give the regular teacher a break, and as practice to keep their hand in, so to speak."

"Yes," I said. "If you like, we can arrive just before the service, then we can leave via a lesser used door so as not to attract too much attention at this early date."

Ben smiled. "I agree! Is the service early?"

"The worship service starts at eleven and ends right at lunch time. I think you'll like our pastor as well. In fact, he is also the principal of our Church school, which is an accredited alternative to the secular schools. As such, we teach a range of Bible classes and religious studies, in addition to all the other subjects students learn in government sponsored schools."

"Interesting," said Ben. "So, this compulsory law permits attendance at religious schools as an alternative?"

"Yes," I said. "Parents and students may choose from any number of private schools of all types. As a side note, that also serves to improve the curriculum in the public schools, as they have some measure of competition".

"How very American!" said Ben, at which we all agreed.

As we finished up the meal and the dessert of strawberry pie Kathy had brought, it was time to take a break.

"Ben, take a little while to get refreshed, if you want," I said. "I have a couple of things to do, and when you're ready, we'll adjourn to the lounge where I want to show you a full length movie. It's a subject of which you are all too well acquainted. It will take a little over two and a half hours, and as I promised, we'll have a snack of popcorn to enjoy while watching."

"I am intrigued about this 'snack' you refer to," said Ben, "so would about an hour be acceptable?"

"That sounds perfect!" I said.

"Fine. Will the rest of you be joining us as well?" ask Ben.

A chorus of 'Of Course', and 'Yes', came from around the table, so the schedule was set.

"Splendid!", said Ben rising, "If you ladies will excuse me, I shall adjourn to my quarters for a short while, and rejoin you in the study."

"Whenever you're ready," I said.

Chapter 25

Friday - First Week

Kathy, Bill and I were in the lounge talking about the day's activities and discussing how to work out the logistics of getting Ben to and from Church. I told them we had planned on driving him to our house on the following evening for a piece of pie and some hopefully relaxing conversation. They had all been to the house before, so I invited them to come as well. Kathy said she'd speak to Miriam and Phillip, as they were in the kitchen cleaning up and preparing the popcorn popper. We frequently used the lounge for such activities on those long days after we'd worked on the mechanisms to do the transfers, and some while back I'd bought one of these medium size commercial kettle poppers for just such occasions. Yeah, it's junk food, but there's just nothing else that goes as well with a movie.

Phillip stuck his head in the door, tablet in hand. "I think Ben will be ready in a few minutes. He's been making notes, presumably about today's events, and he's put all that up now and he's in the bathroom."

"Sounds good," I said.

"Popcorn's ready to pop," said Phillip. When you start the movie, I'll get it going. I've seen this one a few dozen times anyway, so I won't miss anything."

"Thanks," I said. With that, Phillip went back towards the kitchen, and Kathy got up to follow him.

"Back in a minute," she said.

"Bring me a Dew!"

"In your dreams," she said as she went through the door.

Bill laughed. "How you gonna pull this one on her?"

"I'll plead the 'weekend extra', even though it's just Friday. She'll complain, but that'll be it. I just won't get another Dew fix until next week, but I'll survive."

We chatted a few minutes about baseball. The Braves were in a pennant fight along with the Phillies, and we were friendly rivals. I'd been a Braves fan since the days of WTBS, but Bill had always lived in the Philly area and I was hoping this year they would both go to the playoffs. That way, we'd get to see both teams play on the same day as the play would come to CB Park, and the inevitable side bets and trash talk until one of us had to eat crow. I hate crow.

Kathy came sauntering back in with Ben in tow. "Look who I found wandering the halls," she said.

Bill and I stood. "So, Ben, are you ready for your first ever full length motion picture on this new fangled TV box?" I asked with a smile.

"But of course!" said Ben.

"Great! Have a seat here in the honor position", and I pointed to the chair immediately opposite the TV. As Ben sat down, Miriam came in. "Have a seat, M," I said, "we're just about to start."

I sat down on one side of Ben with Kathy on the other. We had arranged the chairs and the couch in a 'U' arrangement so everyone had a good view of the TV, and Bill and Miriam took some of the remaining seats.

"Does Phillip know we're about to start?" I asked.

"He started the popcorn when he saw Ben, so it should be ready before the opening credits are done," said Kathy.

"Great!" I said. "That gives me time to set all this up". I turned towards Ben. "First of all, popcorn, which we'll have shortly, is always available in commercial theaters where these movies are shown on a really big screen in a darkened room, and we try to emulate that when we watch movies here."

"Just what is this popcorn you're so enthralled by?" Ben asked.

"Well," I explained. "Are you familiar with kettle corn?"

"Yes!" said Ben. "I've never actually had any, but I'm familiar with the term. Is that this 'popcorn'?"

"Yes," I said, "at least it's related to it. In reality it is popped corn. The Pennsylvania Dutch introduced it here in the Colonies around the time of the Revolution, even though it's really been around for thousands of years. But it didn't become in vogue in this country until the mid to late 1800s. By the middle of the twentieth century it made it's way into movie theaters, and basically took over as the snack of choice. The strain of corn it is made from contains a seed which contains a bit of moisture so that when the kernel is heated it rapidly expands, or 'pops', into a white or light yellow soft edible flake about the size of the end of your thumb. You salt it lightly, or sometimes add a light coating of butter. I think you'll like it, and there'll be plenty for all of us."

"Ah, yes," said Ben. "another confection discovered by modern folk. I overheard Dr. Ken use the word 'junk food' earlier. Is this another of that category?"

"Most certainly!" I said. "Ken would disapprove unless, of course, he were here watching with us."

"Just what is the subject of this movie we are about to witness?" asked Ben.

"One of my favorites," I said. "The New York Times review of this movie said it was a 'gruesome hybrid, a mix of sentimentality and brutality'. Just right for modern America. The actor playing the lead character, interestingly enough, hails from Australia, which is now an independent country and like our own in some ways. His name is Mel Gibson. I have a picture of him here," and I produced a photograph of Gibson I had procured earlier on the day.

"The story contains a highly fictionalized account of the Revolution from the perspective of the central character," I said, "but some facts are probably accurate. The industry that produces these movies tends to blur the line between reality and fiction, even when treating historical tales such as this, though I believe the actual story would be just as entertaining. But that's an entirely different discussion. Also, there are some special visual tricks the director of this movie used, in particular the use of slow-motion, where a particular event is shown as if time slowed for a moment or two. Just realize that this is all for entertainment purposes, rather than trying to actually tell the story of the Revolution. Suffice it to say, I would like you to view this not only as entertainment, but as someone who was actually there when these events were occurring, and offer us your own critique when the movie is over. I am particularly interested in everyday things such as dress, customs, language, and so forth, but historical accuracy of the Revolution would also be interesting. Many critics have assailed this movie, just as others have praised it for its production, but I think it might give you at least some insight into the mindset of current day Americans as to how they perceive some of the actions of those in your time, so I'm very interested in your comments once it is completed."

Ben nodded his head in agreement. "I shall do my best!" he said. About that time Phillip came in with a rolling table containing a number of bowls of freshly popped corn and drinks.

"The white bowls contain only salted popcorn, while the yellow bowls are buttered," he explained as he brought the cart around. "Take your pick!"

Kathy and Bill took buttered, while Miriam and I took the salted. "Tell you what," I said to Franklin. "How about if Kathy and I share with you for the first few minutes and you see which one you like the best. There's plenty of both."

"Excellent!" said Ben. Everyone chose their soft drink and Ben chose water, after my reminding him he might want to abstain from the soft drink category. I however, grabbed a can of Dew and when Kathy gave me the evil eye, I simply whispered 'Weekend privilege' to her. Her expression didn't change, but she didn't snatch the can out of my hand, so success!

With all the snacks in place, I said, "Everyone ready?"

There were nods all around, including Ben, so as I reached for the remote, I said, "Ben, the movie starts with an introductory interlude including some of the credits of those who produced the movie, but you'll know when the real story starts," and with that I turned on the TV. I had queued up the movie, so the picture was frozen on the 'Paramount' logo, so I pressed the 'play' button and the movie started.

"If you're confused about anything," I said, "or if you have any questions, or need to take a break, just let me know. I can pause the picture and when you're ready, I can start it back up without you having to miss anything."

Ben nodded, and the movie began. I must say, if it had been me in his position, I would have had to stop the picture several times to ask a question, but then I don't have the mind of Ben Franklin. As the movie began, Ben sampled both my bowl of corn and Kathy's, and indicated he liked Kathy's better, so I retrieved a yellow bowl full of popcorn from the cart and handed it to Ben. He nodded, and sat enthralled through the entire movie.

About a third of the way through the movie, I noticed Ben picking at his teeth with his fingernail. I grabbed a toothpick from the box on the table and handed it to him. "You're familiar with toothpicks, right?" I said. Ben just looked at it, then me, then smiled and picked his teeth.

It's the small things that you remember, I guess. Like Ben Franklin watching a movie on TV, eating popcorn and picking his teeth with a toothpick.

When it was over, it was about nine forty-five, and the day was certainly wearing down on those of us, particularly Ben, whose minds had been in overload the last few days. However, Ben was very animated as he discussed the story he'd seen.

"I understand what you meant when you said 'highly fictionalized'," said Ben. He went on to discuss the problems with clothing, language, customs, as well as some of the things the writers got right. I was struck by the fact that he didn't immediately point out the level of violence portrayed in the film. When I asked him about that, he simply said, "War is always bloody. In fact, it is much worse than what was shown here."

We talked for nearly two hours, Ben pointing out the inaccuracies in the movie, as well as some of the things they got right, and I was surprised at the level of both. I guess if you weren't there in 1776 and it's now over 240 years later, it looks much different than to a contemporary. Ben was very interested in how movies were made, and we talked a good while about that. He was particularly interested in how slow-motion worked, and his enthusiasm could probably have gone on all night, until I pointed out it was nearly midnight, at which point, Bill and Miriam said they really needed to go home. We all stood as they said their goodbyes, and Kathy helped Phillip round up all the popcorn and soft drink glasses and wheel them into the kitchen, and Ben headed for his apartment.

As we stood at his door, Ben said, "I must say, Tom, I am struggling to contain all this information you've filled me with the last two days. How am I to take all this in and function in a world so different from where I was just forty-eight hours ago?"

"I know, Ben, and I'm sorry. I so much want to give you enough basic information to be able to function, because I don't want you to be trapped in this building any longer than absolutely necessary."

"I understand, and appreciate that," said Ben. "I shall try to keep up with your pace as much as I can, but would it be possible to slow down somewhat tomorrow?"

"Of course," I said. "I tell you what. Let's take tomorrow morning more slowly. I'll come in around nine, so just take your time in your apartment. There'll be breakfast waiting when you get up. I've arranged for the morning meal to be prepared and brought into the building, where we can keep it warm until you're ready. Just get up and eat at your leisure, and when you're ready, I'll be in my office. Phillip will be here tonight as usual if you need anything, and we'll take tomorrow a little bit at a time. How does that sound?"

"Acceptable!" said Ben. "I am making notes on all I've seen, and I may have some questions, which I'm sure you can answer for me, but for tonight, I think I'll go straight to bed."

"Yes, I'm sure you're at least as tired as I am," I said. "Good night, Dr. Franklin, and have a pleasant night's sleep."

"Oh I will," said Ben, "Especially on this comfortable bed you have provided for me!"

I laughed and said, "You are much kinder than most would be, but I suppose it is a bit different from the type of bed you're used to."

"Indeed it is!" said Ben. "Thank you for the 'entertainment' tonight, and yes, I like popcorn. Please tell your Dr. Ken that he has his job cut out for him, what with all this 'junk food' you are filling me with."

I laughed. "Yes, I may be in real trouble with Ken."

"Goodnight then, sir!" said Ben.

"Have a pleasant sleep, Ben," I said, as he closed the door to his apartment.

I went in Phil's office and switched on the surveillance monitor. Ben started to sit down at his desk, but one look over at the bed was all it took. I know I'd pushed him hard these past two days, but I would never have guessed we'd be at the point we were now, just the second day after his arrival. As I was contemplating all we'd been over the last two days, I looked up and there was Ben, shedding the last of his clothing.

"Good Lord!" I muttered to myself, and turned off the monitor. I went down the hall past Phil's office and said, "He's all yours Phil! And, by the way, I think we can remove the camera from Ben's bedroom, at least until we turn it back into an office.", and headed for the door.

Chapter 26

Friday - First Week

I was glad I'd allowed for a little time the next morning. I was spent, and I can imagine Ben, particularly at his age, was even more spent than me, so by the time I arrived home, I was ready to hit the sack. The lead-up to the transfer had been hectic, and the last two days had been intense. I really appreciated my crew stepping up, and I had planned a Monday morning assessment of how things were going. I was even considering having Ben there as an integral part, but I wouldn't make that decision probably until Sunday night when I'd had time to sort of assess things myself.

Kathy was waiting at the door when I got home – she'd only left a short while before I had – and I know she had some comments of her own.

"How you doin', Hon?" she asked after I'd unloaded my phone and began the getting ready for bed ritual.

"Tired as I can be," I said. "It's been a packed week, not to mention the last two days."

"I know," she said. "I heard about the relaxed schedule in the morning. Do you still have much to discuss?"

"Well," I thought. "Let's see. Computers – I kinda put him off on that one because he needed a bit more background. That and the Internet alone will blow his mind. Then air travel…."

"Finally getting to Orville and Wilbur?" she mocked.

"Yeah, time for the flight twins. I'll let him chew on that for a while before I spring Apollo on him."

She thought for a moment, then said, "You know, as we were talking and watching the movie tonight, I watched Ben as he interacted with us all, and as he watched his first movie, and I have to say, he is an amazing man. I mean, I've read all about him since high school, and we all know the stories we've heard, plus you made me read his biography. But, even with all that information, it amazes me how he just soaks up all this knowledge like a sponge."

"I know!" I exclaimed. "Now you know why I'm so tired. He's decades my senior in actual physical age, yet he seems to only tire about the same time as I. And, add to all that, his amazing character and demeanor through what would be a shattering experience for anyone else. I've placed myself in his position several times over the last forty-eight hours, and I don't see myself being anywhere near his mental and emotional state. I think his natural curiosity, mixed with his highly intelligent mind, just overrides all the terror and emotion anyone else would experience. I keep looking for him to crack, but other than asking for a little slowdown tomorrow morning, it's just not there!"

"I'm so happy you let me be a part of this experience," she said as she hugged me.

"Well," I said, "you were a big part of getting us to this place back when you worked there, so it only seemed fair. Plus, I really need my best critic helping me keep a hold on reality as we go through this."

"Oh, there's lots I want to go over. Where do you want to start?" she asked.

"Breakfast. Tomorrow morning. I'm spent!"

Chapter 27

Saturday - First Week

The alarm clock went off at the earlier-than-usual time I set it to the night before, but I slapped it a couple of times, and took my time getting up. Kathy was already up (she's much more of a morning person that I am) and I could smell the breakfast aromas waffling (pun intended) into the bedroom. I put on my slippers and headed into the kitchen. The shower could wait.

"Mornin' Sunshine!" she said. "How'd you sleep?"

"I don't think I turned once all night long. I needed a good long night's sleep. My battery was about gone".

"Well, have a seat," she said as she grabbed a plate from the counter. "I have the full load for you this morning. Eggs, waffles, sausage and toast. Milk or juice?"

"Juice," I said.

She put everything on the table and we sat down to eat.

"I liked Ben's critique of the movie last night," she said as I buttered my toast, "and it's interesting what we've lost to history, and how much we both understand and don't understand life in the eighteenth century."

"I believe that's just the tip of the iceberg," I said. "I am particularly interested in his take on where the government is now and how it differs from what they intended when they signed the Constitution two days ago."

Kathy smiled. "Yes, that's one thing that just boggles my mind. He literally just walked out of Independence Hall into your building. Talk about fresh in your memory. Does he really have all the same thoughts and memories as the Ben Franklin that he left in 1787?"

"How many times have you heard me say 'bad breath and all'?"

"Yeah, I know," she said as she pondered that. "But it still seems unrealistic that it's exactly him."

"Yep. Every synapse. Every brain wrinkle – all perfectly intact."

"Here's the really big question," she said. "What about his soul?"

Sometimes I'm amazed at how our thoughts dovetail in the same direction. This is the one part of this whole process that concerned me most. I believe...scratch that. I *know* man is a spiritual being, and as such has a soul that transcends this life. As a Christian I'm told that after this life there are one of two destinations – Paradise or Torment – for the soul of man. But, each man has only one soul. To me the biggest paradox of all about time displacement is what happens to that soul?

I paused before eating my next bite. "Yes. What happens to that soul? Does 1787 Ben have it, or did twenty-first Century Ben inherit it? If the latter, what happened to 1787 Ben? I know I've broken some physical laws, at least as Einstein and others understood it, but there's nothing in the Bible that says 'Oh yeah – time travel – don't even think about it', so how does all that play out?"

"I have those same questions," said Kathy. "The fact that he's here, and you weren't obliterated by a Sodom and Gomorrah size firestorm from Heaven gives me hope that God has handled that somehow. But, how are we to know?"

"One thing I don't know," I said, as I took another bite, then a drink of juice, "is the state of Ben's soul in the first place. If he's a believer as are we, have I pulled him back out of Paradise much like what happened to Lazarus, or has something unspeakable happened? I'm also glad that firestorm didn't show up, but did I cause something like that to Ben? That's what's kept me up at night."

"Me, too!" she said. "But here's the thing. I have a strange peace about this. If I thought we'd violated some cosmic law, I'm pretty sure that conviction would be eating at me right now, but for some reason I feel there's a plan to this that we may not know yet."

"Yeah," I said, "now that you mention it. I've not felt that familiar twinge when I'm on the wrong side of the truth either. I guess as long as I'm staying close to the right path, the plan for Ben will come together. I'm just not sure how to approach him with that."

"Well," she said, "let's just leave that up to the Lord, and He'll work it out. He always does. You know, 'All things work together....'."

I smiled at the familiar quote. "I guess that's what we have to hang on to."

We talked about several of the other things we'd thought about, particularly the way Ben was handling things, until it was finally time for me to get ready.

"Don't forget, I'm bringing Ben home with us tonight. I'm considering having him stay in the spare bedroom. How do you feel about that?"

"I was hoping you would," she said. "He really needs to get out of that building. By that time he should have enough information to keep him from freaking out if a plane flies over, right?"

"That's the plan!" I said, rising. "Well, better get going!"

I showered, dressed and headed out for the office. As I drove, I took particular notice of the sights along the way, in case I had to explain some things ahead of time. But, as it turns out, other than much more traffic than he'd seen on our first excursion, the rest was just more of what he'd already seen, albeit different signs, businesses, and homes.

When I arrived, Bill had already relieved Phillip, and he'd gone home for the weekend, so one of the things I had to do was get him ready for the weekend security we had coming. I had made a deal with the folks at NSF to provide security for the next couple of weekends, and they had sent a nice young ex-MP Army officer over several days ago who's security clearance was sufficient to provide what we needed during Ben's first weekends here. Normally we had a security company provide weekend security for us, but they didn't have the necessary clearances, so we just asked them to take a couple of weekends off while we had our own people on sight.

Entering the building and through the internal security door, Miriam was coming down the hall from her office.

"Morning, Tom."

"Mornin'. How's our guest?"

"He's in the conference room scarfing up the Big Breakfast Deal from the Colonial Diner Cafe. He got a good laugh out of the name when he saw the box they brought it in," she smiled.

"Good," I said as I headed down to my office. "If you don't mind, tell him I'll join him in a few minutes."

"Sure thing," she said and headed for the conference room.

I placed my briefcase beside my desk, then went over to the cabinet just to the right of my office window, opened up the doors, and retrieved my computer monitor and keyboard. I put them on my desk, and fished the wires out of the access hole in the top of my desk I'd covered up with a tissue box, and hooked it all back up. Then I opened the bottom right hand computer door on my desk and booted up the small desktop computer there. As the screen came to life, I reached in the desk drawer and pulled out my wireless mouse, clicked the login icon, and logged into the system. It took a few minutes for me to scan the emails in the inbox, but there wasn't anything that required urgent attention, so I logged out, switched off the monitor, and headed into the conference room.

"Good morning, Dr. Franklin!" I said in the cheeriest voice I could muster.

"And a good morning to you, sir!" said Ben.

"How'd you sleep, Ben?"

"Marvelously!" he exclaimed with raised eyebrows. "Had I known beds could be so comfortable, I would have wished to have been born much later!"

"Ah!" I said, "But you were needed in your time!"

"Possibly, possibly," he said, "but I have confidence the Almighty would have succeeded without me."

"Well, it wasn't the Almighty I was concerned about," I said, and we both laughed.

"I must say," he said, "these Colonials who prepared this sumptuous meal seem to be very skilled. The morning meal was delicious!"

"Glad you enjoyed it," I said. "Kathy prepares mine, and I do believe it cannot be topped. Looks like we both fared well last night."

Bill came in with his ubiquitous morning coffee and sat down, followed by Miriam with hers.

"Well, looks like the gang's all here," I said, "so how about we talk about the rest of the weekend?"

"Agreed," said Ben. "What are the plans for today?"

"Well, Ben," I began, "with your permission, there are two, well, two and a half actually, more major items to acquaint you with, and the rest will be primarily up to you. The first thing I want to do is show you one more area of modern communications that would have been much harder to explain had I not told you the history of these electronic devices we now use, and there's a related area that's even harder to explain, but I'll give you the general idea of how it works and give you a demonstration. I think you'll be amazed."

"You mean, I can be more amazed than I have been already?" he asked in half-serious surprise.

"Yes, very much so," I said. "But, the second thing is about transportation, and believe me, it will be amazing as well. In fact, when I get to the phrase 'One small step for man', you will have completely reached the realm of the unbelievable."

Ben's face lit up, his eyes were wide, and he was almost drooling. "I cannot possibly imagine what you have in store, but believe me, sir, you have piqued my curiosity. I am supposing I will sleep deeply again tonight, as I see another exhausting day approaching."

"Well, only mentally, maybe," I said. "I intend to take the physical part of the day pretty easy, and if all goes well this evening, I'd like to take you to my home for one of Kathy's home cooked meals. Does that help your apprehension?"

Ben smiled. "Indeed it does!" he said.

I told him about the new security man coming, and he was intrigued that he was ex-military. We also discussed some of the logistics of the day, and in particular what we might do for lunch. All that decided, I told Miriam she could plan her day however she wished. She decided to take the morning off and do some grocery shopping for the week, and we discussed the weekend's logistics, including that Ben might be spending the night at my house.

"If that meets with your approval, Ben, that is," I said.

"I'd be delighted to see your home, and I thank you for the invitation."

"Well, then, barring any unforeseen problems, we're set for the weekend. If you're ready, let's start in my office, and we'll go from there."

He nodded and rose, as did the rest around the table. Miriam said her goodbye for the morning and headed out. Bill said he'd be in his office if we needed him, and Ben and I headed for my office.

As we entered, Ben noticed the monitor on the desk. "Interesting," he said. "Is that a smaller version of the TV we watched last night?"

"Ostensibly, yes," I said, "though this particular TV is referred to as a monitor. It is used in conjunction with a device I have behind this door in my desk," and I pointed to the door to the computer compartment below the drawer

134

on the right. "This is a keyboard similar to what I showed you yesterday. But, this keyboard has a wire coming out of the back which goes through that access hole and attaches to the device in my desk, as does this monitor."

Ben examined the cables, then nodded.

"Yesterday, we discussed a small bit about computers. I have yet another book of pictures for you," and I reached behind me and grabbed another photo album.

Ben said, "I am still intrigued by how easy it is to create these pictures, but proceed, and I'll try to stay on the subject."

I flipped open the cover to the first picture. "This is the machine that Turing invented during the Second World War to break the German military codes that helped us shorten the war. After the war, there was much interest in these computing machines, and much like the other inventions that have occurred since your time, these began to evolve over the years."

I flipped the page to the Colossus. "This was the next step from Turing's machine. It was able to break the codes even faster that the original Turing machine. Over here in the States, many colleges and universities began experimenting with electronic computing, and in fact, right here in Philadelphia the first fully functional electronic computer called ENIAC was developed. ENIAC stood for, I believe, Electronic Numerical Integrator and Calculator," and I flopped the page to the ENIAC.

Ben examined the picture. "This model, as well as both Turing machines and others before it, ran on something called 'vacuum tubes'," and I flipped the page to a picture and cutaway diagram of a tube.

"These tubes were powered electrically by heating up this element called a 'heater'. This heater would glow, and in doing so would propel electrons which could then be controlled by these other elements. Suffice it to say, by utilizing different types of these tubes, in conjunction with other electrical and electronic components, one could build many of the early devices that were the 'ancestors', so to speak, of the things you've seen today, such as this monitor and last night's TV."

"How does this help one to compute?" asked Ben.

"Well," I went on, "computers utilize something called 'binary language'. In the binary language, there are only two characters. The 'zero', which refers basically to the absence of an electrical charge, and the 'one' which refers to the presence of an electrical charge."

I took out a piece of paper and gave Ben a quick lesson in binary math. Then I pulled out a chart that shows how different binary numbers can be used to represent every printable character of the alphabet, as well as some basic graphic characters. Then I showed him how those graphic characters could be combined to make some rudimentary pictures. Lastly I showed him how binary translated into octal, hexadecimal, and finally the familiar base-10 numbers we all use. I let all that sink in for a few minutes.

135

"Now. Once you have these rules in place, you can manipulate this binary code to do some calculating. They also devised ways of storing for later retrieval of some of these groups of ones and zeros so they could be retrieved and used again."

Then I explained memory to him, and how basic calculations could be accomplished.

"As we now know, these electrons travel over wires, and if married up with a radio, wirelessly, at the speed of 186,000 miles per second. So all this storing, retrieving, calculating and displaying happens virtually instantaneously."

Ben's eyebrows went up and his eyes went wide. "Such speed is possible?"

"Yes, but just hold onto that little bit of information for a later discussion, and just take my word for it. Of course, these electrons are invisible and they pass through most materials and matter without disturbing them, so we just discovered many ways to use their properties in the last century or so."

"I will accede to your request, but you must return to these electrons and help me understand how they operate," he said.

"Oh, I have plenty of information on that, and everything else we've discussed, so you'll be able to delve in as deep to them as you wish."

"Exceptional!" he said. "Please continue."

I then went through ENIAC, other educational institutions and research, government developments, showing him pictures of each until we arrived at minicomputers, the emergence of IBM and it's lines of computers, and I ended up with a picture of DEC's PDP series.

"Around the 1970s, and into the early 1980s, hobbyists, laboratory experimenters, and academic students began tinkering with ways to reduce the size even further. Finally, someone developed a small computer that practically anyone with sufficient resources, primarily money, could build themselves. It appeared in a hobbyist publication and was called the 'Altair 8800'." and I flipped to a picture on the Altair sitting on a desk beside a bespectacled young man.

"This was the first production of a 'personal computer'," I said. "By today's standards it was like comparing your horse drawn carriage to my SUV, but it worked, and many thousands purchased the parts to assemble these computers in their own homes and workshops."

"How did these smaller devices compare to the first ones you showed me?" he asked.

"Again, a similar comparison would be the first Model T Ford I showed you yesterday to my SUV."

"Amazing," said Ben. "What does one do with such machines?"

"Hold onto *that* thought for just a few more moments," I said. "From the Altair, next came several models from other groups." Then I went through the Commodore, the Apple, the TRS-80, and that brought us to the IBM PC.

"In 1981," I began, "the worlds largest computing equipment manufacturer, International Business Machines, or IBM, decided to get into the microcomputer business, so they came out with the IBM PC, or IBM Personal Computer. This was like an elephant jumping into the pond. Suddenly, no other manufacturer mattered, everyone wanted the IBM. As businesses began purchasing these machines for their own use, and they realized that making a mistake by buying a machine designed for a hobbyist might not hold up to the requirements a business needed, they flocked to the IBM PC. As a matter of fact, the saying was 'Well, nobody ever got fired for buying an IBM'. As a result, many of the smaller companies disappeared, leaving only two or three companies to compete. But, compete well they did, and they all soon came out with machines that not only mimicked the IBM, but in some cases were superior, and cheaper."

I then went through a number of pictures of PCs, right up to today's.

"This is the one I own," and I opened the door to the desk rolled back my chair, and showed Ben the Desktop in the desk well.

Ben examined the face of the computer, and of course, it was nothing but an on/off button, a couple of lights, and some USB access ports.

"I know," I said, "it's not very impressive, but what goes on inside that box truly is. Ben returned to his seat, and I shut the door and continued. "Now, you asked what one could do with a PC. The box and its components alone do nothing other than await instructions. This box, and its components, is what we refer to as 'computer hardware', because, obviously, you can put your hands on it. But something has to make this box of parts do its calculating. That is done by something called 'computer software'."

"Hardware and software," said Ben with a smirk. "Who comes up with these terms?"

"Well, usually the first guy there," I laughed. "In fact, when computer software doesn't tell the hardware what to do correctly, that is referred to as a 'bug' in the system. That term comes from the ENIAC days. The vacuum tubes that operated those machines, and their sheer size, would attract all types of crawling varmints, as you might imagine, and sometimes these varmints would get between the wired connections causing the voltages to travel to other components they weren't supposed to, and that was called a 'short', or 'short circuit'. When that happened, the computer wouldn't operate as it was supposed to, so someone would have to find that creature, and extract him. It was known as a 'bug in the system'. That term stuck, and nowadays means any computer, hardware or software, not operating as intended."

Ben just sat back. "My, how the English language has been so maligned over the years," and he laughed.

"Oh, I suspect it has always been so," I said. "Only, we really accelerated the process."

"Tell me," said Ben, "how does this 'computer software' work?"

That was a good half hour discussion. I covered binary language programs, hexadecimal programs, then I went into higher level languages such as Assembly, then into Basic, Cobol, C and it's derivatives, and even talked about how different types of languages could be used in concert for different complementary tasks, and used my mouse as an example of how that would work.

Finally I said, "Today there are a myriad of languages used for anything from teaching children how to create rudimentary software programs, to highly scientific languages, to languages that are designed to manipulate images, and much of the new software is now being done using something called 'artificial intelligence', basically attempting to enable a computer system to make decisions on its own and 'learn' from its mistakes and make its own adjustments. That was very high level stuff until recently, and most of what we see of AI is hidden in smaller parts of software programs, but we can really get far off the mark. So, for now, how about I just show you what I do with my computer?"

"Yes," said Ben. I'd very much like to see that!!!"

I turned on the monitor to the login screen, and explained what it was and why it was necessary. I again showed him my mouse and clicked on the login icon and logged into my desktop. Then I clicked on an icon in the middle of the screen. When the image represented by the icon came up on the screen, Ben's eyes shot up. For on the screen was a picture of the signed copy of the Constitution of the United States of America.

Chapter 28

Saturday - First Week

I took a good bit of the mid-morning to show Ben how computer software worked. I showed him everything from word processors (which he most certainly could have used in his time!), to spreadsheets, to the calculator function. I explained, as best I could, what a database was and how it worked. I even showed him a couple of games, starting with Solitaire, which I explained was so popular because Microsoft had bundled it with Windows to help people get accustomed to the mouse.

Then, I took him back into software history, explaining how before graphical interfaces, everything was done on the command line. That led to a discussion about operating systems and what they were and their function. When I explained that an operating system was just another collection of software applications that allowed humans to interface with the computer, that seemed to make a bit of difference. From there we went into the various OS's down through history.

"The system I use on my computer is called 'Linux'. It's named after its creator, a young man from Finland who created it as an educational exercise, and it basically took off when others caught on to what he was doing. The fact that he published all the instructions that made it work, and that he mandated that it had to be free to anyone who wanted to use it not only made its popularity take off, but garnered him plenty of help in adding features and other software programs. While most people use a system named 'Windows' from a company named Microsoft, the Linux-based systems are the most widely used system in the second part of this story."

Ben sat back and thought for a few seconds. "Before you talk about this 'second part', how many people use these computers today?"

"Everyone," I said. I pulled out my smartphone. "In fact, this cellphone, somewhat similar to the one I showed you yesterday, is actually a portable computer that is primarily a wireless telephone, but also contains some applications. For instance, remember the Solitaire card game I showed you a few minutes ago?"

"Yes," said Ben, nodding his head.

I punched a couple of icons and up popped a Solitaire game I was in the middle of. "Here's the same software program, called an 'App', short for 'Application', on my phone. There are thousands of these Apps you can get for practically any area of interest you may have."

Ben examined my phone for a second as I held it out. "So tiny? You say this is a computer, just like the box you showed me moments ago?"

"Very similar," I said, "though the larger one does have more capabilities. But, their operations are very similar. We'll talk later about how we got these things so small."

"Yet more information," he smiled. "How does one obtain these 'Apps', and how do you know what is available? Is there a catalog?"

"Well," I said, "that's the second part of the story. Imagine that my wife has a computer at my home, which she does, and I have a computer here, and I want to retrieve, or copy, something that is on her computer over to mine. There are several ways to do that. There are storage devices that I can plug into hers, make a copy of what's on hers, then transport that device over here, plug it in mine, and copy it onto my computer. There are several types of storage devices of varying capabilities, but one thing they all have in common: I have to physically transport it from there to here."

"Yes, I can understand that....I think," He said, tentatively.

"Well, what if I could use these wires we use for the telephones we talked about to act as a kind of storage and/or transfer device, and just copy that App over those wires from her computer to mine."

Ben thought for a minute, then a stunned expression came over his face. "You mean, the same way you 'copied' me from 230 years ago and transported me here."

Wow. I hadn't even thought of his making that connection. This guy really was intelligent. Now I was stunned.

"Ben!" I said. "That is an amazing insight you just had. Yes, it is very much like that, though obviously much different in effect, but you ran right to that idea, and I hadn't even considered how similar this concept was to your situation as I was trying to explain copying Apps to you."

Ben sat back, contemplating, and then he sat back up. "Tom, I am afraid you are beginning to rub off on me. You have told me so many things in the past two days, and I fear they're all related to each other in many ways."

Again, I was amazed at his intellect. "You are exactly correct, Dr. Franklin. This breakthrough in your thinking was exactly what I was hoping to accomplish along with acquainting you with the changes since your time!"

We both sat in silence for a moment, then Ben said, "You want to copy something from your wife's computer to yours.....Please continue."

"Yes. So, if I could copy the contents from her computer, all the ones and zeros, and place those same arrangements on my computer, I would save an enormous amount of time. In the 1960s, many colleges, universities, and government agencies, had access to these large computers I showed you," and I patted the photo album, "and there was this desire to be able to share information between these machines without having to do the traveling I just described. There was, and still is, a government military agency called the Defense Advanced Research Projects Agency, or DARPA, that began to research a way to do this. The connecting of computers together is called a 'network', or 'net' for short. This agency created something they called DARPANET. Later the National Science Foundation built on this project and created their own network they called NSFNET based on DARPANET that could be used in their research, which then made its way into universities. Once students became accustomed to using this resource graduated from college, they still wanted access, so colleges granted access to those students, and it just expanded from there. The result is something we use today called the Internet. Virtually every computer in the world is now connected to this network, all traveling over greatly enhanced communications systems, so I can literally connect my computer to any computer in any country at any time of the day."

I moved back over to my computer, and motioned for Ben to come closer. I clicked on my browser and as it came up I explained to Ben what he was about to see.

"This is an application called a 'browser'. It allows me to actually 'browse' through all the information available on this Internet network." Our internal Intranet web page came up. "What you are looking at here comes from a computer down the hall called a 'server', because its function is, literally, like a server in a restaurant – to get what I want and make it available to me. This is called a 'web page', or a 'website', because one of the developers of the Internet created a way to display the information found on the Internet in a more aesthetically pleasing and easier to use method than just typing on a keyboard. He named it the World Wide Web, because in his mind he saw the connections that allow the flow of information between multiple computers like it was a spider web."

Ben looked at the content of the website. It was not fancy – just contained a list of resources available only to us, since it was firewalled from the outside world.

"This particular website just contains information we might use here in our project, and we can update this with newer information as we need to. I can add something to this website and it will instantly be available to everyone else in the office."

"So," he said, "these computers in your office are all connected by wires?"

"Yes," I said. "There are also wireless networks that use tiny radios with a very limited range, yards instead of miles, which is what my phone uses to access this same page," and I pulled up the browser on my phone and accessed the internal website.

"Amazing! Simply amazing!" he said. "Do these wires also connect outside your building?"

"Yes, they do!" I said. "In fact, I literally have direct access to all of the world's history, as well as the accumulated knowledge from down through the centuries, at least as much as has survived, and information that is continually added each second of the day, any time I want to see it. Would you like to see an article from the World Wide Web that might interest you?"

Ben shot me an 'are you kidding' look and said, "Well, of course!"

I had already prepared a link and saved it on my toolbar, so I clicked it. Up came a Wikipedia article with a picture of a distinguished gentleman on the right, and on the left a heading that read simply 'Benjamin Franklin'. Ben's expression changed to one of delight as he viewed his portrait from 1785. He began to read what was written, and I scrolled down the screen as he did. It took a few minutes, since the article is detailed. When we got to the bottom, Ben looked over at me, then back at the screen.

"So much information on one individual among many of my time," he said. "If you don't mind, why are some of these words in blue?"

"Great question!" I said. "These are called 'links'. If I maneuver the pointer controlled by this mouse over one of those links and press the left button on the mouse, the browser retrieves another webpage that this link points to." I clicked on the 'Franklin Institute of Boston' link, and instantly the website for the Ben Franklin Institute of Technology loaded.

Ben's eyes widened and his eyebrows shot up. "There is an institution named for me?" he asked.

"Oh, Ben, there are several things named after you. Schools, streets, commercial enterprises. You are quite famous, Dr. Franklin!"

Now Ben was astonished. He sat back for a moment. Then he looked at me, then down at the floor with a mixture of wonder and humbleness and said, "One never knows how one will be viewed once having departed this earth. I hardly know how to take this."

I thought for a moment, and said, "You know, Ben, one of my favorite stories is a movie about a man who fell onto hard times – an honest man – and his world came crashing down around him in the space of just a few hours. His friends prayed about his plight, and as he was contemplating taking his own life, an angel was sent down to save him. To do so, this angel ended up changing history by erasing this man's life from history and showing him how things would have been had he not been born. The effect one man has on not just those around him, but on history itself is incalculable. It totally changed his outlook as to who he was, and he wanted his life back. When he returned to his family, his friends had rallied to help him out of the trouble he was in. The movie is called 'It's a Wonderful Life', and you have the rare privilege of seeing just some of the things that have occurred as a result of your own life. I do believe I told you this on your first day here."

Ben looked up and said, "Indeed you did, sir. Indeed you did. Whatever doubts I may have had about why I was chosen for this adventure, I now see I have indeed been given a gift. So, whatever feelings I may have had before this moment, I now thank you, sir, for allowing me to see that my life had meaning."

"It still does, Dr. Franklin! It still does!"

Ben smiled, and we both sat there for a second, enjoying the moment. Then, he looked up and said, "What else can you show me?"

"Well, Dr. Franklin. You are going to love this! You were the first Postmaster General of the United States, and that, as we discussed yesterday, is going strong and handles millions of letters and parcels each day. But along with the development of the Internet came another way of exchanging information between individuals. You have seen the web browser, now let me show you an application called 'Thunderbird'. Honestly, I don't know how they come up with these names," and I clicked on the Thunderbird icon on my desktop, "but this particular application accesses one of the most popular and powerful applications on the Internet."

Up popped the window and I noticed there were several messages that I hadn't read yet, but I clicked on one Kathy sent a couple of mornings ago I had already read. It said:

> 'Hey, hon. Just remember, you don't have to teach class this Sunday. We get to sit in our class together this week – how great is that? Don't forget – milk on the way home. We're almost out.
> K'

"This, Dr. Franklin, is called Electronic Mail, or Email."

Chapter 29

Saturday - First Week

I know, I know. I felt a little guilty. Every time Ben thought he had a handle on the latest major change in his world and worldview from 1787, I threw another curve ball to him (and we hadn't even discussed Baseball yet! Though he had seen a home run...) But, the night he arrived, as I drove home, and later as I was drifting off to sleep, and on the drive in the next morning, I kept going over and over in my brain how I would introduce all these major elements to him I had identified weeks ago for whomever the arriving 'guest' might be. It just seemed to me the way to both keep his interest, and make it relevant at the same time, would be to incorporate into each development, as much as was possible, something that he could identify with from his own time. Today, it was his biography on Wikipedia, and the revelation of Email to the first Postmaster General.

Ben was aghast. "But, you say people still use the postal service?"

"Yes, very much so!"

"But, if you can send greetings instantly, why would people still wait for a letter to arrive days later?"

"Well, sir, there are those in our society, primarily those who are heavily into this new technology, that are asking the same question. Partly, I suppose, because of habit, but there are other reasons. For instance, there is a sticky problem with privacy."

"How so?" Ben asked.

"As you remember, this Internet system is all interconnected like the spider web from a few moments ago?"

Ben nodded.

"Well, because of that, and also because the original inventors of the Internet didn't foresee how massively their system has grown, they didn't build into it ways of tracking who could and could not eavesdrop on these communications as they are in transit. On the other side of the coin, and something you would probably agree with, they didn't want those in positions of power keeping tabs on every little thing every single citizen was involved in, at least without some legal probable cause, so it is possible to both be anonymous and 'out in the open' at the same time. I know that sounds impossible, but it seems the more we try to hide what we're doing, the more it seems some out there find ways to track us anyway. And now with everybody connected to everybody, it's the big problem of the twenty-first century – privacy."

Ben pondered this for a moment. "I agree, sir, that unless I wish, no one has the right to my business, particularly some potentate down the way, but I will need to understand more of how all this 'Internet' business works. I assume there is much more to it?"

I laughed. "Yes, you could say that. It is rather complicated, and to tell the truth, practically none of those who use the Internet each day have much of an understanding of exactly how it works, so in that, you're not much different from my next door neighbor."

Ben let a sly grin run across his face and said, "Well, possibly I have come further than I thought, so to speak."

"Oh, Ben, you have no idea how far you've come. As you might imagine, as I was contemplating how I would bring someone from the past into the present day realities, I assumed that by the time we got to the Internet and Email, several days would have passed. But here we are, on your third day, and I must say you have taken great strides – greater than I could have imagined. Would you agree?"

"I would agree that the sheer magnitude of the changes you have exposed me to is all but unbelievable, especially in light of where I was just two days ago, but I will say it does already seem like weeks since we started."

"Well," I said, "I see we're in agreement on that front, at least. Anyway, back to the Email issue..."

"Yes," he said. "How does one choose whether to send one of these Emails as opposed to posting a letter?"

"Much of it has to do with content", I explained. "For example, our government insists on paper copies of important documents that will be or might be part of their duty under the Constitution. Not only that, many companies still insist that paper copies of items convey more an air of authority than some words on a computer monitor somewhere. Then there are the advertisements and newspapers, though the latter have certainly been harmed by instant communications, and books and other printed materials are still very much in vogue. I can foresee a day when much of what's still being sent through the postal service will convert to Email and other means of electronic delivery, but for now, loads and loads of letters, parcels, periodicals, newspapers, and other printed materials are delivered to each post office across the nation each day. The Postal Service you established is actually stronger than ever."

"Delightful!" said Ben. "I would very much like to see a post office. Would that be possible?"

"Oh, of course," I said. "I plan to arrange a tour as soon as we finish your, shall we say, 'orientation'."

"Yes," he said. "I suppose I still need some orienting. Please continue. What other magic are you able to coax from this little box."

I laughed when he said that. "You know, Ben, you just used a phrase I have to tell you about. Years ago a writer of fictional stories with a scientific theme – we call it science fiction – made a comment about the advancement of technology. His name was Arthur C. Clarke, a renowned British writer. He announced three adages he called 'Clarke's Three Laws". Now, while I don't remember the first two, the third says that 'Any sufficiently advanced technology is indistinguishable from magic'. So, I can certainly understand how this all looks like magic to you."

Ben smiled. "But it isn't, correct? At least that is what you have insisted when the subject came up before."

"Correct!" I said. "Remember when I told you there was plenty of documentation to explain, in detail, all of these 'magic' inventions, and how they came to be, and that I would gladly provide them to you when the time came?"

"Yes, and I plan to hold you to that!"

"Well, then," I said. "Let me introduce you to something called 'DuckDuckGo'."

Ben's face wrinkled at the absurdity of the term, which I fully expected, and made me smile when it happened just as I'd imagined it would.

"I told you," I said, "I don't know how they come up with all these terms. Before I show this one to you, a little history. When the Internet first came into existence, there was very little way of discovering what was available. Imagine a huge library – the size of a city block – where anyone could place a book anywhere they wanted in that library, any time they want to, and you just wander in from the street. You would have no idea where to look for a book on Roman history, or on philosophy, or on gardening, or even where the Bibles were kept. So, some college students, who as we discussed, were among the first users of the early Internet, began creating computer programs that would automatically search through what was available and build an electronic index. This information was organized and stored so that by simply asking some questions, or providing some key words on what you were looking for, several matching options would be provided and those magic 'links', like the words in blue from a few minutes ago, would appear and you could browse them to your heart's content. This system became known as a 'search engine'. The word 'search' is self explanatory, but the word 'engine' referred primarily to the ongoing indexing of each and every new volume of information added by someone to the Internet."

Ben thought for a second. "How detailed does this index get?"

"Very detailed," I said. "There are several of these search engines in existence now, and over the years they have grown in scope and detail. Some are not in existence any more because the next one to come along was so much better that people ceased using the old one and began using the latest. There are hundreds for one to choose from, but the most popular include one called 'Google', another called 'Bing', another that's been around for a while named 'Yahoo', and the one I use called 'DuckDuckGo'. I think the name is a play on words for a children's game called 'Duck, Duck, Goose', but I'm not really sure why. The reason I use it is because they guarantee that whatever you are searching for is never stored and associated with you, so you can still maintain some measure of privacy. However, Google is still by far the most popular."

"These students that dream up these things seem to have wild imaginations in linguistic areas as well," Ben laughed.

"That they do!" I said. "But, let me show you how easy it is. Let's take an example of something we've talked about already. I have a search option built into this browser, so all I need to do is tell it what I'm looking for and I'll get some options."

With that, I clicked in the search window on my browser and typed 'automobile engines'. When I clicked the search arrow, a list of relevant articles popped up. Among the articles was one entitled 'Automobile Engines – A Short Course on How They Work'.

"As you see, there are several here." I explained, "So we can choose based on the initial description, then choose that link and see if that article is suitable."

I clicked on the link, and up came the article, complete with a picture of a modern day engine, graphics of its component parts, and even an animated gif that showed the cycle of an internal combustion engine.

"This is an introductory article," I said, "so it just gives the basics, but if you want to look deeper into automobile engines, you can search for, say, engineering drawings". I added the words 'engineering drawing' to the end of the previous search and clicked the search arrow. A few clicks later and I had on the screen pictures of a small engine from several angles, a table with all the engine's specifications, followed by engineering drawings of each part of the engine, all in a printable PDF. I showed Ben how to use the scroll wheel on the mouse and handed it over to him.

He was a bit intimidated at first until I said, "Go ahead, Ben. It won't bite you," which garnered me a nasty smirk. But after some short instructions, he quickly figured out how to make the picture scroll, so I sat back and let him look through the document.

When he finished, he sat back and said, "How many subjects are you able to search through on this 'library', as you termed it?"

"Billions," I said. "Pick a subject you know something about. Any subject."

Ben thought for a moment, and said, "Apple Tansey".

"OK," I said. "I don't know what that is, but let's see what we find." I typed in 'Apple Tansey' in the search window, verified the spelling with Ben, then clicked the search. The third option was '*Apple Tansey recipe from Colonial Williamsburg*'. I had a pretty good hunch about that one so I clicked it, and wasn't disappointed. What appeared was a graphic of the 1754 recipe card for Apple Tansey, so I clicked it, and there was the recipe.

"Would you like to have that made for you?" I asked.

Ben sat back. "What if I had asked for a picture of my pocket watch, which you seem to already know something about?" he asked. I typed in 'Ben Franklin Wagstaff' in the search window and clicked the arrow. Up popped several items, one of which was 'Ben Franklin's Pocket Watch by Thomas Wagstaff, London'. So, I clicked it, and there it was in all it's glory.

Ben reached in his pocket and pulled his out and held it up to the screen. Again, the look on his face was just priceless.

"Dr. Franklin, available on the Internet is all the world's history, all its wonders, all the accumulated knowledge available to mankind from every culture in the world, and all I have to do is tell this search engine what to look for. Now, admittedly sometimes the options are not exactly what you are looking for, and there is a bit of a trick to it, but that's quickly learned, as you see, and anyone, anywhere, on any computer connected to the Internet can find it."

Ben just stared at me for a moment. "Any knowledge?" he asked.

"Yes," I said. "Now, I must warn you, there are some things one just shouldn't see. The Internet is like the wilderness – there are all kinds of things out there, some of which are not, shall we say politely, edifying. It does require some measure of self control, because as flawed human beings we tend to migrate towards things we should stay away from in many instances, but to keep tyrants from censoring and controlling what we are allowed to know, many times we have to allow things that we might wish to be otherwise hidden. But, look who I'm talking to. You were instrumental in delivering the very liberty that would suffer if we allowed government imposition of censorship."

Ben thought about that for a moment. "This seems such a powerful tool to be in the hands of individuals. Has personal responsibility grown in such a manner that such power is not misused?"

"No," I said. "It is still a fact of life that some people will be up to no good no matter what constraints we attempt to place on them. However, there is a quote that is attributed to a gentleman which you know very well, that says *'Those who would give up essential liberty to purchase a little temporary safety deserve neither liberty or safety'*. Are you familiar with this quote?"

Ben smiled and said, "I see you have no compunction in using one's words against oneself, so I concede your point, at least for now. I may wish later to know the extent of this information one shouldn't see, not to see, but to be aware of the dangers that might abound in this magic – and I will continue to refer to it so, for the time being."

"Well, for the record - even though I have a fairly detailed knowledge of how this all actually works - I must confess, it does seem like magic sometimes to me as well."

I looked at the time in the corner of the desktop screen. "It's getting near lunch, so before we break, let me show you one more thing about this computer and the Internet."

Ben leaned forward and nodded, "Continue then, sir."

I cleared the desktop and clicked on an icon I had placed there the previous day. It brought up another browser window and a page from a website I had discovered when I was compiling information on all the possible subjects that might be on my primary list to be transferred.

"This, sir, is the family tree of one Benjamin Franklin from Boston. As you will see, there are relatives of yours that are alive today. All of this information is available from resources on the Internet, and this chart only took me about an hour to compile."

Ben stared at the chart, then back to me. "Tom, you continually surprise me with things like this – one I had not even considered until just this moment."

Yep. Another classic stunned Ben Franklin look, just as I had anticipated.

"Let's eat!" I said.

Chapter 30

Saturday - First Week

As we entered the conference/dining area, Kathy came through the door with lunch. Bill was loitering around the kitchen drinking some tea, so he sat his cup down and helped Kathy unload the box.

"What's on the lunch menu today?" I asked.

"Your favorite sandwich!" she said.

"Ah, great!" I said as I turned to Ben. "Ben, remember the hamburger we ate yesterday?"

"Of course!" said Ben. "Exceedingly tasteful!"

"Well, it's actually a form of something that's become known as a 'sandwich'. The rumor is that the name came from the Earl of Sandwich who, I believe, was a British politician from your era."

"Why yes!" said Ben. "I know him well from my time in Britain. I have met him several times. Why is a meal being served in this time named after him?"

"The rumor is," I said, "that when at the gambling table, Montague would ask for meat and bread, placing the meat between two pieces of bread, and when others would be asked what they would like to eat, they would say '*the same as Sandwich*', or words to that effect, so any meal consisting of an edible substance between two pieces of bread became known as a 'sandwich'.

"Utterly amazing!" said Ben. "I myself have seen the Earl partaking of just such a meal. I confess I may have even had one myself. That simple example has survived to this day?"

"Indeed!" I said. "As a matter of fact, millions of different types of 'sandwiches' are eaten each day all over the planet, primarily for the noon meal."

"Unbelievable!" said Ben. "Am I to understand we will be partaking of a 'sandwich' today?"

"Yes, we will," I said. "Today we are going to eat a filleted chicken breast between two half-buns of bread with a slice of pickle. It is prepared and sold by a company based in Atlanta, Georgia called 'Chick-Fil-A'. It's one of my favorite sandwiches. I hope you like it."

As we sat down, I blessed the meal with a quick prayer, then Kathy brought each of us a small tray with a Chick-Fil-A sandwich, some fries, and a cup of ice.

"You can pour your own drinks this time, gentlemen. Dr. Franklin, it's time to learn that we women are no longer slaves to you men!" she said laughing as she pointed to a pitcher of tea beside two 2-liter soft drink bottles.

Ben smiled and said, "I appear to be put in my place! I shall, therefore, pour my own 'iced tea'," and he reached for the pitcher.

"See, hon," she said to me. "Some people learn rather quickly!" and she sat down with her meal and a cup of tea she'd already poured.

"Yeah yeah," I said. "Way to rub it in!" and I reached, of course, for the Mountain Dew. "Just for that, I'm drinking Dew!"

She looked at Ben and said with a smirk, "Some people never learn, Dr. Franklin!"

He laughed and we dug into the meal. Dr. Franklin looked over at Kathy.

"I understand your house is running out of milk," he said. "Is there no delivery today?"

Kathy looked a bit confused, until I said, "Today's lesson on Email. Yours from a couple of days ago was the one on the screen. Ben, milk is no longer delivered. We have to go get it, but we'll discuss all that later."

She laughed and said, "Well, as it turns out, we need more milk, so pick some up on the way home", then she looked at Ben, "And you just make sure he follows his instructions this time!"

"Oh, I will, dear lady. After the stern warning you just gave me I dare not cross you today!"

We all laughed. For the next half hour as we ate and finished our meal, we talked about how far Franklin had come since Thursday. He admitted once again that the sheer amount of information that he'd been exposed to almost made his head swim, but that the excitement of all that had transpired since his time had completely captivated his imagination.

"I fear it shall take me the rest of my life just to catch up on what, apparently, twelve-year old boys now accept as just a normal part of life. Tom here tells me there is plenty to read and understand, and I cannot see how there will be time enough to learn all I should like to."

"I agree," said Bill. "My teenage son knows more about cellphones and computers than I can learn in a lifetime. As a matter of fact, when one of these things is not acting like I think it should, I just take it to him and tell him to fix it. I'm afraid we've 'invented' ourselves out of the picture."

As the discussion began to wind down, Kathy looked at Ben as we rose from the table and said, "Remember, Dr. Franklin, everyone's coming to our home tonight for a nice home cooked meal, and you'll be spending the night in our spare bedroom."

"And," I finished her thought, "We'd like to invite you to attend our Church services in the morning, if that meets with your approval."

Ben smiled and said, "I'd be delighted! Though, I am a bit apprehensive about mixing with the general public with such limited information about today's social etiquettes. I should not like to be a distraction to your minister and his service."

"Don't worry about that," I said. "We'll enter and exit as unobtrusively as we can, and I can help you through any issues that come up while we're there. I just thought this might be a good first outing, and I'd be interested to hear your observations afterward."

"Wonderful!" said Ben. "I shall look forward to meeting your friends."

As the meal broke up, Miriam and Kathy cleared everything off, and I told them we had a couple of more items before we left, and I told Kathy we'd be along in a few hours. She told me not to worry about the milk, she'd go ahead and get it, and I got that 'you'll pay later' look she's so good at. Ben laughed at the exchange, but didn't needle Kathy about the change. I'm guessing he wasn't comfortable with the interaction between the sexes just yet, particularly between married couples. I know things were much more formal in his day, but the way he was progressing in other areas, and knowing his acumen in diplomacy, I had no problem with him acquiring the necessary skills in short order.

"Ben," I said, "let's go sit on the patio, if that's OK. There is one more major piece to be put in place before we transition to letting you loose on the world that I'd like to get started on. Would you like something to drink while we're there – coffee or hot tea?"

"Yes," said Ben, "a cup of that coffee I smell would be welcome!"

Miriam was standing at the door to the kitchen, and before I could head that way she said, "You two go on out to the patio. I'll bring the coffee. You want anything, Tom?"

"No, thanks. I'm fine." I said and we headed out to the patio.

It was another nice sunshiny day and the temperature was again mild enough that coats weren't necessary. We sat at the patio table until Miriam came out, and Ben stood as she poured him a cup of coffee then put the coffee pot on the table.

"If you don't mind, I'm going to head out," she said. "I think you two have everything in order. Call if you need anything."

"Will do," I said. "Thanks for all your help this weekend. See you and Charlie tonight!"

Ben bowed slightly and said, "My thanks to you as well, Madam. Have a pleasant day!"

"Thank you, Dr. Franklin," she said, "and please have a seat. We're all very informal around here. I guess that's something else you'll get used to before long." With that, she left, and Ben sat back down.

"Yes," he said. "I suppose there are many things I must become accustomed to, and old habits to break as you, how did you say it, 'let me loose on the world'?"

I laughed. "Yes, I know the customs have changed in many ways, some not for the better, but as we say these days, 'it is what it is', and I'll be glad to help you through that transition as well."

"Tell me of this 'one major piece' you referred to. I shall not even try to guess in which direction you are to take me now!"

"I actually thought you might guess this one," I said, "but with so much else going on, I'm amazed at the information you've been able to absorb thus far. Let me tell you about two brothers from Dayton, Ohio in the Midwestern United States, and a small town in North Carolina called Kitty Hawk."

Ben sat up in his chair, because by now he had become accustomed to my openings when a new subject was about to be introduced.

"Their names were Orville and Wilbur Wright. You remember our discussion about the evolution of automobiles how one of the transitions from horse to horseless was the bicycle?"

Ben nodded, "Yes, interesting method of travel. Please continue."

"Orville and Wilbur were not highly educated young men, but like you they had a boundless curiosity. They actually built their own printing press and started a weekly newspaper in the late 1800s. The newspaper didn't last long, but they did put the printing press to good use doing commercial printing. They also became involved in the national interest in bicycles and began manufacturing their own brand. However, this was not their primary interest. Bicycles and printing just became a way for them to make a living while they worked on their real passion – flying."

"Flying?" asked Ben. "You mean, like a bird?"

"Yes," I said. "Surely you are aware of Leonardo Di Vinci's drawings of flying machines and how he had envisioned them, and of course you know something about kites, but I understand you experimented some with lighter than air balloons in your time. I believe there's a famous quote where, when asked what they could be used for, you said, '*What is the use of a new-born baby*'?"

Ben's eyes shot up. "Yes, I said exactly that. Are you to tell me that that baby has grown up?"

I laughed, "Oh not only has that baby grown up. He's flying!"

Ben was hooked. I started with balloons and described how they were a novelty that primarily found their place in fairs and expositions. Then I went on through airships and how they're still used in public events more, again, as a novelty today. From there I started with the Wright brothers first flight at Kitty Hawk and how that changed everything.

"Once they had that short flight in 1902, only about 800 feet, the world had changed. When word got out, and newspaper stories appeared how these two brothers from Ohio had demonstrated that human beings were no longer shackled to the ground, everyone wanted in on the act. By 1914 hundreds of 'aviators', people who had learned how to control these flying machines, were flying their 'airplanes' all over the country, and advances in their abilities were being made almost daily. Then came World War One."

"Were these flying machines useful in war?" asked Ben.

"Yes, though because they were still in their early development, they were primarily used for intelligence gathering. As you can imagine, if you can get way up in the sky, you can see what your enemy is doing far in the distance. However, along with other developments in the instruments of war, guns have also progressed. These airplanes were outfitted with guns that the men flying them, called 'pilots', could remotely fire so they could fire their weapons at soldiers on the ground as well as on other airplanes. Not only that, explosives have also developed over the years to the point that these pilots could drop explosives on the ground troops. But, airplanes were not a deciding factor in the First World War."

Ben thought about that for a moment, then asked, "Then, from the way you expressed that last part, am I to assume their effectiveness changed?"

"Oh, yes!" I said. "But, there was much to change between the two world wars. The speed, agility, distance, and overall performance of these airplanes would grow by leaps and bounds. There were obvious peacetime uses as well, as the size and safety of these airplanes grew. All of a sudden, not only did you not have to travel for days on a horse when you could go the same distance in a motorized vehicle on the ground, you could travel in the air for just a few hours in what would take days or even weeks on the ground or on the ocean. They also began carrying the mail rather than by horse or car. In the late 1920s an air-mail pilot named Charles Lindbergh flew his airplane from Long Island, New York, to Paris, France, 3,600 miles, without stopping in just over thirty-three hours. It was the first transatlantic flight, and he instantly became a national hero."

Ben sat back in astonishment. "I assume, then, that traveling in the air to Europe is still being done today?"

"Every day," I said. "First it was using engines similar to what are in our cars and trucks, but there was an invention in the late 1930s called a 'jet engine'. This new engine greatly increased the power that propelled these airplanes through the air, thus increasing their speed. Today you can fly from an airport in New York to an airport in London in just over seven hours. We could eat breakfast in New York, then dinner in London, then be back by breakfast the next morning with time for some sightseeing in between."

I reached down and pulled up a file on my cellphone with a number of pictures. "By now you already know my phone here has some useful features, and one is the ability to display pictures that I've saved, so we won't need the photo album any more. Here is a picture of the Wright Brothers first airplane that flew that 800 feet."

From there I showed him the bi-planes, then mono-winged planes, then planes with multiple engines. Then I went to pictures of the first prop driven commercial airliners and their development. Next came the first jet engines, single and multi-engines.

"Once these engines had been perfected, and the structures of these airplanes refined, the companies that provided air travel to the general public began improving the safety and comfort of passengers in their care. Let me show you a modern-day airliner that might take passengers to London."

I pulled up a picture of a large airliner. "This is a picture of the Boeing model 777. It can carry as many as 390 passengers, along with all their luggage, the meals they'll consume while in flight, and all the fuel necessary, for any destination on the planet as far as 8,000 miles away without having to land and refuel."

Then I pulled up a picture of the interior. "This is what the interior looks like. There are toilets in the front and rear, and employees of the airline companies that operate these airplanes have areas to prepare meals and store items that might be needed for the passengers like pillows, blankets, and such."

Then, I pulled up another picture. "Here are the pilots and the area in the front of the airplane where they work. They call this area the 'flight deck'. This particular airplane cruises at an altitude of over five miles, and at a speed of over 500 miles per hour. They can go higher and faster, but this is their normal operating speed and height."

I expected to see gray matter all over me any minute, and I was sure Ben's brain was about to explode. "I'll let you think about that for a minute. If you thought instant communications and motorized vehicles was a big change in the way the world works, the ability to jump on an airplane and travel half-way around the world in a single day changed everything."

I put the phone back down on the patio table and suddenly wished I had something to drink. "Tell you what, Ben. Let me get something to drink, then you can pepper me with your questions. I know you have some!" and I rose and went back into the kitchen and poured myself a glass of tea. No use getting Kathy any angrier with me than she already was with her monitoring of my soft drink intake!

When I came back out, Ben was standing at the patio looking up into the sky.

"At night, you can see airplanes with their navigation lights on as they criss-cross the sky," I said. "Tonight, if you like, and if it's not too cold, we'll sit on my patio and look for some. As a matter of fact, airliners flying from New York to Washington, D.C. and places south go right over Philadelphia, so there should be plenty to look for."

I purposely left out the part about the flight tracking app I had on my phone. I didn't want to give him a heart attack just yet.

As he stood there looking, he asked, "You were talking earlier about how these airplanes were not useful in the First World War, and your implication was that they became more useful. Am I correct in that assumption?"

"Yes, Ben, you are. Man has always devised ways of using inventions meant for peace to kill each other. Airplanes are no exception. Let me show you some examples."

Ben came back over and I pulled up a series of pictures, starting with bi-planes in WWI. Then I progressed to the beginning of World War II.

"Do you recall our discussion of Israel and how the story of the restoration of Israel had part of its beginnings in our fiftieth state in Hawaii?"

"Yes, and I meant to return to that issue. Please explain."

"As you recall," I said, "we have a naval base there in a harbor named for the town it's adjacent to - Pearl City. It's called, of course, Pearl Harbor. One of the developments in the intervening years between the two wars was the ability for airplanes to take off and return not just to land, but to specially designed ships, called aircraft carriers." I pulled up a picture of the USS Langley. "This was one of the first. You can see the large deck built onto the top of an existing ship. It was long enough for airplanes to take off and land there, though it was a treacherous undertaking each time, but eventually these pilots developed ways to do so."

Then I went through the other carriers right up to the ones in operation in WWII. "This is the aircraft carrier Akagi, built by the island empire of Japan. On December Seventh 1941, the Akagi and five other similar ships, all laden with war-equipped airplanes, had sailed within striking distance of our bases in Hawaii, and on that Sunday morning, without warning, they attacked our naval installation there, as well as other military targets, killing or wounding nearly 3,000 Americans and a number of civilians. Since it was a surprise attack so far from Japan, and on a Sunday morning, we were completely unprepared. Our nation was outraged, and that single act propelled us into the Second World War. In that war, aircraft were the deciding factor on both sides in fighting the war."

I then showed him pictures of Pearl Harbor before and after the attack.

"In addition to Japan, the nation of Germany declared war on the U.S. as well, and suddenly we were on a two-front world war. The leader of the German forces, a man named Adolph Hitler, hated the Jews, and he and his cohorts attempted to completely eradicate the Jews from the face of the earth. They murdered, in a most calculated and systematic way, over six million Jews from all over Europe and the Middle East. Once the war was over, though, the Jewish people recognized they could never let this happen again, and began to fight to win their own country. As we discussed, they are one of our strongest allies and we back them with supplies and, if necessary, our own military whenever enemies of theirs, and ours, attack."

I let that sink in for a moment.

"You see, Dr. Franklin. The United States is no longer isolated from the rest of the world by oceans. December Seventh changed all that. Our enemies are just hours away, and if they use ships at sea to transport highly effective weapons, just minutes away. Because of this, we have had to maintain an Army,

Navy, Marine Corp, Air Force and Coast Guard forces not only to guard our own land, but capable of inflicting terrible damage anywhere in the world as a deterrent to attack. We call it 'peace through strength'. We intend to be so powerful and so capable that no one would dare attack us. For the most part, since World War Two, it has worked, but I want to save some of those instances for another day, if that's OK. There is much history in war, and I'd rather focus on things that will help you to assimilate in the world we currently interact with."

"So, you're saying that without that attack that brought our country into the war, Israel might not exist?"

"I'm saying that had the United States not entered the war, Hitler and his criminals could have won the war, and yes, Israel not only would not have existed, but many millions more of them would have been murdered."

Ben thought for a few moments about all this, then said, "Just three days ago I signed a document we hoped would bring peace to our country." He looked directly into my eyes with an almost pained expression. "How were we to ever know something like this could occur? What could we have done had we known?"

"Ben, if a swordsman from ancient Israel were to see what you fought the Revolutionary War with, he would say the same thing. What you must understand is that the document you signed three days ago gave us the framework to change with the times, to meet these challenges, and to keep, for the most part, that liberty you established those days when we were only thirteen states. You could not have known. But, you prepared very well for what you could not see. The Constitution is a miraculous document, and is the single reason our country has outlasted every other form of government on the earth."

That pained expression turned more contemplative. "With such powerful weapons, I can only shudder when I think of what King George would have done with such power."

"Sir," I said. "King George couldn't hold a candle to the atrocities committed by the enemy forces in World War Two. Because of all these events, and the ability of our country to meet those challenges, we are strong. If we fail, it won't be because some outside force defeats us. It will be because we defeated ourselves. Let me show you one more aircraft."

I pulled up another picture on my phone. "This is a special airplane. There are actually two of them, so if one is out of commission, the other can be used. It is used when our President is traveling so that he is never out of communication with the other branches of government, other world leaders, or the leaders of our armed forces. When he is aboard, and only when he is aboard, this aircraft is known as Air Force One!"

Chapter 31

Saturday - First Week

Ben stared at the photograph of the President's plane. "How much travel does the President engage in?" asked Ben, as he looked up at me from the picture.

"Quite a bit," I said. "In fact, he is in California on the west coast today, and will be flying back along the southern border to Texas this evening to speak at a political event there, and I believe he is due to fly back to the Capitol sometime tomorrow to be ready for a meeting with the press on his new proposal to reduce the size of the federal government. Last week he was in Europe for a few days meeting with our allies on economic issues."

Franklin looked back down at the picture of Air Force One. "So many miles in such a short time," he said. "Doesn't he tire of all this travel?"

"Well," I said, "I suppose he does. But, he does travel in comfort," and I pulled up several pictures of the inside of the aircraft, including his office, the conference room, and his bedroom.

"There are accommodations for many members of his staff, special guests, and representatives from the Press, as well as the presidential security detail."

"The presidential security detail?" asked Ben. "I suppose that might make sense when traveling abroad".

"Well, let's not get too deep into that discussion right now, but suffice it to say the President is always accompanied by men and women tasked with protecting him. Remember, as the most powerful country on earth, his position is extremely important, so every precaution is taken to make sure no harm comes to him while he is President. But, let's leave that discussion for later. Right now, I want to focus on these last few details that might come up in every day conversation."

"Yes, priorities," said Ben. "How many citizens avail themselves of this travel through the air?"

"Brace yourself for this number, Ben. There are an average, on any given day, of nearly 200,000 passengers traveling on various aircraft in, from, or coming to the United States."

Ben was aghast. "So many?" he asked. "Does everyone travel by air?"

"No, not quite," I laughed. "Let me put that in perspective. Since your time, with the expansion of the nation, immigration from other countries, population increase due to childbirth, etc., the current population of the United States is over 350 million people. Of those, many are what we call 'frequent fliers', meaning they travel regularly on aircraft. I would say about one in ten have ever traveled on an aircraft. Travel by motor vehicles is by far the most used form of travel."

I could see the calculator in Ben's mind working now. In a few moments, he said, "Since you told me of the expanse of the nation, I had assumed our population was greater, but these many millions? How does the nation sustain such a mass of men?"

"Well, do you remember our discussion of the automobile and it's production, how mass producing vehicles drove the price down so the average citizen could afford to own one?"

"Yes, of course," said Ben.

"Well, in much the same way, we have, in the intervening years, streamlined our production and distribution of everyday items required for life – food, of course, clothing, personal hygiene and health care products – well, practically everything you can think of. As a matter of fact, some of the places I wish to take you next week are large stores where one may buy almost anything you would need."

"I would very much like to see how people are able to acquire such items," said Ben. "I suspect that automobile invention has much to do with one's ability to resupply?"

"You are exactly right. As a matter of fact, there is an entire industry built around the distribution of goods from manufacturers to retailers as well as directly to homes." I looked at the time on my phone, and said, "As a matter of fact, we have just missed a visit from a pickup and delivery service that comes to our office once a day. In addition to the postal carrier, there is another service, several actually, but one that we primarily use called United Parcel Service, or 'UPS'. They also carry millions of parcels each day."

Ben's eyebrows shot up. "So, in addition to the postal service, there are other organizations that deliver the mail?"

"Well, not exactly the mail," I said. "While they do handle some envelopes with important documents, they are primarily premium services that charge more than the postal service because they guarantee a delivery date and time. Also, because of air travel, one service is actually called "Federal Express", even though it has nothing to do with our government. This company guarantees delivery of any envelope or parcel anywhere in the country by noon the next day."

"Overnight?" Ben asked incredulously.

"Yes, overnight. The man who started FedEx had the idea and submitted it as his college thesis. His professor told him it wouldn't work. This man then proceeded to start a company that proved his professor wrong, and today it is one of the most successful delivery services in the world – and they do deliver literally all over the world."

"Do they guarantee overnight delivery anywhere in the world?" Ben asked.

"Mostly, yes," I said, "though there are some parts of the world that are still difficult to get to, but they can tell you where those places are. In those cases, it might take an extra day," I said with a smile.

Ben sat back in his chair again, and stroked his chin with his fingers. "Tom, the changes you keep revealing to me are beginning to tax my ability to assimilate. I have seen a lot in my life, but this is several lifetimes of change. I do not know how much more I can take in," he said with a small chuckle.

"Well, Ben. There are still several things you haven't been exposed to, and many of the gaps to fill in, but my thinking is that if I can get the really big changes explained, maybe it won't be so hard to 'assimilate' the others."

"I have my doubts," Ben said. "How many more of these 'really big changes', as you say, are there?"

"The question I struggled with before I started this enterprise was what constitutes a 'big change', and what constitutes an 'incremental change', or smaller changes that 'fill in the gaps'. So, let me recap for a minute. We started off with electrically operated devices – lights, the watch, the music player. Ice cubes! Then we went to foods, running water, toilets and showers. You even had pizza and Mountain Dew along the way. Then came automobiles and ground transportation and all the ways transportation had changed. Then, all the changes in communications, and computers, and the Internet. Now air travel. Each of these have elements and details that we haven't talked about, and which you will discover as you use them. It is also possible that something I consider to be more mundane, you might consider to be monumental, so we'll cross that bridge once we get there. There is one more major piece of information that changed the world in ways that will most certainly amaze you. But before we get into that one, what do you say that we just fill in a few gaps. Let's wait until this evening to discuss that one, if that meets with your approval."

Ben had listened intently as I went over the list, nodding, and when I had finished said, "Agreed. At this point I don't know how much more my brain can take."

"I understand!" I said. "Let's fill in a couple of gaps, then let's get the things you'll need for the rest of the weekend, and I'll take you to my home where Kathy will have a nice home cooked meal and we can sit under the stars this evening after dinner and finish the discussion."

"I accept your proposal!" said Ben. "What gaps do you wish to fill in?"

"The kitchen," I said.

"The kitchen," Ben echoed.

"Yes. You'll see mine this evening anyway, so let's just get that little bit out of the way, then we'll head to my house."

"Then proceed, sir!" said Ben as we both rose.

I took him back inside the hallway, being careful to lock the outside door as I did, and opened the side door to the kitchen. Most businesses have a break room where one might find a microwave, a small refrigerator, a sink, and maybe a few other small items. When we had this facility built out, I had insisted on a full kitchen so we could handle anything that might come up. I didn't go commercial, because I wasn't planning anything as big as a banquet – we would just have those occasions catered. But I did want the ability to prepare anything the staff might want, particularly on those long days where our discussions and our work might have stretched much longer into the night had we not had the ability to prepare things on site, and we'd had a number of those!

As we walked in the door, we walked into what might be a galley-type kitchen in any suburban home. I led Ben to the center of the kitchen.

"The sink, you already know about," I began. "Obviously, every kitchen would have one. But there's where the similarity ends." I went over to the stove. "This is a combination stove top and oven, called a kitchen range. It is electrically operated. These circular areas on this stove top are called burners, and when turned on they get quite hot very quickly." I turned on one of the burners as I was talking. In a few moments it glowed bright red and the heat could be felt even a few feet away.

"If you place a cooking pan with water on this element, the water will begin to boil in just a couple of minutes. You can see the relative settings on this control here, 'Hi', being, of course, the highest setting, wherein the burner stays on almost constantly. Lower settings cause the burner to come on and go off periodically, depending on the intensity of the setting. This is a four burner stove, so you can cook four different items at a time." I turned off the burner then opened the oven door.

"This is the oven. You can see the large burner element on the bottom, and there's another one on the top. You can turn this knob," and I turned on the oven, "to whatever temperature you want the oven to warm to, depending on the meal you're preparing, and the bottom element will come on until it reaches that temperature, then go off, then back on, and so forth, to keep the temperature at that level. There is also a setting for 'broil' that turns on only the top element."

Ben warmed his hands on the heat coming out of the oven. Then he looked at me and said, "I assume a full meal might be prepared in a much shorter amount of time, then."

"Absolutely," I said. "And by precisely controlling the temperature, it's much harder to burn or under-cook meals, though I seem to be able to do both."

Ben laughed, and I turned off the stove and shut the oven door. Then I motioned him over to the refrigerator.

"This invention probably saved as many lives as some modern medicines," I said. "This is a refrigerator. Do you remember when we discussed the air conditioning unit outside?"

"Yes," said Ben, "and I am very much enjoying the 'weather' in here!" and he scanned the ceiling as he laughed a bit. I had to laugh as well!

"Well, this is a miniature version of that air conditioner. Just like we learned how to control the temperature on the inside of this building, we can control the temperature on the inside of this appliance, just like we control the heat on the stove and oven, so that today we have something here that every household has. This is a side-by-side refrigerator/freezer with built-in ice maker."

Ben's eyes shot up. "Ice maker? Is this the contraption that has produced all this cubed ice you are so fond of and have now hooked me on?"

I laughed and said, "Exactly! Let me show you." I reached up into the cabinet on the opposite wall and grabbed a plastic cup. I placed the cup in the ice dispenser area of the freezer and pressed it up against the activation lever and several cubes of ice plopped into the cup. Then I punched the selector button on the front from 'ice' to 'water' and filled the glass with water. I then handed the cup to Ben.

"Glass of ice water, Dr. Franklin?"

Ben laughed, took the cup, and took a swig of the water. "Absolutely amazing!" he said.

"Well," I said, "Let me show you the inside." I opened the door. "This is the refrigerator portion. As you see, we have several food items here - butter, eggs, soft drinks, some lettuce and cabbage. There's milk in the back and various other items. These stay cool at a constant temperature of around forty degrees, and there's a rumor that this little light goes out when you close the door, but nobody's ever been inside to verify it," I said as I laughed.

Then I opened the freezer door. "In here are the frozen foods. As you can see we have meat here – this is ground beef, which is what the hamburger you ate yesterday is made from. We also have frozen milk products called 'ice cream' which you haven't had yet. I'll see if we can get some tonight. These other items are frozen foods purchased at the local grocer. These can stay here indefinitely, though the ones that have moisture still in them, particularly dairy based items, might suffer from something called 'freezer burn' where they have been exposed to air and are damaged by dehydration and oxidation, but that's fairly easy to spot. Some of the items in this particular freezer have probably been here for months."

Ben looked up and said, "So I am to understand that one could obtain any foodstuffs, place them in this freezer and keep it for months without it going bad?"

"Yes," I said. "It has greatly reduced not only the need to quickly consume something grown or purchased, but almost eliminated disease and sickness from eating foods that have ruined or gone bad."

I closed the doors to the refrigerator and freezer and said, "Let me show you one more invention that occurred in my lifetime."

I motioned to something hanging from the under side of the cabinets on the other side of the room. "As you know, I enjoy my radio set. That radio set works by sending out electromagnetic waves that travel through space to whatever destination they can reach. Years ago, a technician working on a particular radio device that produced a particular type of electromagnetic wave noticed that when he turned it on, a piece of candy he had in his pocket would melt. He began experimenting and discovered that by controlling this wave, and containing it within a metal enclosure, he could rapidly heat foods. A company called Amana began producing a version of this device for home use. It's called a 'microwave oven'."

I went back over to the refrigerator and retrieved a slice of bacon. "This is a thin slice of pork bacon," I said. I placed it on a paper towel and put it in the microwave and closed the door. Then I set the dial to forty-five seconds and turned the oven on. The light and the blower came on and forty-five seconds later the 'ding' sounded and I took the bacon out of the oven. The paper towel was soaked with bacon grease and the bacon was almost too hot to touch. I blew on it, then tore it in half and handed half to Ben, and ate mine.

"Bacon, Dr. Franklin?"

Ben looked at me, then the microwave, then the oven. He took a bite of the bacon and smiled. "From cold to hot in just seconds?" He asked.

"Yep!" I said. "Amazing, right?"

"Truly!" he said. "I suppose every home has one of these, as well?"

"Yes, and there are commercial versions used in restaurants as well. When you want something quick, you microwave it!"

Chapter 32

Saturday - First Week

We packed the clothing Ben would need for an overnight stay, and I insisted he wear his pajamas at my house – I still couldn't get the picture out of my mind from the surveillance monitor the other night! He agreed that might be a good idea as well, so at least we were on the same page there. As we entered the foyer area, the security guard the NSF had provided was in a chair just inside the main entrance on his cellphone. He started to hang up when I stopped him, made sure he had all the weekend contact and emergency info he needed, then bade him a good night, and we headed out into the parking lot.

Ben had no trouble getting in the Tahoe, but a little finding the latch for the seatbelt, so I helped him get that squared away, then I buckled up and away we went. I still had the cover over the LCD display in the center console, so I just left it because I wasn't quite ready to reveal its capabilities. Besides, I wanted him to focus on the ride rather than the gadgets.

"I do believe I was to remind you of the shortage of milk at your home, Tom," Ben said. "I would not want to cross your wife. She appears to be able to hold her own with any of us!"

"Oh, that she can, Dr. Franklin! That she can. But, just before she left she told me she had taken care of the milk, so I think we're safe. Thanks for the reminder, though."

As we drove, Ben commented on some of the sights along the way. It was getting dark and many of the lights were coming on, not to mention the traffic lights, the stop and yield signs, and all the other things we all take for granted and thus ignore. He was particularly impressed with the amount of traffic headed out of town, though it thinned out some the nearer we got to home. At one point we crossed over some railroad tracks and I pointed them out, as well as the crossing bar, and explained how that worked. I had hoped we'd see at least a train on the way home, but I normally didn't see one this time of night. Maybe Monday.

I turned down the road to my house and up to the mailbox at the end of my driveway and retrieved the mail. "Dr. Franklin, here's today's delivery from the U.S. Postal Service." I thumbed through the mail and pulled out three envelopes.

"This is junk mail, so it'll get tossed into the trash as soon as we get home," I said.

"Junk mail?" he asked. "Please explain. How do you know what is in these before you have read them?"

I laughed and said, "I guess that doesn't sound very good to the man who practically invented the post office, but these are all advertisements and solicitations that various companies and organizations have produced and sent to thousands all across the country. This one, for example, is from an insurance company. I know because of the logo on the outside. I know this company, but I already have insurance, and I can tell you exactly what this is going to say because I've seen it many times before. After a while you know from the type of letter and the writing on the outside which pieces of mail are important, and which ones are, well, junk."

Ben nodded thoughtfully. "Perhaps I understand your point. It's just that I am accustomed to receiving mail that someone took time to write and mail to me for a purpose, so I see each as something of importance. I suppose that's another of the things that have changed?"

"Yes," I said. "Just like automobiles and other things that we use on a daily basis, these types of advertisements and solicitations are mass produced by the thousands and carried to the post office in boxes. They are about as impersonal as they can get. Still, out of a thousand or so, one or two may lead to some business for these companies, so they can justify the cost based on the return they receive. It literally is a free economy in practice."

We pulled up to the house and I thumbed the garage door opener mounted above the mirror and pulled in as the door opened. Of course, there was the tennis ball on a string hanging from the ceiling that I pulled up to and stopped as it touched my windshield, then I thumbed the control again and the door closed. Ben observed the whole process, so as we got out of the vehicle I explained in intricate detail how it all worked. The tennis ball amused him. Obviously he'd never run a vehicle into the shelves on the wall and dented his hood before.

As I entered the door to the mudroom Kathy met us in the hallway.

"Good to see you again, Dr. Franklin! Welcome to our home. What would you like to drink with your meal? We have tea, coffee, water, or even milk if you prefer."

Ben asked, "What is your custom?"

"My custom is to drink whatever I want, but generally I drink iced tea with the meal, then maybe a cup of coffee afterwards, but I'll prepare whatever you wish."

"I'll have what you're having," said Ben. "That sounds wonderful to me".

"Great then!" said Kathy. "Everyone else should be arriving in a few minutes, and dinner will be ready shortly. Tom, you want to give him the tour?"

"Sure," I said as I put my briefcase on the floor by the door. "Ben, let me show you around." I picked up the small suitcase with his clothing and had him follow me. I showed him the living room, complete with my big screen TV and dual recliners. Then the kitchen and dining room where dinner was smelling pretty good. Then we went down the hallway to the bedrooms.

"Here's yours for tonight," I said as I placed the suitcase on his bed. "It has it's own bathroom with shower, so you should have everything you need, particularly if you need to get up to use the toilet in the night. Our room is just across the hall," and I showed him our bedroom.

"This is quite luxurious," he said. "Your wife has excellent taste and refinement. This chest of drawers is particularly well crafted."

"Yes, we spent a bit of money in the furnishings here, since we spend one third of our lives here, although we're sleeping so all of a sudden that doesn't seem to make much sense," I said with a wry smile. "But, I continually remind myself that women are the stabilizing influence in society. I've seen how a bunch of men live, and this is much better, so I guess it's worth the cost."

Ben laughed, and we headed back out and down the hallway. "This is my room," I said, as I opened the door. Inside was my amateur radio equipment, as well as a bookshelf full of books, my guitar in the corner, and a combination printer/copier/scanner on a floor stand to the left of the desk.

Ben surveyed all the equipment. "This is much more impressive than the radio you have at your work! Is there an increase in what you can do with all this over what you have at your work?"

"Yes, and no," I said. "There are some additional functions that some of this equipment has, but to tell the truth, that same gentleman I talked to in London would have not sounded much different on this equipment as he did there. Folks who enjoy this kind of pastime tend to accumulate more and more equipment, some of which does the same thing as equipment you already possess. I think we just like all the shiny knobs, lights, and buttons. Besides, it does look more impressive when you walk in the door."

Ben laughed. "I suspect that each endeavor one does for enjoyment is that way, though there are many lights, knobs, and buttons, as you say."

"Tell you what, Ben. Next chance we get, if you want, we'll see just who we can find from around the world on these contraptions."

"Yes, I'd like that," he said. He looked at the guitar in the corner and asked "Are you a musician as well?"

"Well, you could say so, but I play more for enjoyment. When I was younger I would lend my talents, such as they are, to our Church services, but we have more talented younger people for that now. I primarily just play for my own enjoyment, though I must admit, I've played less frequently these days."

"Yes," Ben said. "It seems our interests grow as we age and find it more difficult to return to earlier endeavors."

"Exactly!" I said. We exited that room, and I opened the door on the opposite side of the hall. "This is where Kathy likes to spend some of her time. She's into calligraphy and card making. Here are some of her creations." Ben looked at some of the cards she had on the desk.

"This is exquisite work!" he said.

"Yes. She uses her talents to create get-well and greeting cards for friends and acquaintances. Also, since my daughter is a photographer, she likes framing and making albums of her photos." I pointed to the wall on the left of the door. "These are photos of my family. This is my oldest daughter and her children, and here's my youngest and hers. They both live not too far from here, and come by regularly to visit Mom and Dad."

Ben took time to look at each photo, commenting on how handsome the boys were, how beautiful the girls were, and asked several questions about each, what they did, etc., and we spent several minutes talking about my family, and I shared a couple of humorous stories of their childhood. I was in the middle of telling him what my sons-in-law did when Kathy came in and said everyone else was here and we were holding up dinner. I didn't need a second invitation.

"Let's eat, Ben!" I said.

"As you lead, Madam!" he said.

We went into the dining room and introduced Ben to Miriam's husband Charlie, and Bill's wife Linda. They were both as wide-eyed as Miriam had been at her first introduction.

"It's a pleasure to meet the families of those who have been taking such good care of me," said Ben.

Charlie said, "Never in my life would I have imagined this. Too bad I can't tell anyone!"

Linda got the traditional bow and kiss on the back of her hand, and you could almost see the 'I'll never wash this again' look on her face.

"So pleased to meet you as well, madam," said Ben.

"It's an honor, Dr. Franklin!" she said.

Ben smiled and said, "Oh please. My name is Ben!" and everyone laughed.

Phillip said, "Ben is beginning to get a handle on this more informal world. Welcome to the twenty-first century, Ben."

Well, I'm not sure about this 'handle' you're referring to, " said Ben, "but I am getting a bit more comfortable, especially with this group."

"Glad to hear it!" said Kathy.

Introductions done, Kathy pointed everyone to a seat, and I offered a prayer for the meal and our time together.

"Tonight we have baked Turkey and dressing, with cranberry sauce, mashed potatoes, green beans, and iced tea all around." Kathy instructed. "Tom, if you'll start with the turkey and pass it around...."

As we ate we discussed Ben's day and his constant amazement at all the new sights, sounds, and wonders he'd been exposed to in the last three days. As we listened to him describe each discovery, he became more and more animated, and I was gratified to see that he seemed to genuinely be enjoying himself, maybe for the first time since I'd 'snatched' him out of his world. At the same time, I still had this nagging guilt for having completely upended his life, even though I didn't really. The paradox of duplication through time, I could see, was going to be problematic, and I was constantly concerned about how all this was eventually going to turn out.

Either way, we had a nice meal, and there was plenty of discussion and genuine laughter as Ben's impressions of all he'd seen put each episode of discovery in a bit of a different light. By the end of the meal, I was feeling a bit better about the whole undertaking. Kathy cleared the plates off and told us there was a nice dessert she wanted us to try. She brought back several small plates of something I had seen the day before. As she put Ben's down, we both watched as he stared at it for a moment, then looked back up at us.

"Apple Tansey," Kathy said. "I assume you are familiar with this, Dr. Franklin?" The wide smile on Ben's face confirmed the answer.

"Kathy," he said, "you and your husband continually surprise me. It has actually been a while – in my time – since I have had any. Thank you for this nice surprise!"

"You are certainly welcome," beamed Kathy.

"This is good!" I said after taking a bite. That sentiment was echoed around the table as we finished off the dessert.

"You all are spoiling me. With all the new foods you have introduced, I am beginning to like this twenty-first century! You already had me drinking cold tea, which is something that in my day might get you hanged in an alley."

Now it was our turn to laugh. We all devoured the dessert, and when we finished, we adjourned to the living room where Kathy served coffee. I had asked the others to keep the night short since I had some other things to cover with Ben, so after about a half hour, they began to leave.

"Tell you what," said Miriam. "Since we're going near the office, how about I take the new security guy a plate. I'm sure he'd appreciate it – after all, it is such a nice meal"

"That's a great ideal. Thanks!" I said. "Be sure to put some of that dessert in his box as well"

Goodbyes said and the place empty of everyone but Ben, Kathy and me, I said, "Well, Ben. If you like, it's a nice night out, and we can sit on the patio and see what's in the sky tonight, if you like."

"Yes, I like the outdoors on a pleasant night."

"I'll bring your coffee out shortly, then," said Kathy.

"Thank you, kind lady!" said Ben, as he rose and bowed slightly at Kathy. "This was a most enjoyable meal, and the company is unsurpassed by anything I've experienced in the last 200 years!"

Now we all laughed. We headed out to the patio, and on the way I grabbed my Android tablet from the table beside my recliner. As we sat down, I pulled up an app on the tablet called 'Plane Finder'. As it started, it found our position via GPS and began displaying all the aircraft in the air above us. I placed it face down on the patio table as Ben sat down and was looking at the sky.

There were several planes visible, and I watched Ben as he began tracking one of the flashing lights as it moved across the sky.

"That's an airplane in flight," I said. "The lights are called 'navigation' lights, and they're flashing to help other aircraft in flight avoid crashing into them."

Ben looked at me, "Is crashing a frequent occurrence?"

"Well, more frequently than we'd like. But, I suppose getting thrown by a horse in your day was the same way. It's just a chance you take to keep from having to walk everywhere. But, as it turns out, flying in a plane is actually one of the safest ways to travel. As a matter of fact, you and I just did the most dangerous thing people do these days: Travel in an automobile."

"Yes," said Ben. "I can see how that could be a problem. I was amazed at the speed automobiles were traveling, particularly as they passed each other going opposite directions, and especially how close to each other you are when doing so. How often are people injured when these collide with each other?"

"Too often," I said. "We've had to enact laws that set standards for vehicle safety. For instance, if you operate a vehicle on the public highways, you must have certain lights of a certain brightness on your vehicle; you must signal a turn with a flashing light; and all the passengers in your vehicle must be protected by seat belts. In addition, built into the front panel of the inside of each vehicle is a pop-out compartment that deploys an air-filled balloon-like bag the instant a crash is detected to further protect the occupants. But, even with all that safety, many people are injured and killed across the nation each day."

Ben pondered that for a moment. "I suppose that some safety is sacrificed for much of what we do in life," he said. He returned to looking at the moving lights in the sky. I picked up my tablet and looked at the screen for a moment.

"Ben, you've seen my hand-held tablet at work. This is my personal tablet here at home. I have an application running on it that shows me every airplane in the sky right now over the Philadelphia area."

I handed Ben the tablet and pointed to one of the plane icons on the screen. "This is an airplane owned and operated by American Airlines". I pointed to that spot in the sky, and said, "There it is. You can see the navigation lights." I fingered the icon and the flight number and other information was displayed. "This is a flight going from Atlanta Georgia to New York City's La Guardia Airport."

Ben looked at the information on the screen, then back up at the aircraft. "How many people are traveling in that airplane?"

"That's an aircraft manufactured by the Boeing company, their model 767. It's a mid to large size aircraft, so there could be as many as 200 people on board. There's no way to know unless you look at the passenger list, which, of course, varies from flight to flight."

Ben nodded, and I could see that was just another of the new wrinkles his brain was going to have to absorb. We pointed out and talked about the flights in the sky for several minutes. As we were doing so, Ben noticed something standing at the end of my patio.

"Why, Tom, is that a telescope?" he asked.

"Yes, it is. I don't know what telescopes you've seen before, but I would wager this one is much more capable than anything you've ever encountered. Do you want to see it?"

"Of course, of course!" Ben exclaimed as he rose from his seat. We both went over to the telescope, and I took the remote and turned it on. The motors began to whir as the telescope moved back and forth trying to orient itself.

Ben watched in amazement as it moved back and forth on its own. "It has a small built in computer that's looking for certain stars in the sky – Polaris, for example – to align itself. When it's finished, I can instruct it to find any star in the sky and it will automatically move to that star. I can also manually move it if I want."

Ben looked at me as if I was a nut-case, then back at the telescope. Finally, it stopped and the remote prompted for instructions.

"OK," I said, "Let's look at Jupiter."

I selected Jupiter from the list of objects, and the telescope whirred to that point in the sky and stopped. I peered into the eyepiece and sure enough, there was Jupiter.

"Take a look!" I said.

Ben walked over to the telescope and looked in the eyepiece. "My my!" he said. "That is certainly clear!" He removed his eye from the eyepiece and looked up into the sky in the direction it was pointed, then back to the eyepiece, then up again, then back to the eyepiece. It would have been humorous, but I had done the same thing the first time I used it.

"This is stupendous!" he said. "Instruct it to find another."

"How about the rings of Saturn?"

"Yes, yes!" said Ben.

I selected Saturn, and the telescope found it almost immediately and Ben went back to the eyepiece. While he was doing that, I punched up another app on my tablet. When it came up, I clicked one of the options on the app and a picture appeared full screen in the tablet.

"Ben," I said, and he looked my way. I held up the tablet. "I have a small video camera attachment on the eyepiece that sends the picture of what you're looking at to my tablet. It is much easier to look at than the eyepiece," and I held up the tablet. There was a picture of Saturn and its rings, exactly as Ben had been viewing.

About that time Kathy came out with the coffee, so Ben and I left the telescope, and we sat back down at the table and Ben took a sip of his coffee as I selected several other stars and planets that we then viewed on the tablet, from Polaris, to Mercury and Mars, and even a couple of distant objects in the solar system. Finally, I thought it was time to drop the last bombshell on Ben.

I sent an instruction to the telescope, and it moved over to the largest object in the sky.

"Ben, this is, of course the moon. But, I have selected a particular spot on the moon for tonight. As we've mapped the moon over the hundreds of years, we've assigned names to certain parts, much as we do on earth, to keep up with all the various places there."

I paused for a moment as he oriented himself to what we were looking at.

"This," I said, "is an area on the moon named in 1651, 'The Sea of Tranquility'."

Ben nodded, and said, "Yes, I am familiar with that name, as well as others on the moon."

"Well, this one is very special," I said. "In 1969, perhaps man's greatest achievement occurred. Three men, named Neil Armstrong, Edwin Aldrin, and Michael Collins, took off from the state of Florida in a craft named Apollo Eleven.

I pulled up a video of the liftoff of the giant Saturn V from the Cape.

"This is a rocket, which I know you're familiar with. Only, this rocket is over 350 feet tall. On top," and I pointed to the area where the capsule was located, "are the three men. For this function, they are referred to as 'Astronauts', because this craft propels them above the earth's atmosphere into orbit around the earth. Hours later, another blast sent them into space beyond the earth, and four days later, Neil Armstrong became the first man to set foot on the moon, followed a few minutes later by Aldrin, with Collins waiting in the primary craft in orbit above the moon. Armstrong and Aldrin were on the moon for twenty-one hours, after which they left, rejoined Collins, and returned to earth four days later, landing in the Atlantic Ocean where they were picked up by an American Navy ship and returned to the United States. We now call this area of the moon "Tranquility Base".

Ben sat stunned.

"Do you remember yesterday when I told you we would come to the phrase 'One Small Step' you would have reached the realm of the unbelievable?"

Ben nodded slowly.

As I was talking, I went back to the home screen and clicked an icon where a video came up ready to play. I turned the tablet so Ben could see it, and pressed the play icon, and there was a picture of Eagle, with Armstrong standing at the base of the leg of the Lunar Excursion Module, or LEM.

"Houston, I'm going to step off the LEM now." He did the small jump from the base of the LEM onto the surface.

"That's one small step for man, one giant leap for mankind."

Chapter 33

Saturday - First Week

It took a while to go from Wilbur and Orville to 'One Small Step', and there was quite a rehash of some history we'd already gone over. Goddard, Von Braun, Gagarin, had to include Yeager – he was just too colorful – but the hot war, followed by the Cold War, then Sputnik, Vostok, Mercury, Gemini, Apollo, the Shuttle, there was lots of stuff. Ben was particularly impressed by the fact that, right now, men were floating in a tin can 250 miles above us that passes by somewhere in this part of the world every ninety minutes. In spite of all the world's tensions, we still have people from multiple countries cooperating to keep this very complex project working, virtually without conflict. Even as I was explaining all that to him, I was impressed we'd been able to pull it off.

In the middle of all this I dropped in satellites and when I got to Telstar, all the manned stuff fell away for a while as we discussed how the increasing capabilities of satellites brought us all the way up to present day. I pulled up Google Earth on the tablet and, as he watched, started off way out in space, then click by click, brought the picture closer and closer until finally we were looking at a picture of my house – the place where we were sitting right now – from space. My wife's SUV was even in the driveway.

"How do these pictures become so clear?" Ben asked. "Do these 'satellites' dip down this far to take these photographs?"

"No," I said. "These photos are taken from a satellite that is never any nearer than 300 miles in space. What you have to understand is that the capabilities of image producing equipment, especially the optical lenses, has grown as much as our ability to place them in the sky in the first place. Our government has some cameras that can read the license tag numbers on the back of a vehicle, in motion, from that distance – maybe even better than that!"

Taken aback was starting to be Ben's default mode by now. He looked at the picture on my tablet, then the telescope at the edge of the patio, then the moon, then a quick glance at the rest of the sky, and finally back to me.

"I know this is, once again, a lot to take in," I said. "Each of the things we've talked about the last three days were amazing changes in and of themselves. But, putting them all together - seeing how one piece affects another, seeing the totality of where we are today compared to 200 years ago – I must say, Ben," and I leaned forward, "I shudder to think, even with the accumulated knowledge I've had in my lifetime, how I would handle such shocking changes were I to go forward in time. Your ability to take each piece, assimilate it to the point you have, and even become almost instantly conversant in the words we use to describe them, is just proof that the man we all thought you to be – even that was an underestimation of your intellect."

Ben just stared at me for a moment, then said, "Sir, the intellect, as you say, of those individuals that created these inventions, far surpasses my ability to comprehend. And you tell me that even youth in this country use all of these without a second thought. This, sir, is what amazes me."

I smiled, and said. "Well, then," I said, "Would you like to have a little fun?"

"Fun?" asked Ben, with a quizzical look on his face.

"Sure," I said. Give me a moment," and I rose, went into the house, grabbed something in the cabinet under the TV, and brought it back out and plugged it into my tablet.

"This is something called a 'joy stick'. I'm not even sure where the term came from, other than it resembles something airplane pilots use to control their aircraft, but it is used in several computer games, one of which I have on my tablet."

I went back to the home screen and clicked an icon. In a few seconds the screen filled with a black maze with blue dots, and some lettering across the screen.

"This is a game my wife and I played on our first date. I took her to a place not far from our hometown that served pizza and beer, and we played this game while we ate. It's called 'Pacman'. It was hugely popular back then, and people like me still like to play it today."

For the next few minutes I believe I hooked Dr. Ben Franklin on keeping Pacman from getting eaten by ghosts while I coached him and told him about the bonus fruits scattered on the maze and what they did. I watched in delight, and we both laughed, as Ben was destroyed over and over again as the ghosts eventually closed in and just overwhelmed his ability to outmaneuver them all.

After he'd played a few games, I said, "So, what do you think?"

"I believe this contraption is most certainly descended from the dark crafts!"

I laughed, as he handed me back the tablet.

"Tell you what, Ben. I want to show you how useful all these satellites we talked about are. First, all of the television programs we are able to view are sent up to several of these satellites where they are resent down to earth from their great height to receiving sets like the one in my home. Come, let me show you."

We went in and I grabbed the remote and turned on the TV. Up came an old black and white movie from TCM, which is one of my favorite channels. I pulled up the program guide, and explained the channels as I moved the cursor up and down.

"The system I have here receives over 800 channels of programs of all different types in multiple languages," and I flipped to a Spanish speaking broadcast. I left it there for a second, then muted the speaker, and went back to the guide. "I can choose any of these programs and be entertained, informed, challenged, even frightened, if you pick some of the stories in the horror genre. All of these come from a series of satellites that are a little over 22,000 miles in space," and I explained geostationary orbiting to him.

"But," I said, "one of the more amazing uses comes from our government, which operates something called the Global Positioning System, or GPS."

I gave Ben a quick explanation of how radio signals and precise timing could be used to triangulate the location of something.

"These are so precise that these GPS receivers can tell you where you are on the planet within six feet of your actual position. Would you like to see a demonstration?"

"Yes," said Ben, "I may as well. Just one more thing for me to disbelieve, even though I am looking directly at it."

I laughed, and said, "Then, let's go for a short ride." We walked through the kitchen and I asked Kathy if she'd like to go with us.

"I thought we'd stop for ice cream," I said.

"Yes, you mentioned this ice cream before," said Ben.

"Yes," I said. "It is exactly what it sounds like. It's flavored cream with milk and sugar that is then frozen. You'll love it!"

"I'm on board!" Kathy said, and I motioned her on, so we went out to the Tahoe and got everyone situated, with Kathy sitting behind me and Ben in the shotgun seat. Just before I cranked up to leave, I peeled off the cardboard cover that I had placed over the LCD display in the center of the console.

"Ben," I said, "I'd covered this up until we could finish our talk on travel, because this vehicle, along with most vehicles these days, comes with a GPS device built in, along with a mapping application that it interacts with."

Then I turned the key, cranked up the vehicle, and the console came alive. I clicked the Navigation function, then the 'Address' icon, and it prompted me for an address.

"Since I don't really know the actual address of the local Dairy Queen we're going to for ice cream, I can have it search for those that are nearby," and I pulled up the on-screen keyboard and typed in 'Dairy Queen'. When I clicked the search icon, it displayed a number of them in the Philadelphia area.

"This is the one I normally go to, on Grand Avenue," I said as I pointed to the nearest one. "But, just to give it a test, let's go to the next closest one," and I punched that one on the screen. Up came the route from our house to the DQ I'd selected.

"The little built-in computer has determined this is the best way to get there from here. I can, of course, go any way I want, and if I do, it will constantly re-calculate how to get there. But, I think I'll drive by our Church first and show you where that is, then we'll go to the Dairy Queen for the ice cream."

Ben looked intently at the screen as I started to back out of the driveway. "How does this contraption know how to get there?" he asked.

"The people who designed the software that makes this work have gathered and stored all the highways, roads, dirt roads, and even field roads in the entire world along with the speed limit on each one, and a wealth of other information so when I indicate where I want to go, it sorts through all that information and calculates the best path to get there."

Ben looked at me with a somewhat quizzical look on his face and said, "You talk about this machine like it is human!"

"Yes, I do," I said. "Years ago when I started playing with computers, I found it easier to relate to and explain what was going on if I just assigned it human qualities. Most people will understand how to get from one room to another in a building, so sometimes I'll talk like that's what this computer is doing. In reality, it's just electronic ones and zeros being manipulated by the components in the computer based on what the creator of the machine designed it to do. Sometimes I even refer to it as 'he' or 'her', depending on how obstinate it's being."

Kathy slapped the back of my chair and said, "Hey – be careful up there!"

We all laughed. Ben watched the screen as we turned out onto the street and headed towards the Church. As we did, the route changed, but I had the onboard voice instructions muted. No sense in overloading Ben just yet any more than I already had.

In a few minutes we were at the Church, so I pulled in the parking lot and stopped. "This is the Church we attend," I said. "If you still feel like it in the morning, we'll go in that side door," and I pointed to a white single door off to the side of the building, "and find our seat for the service. We can come out the same way and avoid most of the crowd and the inevitable questions. I think you'll like our Pastor. He's a really nice man, and he's a history buff, so we'll have to be a bit careful around him!"

Ben nodded and said, "I assume my presence here would be as much a shock to your contemporaries as it was, and still is, I must say, to me three days ago."

"That is exactly the reason we need to tread carefully," I said. "Until we decide how and when, or maybe even if, to present who you really are to the public, any premature revelation would result in attention neither of us would want to have to deal with. But, I think we can make a couple of low-key appearances without arousing any suspicion."

"I am up to a bit of subterfuge!" said Ben. "I am, after all, a revolutionary!"

"Here here!" said Kathy from the back seat, and we all had a nice chuckle.

"OK, one more little surprise about this GPS before we go get that ice cream. One of the things we've taught – see, there I go humanizing them again – these computers is how to simulate human speech. It comes in handy when you use them for just such a purpose as this one. I'm going to turn on the voice function, and this little device will literally tell us how to get to the DQ!"

Ben watched as I unmuted the onboard voice and put the vehicle in gear to head out of the parking lot.

"Turn left on First Avenue and drive for one mile," the voice said.

Ben slapped his legs and said, "Well, Milk the pigeon!".

"Well", I laughed as I turned left onto First Avenue, "Am I to assume you find that interesting?"

"I find that impossible!", said Ben.

"Well, Dr. Franklin," said Kathy from behind me, "I think you have just witnessed the impossible!"

"Yet again!" I said.

"Indeed!" said Ben. "I don't know how many more impossible things I can possibly believe!"

"In One Thousand feet, Turn right onto Apple Road".

Ben laughed again, and said, "I do believe, sir, it is now commanding you!"

"And I will follow!" I said as I turned on my blinker.'

"Turn right," and I did.

"Drive one and a half miles to Wolf Road."

As we drove, Ben stared intently at the moving icon on the GPS map. We made three more turns, then the voice said, *"In one quarter of a mile turn left onto sixteenth street, and your destination will be on the right."*

"This GPS magic even knows which side of the road this 'iced cream' is dispensed??" asked Ben incredulously.

"Sure does," I said, "though it doesn't know what's there. It just knows that's where I told it I wanted to go."

As we pulled into the drive-through lane, I asked Ben, "Are you up for a little more adventure in desserts?"

"More desserts?" he asked.

"Of course!" I said.

I pulled up to the window.

"Three small vanilla cones," I said to the young girl at the window

"That'll be six dollars, ten cents," and I handed her my credit card.

She ran it and handed me back the receipt and went to get the cones. Ben looked at the receipt and the card, and I just said, "Let's talk about this later on. It's a simple way to pay if you don't have any paper money or coins."

I guess by now Ben was becoming accustomed to me pulling small rabbits out of my hat, so he just nodded. In a few moments, the girl came back to the window with the cones . I took the one and handed it behind my head to Kathy. As I did the girl came back to the window. I took the last two and handed one to

Ben. Then I took the napkins she had in her hand, handed one each back to Kathy and then to Ben.

"Thanks!' I said.

"You're welcome! Come again!" she said, and I drove over to an empty spot in the parking lot.

I handed Ben the one of the napkins she'd handed me with mine, and said, "Hold it with this in case it starts melting down the bottom of the cone."

Then I showed Ben Franklin how to eat ice cream. I'm guessing that was yet another historical first.

As he took his first taste, his eyes brightened and he said, "This is delicious!"

"Well, then, Dr. Franklin," said Kathy, "you are officially a vanilla ice cream fan!"

"Why yes, I do believe you are correct, madam!" he said.

I pulled from the parking lot as we finished our ice cream. I noticed Ben had quickly consumed the top part of his cone.

"Ben, the cone is edible as well. It's a sugared wafer. Just don't eat too far past the ice cream or it'll leak out on you"

Ben took a bite and said, "Well, this is much better than chasing the remainder with my tongue!"

"Yes. Yes it is!" I said and heard Kathy laugh from the back seat.

As we drove back to the house, I could tell Ben was enjoying himself as he watched the houses and shops pass by and enjoyed the last of his ice cream. In a few minutes I pulled back into the driveway.

"So, Ben. What do you think of GPS?"

"You say this can give me directions anywhere in the world?"

"Yes," I said, "though, it wouldn't make much sense trying to drive across the Atlantic, but I do believe it has the whole world mapped. I have a similar mapping system on my computer in the house if you want to see."

"Maybe after we have attended your Church services on the morrow," said Ben. "You have once again drained my abilities, and I confess I am ready to retire for the evening."

"I apologize, Dr. Franklin," I said. "I know the last three days have been intense, but I can assure you that your initial 'orientation' is almost over. Let's get your wardrobe laid out for in the morning, and we'll call it a night."

"Thank you, Tom," said Ben. "And thank you, madam!" he said as he looked back to Kathy. "Tonight's meal and festivities were well worth a 200 year wait."

Kathy smiled and said, "The pleasure is mine, Dr. Franklin!"

We exited the Tahoe and headed back inside. Once there, we all went back to Ben's bedroom and looked through the clothing the tailor had provided, and decided on something appropriate for the service.

"I'll just press the wrinkles out of these. I'll be back in a few minutes," said Kathy as she exited the room.

Ben looked at me and said, "What am I to expect from the services tomorrow?"

I went through the normal order of service. Since our Church is more traditional, we don't have a band or orchestra, so I didn't have to explain that, but I did have to warn him that there might be some recorded music, but since he'd already heard that, it wouldn't be much of a shock. I told him the service would be finished by lunch, and then we'd get something to eat and maybe take a little drive and do some sightseeing.

"So, Ben. How do you feel about everything right now? Do you think you can manage life in this new world that you were so instrumental in creating?"

Ben pondered that for a moment, and said, "To be quite frank with you, sir, I am not so sure. There is so much to learn about how life works in this day, and so much to become accustomed to. I may need quite a bit of help!"

"Well," I said, "I got you into this, and I will help you every step of the way, as will Kathy, and the rest of my group at the office. I want you to know that, even though we've shown you a number of things, I am anxious to get to the point where you can take over and start teaching us some things."

"I fear what I have to teach will not compare to the things you've shown me since I arrived," said Ben. "But, whatever knowledge I may have I will gladly share, though I must confess I believe the scales are tipped very much in your favor!"

"It may seem that way now, Dr. Franklin, but I believe there is much you can help us with."

"We shall see," he said.

In a few minutes Kathy came back in with the pressed clothes, and we bade Benjamin Franklin a pleasant night's sleep, and Kathy and I headed back into the living room.

With most of the major items I needed Ben to be aware of out of the way, realizing there were millions of details, both large and small, that he would have to navigate, I prayed that what I had said was true. That there was much twenty-first Century America could learn from Dr. Benjamin Franklin.

PART 2

Citizen Ben

Chapter 34

Sunday Week 2

We pulled up in the parking lot at the Church at ten forty-five, plenty of time for us to get in and find a seat before the worship service started, but not too much time for a lot of questions about Ben. The exit strategy was that we had somewhere to be so we could get past inquiring minds, and we'd go out the same side door where we'd parked the Navigator and make as much an unobtrusive exit as we could. The point of the exercise was to give Ben his first foray into the population with as little interaction as we could manage. It would not only give Ben the experience and allow him his first real bit of freedom, but it might help us identify issues we might have to address.

We went in the side door as we had planned and started to make our way to the main sanctuary when Joan Danbury, one of the members of my Sunday School class spotted us.

"Missed you in class today, Tom. Who's your friend?"

"Joan, I'd like you to meet Ben Folger a visiting colleague from England. Ben, this is Joan Danbury. She's in the class I teach each Sunday. Joan runs an accounting firm here in town."

"It's a pleasure to make you acquaintance," said Ben, as he offered his hand for her to shake. We'd addressed this at home before we left, and he'd practiced this with both Kathy and me. He did it perfectly.

"Nice to meet you, Mr. Folger. Are you enjoying your stay here in the States?"

"Immensely," said Ben. "But, I've been here before, just not in this particular area," and he shot me a look that almost made me laugh.

"Well, welcome to our community, and to Northside Baptist. I hope you enjoy our service. Will you be in town long?"

Ben shot me another look, and said, "Well, it depends on how well our little project progresses, but I hope to be here for a while."

"Then I hope to see you again. Tom, Kathy, nice to see you as well. Enjoy the service, Mr. Folger."

"Thank you, Mrs. Danbury. I am looking forward to it."

"Yes," I said, "we better get in there if we're going to get to our regular seats. Talk to you later, Joan," and we headed to the sanctuary. The Pastor, Rick Chandler saw us as we came in and came over.

"Morning, Tom, Kathy. I was afraid we'd miss you this morning, so glad you're here. Who's your friend?"

We went through the same basic conversation with Brother Rick as we had with Joan, and again, Ben handled it perfectly. That done, and a couple of more greetings from those sitting around us, and it was time for the service to start. I had already given Ben the order of service, and warned him about the music and the graphics that would be on the screen, so even though he was fascinated with it all as we found out after the service, he kept a pretty good poker face during the first half of the service.

The Pastor's sermon today was on the Lordship of Christ, and was based in the first five verses of the Gospel of John. His main point was that Jesus was God in the flesh – not just a new prophet or a great teacher, and that as such, He was to be worshiped as God Himself. I had purposely not had a conversation with Ben about his personal beliefs, because I wanted that to be his idea. I had read that most modern historians regarded him as a Deist - someone who believed in a God out there somewhere, but not someone who was personally involved in each of our lives. They also rejected the idea that Jesus was a deity, and considered Him to be at most one of the greatest philosophers who had ever lived. Brother Chandler's sermon was powerful, and his thread of Biblical logic very well thought out.

Ben was very attentive during the sermon, and seemed to be taking in the message, something I had prayed that he would. My hope was that this sermon, the subject of which I was unaware until the Pastor announced his text, would spur a conversation I was very much looking forward to. For me, personally, Ben's take on Christianity and Christ Himself was important, though I had not formerly thought of it as a reason to bring someone in from the past. Not wanting to second-guess the Almighty, I would try as much as possible to leave these types of conversations to Ben, since he'd lived a full life in the past and had all the opportunities he needed to make his eternal decisions. Lots of philosophical questions here, and I had a big enough task as it was.

The sermon ended, and the invitation was given. A couple and their young daughter responded with the desire to join our Church, so Brother Chandler went through the process of presentation and the vote of the congregation, which was unanimous, and just like that our Church family grew by another three souls. All in all, it was a great service, and I was glad we'd been able to bring Ben.

We exited the building as planned with only a couple of 'how are you today' comments and headed out of the parking lot. The plan was to go to a local restaurant and get lunch and then a driving tour of Philadelphia. I was anxious to see Ben's take on the town that he had known so well, and in particular of the sites he was so familiar with but were no longer in place. I really wanted him to see Independence Hall, where he had been standing literally some 230 years ago in our time, but only four days ago in his. It was going to be a surreal experience for Ben.

We ended up at a Cracker Barrel several miles away in the hopes that we wouldn't run into anyone we knew. I explained to Ben the concept of a restaurant chain and how you could order the same food anywhere in the country and it would, for the most part, taste exactly the same.

"How many of these establishments exist?" he asked.

"I'm not really sure, but I know it's in the hundreds located all across the country. Hold on a minute, and I can tell you." I took my cell phone, went to Wikipedia, and looked it up.

"As of right now, over 640 locations."

"That many? And you were able to find that information that quickly?" asked Ben.

"Yes, and that's a small number compared to other restaurant chains. McDonald's, for example, has thousands. And yes, as you remember, these so-called 'search engine' programs are very powerful!"

"How many such companies as this exist?"

"Hundreds. As it turns out, Ben, the liberty you and the rest of the Founders gave us had the effect of unleashing an economic force that literally changed the world, from small businesses to large corporations. Given the freedom to act, people will sometimes amaze you at what they can achieve."

Ben thought about that for a moment. "Who owns these companies?"

"Most are corporations, owned by those who invested in them and run by management chosen by the investors. Some are privately owned and run by their owners."

Ben looked around at all the paraphernalia hung on the walls and placed around the room. "Some of these tools I recognize," he said, "though even the ones I don't recognize look old. Why do they place them on the walls?"

"They're here for decoration – kind of a reminder of simpler times, I guess. They actually make these things in a factory to look old. Most of these are actually just a few months or years old at the most. I know that sounds strange, but it's common in this day and time to look to things of the past as reminders."

"I suppose I understand that somewhat," said Ben giving me a knowing look.

The menus were given to us when we sat down, but shortly the waitress came over and took our drink orders. We looked over the menus, selected our meals, and when the waitress came back gave her our selections, then sat back and waited on our meal. The restaurant was full, so it would be a bit longer than normal before our meals came.

"Your church service was interesting," said Ben. "I especially liked your Pastor's sermon and his use of the Scripture to make his points. He makes the assertion that Jesus was actually God, but in human form. I have heard others refer to him that way, but my impression has been somewhat different. Still, your Pastor's sermon was very well thought out and documented. I see your sect relies much on the Bible, which I must say is an excellent practice."

"It's at the core of our belief," I said. "Once you make that leap and understand who Christ really was, it changes everything."

"I concede that," said Ben. "I am not sure I am ready to make that leap. God seems too immense for such a thing to be possible"

"There are many who have exactly that issue," I said. "But when you understand the fallen nature of man compared to the perfectness of God, if we were to be able to survive beyond this life, there had to be a reconciliation. The only way to bridge that gap was for someone sufficiently worthy to make the sacrifice necessary to atone for man's fall. As it turns out, there are no humans, or even any group of humans, who could sufficiently bridge that gap from completely fallen to absolutely perfect. So, God did it Himself. Through the crucifixion of Christ on the Cross, the payment was made. All we have to do is accept that payment. Unfortunately, most won't."

"Are you saying that only your sect will accept this 'payment'?"

"Absolutely not!" I said. "In fact, you don't have to belong to any sect. A slave in Africa, or a President in America – God is no respecter of persons. All who believe will be saved. In John's Gospel, Christ put it this way: "For God so loved the world that He gave His only begotten Son, that *whosoever* believes in Him shall not perish, but receive eternal life". That's the Gospel in a nutshell. Our 'sect' - we actually use the term 'denomination' - exists to celebrate this fact, and to learn more of who God wants us to be."

"I see," said Ben. "I shall ponder these points. It is a very interesting concept."

The waitress arrived with our food, and we enjoyed the meal as Ben watched those around him, especially the children who were there with their parents.

"I like the way society looks in this place," he said. "Everyone seems to be so happy and peaceful".

"Well, I agree, but there is still plenty of evil in the world, and times like this come at a price. We are still trying to figure out how to make this all work. Sometimes we get it right, sometimes we don't."

"Yes," said Ben, "I have many questions about how 'all this', as you put it, functions."

"That," I said, "is what I believe is a primary purpose you are here. But, we need to hold onto that discussion until we have time to go into it fully. It is complicated."

"I am becoming accustomed to complicated!" said Ben with a chuckle.

Chapter 35

Sunday Week 2

The meal completed and the check paid, we headed back out to the Navigator and drove towards historical Philadelphia. Being a Sunday, the traffic was not too bad, though since this was a historical town, there was always traffic here. Still, it was light enough that we could 'rubber neck' all we needed to with Ben in the front seat seeing his home town 230 years later.

As we approached the historical part of town, I told Ben, "I know in your lifetime you've seen towns and communities change as people moved in and commercial interests built and expanded, but in this case you need to remember that it's been over 230 years since what you saw only a few days ago existed. As you have already noted, much has changed in the area you lived most of your life. But, I'll try to point out the location of some of the sites that are now important historically to us in the present day that were much different in your time. I'm very much interested in your narration of these differences and your description of how they looked in your time as compared to now."

"Yes," said Ben, "I am highly intrigued at the changes you have described myself, though I must confess I'm a bit disoriented already, so perhaps your orientation will help me as well."

"I concede that," I said, "so, let's do this together." I pulled my smart phone out of my pocket, thumbed on the screen, and swiped to a screen with a recording app. "If you don't mind, I'd like to record our conversation as we do this so I can remember it later. One of the things I'm required to do is keep a journal of how this project is progressing, and this will help me maintain that accuracy after we return."

"Then I have two questions," said Ben.

"Sure, what are they?"

"First, that little device will keep a record of all we say?"

I chuckled a bit, "Oh, yes. Even if we talk for hours."

"I am still amazed at all these inventions," said Ben. "Second, will you allow me to read your journal."

"Of course!" I said. "As a matter of fact, at some point I'm going to ask you to add content and help me edit the final draft. I understand you have some expertise in that area."

"Indeed!" said Ben with a laugh. "I thank you, sir!"

"Oh, once again, the pleasure is mine," I said. I pulled up the app and put it in 'record' mode, then announced the date, time, and purpose of this particular recording. As I was doing that, I reminded myself I was going to have to make some hard decisions about some of the footage we'd videoed of Ben in our offices, particularly in his apartment, but that was for later....

As we exited the expressway and came down the off-ramp to the street, just before I turned I pointed to a park across the street and said, "Ben, that park over there has an interesting name. It's called 'Franklin Park'."

Even though Ben was partially prepared for some historical points of interest, I suppose it's a shock when you find that it's been named after you. I got another of those trademark surprised faces I'd witnessed in the last several days.

"Down the street is another park called Washington Park, so you're in good company, Ben," I said with a chuckle.

We passed the National Constitution Center, the Independence Visitor's Center, and the Liberty Bell, all the while Ben was doing the rubber-neck thing, looking for points he might recognize. I didn't hold out much hope for him, at least for a few hundred more feet. Then, we approached the intersection of Sixth and Chestnut, and I pointed ahead and to the left a bit and said, "Ben. Here's a place you might recognize."

Ben's eyes shot open wide, along with his mouth, and he looked at me, then back to the building just ahead, and said, "I was just here a few days ago, though the building looks to have been changed over the years! I was right there speaking to a woman who approached me as I was leaving and asked me a question. I was just before answering when I found myself sitting across from you, completely bewildered and, I must say, very much frightened."

Now, it was my turn to be surprised. "Wait a minute," I said. "You say you had just left the building and you were answering a question asked by a woman? Let me ask you this: Was she asking what kind of government you had given them?"

Ben's eyebrows shot up and he said, "Why yes, that was exactly the nature of her inquiry."

I swallowed, and said, "And you were about to answer 'A Republic, if you can keep it'?"

A shocked look came upon Ben's face. "Why yes. I was forming those exact words when I was no longer in front of her! How could you possibly know this information?"

"Because that encounter is famous. It is because of this encounter that we knew where exactly you would be standing that day!"

Ben just stared at me for a second, then back at the front of Independence Hall, the very building he had just exited days ago after signing the Constitution!

"Sir," said Ben, "I may be forced to reconsider your Pastor's sermon this morning. Perhaps the Almighty is more involved than I had hitherto considered!"

I was about to say something when the car behind me honked his horn. Kathy, in the back seat and silent until now, quietly said, "Maybe you should drive, dear. You're stopped in the middle of the street."

Chapter 36

Sunday Week 2

As we exited the Independence Hall area, it took a few minutes for us to regain our composure. I pulled over into a parking lot for a minute while we did.

"I had never really thought of the time when you were transferred," I said. "That encounter just as you exited Independence Hall, and that quote of yours is used many times these days to explain the difference between a democracy and a republic. That's why I am so familiar with it."

Ben nodded and said, "For a moment I wondered if you had developed some method of accessing my thoughts! You spoke to me the very thoughts I was having just before meeting you Thursday last. I would never have thought that simple encounter would be something of mine that lasted to this day."

"Well, it certainly has," I said as I looked around to see which way to go. "Tell you what. Let's go back towards the expressway and let me show you some of the sights that commemorate what you and the other Founders did that day."

Ben agreed, and began telling me about his daily routine as he would leave the deliberations, and that where we were sitting right now was a place that was familiar to him then, with the exception of the obvious changes over the two centuries.

As we drove I would show him something he was familiar with, and Ben would expound on his first hand knowledge of each site, along with a number of remembrances of not only those events, but other events that surrounded them. I was certainly glad I had the recording app going, because some of this information was priceless.

We spent the better part of three hours tooling around the historical district with Ben's sometimes animated narration of each place, plus a wealth of trivia surrounding each, and I made a note to look up some of the individuals and events he'd mentioned and see how much of that had survived history.

As we finally exited street level and entered the expressway, I asked Ben, "When you get fully settled, would you be willing to sit down with a stenographer and possibly narrate something like an autobiography? I still don't know if it's something we could release to the general public without compromising the security of our operation here, but I can tell you there are many in the halls of government and research who would be interested in some context concerning the time in which you lived."

"I assume a 'stenographer' is someone who would do the writing for me?"

"Yes, sorry, it would be someone who could transcribe what you're saying at your regular pace without your having to slow down, so you can literally 'speak' your story into print." I didn't want to have to explain speech recognition software right now.

"Why, of course sir! It is often said that one's favorite subject is one's self."

I laughed and said, "We use that same expression today! I'll set that up sometime when you've had a little more time to get settled."

"Excellent!" said Ben.

Kathy, who had been pretty much silent in the back seat spoke up and asked Ben about his impression of the changes in the role of women since his time.

"I must say, the first time I saw your Miriam in your office, I was taken aback that a woman would wear pantaloons, but I now understand that is normal in this society. People seem to be much less formal in this time than in mine. I am not sure I am entirely comfortable with this, especially when I see so many of the fairer sex in positions outside the home. May I ask you how this has affected life in the home?"

"There have been many challenges, I'll admit," she said. "The change primarily took place during the Second World War when so many of the men were overseas fighting, and the shortages of workers here, along with the demand for war materials, forced women into the workforce. The next generation began to rebel against older 'stereotypes' and there was a very powerful women's movement that took place, and still is to a large degree. To be honest, we're still navigating those changes. It has its positive elements, but it has its drawbacks, particularly in the family."

"I would assume so," said Ben. "However, I will not pretend to criticize a society which I have only known a few days. We had issues of contention in our own time as well. I will say, though, that some relationships outside the home have deepened, and I admire the interaction between yourself and your Tom here."

Kathy beamed. "Well, thank you, Dr. Franklin. We work hard at growing our relationship, and I'd like to believe it shows in our children."

"Speaking of which, I should like to meet your children. Would that be possible?"

"Well," said Kathy, "I'd love to introduce them to you, but they are actually unaware of the work my husband is involved in, though they are, of course, aware that I was an early assistant in this work, so we'll have to figure out some way of crossing that bridge. What do you think, Tom? Can we make that happen?"

"I don't see why not," I said. "As a matter of fact, it might help us in finding ways to introduce Ben to others who are as yet unaware of what we're doing. Let me think about that and we'll see if we can set up something in the next few days."

As we were talking, what Kathy had just said caused me to take a different tact back towards our home. "Ben, I want you to take notice of the signs along the way. We're going back a different way home, and you might see something of interest in a minute."

A few minutes later, an exit sign arching over the highway came into view. It said 'Ben Franklin Br', with an arrow to the right. I saw it evidently before he did, but when he did he sat up in the seat and looked over at me.

"How many places have my name attached to them in this town?" he asked. "And what does 'Br' refer to."

"Well, you are quite famous here still, Ben. And I'll show you the 'Br' in a few moments."

We exited one expressway via the off-ramp onto another that headed us in a more westerly direction. As we rounded the curve and entered the next expressway there was a small rise in the highway and another curve to the left. As we began that slow turn to the left you could see in the distance the superstructure of something that straddled the highway and an archway just ahead. In a few thousand feet it became apparent what we were looking at.

As we passed under the archway I pointed ahead and said, "Welcome to the Benjamin Franklin Bridge. It spans the Delaware River on the way to Camden, New Jersey. It's been here over one hundred years, and is an iconic structure here in Philadelphia. It was named for you in, I believe, 1955."

As we entered the bridge itself and crossed the Delaware, Ben said, "Well, at least it appears to be well constructed, not unlike myself."

We all laughed at his joke, and after crossing, I headed south to catch another crossing at the Walt Whitman bridge a few miles away and headed back east towards home. On the ride home Ben was quite animated on all he'd seen that day, and expressed his desire to get a better view up close. In particular he wanted to enter Independence Hall and see how that had changed from his last view inside just a few days ago.

"Yes, I have that on the agenda as soon as we can get some other things in place. Tomorrow, for instance, I have a man from one of our government agencies coming by to begin the documentation you need to live in the present day. We're going to have a birth certificate created, as well as a Social Security account and a photo ID. These three documents will allow you to do almost anything you might want to do as a U.S. Citizen."

"You will need to explain the purpose of these documents," said Ben. "I know much has changed since my time, but are all citizens required to have these items?"

"Yes, I'm afraid so, and it's pretty much an invention of the twentieth century. Until after the Second World War, practically no documents were necessary. Now, these are issued at birth and you'll need them for the rest of your life."

"You know, the Almighty warned the Hebrews about taking their first census." said Ben. "I believe that's another thing He might have had some insight into."

I smiled and said, "Oh, I totally agree with you, Ben. But you know as well as I do that once the government requires something, it's hard to do away with it. By now it's so ingrained into our society that most people don't think too much about it.

"I have a certain perspective on that," he answered, "so maybe at some point I can express my views on such a subject – after, of course, familiarizing myself with the reasons for and effects of such requirements."

"I have no doubt you do have a valid perspective," I said. "And I'll do all I can to get you into the offices of individuals who might need to hear your views. But, before then, there is much for me to do to get you ready. For instance, one of the first things we need to do is find you a permanent dwelling place. How do you feel about doing some house hunting tomorrow?"

Ben perked up. "I'd be delighted!" He turned to Kathy and said, "Can I count on you, madam, to assist me in that endeavor as well."

Kathy beamed and said, "I'd be more than delighted to help you, Dr. Franklin!"

"Please," he reminded her. "just call me Ben!"

Chapter 37

Sunday - Week 2

For the rest of the day we basically discussed the day's events, and Ben, of course, had plenty of questions about some of the sites he'd seen, especially the way we traveled from one location to another. He was amazed that we could cover so much territory in such a short period of time until I reminded him that until ownership of horses and buggies became available to the general population, people pretty much walked everywhere they went.

But, there was much discussion of how much Philadelphia had changed since his day. While Independence Hall was still in place, his own house was now Franklin Court, and there were only fragments left, and a small park dedicated to his memory. We had passed within a block of that location on our excursion, but I had not wanted to get too deep into sightseeing until we'd had more time to prepare. Ben understood this, so we agreed to do a much more thorough tour at a later date.

The day and evening gone, Ben agreed to spend another night with us, and he and Kathy would be going house hunting in the morning. I had tasked Miriam with locating suitable housing, so she would be joining the pair as well. Before it got too late, Kathy and Miriam spoke and had the day planned out.

The next morning, we all arose, had breakfast, then Ben and I headed for the office. Bill and Miriam were already there planning for the day's events when we arrived.

"How'd Church go?" asked Bill when we entered.

"It was a most illuminating service," said Ben. "I enjoyed it immensely, especially the music. My, how much has been improved over the years. The style of the compositions is much different than I am accustomed to, but I still found it very....uplifting!"

I laughed and said, "Well, I think that was the goal."

"Yes, I suppose it was," agreed Ben. "I would very much like to attend another of your services and spend a bit more time, if that would be possible."

"Of course," I said. "New attendees are always welcome, especially those with as much life experience as yourself."

Ben laughed, "I suppose I do have that. However, much of what I know is not applicable to the current environment!"

"You might be surprised," said Bill. "I think you may have more to contribute than you think."

"Well," I said, "let's get started."

We all sat down for the Monday Morning Meeting, where we sketched out the week and what we were expecting to accomplish.

"Obviously," I began, "we'll be starting with the Credentialing Specialist who will be here in about an hour. He'll be getting Ben set up with all the documentation he'll need to move about in society, including proof of citizenship. Ben, I know all this sounds foreign, but events in the intervening years have made this documentation necessary, and once we have you 'legal', as it were, I'll go over each of the documents, what they are, and why they're needed."

"I am very much interested in having that conversation," said Ben.

"I know you are, and I'll get all your questions answered. The first thing the Specialist will do is take your photograph, because sometimes a picture-ID is necessary. Then there'll be fingerprinting, something we haven't discussed yet but will be simple and painless, though a bit messy. Finally, we'll get something we call a 'legend' prepared for you. It essentially is a 'back story', or a feasible story of who are and how you got here for those who won't be privy to the actual details of your existence. And before you ask, yes, it's basically a lie, but it's intended to prevent harm rather than inflict it."

"Oh, I have no issue with contrivances when necessary, so long as those in authority are aware of the truth."

"Oh, they will be," I said, "though that number will be very small, as you might imagine."

"I concede that point," said Ben.

"After that and lunch, Miriam and Kathy will be taking Ben house hunting. Bill, you'll do the driving, if that's OK, and make sure no problems come up. Once Ben has had a chance to decide on a place, we'll go through the acquisition paperwork. The budget for this part of the project is relatively liberal, and Miriam already has the guidelines, so take your time and get it right."

Ben spoke up, "How much influence shall I have over this selection?"

"Oh, Ben, you are the one we have to satisfy here. Bill will assess any security issues and will have veto power in instances where that might be a problem, but other than the price guidelines we have to stay within, the decision will be yours."

Ben smiled. "Wonderful! I shall be frugal, but practical."

"I expected nothing less," I said. "Any questions?"

"Yes," said Bill. "Will Dr. Franklin be driving himself, or is that part of my responsibility?"

"Ben, we haven't really talked about that. Would driving a vehicle yourself be something you'd like to learn?"

Ben considered that for a moment. "I am not sure I can master this 'driving'. Not having seen these vehicles until a few days ago, frankly, it gives me some trepidation. However, I do not want to upset Bill's life with my excursions, so if I must I can attempt it."

"Well," I began, "when this all came up in our planning sessions, we always assumed there would be a driver assigned to you who would be available whenever you needed to travel somewhere. As a matter of fact, the thought was we'd treat you like a visiting dignitary, which is exactly what you are. As such, a government assigned vehicle and driver would be available to you, and the driver would double as your personal security, should that ever be necessary. Essentially, you'd be traveling in luxury!"

Ben smiled. "I like that idea, but would this not be a bit obvious to those outside this building?"

"That's a good point," I said, "but as a member of what we call a think-tank, basically a research facility, your stature would be sufficient to justify that, while at the same time not rising to the level of someone who has to live separate from the rest of society. You'd be in that middle-ground area that should suit both you and those around you. This 'legend' we're working on should cover those issues."

"Splendid," said Ben. "Then I shall accede to this plan, assuming you can make it both believable and livable."

"That we will," I said. "To answer your question, Bill, if you can perform this function for the next few days, we'll get a permanent driver for Ben and that should handle that issue."

Bill smiled. "Works for me!"

"Great. Anything else?"

Nobody had anything, so we adjourned until the credentialist was scheduled to show up. Ben went to his apartment to unpack his belongings and make some notes in his journal. I had some phone calls to make and emails to attend to, as did everyone else, so we went our separate ways.

At nine, right on the dot, the credentialist arrived and we ushered him into the conference room. As we did, I began to take note of all the people who were now in on the secret, and it was growing larger than I had hoped at this time, but all these individuals had been thoroughly vetted, so whatever fears I had would have to wait until later.

Al Sanchez works for the U.S. Marshall's service, and is the go-to guy for documents for those in situations like those in the Witness Protection Program. His visit had been arranged by the higher-ups in NSF as someone as an expert at manipulating government records for those who needed new identities. As with the others, he had to be in on what we were doing, because there's just no hiding who Ben Franklin is at this stage, but that was going to be his job to change.

He was an amiable character, and not at all what you would expect from who, in any other venue, would be not much more than a really talented forger. We had not met in person, and had only spoken on the phone a couple of times setting today's meeting up, but after a few minutes it was obvious this guy knew his stuff.

We did the obligatory introductions and he, like everyone else thus far, was sufficiently awed by the presence of one of our preeminent Founding Fathers. Ben, like with everyone else, put him at ease in short order, so Al got to it.

He took a couple of minutes to tell Ben what he would be creating for him, and a little bit about what each document would be used for, something he may have had to explain to some very significant crime figures in the past! I know Ben had some questions, but I had asked him to save most of his questions for me, since I didn't want to complicate this meeting.

"Dr. Franklin," said Al, "the first thing we need to do is get a good set of pictures. Then we'll get your fingerprints, and I'd like to do a scan of the bottom of your feet."

"My feet?" asked Ben. "Whatever for?"

Al gave me a glance then explained, "When someone is born, many times they get an imprint of the newborn's feet much like we're about to do with your fingers. This is helpful in identifying a single infant in a ward where there might be dozens. If someone was really curious, they could get a copy of your footprints and compare them with your birth documents and find a difference. We are, sir, very thorough. I can use a computer software program to take your current footprint and make it look like a newborn's."

Ben shot me a glance, then shook his head. "Yet another item with which I am sufficiently amazed. Let us proceed then, sir!"

Al assembled and opened up a green-screened backdrop and a couple of lights with diffusers, then had Ben stand for front and side pictures, then for some posed shots, both sitting and standing. We had grabbed a couple of extra shirts, and we had Ben change into each of them and have additional shots made so not all his pictures would show the same shirt. He even took a couple of shots with Ben's back to the camera looking to the side or back at the camera. Al could digitally change the background several times for each shot so that, in the end, he would have multiple combinations. Using a graphical manipulation program he could also make Ben appear to be younger and possibly thinner. When everything was said and done there would be several pictures of Ben, some of which would have different backgrounds – vacation shots in front of outdoor and indoor images that Ben's picture would be superimposed on. Ben would have a virtual scrapbook of pictures he could show someone as proof that he wasn't the Ben Franklin in all the history books!

Then for the fingerprints. Al did the same with fingerprints, getting several copies of each finger so all his fingerprints wouldn't look the same. I had no idea what he was going to do with all these, but it was abundantly clear he was very practiced in creating new citizens out of thin air. Ben had the most fun getting his footprints done. He did several, but Al only really needed one good pair, since practically no one has more than one set of footprints. He just wanted, again, to be thorough.

Then he got to the documents. Al had already done much of that work. From his briefcase he pulled out three copies of Ben's new birth certificate, and a couple of copies of his brand new old social security number. Since Ben was eighty one on the day we had grabbed him, that meant his birthday would have been in the late 1930s. Al explained that he couldn't keep, for our purposes, his current birthday because that would be too coincidental. So, he had chosen a new birthday, August 6, 1948. This would put him in his early seventies.

"I chose that date," said Al, "because I wanted to get as far away from your actual birthday, as well as some of the other Founders, and I wanted to make you a bit younger, since you are applying for Social Security."

"I keep hearing of this Social Security," said Ben. "What exactly does that mean?"

My turn. "Ben, just hold onto that discussion for a bit later. Essentially, though, it's a retirement plan that Americans pay into to take care of them in their old age. When it starts, part of what you'll receive each month will come from this fund. The rest will be a private retirement fund NSF has set up for you. This will allow you to live in comfort without having to worry about money for the rest of your life. In addition, we'll have a financial counselor available to you should you have any questions."

"But, I haven't paid anything into this fund," said Ben.

"Don't worry about that," said Al. "We have a program set up to make allowances for those we're putting in that program. Nobody will be shorted any of their retirement as a result."

"Besides," I said. "based on what you've done for your country in your life, nobody in America would object!"

Ben smiled. "I appreciate your sentiments, sir, but I would not like to be a burden on anyone who has worked all their life expecting their proper due."

"Which is why," said Al, "you are revered in our country. Believe me, this has all been taken care of."

Ben gave Al a solemn nod, and Al finished explaining the basic purpose of each of the documents he was receiving.

"One thing we're providing is a picture identification, since you are not receiving a driver's license. That is normal for many people who live in metropolitan areas who use public transportation and thus never learned to drive. It is not as prevalent in Philadelphia, but it is not unusual."

When all was said and done, Ben ended up with an ID, his birth certificate, a social security card, that interestingly enough, looked decades old. "We aged these to make them look authentic," explained Al.

Finally, Al presented Ben with some credit applications. "I just need you to sign these," said Al. "These will be used to obtain credit and debit cards you can use in lieu of cash. Additionally, I need you to sign these papers. These I will use to establish a bank account for you, into which your monthly retirement funds will be automatically deposited. There'll be two deposits. One at the first of the month, and the other on the fifteenth. That way you'll have a regular funds influx for you to use as needed."

Ben looked at the papers, then said, "I'm still not sure about taking such funds, but I would not even know how to begin to make a living in this still foreign environment."

"Look at it this way," I said. "You will actually be earning this money, and then some, with the advice, perspective, and historical context you will be bringing to the country you helped establish. If anything, you should be paid much more. But, the idea is to basically hide you in plain sight, at least to the general public. I expect you're enough of a thespian that you can make this believable!"

Ben chuckled and nodded. "The role of my lifetime, I suppose. Would you care, Mr. Sanchez, to go over each of these documents with me as I sign them?"

"Of course," said Al, and over the next several minutes Al carefully explained each document, why it was needed, and what the end result would be. I know that this created more questions for me later than it answered for Ben now, but that was nothing I hadn't expected.

Finally, it was all done, and Al rose to leave. As he did, Ben stood and said, "It has been an honor, Dr. Franklin. I have enjoyed meeting you immensely, and I hope to meet you again."

"Indeed, the honor is mine," said Ben. "I thank you for the work you have done here today, though I must admit much of it still perplexes me, but I am certain Tom here will eventually explain it all to me."

"I expect he will," said Al. "Before I leave, I would like to perform a ceremony for everyone I do this for, though this time it will mean much more to me."

"Of course," said Ben. "What is the purpose of this ceremony?"

"Well," said Al. "this is the citizenship oath we administer to each immigrant who enters the country when they become a citizen. While Ben Franklin is technically already a citizen, Ben Folger is not, technically. Either way, I like to be thorough."

Ben smiled. "Well then, sir, I would not like to hinder your duties, so please proceed!"

"Thank you. Now please raise your right hand." Ben did so with a smile.

"Please repeat after me: 'I hereby declare, on oath, that I absolutely and entirely renounce and abjure all allegiance and fidelity to any foreign prince, potentate, state, or sovereignty of whom or which I have heretofore been a subject or citizen; that I will support and defend the Constitution and laws of the

United States of America against all enemies, foreign and domestic; that I will bear true faith and allegiance to the same; that I will bear arms on behalf of the United States when required by the law; that I will perform noncombatant service in the Armed Forces of the United States when required by the law; that I will perform work of national importance under civilian direction when required by the law; and that I take this obligation freely without any mental reservation or purpose of evasion; so help me God.'"

As he did so, he paused every few words for Ben to repeat. When he was finished, Al extended his hand and as Ben shook it, Al said, "Congratulations, Mr. Folger. You are now a citizen of the United States of America, and I would like to be the first to welcome you back!"

Ben smiled, and said, "Thank you Mr. Sanchez. Please, just call me Ben".

Al laughed and said, "Thank you, Ben. Please call me Al."

Chapter 38

Monday - Week 2

The events of the morning brought on questions about the reason for all the paperwork Ben had just signed, and even though Al had explained things very well, everyone knows it's much deeper than that. I had some email to attend to, so I went back to my office, answered all the emails that had to be taken care of, and copied several attachments from one of the emails onto a thumb drive. Then I took an MP3 player out of the drawer of my desk, attached it to at cable that would interface with my thumb drive, and copied the files to the MP3 player. There was some other administrative work, and just before returning to the conference room, I retrieved several binders from a shelf in my office and carried them with me.

Since it was almost lunch, I deposited the binders on the table by the door, and went into the kitchen to see what was up. Bill was there unpacking today's lunch from the food delivery service I set up. I had a standing order for each day of the week, being a creature of habit, and today was Reuben day. Our delivery service would make the rounds of the lunch places in town, collect everyone's lunch orders, then bring them to the office. I had ordered another sandwich from Chick-Fil-A for Ben, since he'd indicated he'd really liked those, so I took those two meals with drinks into the conference room. I retrieved Ben from his apartment, where he was working on his journal again (that thing was getting long and I made a mental note to make sure he had plenty of journal books), and we went into the conference room for lunch.

"Ben," I began after wolfing down a couple of bites of my sandwich, "I have something for us to go over after lunch, and I think it'll be something I know you've been wanting to get to."

"Very well," said Ben. "What might that be, if I may ask."

"In anticipation of this event, I had Miriam work with a well known historian and they put together a team of individuals whose work, after my initial reading, I have a great deal of respect for. They prepared for you a semi-detailed summary of American History since the Revolution. It's pretty daunting, since you already know that much had transpired, but there's plenty of information there without getting too deep into the details. As you go over this information, you may have questions about some of the events, so I'll show you sometime this week how to use the search engine for the Internet, as well as a course on how to navigate all the disinformation out there – as you know freedom of speech is a wonderful thing, but has its own set of issues – so you can look up some details as you wish."

"Excellent!" said Ben. "I have many questions and more than a few concerns, so I trust many of these will be addressed in your 'summary'."

I pointed to the binders on the table and said, "It might take you a while".

Ben's eyebrows raised as he saw the binders. "Indeed! I may need new eyeglasses after all this reading is completed!"

"Funny you should say that. I almost forgot. You have an eye appointment in the morning, and we're going to get your vision perfected. But, you won't have to read every word. Do you remember the music player I showed you the first day?"

"Of course. I still marvel that such a small device even exits."

"Good," I said. "Miriam also had the historical team employ someone who makes a living in the spoken word. I just received copies of his work. Every word in those binders is read by this gentleman and stored on that player so you can just listen to it. You can just listen to the spoken version, or you can read and listen, or you can just read – whatever works best for you. The player will let you go backwards and forwards, and each of these is well indexed so you can easily find different chapters. Plus, it will remember where you were the last time you stopped and return you to that same place when you next want to listen."

"Incredible!" Ben said. "I trust you will instruct me in its use?"

"Of course, but it won't take long. It's fairly intuitive once you've used it a couple of times."

"Excellent! That may help get through all this history you've accumulated for me," he said as he nodded towards the table.

"Oh, I find it invaluable. As a matter of fact, most of the 'reading' I do these days are actually audio books that I can listen to as I'm driving or working. I'm afraid it's almost ruined written books for me. But, not everyone likes it that way. So, you'll have the choice."

"I am most interested in the material, and I am again in your debt."

"There is no debt," I said. "Just let me know if you need any help. In the meantime, you, Kathy, Miriam and your temporary driver over here have some house hunting to do this afternoon. Kathy should be here in a few minutes."

Miriam and Bill had been pretty much silent for the last few minutes, but Miriam spoke up as her name came up in the conversation. "I am looking forward to this afternoon. Gets me out of the office, and I love looking at houses." She looked over at Bill. "I suspect Bill is not as eager as I am".

Bill looked up and said, "Oh, I don't mind. Gets me out of the office, too. We'll have fun."

We finished the meal, cleaned up, and as we were finishing, Kathy sauntered into the room looking loaded for bear, ready to house hunt. I know she and Miriam would have a great afternoon. Ben would as well, since it would be his permanent home. Bill would be bringing up the rear of the 'thrilled' train. But, he was paid well, so I wasn't feeling too sorry for him.

"You guys ready to go?" asked Kathy.

"Absolutely," said Miriam.

"Sure, why not," said Bill.

"I don't know what I shall be looking for, so I will assent to your direction, Kathy and Miriam. I trust you will lead me in the right direction."

"We'll do our best!" said Kathy. "Let's get to it!"

"Oh, and Kathy?" I asked.

"Yes?"

"Please drop this envelope off at the Post Office on your way. Carry Ben in with you."

With a sparkle in her eye, she took the package.

I bade them goodbye, and they left for the afternoon. That worked well for me, as I had lots of work to catch up on since I'd been somewhat occupied the last several days. I had, of course, prepared for the time to be spent with our new 'guest', but not everything would wait. I reviewed my email and saw that the DNA results had been emailed from my daughter with a snide remark about doing a stranger's DNA tests, so I forwarded it to a contact I had inside the NSF who could do the comparison for me. I told her it was urgent, and an hour later I received the confirmation. It was, indeed, DNA from an ancestor of known Franklin descendants. That done, I initiated a secure conference call with my superiors to bring them up to speed. That took most of the rest of the afternoon all by itself, and the guys in the D. C. office were beside themselves.

But, the call went well, and all those on the call were not only pleased, but surprised at the progress so far. One of our concerns was the mental well-being of our 'guest', so one of those on the call was a psychologist who asked several probing questions about Ben, his behavior, and his attitude. We had toyed with the idea of having an early sit-down session with Ben, but it was decided that for now my observations would suffice unless there were any red flags. There weren't, and as a matter of fact, Ben's enthusiasm and willingness to learn more were very encouraging. Once completed, I wrote up my notes on the call in my daily log, and answered a number of emails.

The afternoon was almost gone when the group came back, and I heard them talking as soon as they came in the door. Ben was very much animated, and there was some laughter as well. I joined the group in the conference room and we all sat down to see where we were.

"Well, Ben. How did you make out?" I asked.

"Very well, sir, very well indeed!" said Ben. "These well-prepared lovely ladies carried me to a number of residences, and I believe we have decided on a very fine abode. Oh, and Kathy took me by the Post Office on the way. I must say, it seemed very well organized. I liked their uniforms as well. I was proud!"

I grinned. "Yeah, I told you we'd get you by one."

I turned to Kathy. "So, what's the deal on the house?"

"Well," she said, "it's not too far away, an easy commute both from here and from the shopping district. It's on a somewhat secluded lot, but not hermit-like, and has plenty of room for Ben to make a home, as well as a nice office/library just off the living area that should do him well, and a small building in front that could be used by the security staff. All in all, it's a nice place, wouldn't you say, Ben?"

"Indeed!" said Ben. "It reminds me a bit of my residence in Philadelphia, but a bit more private. I believe I shall like it." He looked at Miriam and said, "How do we acquire this residence?"

"Oh, you leave that to me," she said. "Tom, I've spoken to the Realtor, and already negotiated a price. It's well within the budget we were given. If you approve, I can get back with her and begin the closing."

"OK," I said. "Show me where it is."

She rose and started over my way. As she did, Ben also arose. "Are we going back now?" he asked.

"Oh no," I said. "Do you remember our talk about satellites orbiting above us all the time, and how Google Earth works?"

"Oh yes, of course," said Ben.

"If you remember, they literally have almost every inch of the planet photographed and available to anyone with access to the Internet."

As we were talking, Miriam had pulled up the house on her tablet. She walked over to Ben and showed him the tablet. "Here's the picture from space," she said. "If I press this object, then the street the house is on, it switches to a street level view that was photographed by vehicles and assembled together. We only have a picture of the end of the driveway because they didn't get pictures of the house, but I took some while I was there." She switched to the street view, then rotated the image to show the neighborhood and the entry to the drive, then she pulled up the pictures of the house. She switched back to the aerial view and showed me where the house was located, along with zooms in on the property from three different directions.

"Yep. Looks good to me," I said, "as long as Ben likes it."

"I find it very pleasing," said Ben.

"I drew a quick floor plan," said Miriam, as she produced a very nice looking hand-drawn floor plan of the house.

"Bill," I said. "What about personal security?"

"Well," said Bill, "the property is, as Miriam said, secluded, but not too much. There's another residence behind his on the next street, but it's far enough away that Ben will have plenty of privacy. There's a nice fence around the back yard, so access can be controlled. We'll, of course, install our usual alarm systems with on demand monitors, and our security contractors will serve as on site monitors. I don't see any real problems."

"I don't understand all you just said, Bill," said Ben. "Are you expecting trouble?"

"Oh no," said Bill. "But, you are a significant individual in our world right now, so we just want to make sure there's plenty of attention to detail. Your privacy will be absolutely maintained, but should there be a problem of any kind – health, fire, or God forbid, unwanted individuals, this will allow the proper response to be dispatched immediately."

"I see," said Ben. He looked at me. "Another conversation for another time, I assume?"

I chuckled. "Yeah, these 'conversations' are stacking up, aren't they?"

Ben laughed.

"Tell you what," I said. "How about we all go out for a nice steak tonight, my treat. Bring Charlie, Miriam. Bill, bring Linda. We'll call it a day, and Ben, we'll work on those history documents in the morning.

Everyone nodded. I looked at Miriam and said, "Sounds like we have a house. Go ahead and acquire it, get the keys, and let's get our new citizen here situated. Ben, how do you feel about moving into your new residence first of next week?"

Ben smiled as he said, "Citizen Ben." He looked around the room and continued, "I thank you all for your care and assistance. I shall not take all this for granted. I assume you will each visit once I am established?"

"Oh, we'll do better than that," said Kathy. "I think we'll have a housewarming party. We'll help you get all the things you need and get you settled, and get you started off right."

Be smiled. "I very much look forward to that. Thank you all again!"

"You're welcome, Citizen Ben!" said Kathy.

Chapter 39

Monday - Tuesday Week 2

Now Ben had a house, and we'd spent a great evening at the restaurant. We carried Ben back to his apartment at the office and Phillip and Ben settled in for the night. We said our goodnights, and headed home. The next morning I arrived at the office just as Phillip and Bill were changing shifts and spent a few minutes with them going over security while we did the transition from Ben's apartment to his new home. Phillip left, Bill went to his office to get set up for the day, and I collected Ben and headed to the optometrist's office for his first ever eye exam. Since the optometrist was not in on the secret, we left Ben's trademark spectacles at the office, and dressed him in as innocuously as we could, hoping the folks at the clinic wouldn't get curious. They did give Ben a second take as he came in, but the office was busy and it all went well. I had already prepared Ben for the equipment they'd be using and told him to just do what the doctor said, but not to volunteer any information.

We got the prescription from the doctor and headed over to a building in the industrial district where I had a special arrangement set up. The government had a contract with an optical laboratory on an "immediate" basis. The contract was primarily for security personnel who had immediate needs of emergency eye wear due to ongoing security needs, but the lab personnel were not permitted to ask questions. We dropped off the prescription and were told the lenses would be available by early afternoon, all fitted into the frames we'd picked out late last week and had overnighted in. The lab agreed to call as soon as they were ready.

Back at the office, I sat down with Ben and went over the historical materials, as well as the operation of the MP3 player with the audio versions. It took him a few minutes to get the hang of finding the subject matter, starting the player and adjusting the volume, as well as going backwards and forwards in case he wanted to listen to something all over again. It was a little after ten before he got started, and was anxious to get into the details of what had transpired since he was on the street in Philly last Thursday. That done, I left him to it and went into my office to catch up on some more of the work that had been piling up.

The rest of the morning went pretty quick, and before I could turn around twice it was lunch. Kathy was eating with us today, so she came in promptly at twelve and we all sat down to eat.

"So, Ben, how far along did you get?" I asked.

"I am fascinated with how history has portrayed some of my friends from the debates," he said. "I was just reading about my interaction with Adams whilst in Paris, and I must say I am amazed at how those events seem to have transpired and I am not so sure I feel very good about how history says these things happened. Mr. Adams is a great man of integrity but, I must admit, I understand how many would see him as rigid and uncompromising. The conversations he and I had during the debates made us close allies in the fashioning of the Constitution."

He paused for a moment, as if considering how he wanted to say something. "I am not certain I wish to become too fully immersed in how history has seen me to be. I should say the same about Mr. Adams!"

I thought for a minute, and said, "You must realize that most of the history we have is from people who weren't there. Any time you're reading history you must understand it is history from the perspective of such people, and should be used primarily as guidelines rather than gospel. I would advise you not to get too caught up in how events you are intimately familiar with are portrayed, other than to use those portrayals as a point from which to correct the record. Also, the hard part for you will be wishing to correct some things that might be accurately portrayed in these histories to the way you wish it had been. As you may have seen, we have the histories broken down into periods and subject matter. Use the space we've provided in the documentation to make your own notes and we'll discuss each of these as you finish and, if necessary, have the authors come in for consultation and clarification. Miriam could also help in this area."

"Oh, I have already made some notes," said Ben. "I had hoped for some access to those who prepared this material. I must say, though, that it is presented in a most interesting manner, so even those areas in which I have some trepidation seem to be helpful in understanding current thinking on those events."

"Well, bear in mind any notes you take will also add to our understanding of those times. As you get to events outside your own experience, I expect those notes will change more into questions than comments."

"Indeed!" said Ben. "I had already considered that."

"Is the MP3 player useful at all?" I asked.

Ben smiled. "I am afraid I am a creature of habit, and while I toyed with it for a few minutes, for now I prefer to read the material, especially since I have so many notes to make."

"I understand," I said. "I expect it will become more useful later when the material is informing you about events you are not familiar with."

"Perhaps," said Ben. "It is gratifying to know I have the option."

He turned and looked at Kathy and Miriam. "Ladies, I had the most peculiar experience this morning. This young lady, who didn't seem to be much older than someone still in their teenage years, gave me the most professional ocular examination using some amazing devices wherein she could change the clarity of my vision in an instant. I must say, I am so impressed with the instruction she must have received to be so proficient at her assigned task. Am I to assume that many such young women perform other similar functions?"

Miriam took this one. "I remember the first time you saw me, Dr. Franklin. I'm guessing my function here is not as shocking as it was last week?"

Ben laughed. "Touché my dear. Touché. I fear I am trying to bring the societal norms from my day into the current day, which would be just as absurd as trying to bring societal norms of Christ's day into mine. I hope you will overlook my error."

Miriam and Kathy both smiled. Kathy said, "Ben, that is not as uncommon as you think. In my lifetime women have gone from house moms to professionals, and some of the men in our day are still struggling with those changes. So, don't feel bad. You're in good company."

Miriam spoke up. "And, to answer your question, yes. When you go see a professional, the odds are more and more in favor of seeing a woman there as a man. There are hardly any gender-specific vocations any more, so don't let it surprise you."

"Well I must say, she was very proficient, and I am anxious to see the outcome when the new eyeglasses are received later today. As you may know, I do have some expertise in this area!"

"Yes, we are very aware!" said Miriam, "and had the doctor today been aware of who you really are, she would have had many questions for you, since you practically invented eyeglasses in the first place."

Ben smiled. "From what I have read today, I am best known in that area for bi-focals. I am much interested in seeing how that invention has progressed."

"Oh, I think you'll be sufficiently impressed," I said. "They should be here tomorrow.."

Just then my cellphone rang, and the caller-id said it was my supervisor in Washington.

"Tom, I have some news for you. Is Dr. Franklin sufficiently aware of technology that he could be added to this conversation?"

"Well, yes he is. As a matter of fact he's right here with the rest of us eating lunch. Do you want to speak directly to him?"

"Just put me on speaker. This is something you all should hear."

"Sure, hang on a second."

I looked around the table. "This is Dr. Lawrence Freeland in Washington. Ben, he is my contact at NSF and my immediate superior. He has something he wants to tell us". I punched the 'speaker' function on my cell and placed it in the middle of the table.

"Dr. Freeland, you're on speakerphone with Dr. Franklin, Miriam, Bill, and my wife Kathy is also here eating lunch with us. She's cleared for anything you have to say, so please – what do you have for us."

"Well, first, Dr. Franklin, Tom has been keeping me up to date on your progress there, and I have to say it is impressive. I am very much looking forward to meeting you later this week."

Ben spoke up, "I would be delighted!"

"Thank you, sir. I have news you all might find interesting. One of the things I do each week is send a summary of NSF activity to various agencies, and this last week I sent the latest update on your project to the Office of Science and Technology Policy. This morning I received a call from the Deputy Chief of Staff in the White House. She would like to arrange a meeting between you Tom, and Dr. Franklin as soon as you and I sign off on it. The President has been briefed on your project and when informed of Dr. Franklin's presence, he immediately asked how soon we could arrange a meeting. Dr. Franklin, the President is very much looking forward to meeting with you."

There was silence around the table for a couple of seconds until I regained my faculties, and I said, "I don't know about Dr. Franklin, but that's extraordinary! I had no idea he was aware of our project."

"As soon as I knew you were attempting a historical transfer, I had the President's Science Advisor briefed, and he in turn briefed the President. This was all very much theoretical until last week. What do you think, Dr. Franklin? How would you like to meet the current President of the United States?"

Ben did not hesitate. "I would very much like to meet him, and to see this White House I have heard so much about in the town I had only spoken of in the most esoteric terms only a few days ago. I would be delighted and, of course, honored. I will leave the arrangements to Tom and yourself, as I am aware of certain considerations that my presence here has precipitated."

"Excellent," said Dr. Freeland. "I will immediately inform the President's Deputy Chief of Staff, and we'll talk about timing when I come to your office later this week."

"I shall anxiously await your arrival," said Ben.

"Yes," I said. "Look forward to your coming, Larry. Friday?"

"Yes, Friday will work," he said. "I'll see you all then. Goodbye."

"See you then, sir. Bye," I said, and terminated the call. "Well, that was unexpected. I thought we'd eventually wind up at the White House, but not this soon. Ben, we have some work to do. We'll get a briefing on the subjects the President will want to touch on, as well as how long we'll have with him, so until then, the best thing is to continue your updates on history. It might not be a bad idea to take a look at some other information I have as well about the current organization of the U.S. Government. I had hoped to wait until you'd had time to take in the history you're reading now, but we may need to speed that up."

"I agree," said Ben. "I am certain I will need the new spectacles now, as I may be wearing out this pair," and he pointed to his original bifocals he was wearing.

Chapter 40

Tuesday - Week 2

Ben spent the rest of the day and into the night reading through the history documents. We didn't see much of him other than at the evening meal, which I also had brought in via the delivery service. He wasn't very talkative, but I could tell he was more in a contemplative mode as I was sure he was digesting the material he'd been reading.

As we finished the meal, I told Ben, "I'll come into the office a bit later in the morning, as I'll be going by to pick up your new eyeglasses. When I get here, I've asked the staff to meet in the conference room for a, probably not more than ten minute, meeting. I'd also like to do that every day while you're transitioning between being our captive to being a private citizen. It'll be more of a heads-up meeting just so everyone knows what's on the schedule and to discuss any issues that might come up. Will that be OK with you?"

Ben smiled and with a smirk said, "To clarify, then, 'heads-up' means you wish us all to pay attention?"

I laughed. "Yes. It's another colloquialism. It does indeed mean to pay attention, but it can also be a euphemism for getting an update, or getting informed."

"Then yes," said Ben, "that would be 'O-K' with me."

I smiled again. "Getting used to the new lingo there, Dr. Franklin?"

"Yes," said Ben, "and I must admit I am enjoying the acquisition of this new 'lingo', as you say, which leads me to a 'heads-up' of my own, if I have that term correct. I would like to spend some time discussing these events I have been studying. I have many questions, the answers to which will hopefully provide some understanding."

"Of course," I nodded. "Let's make that a topic of discussion for tomorrow, and we'll decide the best way to get you the answers and clarifications you need."

"Excellent!" said Ben. "I should return to my studies, then, if I may take your leave."

"Absolutely," I said. "I have some things to do at home.. Let me know if you need anything. Either Bill or Phillip will be here around the clock, so let them know if you need anything. ."

"I shall return to my appointed duties then," said Ben as he arose to go back into his apartment.

"Good night, Ben. I'll see you in the morning, "I said, then left for the evening.

The next day, I went by the optical laboratory and picked up Ben's new glasses. While there, I asked them to prepare another pair as a backup and just send them over to the office. That done, I headed into the office, getting there around ten. As I entered the office area, Ben was at the conference table with his materials spread around him, and he was actually listening to the MP3 player! As I came in, he fumbled for the controls and finally figured out how to stop the playback.

"I hope you don't mind my use of your nice conference area," he said. "I find it a bit more useful to spread this material out as I study it. I have also discovered this little device is actually quite useful. It certainly is easier on my eyes."

"Of course, Ben. You can use anything in these facilities that you may need. You're one of the main reasons you're here. Speaking of your eyes..."

I pulled out the eye-wear I'd picked up and handed them to Ben. "Try these and let me know what you think."

He removed his spectacles and put on the new glasses. As he adjusted them on his face he looked around. "My, this is an improvement!" He opened one of the binders and began to read the contents. Then he looked up at me, then back down to the binder.

"I believe you have measurably improved my vision!" He picked up his original eyeglasses and looked at them. "I shall probably not require these any further."

"If that's the case," I said, "I may know an institution here that might wish to have them."

Ben looked at me and smiled, then said, "May I assume that institution has the name of a certain famous 'Founding Father' affixed to it?"

"Yes, you may," I said. "The real problem is explaining to the Franklin Museum how I obtained these."

"Simply tell them you came across one of his descendants," we both laughed as Miriam, Bill and Phillip came into the room.

"Right on time," I said, as I took a seat at the head of the table. "Let's get started." For the next several minutes we discussed the events of the week and Ben's need for getting the blanks filled in. The goal was to get Ben ready for his visit to the White House, which meant there was much more background to be absorbed. Since Ben was anxious to be ready for the trip, we all agreed to help as much as possible. Ben had also indicated he was warming to the MP3 version of the material, so he intended to use it as the primary source, and use the printed material for notes and for reference.

With that, everyone got back to their day. Throughout the day, Ben would pause his player and seek one of us out for questions. One of the things that concerned him was the contention between the newly formed political parties in the early nineteenth century. It had been something some of the Founders feared, particularly Washington. The contentions between these 'factions', as they had termed it, were seen as detrimental to good republican government, and I could see more of these conversations coming the nearer we got to present day.

We had already talked about the War of 1812 and Ben was surprised to find out that James Madison had been President and that his wife Dolly, the First Lady, had been the one to rescue the famous painting of George Washington. Ben, of course, knew Madison, and as he studied his presidency he recognized his friend's actions from the conversations they'd had, literally, a few days earlier.

Ben's consternation with some of his fellow Founders began to show as he read of the shooting of Alexander Hamilton by Aaron Burr, and as he saw the direction some of his contemporaries had taken after the signing of the Constitution. But in a candid conversation with all of us sitting around the conference table that evening just before we left, he didn't seem to be surprised at some of the things he'd read.

"The passions of man were something we always knew would present problems to a free people," he said. "I am not as surprised at some of the things I have read thus far as I am at some of those involved. Many conversations I had with others involved in our endeavors were concerned with limiting the abilities of such passions to affect the liberty we had hoped to establish. One thing that is entirely gratifying is that here I sit, some 230 years from the Foundation, in a country that has not only survived, but apparently thrived."

"Well," I said, "you need to be prepared for some of the events that led us here. Not all were perfect, and not all were foreseen."

"I am most certainly aware that our country is not perfect," said Ben, "but we never thought it would be so. What we most hoped for was to provide a situation where free men could decide their futures for themselves unencumbered by tyrants. Apparently we accomplished at least part of that purpose."

"That you did, Ben," Miriam said, "that you did, and I for one am grateful to have this chance to learn more of our history from you."

"You, my dear lady, are a product of that history!" Ben exclaimed. "That you are here in this office, performing the duties that you perform, along with the rest around this table, convinces me that our deliberations were not in vain."

"Here here!" I said. "With that, let's adjourn for the evening. Ben, would you like to come to my house for a nice meal? Kathy would certainly relish the chance to spend another evening in your company."

"Thank you, sir. It would be my pleasure."

With that we all split up and went our separate ways, Ben in the Tahoe with me. Phillip came with us and agreed to bring Ben back later that evening on the condition that Kathy would include him in the meal. That agreed to, we left in separate vehicles. For the next few hours we had a great time listening to Ben regaling us with stories from his youth, and some stories about his friends that you just won't find on Wikipedia.

As I walked him to Phillip's vehicle at the end of the evening, Ben asked the question I know he'd been waiting to ask.

"Tom, how do you see the rest of my life here in this future time, so removed from all that I knew just days ago?"

"Ben, as I told you a few days ago, you have the unique chance to change the direction of the country you helped establish. My fear is that you won't enjoy the journey, and I'll do whatever is in my power to help you enjoy it. But, your immediate chance will be when you meet with the President in a few days. As you might have deduced, the President of the United States is the most powerful single individual in the world, and even though he is answerable to the Congress, the Courts, and the People, he still wields much power and influence, and his opinion on any subject can, literally, change history. My prayer is that you will help him with those opinions, particularly the role of government and the dreams the Founders had for our country."

Ben smiled. "I shall do my best, and do not be too concerned with my 'enjoying the journey', as you termed it. Discovery is my great journey in life, and you have added to that immeasurably. I do not know how long the Almighty has determined my existence to be on earth, but He has certainly determined to fill my days with that discovery I enjoy. As for your, 'our', President, I shall speak truth. There is nothing more I can do."

"Well," said Phillip. "That should do it!"

Chapter 41

Middle of Week 2

The rest of the week went pretty much the same. Miriam and Kathy were busy outfitting Ben's house and handling the purchasing documents. Periodically they would consult Ben on furnishings, styles, accessories, etc., generally around lunch time, and it was fascinating watching him trying to decide about styles about which he knew little. But, the two ladies did a masterful job guiding him through the selections and, in the end, I think he would be well pleased with his new home.

Ben spent much of his time studying, listening to the audio history, and asking questions. In his documentation, I had placed a single piece of paper with the words 'STOP – Talk to Tom' emblazoned in the middle. It was the beginning of the Nazi era and, as a World War II buff, I wanted to have that conversation with him. I had been heavily involved in the material selection for this part of his education because much of what happened in that period of time defined who we are today. When he got to that point he sauntered into my office.

"Apparently," he began with a smile, "you are to enlighten me on the next period in our history," and he held out that paper he had simply ripped from the book.

"Yes!" I said. "I wanted to go over this period with you because of the way it has affected the United States up to and including today."

"In that case, sir, I await your instruction."

"Let's go into the library."

I had Ben sit in the chair opposite the TV while I loaded a DVD into the player.

"I have a video presentation for you, Dr. Franklin," I began. "The first thing we're going to view is the attack on the Hawaiian Islands by Japan. But, let me give you a bit of history leading up to that first. Please stop me if I fail to explain it all, and ask any questions you have at any time."

I began with the end of the First World War, and how that had served to simply set the stage for the next war. Even though we had already talked about the Balfour Declaration and the establishment of the nation of Israel, I didn't leave that important point out of the discussion. From the first overt attack on the Jews in Germany, Kristallnacht, to the invasions of the surrounding countries culminating in the Polish invasion that brought Great Britain into the war.

When I got to 1941 I told Ben, "This video is part actual video, and part dramatization, but extremely accurate. It was prepared by the same historian who prepared your written material," and with that I started the video. When it was finished, I set up the next video that described the two-front war, showing the struggle in Europe and the island hopping campaign in the Pacific, which started with one of my favorite stories – Dolittle's Raid on Tokyo. It ended with the surrender of Germany and the death of Hitler.

"You are very fortunate to have history available in such a form," Ben said. "I presume this is used in educating our young citizens?"

"Yes," I said, "but education is a problem area that we'll cover later, if you don't mind. Right now, I want to tell you about an event I alluded to the other day when I told you there was another event that was even more spectacular than the establishment of Israel. This is a story of one of the greatest, and most dangerous, scientific achievements in history. And it all starts with a German expert in the area of physics named Albert Einstein."

For the next several minutes I explained the elementary elements of nuclear fission and how that translated into the Manhattan Project. The secrecy involved, the funds expended, the scope of the project, and the run up to the first test in New Mexico.

Then it was time for the next video. "Ben, this is an archived video of the first test of what we call a nuclear bomb." With that, I played the video. When it finished, Ben sat there for a few seconds.

Finally he asked, "You are telling me, then, this explosive event actually happened on American soil?"

"Yes, not too far from San Antonio, Texas, in the desert in New Mexico. The flash was so bright that a partially blind woman fifty miles away saw the light. The heat generated was so hot it instantly turned the sand into glass and completely vaporized the tower and all the equipment on the site. It generated an explosion roughly equal to 44,000 pounds of high explosive."

Ben gave me another of those astonished looks and said, "What did we do with this invention?"

"Excellent question. That's the subject of the next video." I started the next video which chronicled the deployment and use of the first nuclear bombs. Little Boy, Tinian Island, Paul Tibbets and his crew, and the trip to and dropping of the bomb on Hiroshima, including the jumpy videos taken from the aircraft that day immediately after the explosion, followed by the Nagasaki bomb, this short video covered it all.

"Ben, the decision to drop the bomb was made by President Truman," I began when it was over, "because the estimates were that millions would die in an invasion of the Japanese islands, including perhaps a million Japanese. I once read that the military planners had ordered a half million body bags to hold all the dead American soldiers that would occur in such an invasion."

I paused for a moment to let that sink in, then I began the last WWII video that chronicled the warning leaflets dropped days before the bombs, followed by a short edited documentary of the on-the-ground effects in both cities. The last frames showed the final casualties in both towns finishing up with the complete surrender of the Japanese military on the USS Missouri.

Ben was aghast. He sat for a full minute. Finally, he asked, "Are there more of these bombs today?"

I nodded.

"Have they been used again?"

"Well," I said, "That's the second part of the story. Right now, as we sit here, there are literally thousands of these weapons, hundreds and thousands of times more powerful, in existence today in eight countries, with more trying to build their own. Yet, not a single bomb has been dropped on another country since 1945. To date, the United States is the only country to have used this weapon against an enemy. But, its use was so terrible that no other country, including ours, is willing to use them."

I went on to explain Mutually Assured Destruction, the Cold War, the rise and fall of Soviet Communism, then China, and the other nuclear powers, and ended up fast-forwarding to present day where some countries, particularly Iran and North Korea, are trying to obtain these weapons and might actually be willing to use them.

The discussion was lively, and I found myself defending the United States for using such a terrible weapon. Ben was desperately trying to understand all the elements that went into the decision to even create nuclear weapons in the first place. Finally, he began to understand the inevitability of someone building such weapons.

"Let me put it this way, Ben," I concluded. "Once the science was available, it was inevitable someone would build such a device. Rightly or wrongly, the United States was the best possible choice to be the first nuclear power, and they were only used because not to would have resulted in many many more deaths. Now we live with all the decisions made to end the largest war ever on the planet, including the decision by President Truman to use it at all."

Ben thought about that, then said, "Such a terrible decision for one man to have to make."

"Yes," I said. "That's why the Presidency is called the loneliest job in the world."

Ben once again considered that before speaking, then said, "We were so concerned about the establishment of an office that might lead eventually to a monarchy, but saw no other viable option."

"Oh, I wouldn't worry about it, Ben," I said. "It has worked pretty well for over 200 years. We all think you did a pretty good job."

"I do suppose that the country has lasted this long speaks well for some of our efforts," he finally said. "Still, when I see the struggles, and the conflicts that have beset our country, I stand humbled by the men who have guided her through the years."

"Well, in a few days you will get to meet one of those men. What will you say to him?"

Ben laughed. "I haven't the faintest idea. I suppose I have some thinking to do. With today's new knowledge I believe I still have a half century to go. Perhaps I should get to it."

"I would suggest you review the printed and recorded information on this time period before continuing," I said. "The last fifty years are very much still tied to the two world wars. Also, there are some changes in the way our country views itself, its Constitution, and its place in the world that we are still struggling with. I suspect that information may influence your talk with the President very much as well."

"Intriguing!" said Ben. He took out his Wagstaff, looked at the time, and said, "I may have time between now and evening retirement to review. However, I do believe I shall retire for a short nap before continuing."

"I can't blame you for that!" I said. "You've had a busy couple of days. I have a couple of things to do before going home. If you'd like, I'll take you down the street to a diner for an evening meal before I go home."

"I'd like that," he said. "But I do have an inquiry."

"Sure. What is it?"

"How does one obtain one of these little cards you carry around that allows you to purchase food?"

"Oh," I said. "A credit card?"

"Yes, that!"

I laughed. "That will be coming in a few days from now. The NSF is working on establishing your identity and credit rating, but first, they are establishing a bank account for you, and next week your account will receive the first payment as a consultant, and with that you will be issued something called a 'debit card'. It looks just like a credit card, but instead of the balance being due in thirty days, it immediately removes the funds from your bank account."

"Interesting," said Ben. "I trust you will show me how to use these items to access the funds?"

"Of course," I said. "We'll guide you through all that."

"Excellent!" he said. "When I think of a bank, I think of my friend Alexander Hamilton." He shook his head slightly, then said, "Shame about that incident between him and that Burr fellow. I knew Burr's father, but never really trusted the younger Burr. I suppose that was a wise move on my part," he said with his eyebrows raised.

"I guess Hamilton would agree with you!" I said.

"Indeed!"

216

With that, we both adjourned to our respective tasks, and later I carried Ben to a diner and we had a nice evening meal. Then, Ben back in his apartment, I headed home. When I walked in the door, Kathy asked my how the day went.

"This afternoon was a bit intense. Ben got to the Second World War, and I ended the evening with Hiroshima, Nagasaki, and the arms race. That's a lot for one individual to absorb in one afternoon, so I'll be interested to see how he handles it."

"What?" she said. "You think he'll handle it any better or worse than the rest of us?"

"Good point," I said nodding. "He's pretty much taken everything in stride so far."

"Well," she said, "wait until you tell him what we've done to the Constitution and the massive government we now have. I expect that explosion will make Hiroshima look like a firecracker."

"Yeah."

Chapter 42

Friday - Week 2

Friday came and Ben had gone over the material he had and that brought him up to present time. All the wars, the threats to national security, enemies, friends, and even many of the struggles the nation had gone through internally. There had been lots of questions about social issues, and he was particularly interested in the residual racial issues stemming from the Civil War.

"It appears," he said, "that many believe we failed in our societal construction because of the slave issue." He paused for a second, then said, "I cannot say they are entirely wrong. It was a contentious issue. It is very easy, however, to look back in time at our decision and assume they could have done better. In that belief, they are not entirely right."

I was instantly impressed with his logic.

"They weren't," I said. "Turns out, the issues are still being settled. It seems, Ben, that the more we increase our abilities to communicate with each other, the less communication we actually do. Turns out human nature hasn't really changed in thousands of years."

"That does seem to be the problem," Ben agreed. "As a matter of fact, human nature was one of our primary concerns in the establishment of a new nation. How to govern ourselves, when we all are flawed and prone to selfish aggrandizement. As you have seen in your own century with this Hitler fellow and others, you are correct. Nothing has changed."

I sat up and looked into Ben's eyes and said, "Dr. Franklin, tomorrow we are going to discuss the country we have built. Not the one you have built - the one we have built. You may have noticed that detailed information about the current structure and scope of the Federal Government was left out of your material."

"Yes, I was about to ask you about that."

I nodded. "This was on purpose. Before we could attack the changes in government in detail, we needed you to have a sense of the historical background that contributed to these changes. Some were external in nature; some were internal in nature. I am afraid you will not like much of what you see, and like the social issues, we struggle on an almost daily basis with the governmental issues."

"I, then, am highly anticipating that discussion," said Ben. "I am most curious to see the evolution of what I was a part of just days ago."

"That," I said, "is exactly why your perspective will be so beneficial to the future of our country. Ben, as I keep saying, you still have much to contribute. We need first person perspective, rather than those assumed by historians. It all starts with your meeting with the President."

"Agreed," said Ben.

"However, today, my superior at NSF will be here, and he will be most anxious to meet you. He is a very intelligent man, and the one who first reached out to the White House. I think you'll like him. He is fully informed of the program here, and I've been sending him regular updates, so there are no boundaries in your discussion with him."

"Wonderful," said Ben. "A time like this is not one for duplicity, and I most certainly want to make use of the time granted me. I shall be myself!"

"That should do the trick," I said with a chuckle.

A few minutes later in my office, Miriam came over the intercom to inform me Larry had landed and was on the way. I gathered the group in the conference room, went over protocols, and we prepared for his arrival. Shortly later, Larry came in with his driver where we were all waiting. I was up front to meet him.

"Larry, good to see you," I said as I extended my hand.

"You too, Tom," said Larry as he shook mine.

"You know all the staff here," and Larry did a quick acknowledgment and handshake with each.

"But I know the one you really came here to see is this distinguished gentleman." and I turned towards Ben.

"Ben, I'd like you to meet Dr. Lawrence Freeland, Deputy Director for the Physics Division at the National Science foundation. Dr. Freeland, Dr. Benjamin Franklin of Boston and Philadelphia, freshly arrived from 1787."

Larry stepped forward and extended his hand. "Dr. Franklin. I cannot express my honor to finally meet you in person."

Ben shook his hand. "Oh, Dr. Freeland, the pleasure is mine. You are, after all, a major reason that I am standing here today. And, one thing I have learned since being here is that salutations are much less formal than in my day, something I am still acclimating myself to, so please, just call me Ben."

Larry laughed. "Yes, I imagine that is a change. In that case, please call me Larry."

We all sat down at the conference table, and Larry began. "I understand you have been pouring over the historical material Tom had prepared. How are you finding it?"

"Most interesting," said Ben, "...and troubling. So much we could not see. So many ripples in history. You know, sir, seeing the effects of actions I and others had taken those many years ago has caused me much reflection. Some troubling, but some hopeful as well."

"Well," said Larry. "Knowing what you know now, what would you have done differently?"

"Oh, sir, that would be a dangerous proposition. Such an exercise serves only to castigate those who made such decisions when that information would never be available. It is many times nothing but a shortcut to those unwilling to understand circumstances at the time." Ben leaned forward and in a quieter, much more serious voice, "It is much more important to make one's own decisions wisely."

Larry smiled. "I knew it wouldn't take long for the wisdom of Benjamin Franklin to appear."

Everyone around the table smiled.

Larry sat back. "Let's talk about your pending visit to the White House and your meeting with the President."

For the next couple of hours, we held what is probably best described as a full debriefing. The conversation was detailed, but amicable, and some of Ben's insights into how things were going were very helpful in planning the next several days. As a result, we set the date for the visit to the President for two weeks in the future. Catching the President on a, hopefully slow news day, would be more likely on a Friday when everyone was trying to get out of town. Larry would have a Secret Service representative come by and set everything up. The last thing we wanted was for anyone to have a clue that the President was meeting someone that afternoon, and we certainly didn't want any pictures appearing in the Press. I could only imagine the speculation that would occur if someone who looked like Ben Franklin were to be found in a meeting at the White House. Fortunately, the Secret Service was practiced in these covert meetings, so we felt pretty confident the clandestine meeting would come off OK.

At lunchtime, I had prepared a private dining room at a local restaurant to be made available, so Larry, Bill, Ben and I rode in my Tahoe, and the rest in Miriam's SUV, and we had a really nice lunch. After lunch we went back to the office and went over travel details to and from D.C. Larry had already been clued in to Ben's lack of knowledge about current governmental operations, so he kept it simple. I knew that lack of knowledge would not be the issue in two weeks, and might in fact be the subject of the meeting, but that was in two weeks.

I did find out something out about Larry that I didn't know. He was an autograph hound. He had brought a restored copy of Ben Franklin's autobiography from the early 1800s, as well as a nicely bound reproduction for Ben. He had Ben sign the restored copy (instantly making it irreplaceable!), and presented Ben with his personal copy signed over to him on the inside cover by Larry. I saw the starstruck fan come out in Larry for a few minutes, something I tucked away to kid him about later.

Finally, the visit done, Larry was sorry to leave, but anxious to get back home for the weekend. Before going, he pulled me to the side for a quick word.

"I understand you're about ready to move Ben into his new home," he said. "Are there any details we need to talk about?"

"Well, I am still a bit concerned about security. I want to make sure there'll be no problems, but at the same time I don't want him to feel like a hostage any more. It's something we'll have to work on once we get him ensconced."

"I read his comments on his being a prisoner," Larry said. "Have you made inroads in his perception in that area?"

"I think so," I said. "Getting him his own place is a major part of that. Once he has access to his own funds that would go a long way as well, so I want to foster that without sacrificing security. Handling this perception with Ben was one of my major concerns before we got started on this project, and a major conversation with the psychologists at the time. They helped a lot, so right now I think we have a handle on that."

"Good. But, don't hesitate if you have any problems."

"Oh, I won't." I promised. "I am very grateful for the support you've given me and the team. This is a dream come true, and your office is responsible for a lot of that."

"Tom," he said, just before going out the door, "maybe at some point you'll get a sense for just how monumental this project is. Perhaps when you're in the Oval Office with Ben."

"I hadn't even thought of that," I said, surprised. "I was concentrating on Ben's visit I forgot I might be there as well."

"Tell Kathy she's invited, as well. Do you think she might want to meet the First Lady?"

I was astonished. "Are you kidding? Of course she would."

"Well, tell her. Just tell her she can't ever tell anyone else."

"Ha!" I chuckled. "That'll hurt, but she's good at keeping secrets. Thank you very much, Larry!"

He smiled, and said, "See you in D. C."

"Yes. See you there. Have a safe trip back," and with that, he was gone.

Now, I couldn't wait to get home. I went back in the office and told everyone else to take the rest of the afternoon off.

"We've been on go for over a week now, and it's time to take a breath. Tomorrow Ben and I have a long session on the Government, but none of you have to be here for that, except for Phillip, at least until the weekend security shows up tomorrow afternoon. Monday is moving day, and I expect we'll all spend the entire day getting Ben into his new home. So, get a good night's sleep, and take it easy this weekend."

They all nodded and began their individual exit strategies. I looked at Ben.

"What would you like to do the rest of the evening, Ben?"

"Well, sir, I believe I will spend the rest of the evening reading my autobiography which I hadn't yet authored. I should like to see how it turns out!"

Bill heard that and laughed out loud, as did I. Ben had that trademark smirk on his face, and it occurred to me just how right he was, and how strange that would be.

"Great, then," I said with a chuckle. "I'm going home and tell Kathy she gets to go to the White House with us in a couple of weeks and meet the First Lady!"

"Well, then," said Ben with a devilish look on his face, "I suspect you shall have a great evening yourself!"

I shot him a dirty look, then said, "See you in the morning Ben." and headed out the door.

At home Kathy was in the middle of preparing the evening meal when I walked in the door. She looked at the time on her phone then asked, "What are you doing home so early? Larry didn't fire you, I hope?"

"No – the meeting went really well. I just gave the team the weekend off and came home early."

"Wonderful!" she said. "Dinner's not yet ready, so take it easy for a bit."

"Oh, I will. By the way, what are you doing two weeks from today?"

"Not anything I can think of. Why?"

"Ben has this meeting with the President that day, and I'd like you to go to D. C. with me."

Kathy smiled, and said, "Great! I was hoping to not be left alone. I can do some sightseeing while you're in your meeting."

"Nope. You won't have time?"

That got a frown. "Why not?"

"Well, you have some babysitting to do."

She put her hands on her hips. "Just who are you expecting me to babysit?"

Smirk time. "The First Lady of the United States."

Turns out, Ben was right!

Chapter 43

Saturday – Week 2

I arrived at the office around nine to find Ben sitting at the conference table with Phillip. They were both sipping on coffee, Phillip working on his laptop, and Ben reviewing the history he'd already covered in the binders.

"Mornin', gents. How's it goin'?" I asked.

Phillip spoke first. "Fine here. Just working on my weekly report. You?"

"Oh, I'm great!" I said, maybe a little too enthusiastically. "Ben – you ready for a long day?"

Ben closed his binder and said, "Most certainly. I have many questions."

"Yep. I figured you would. Let me get the materials we'll need and we'll get started."

I went to my office, grabbed my tablet, and went back into the conference room. I turned on the ceiling-mounted projector and established the wireless connection to it with my tablet. As I was doing so, Ben spoke up.

"Sometime soon you must familiarize me with these devices you use. I have surmised that they allow one access to a wealth of information."

"Well, that they do," I replied, "and yes, probably after today's session, I can familiarize you with how they work. You will definitely have access in your new home, but there are some pitfalls you need to be familiar with."

"Excellent," he said.

In another minute I had my first presentation ready to go, so I began.

"As you know, Ben, I told you the information since the First World War had, and still has, a major impact on how our government works today. I must say, this is another of those sessions I dreaded."

"How so?" asked Ben.

"Well, Ben, I'm afraid that the government you gave us will barely resemble what we have today. The first thing I want to show you is a current copy of the Constitution."

I went over to the cabinet and retrieved a large bound volume and plopped it on the table.

"This is what's called the 'Annotated Constitution'. It is nearly 3,000 pages long. It contains the original document you signed just days ago and all of the amendments since then. But the majority of what you see here are all the court decisions, opinions, acts of Congress that the Court has not ruled on, as well as opinions and regulations issued by the various departments of government. This is what members of Congress look to when proposing and passing legislation to determine if something is Constitutional or not. This is your copy."

Ben pulled the book over to him and leafed through its pages for a moment, then looked back up at me.

"This is not what I just signed!"

"Yes," I said, "I know. That is why I dreaded today's discussion. I have lived most of my life thinking the Constitution was around 4,400 words or so, and even after I began working for DARPA it took a while before I was introduced to this behemoth. What I want to do is lead you through how we got from 4,400 words to 3,000 pages, and what your role in all this might be."

Ben sighed. "We were never under any illusion that the Constitution would remain its original size, which is why we introduced two ways to amend it. But I can assure you, sir, not one of my contemporaries envisioned this," he said as he pointed to the bound volume.

"I know," I said. "I know. But, let's start with the document you and your contemporaries gave us, and bring you up to the present day and this....thing."

I started with the Bill of Rights. Ben was, of course, in agreement with those amendments, including the one still pending from 1789 that would have strictly regulated the size of House districts. He agreed with the amendments that resulted from the Civil War, but had real heartburn when we got to the Sixteenth Amendment.

"What possessed the legislatures to agree to allow direct taxation by the Federal Government?" he asked incredulously. "We had extricated ourselves from an oppressive government that confiscated our wealth without our consent. Why would we once again allow this to occur?"

"Simple," I said. "They were told it would be voluntary and would only be a minor amount on the wealthy. Let me show you something."

I pulled up a picture on my tablet and put it on the screen.

"As a result of the Sixteenth the government established a department called the Internal Revenue Service. Their job is to collect and enforce collection of all taxes. What you see here is a picture of the current IRS tax code that has evolved since then. Virtually everything in the United States is taxed at some level, and some things are subject to multiple taxes. Either directly, or as a result of taxes that are taken from individual incomes."

"Income taxes?" he asked. "How many citizens are taxed."

I pulled up another picture. "This is my youngest daughter's paycheck record she receives from the firm she manages. Note these areas I have circled and numbered. Number one is the amount she made this pay period before taxes. Number two is the amount of Federal income taxes held back by her employer that are sent to the Federal Government. Number three is the amount held to cover her health care expenses after age sixty-five, also sent to the Federal

Government. Number four is the amount held out as a small retirement fund after age sixty-two, another Federal Government program. Number five is the amount held out for her taxes to the state of Pennsylvania. Finally, number six is the amount she was actually paid."

Ben looked back at me with an expression that can only be categorized as astonishment. I continued.

"If you have a job in the United States, your paycheck will look similar to this. In fact, the funds you, Ben Franklin, are going to receive will also be the remainder after these taxes are deducted from your gross pay. These numbers are based on one's marital status, the number of children one has, and that tax bracket the income places you in. Each April fifteenth, every citizen with any measurable income is required by law to file a series of forms with the IRS that reconciles these taxes, wherein you either pay the amount of shortfall, or receive a refund for taxes overpaid. Most Americans receive a refund of some sort, but many have to pay additional taxes into the system. In addition, there are business taxes, excise taxes on such things as automobile fuel and tires, corporate taxes, and a host of others."

Ben stared at the picture on the screen for a second, then back at the Annotated Constitution, then back at me.

"How much money is confiscated from our citizens each year?", he asked.

"Last year, over three and a half trillion dollars."

Ben sat back in his chair, and exhaled, then softly, "This was not what we envisioned."

"I know," I said. "Unfortunately, this is not the worst of the news. Now you see why I dreaded this day. But, one thing you need to understand. Even with all these issues we will talk about today, the United States is the strongest, richest, has the most liberty, and is the most powerful nation in the world. The good news is that you placed your bets on the People, and they have excelled."

"Yes," he said, "but where will all this lead."

"This, Ben," I said, "is why I am glad you were the person we brought across time. Your eloquence, experience, and wisdom, coupled with your personal stature, may be just what our nation's leaders need to hear to take a good long look at what has been done in, many times, the name of making things better."

We sat in silence for a few minutes. Then Phillip spoke up.

"Ben. We have a great country. I would like to see it remain great. But, some of the decisions that are made in Washington make me wonder if our leaders feel the same. You may be just the man to change that perception."

Ben thought about that, then smiled a bit and said, "Every time you say 'Washington', I think of a general, not a city."

"Well," I said, "sometimes we don't even think of a city. We think of a group of faceless men making laws. How would your friend George react to what you've seen today?"

Another smirk. "Probably attack at dawn."

Chapter 44

Saturday – Week 2

The rest of the day didn't go any better. Each time I would bring up yet another government department, Ben would go right back to the Constitution (the original one, not the Annotated monstrosity), and several times he asked just where the authority for such an entity would come from. The Department of Education was a real sore spot.

"It is not the federal government's business to educate the young!" Ben exclaimed. "In actuality, such a practice is supremely dangerous. I would make the argument that the People would be better served that education be performed by those opposed to government than those in government. Otherwise the government's interest is supreme rather than instruction."

This turned into a lively discussion of the origins of public education, and the decisions that led to the Education Department.

"There are many in the nation who agree with you, Ben, but the current establishment is so entrenched, and the teachers' organizations so prevalent, that changing from the status quo is very difficult."

"Exactly my point!" Ben said, almost in a shout.

Department after department, it just got worse. But the real kicker came when we began to discuss what some of these departments actually did. Finally Ben, exasperated, asked the salient question.

"Tell me, Tom. How did the People let this government become so large and all encompassing?"

"Much the same way as it happens in every other government," I said. "One thing at a time. It all started almost immediately. The Supreme Court ruled in 1803 that it had the sole authority to strike down laws, statutes, and some government actions on Constitutional grounds. Many consider that the most important decision made in American jurisprudence, and it was a decision made in a case between a supporter of President John Adams as he left office, and James Madison, Secretary of State for the incoming President, Thomas Jefferson. Many believe this case to have been wrongly decided, but it has served as the benchmark for Supreme Court authority since.

Ben just shook his head.

I continued. "With the Civil War and all the wars in between, the expansion of the country, racial and political divisions, and you add in the explosion of inventions that totally changed how people interact with each other, there were a myriad of issues that came up for government and the courts to deal with and, unfortunately, one at a time, Constitutional absolutes were turned on their head. And remember, for you the Constitution was last week. For us it was 230 years ago. A lot of things have happened. Every major war, emergency and large disaster has further added to the expansion of the Federal Government, including the most recent emergency that resulted in almost shutting down the entire country."

Ben thought about that for a moment, then said, "That is a very good brief history of usurpations, but usurpations nonetheless. Your statement just now indicates that you, and I assume others, are aware of these aberrations, so my bewilderment is with the People. Why have they not demanded reclamation?"

I thought about that for a moment. "Ben, a British politician in the nineteenth century made a statement that I believe applies, at least partially, to your question. He said, '*Power corrupts, and absolute power corrupts absolutely*'. I believe you and your compatriots made the case that governments, if allowed, would always grow into oppressive ones. The good news is that we are not there yet, but we are in the process, and unfortunately, many times the Supreme Court is leading the charge."

"Apparently!" said Ben.

"Well," I said, "let me take you the rest of the way to where we are now, and just how bad it is. Knowing who you are, and having some knowledge as to your personal beliefs in general and regarding the Constitution in particular, I have dreaded this day. But, you deserve to know all the truth. So, let's get to the worst of it. Let me introduce you to a Supreme Court decision made in the 1970s in a case called Roe versus Wade."

In short order, we both had tears in our eyes. I don't know about Ben, but every time I considered the number of children our nation had killed in the name of convenience, I tended to tear up. This time, though, here was a Founding Father who's heart was breaking because of what had been done in the name of the nation he helped create, and my heart was also breaking for him.

The bad part was this was the first of many such instances of what we went over for the rest of the day. By the time we decided to break for the day, Ben's 'countenance' had fallen, and I was emotionally exhausted. I wound up the discussion by trying to get Ben back on track for his upcoming session with the President.

"Dr. Franklin, I believe with all my heart that your being here at this time in our history is no accident, nor is it a coincidence. As you may already have surmised, I believe in Providential direction, the act of God directing history. The funny thing is that, even though we've spent the last several hours decrying how far we have strayed from what you Founders created for us, you are here as the result of the actions of two agencies of the Federal Government! We can discuss whether these agencies are proper or not – I believe they are – but the fact is that you have a point of view backed with experience that nobody on the planet can approach, and in a few short days you will begin to bring that point of view to the very center of the United States Government – the office of the President. Let me make a suggestion."

"Please!" said Ben.

"Let us take the rest of the weekend to relax and contemplate what we've talked about and a proper path forward. Monday, you will be moving into your new residence, so let's table all these issues and reconvene Tuesday to put a plan together. Make no mistake, this will not be my plan, and it won't even be our plan. It will be your plan to bring some, how did you put it – reclamation? That, sir, is exactly what we need, but those in positions of authority are too entrenched in the current paradigm that they have difficulty seeing a way back. You can bring that vision to them."

Ben thought about that for a moment, then said, "That may be an exceedingly difficult task."

"Could be," I said, "but if not now, when? And if not you, then who?"

Ben sat back. "You put that much responsibility on an old man?"

"No!" I said. "I put that much responsibility on the right man."

Ben smiled. "Then, let us put together my battle plan. First of the week will be an excellent time to start."

"And," I said, "I will certainly be praying for you. Ben. Considering my firm belief that God Himself ordained this event, I should certainly be asking for His guidance."

Ben chuckled and said, "I shall most certainly accept it!"

Kathy came in through the door. "Are you two about finished?"

Ben stood up and said, "No, madam. We have just begun!"

Chapter 45

Saturday Evening – Sunday – Week 2

We went out to eat that night and while we were eating, Ben asked about my showing him how to find out information on his own.

"I should like to delve deeper into some of these subjects," he explained. "The dissertations you have given me are excellent, but I desire some deeper understanding."

"Yes," I agreed. "You need to be able to access the wealth of information that is available to everyone else on the planet now. So, how about after Church tomorrow, we sit down and let me give you an initial lesson on how to use the computer and search engines to look up what you are interested in?"

Ben brightened up at that suggestion. "I would like that very much! Are you certain I can become capable of this?"

"Oh, very much so. If my six year old granddaughter can do it, you certainly can. Once you've used it a couple of times, it becomes more and more intuitive. Also, I can have a person available for you to answer questions in case you have difficulty, and I'll show you how to get in touch with that person."

"Excellent!" he said with a smile.

"You're moving into your new house Monday," I said. "I believe everything is ready to go, and we'll have all the other provisions in place – food, utilities, security, et cetera – and you can get settled in. You'll have your own computer setup there, so tomorrow would be a great time to learn that. There'll be more in-depth instruction later, but I'll get you started."

"So," he said. "I will have officially moved into the twenty-first century, then? I must say, none of my contemporaries are able to make that statement!"

I didn't remind him we could, indeed, transfer another of his friends (and we had no such plans to do so!), so I just agreed. Phillip carried Ben back to the apartment, and Kathy and I went home. Ben decided to forego Church the following day to prepare for his move and to finish some of his reading and notes, and I told him I'd be back after lunch to dive into the world of computers.

Church was great, as usual, the next morning, and I made a mental note to show Ben how he could view the service as it streamed online, or even watch it later if he wished. I had no idea if he'd be interested, but it would serve as an example of some of the things he could do once he had some basic computer skills.

Kathy and I had a leisurely lunch, then we left to go to the office. Kathy was fascinated with Ben's ability to pick up new skills, and she took a book with her to read if things got too boring.

When we got to the office, I set up a computer in the conference room and connected it to the projector so we all could see without having to crowd around a monitor. I did have a monitor as well, so Ben could get used to seeing things on a smaller screen.

One thing I was concerned about was exposing Ben to some of the seedier things one could find online, so I'd had our IT guy install a fairly strict filter, the kind you would have for your kids, and had him customize it so it would be unobtrusive, but keep those subjects away until Ben was more acclimated to the much more liberal lifestyles of modern society. I also had a remote access program installed so if Ben got into trouble I could access his desktop and fix whatever problem he was having. The support desk would also be able to do the same. The further we got into Ben's acclimation, the more people we were bringing, at least partially, into the loop, but the Help Desk guys only knew him as Ben Folger, an elderly man who was just learning computers. Ben would, of course, be instructed to not divulge in any way his true identity.

Once settled in, we began the lesson. Turn the computer and monitor on. Wait for it to 'boot up' (that was a fun explanation!). There was no login – I had it boot directly to the Desktop. Fire up the browser. Using the mouse. How to input information. It was a good thing Kathy brought a book, because the things we do every day without thinking about it were certainly boring to watch someone else learn for the first time. There were some moments of levity as Ben discovered some things, but it took the better part of a couple of hours to just get him where he could turn it on, do some simple searches, then turn it off. He was fascinated by the on/off switches for some reason. I guess if you've never had access to electricity, using it the first time would be fascinating, and it was not lost on me that this man had discovered it in the first place!

Finally, we got to the point where we could actually look some stuff up. Wanna know what his first search was? 'Benjamin Franklin', and Kathy and I both laughed because I guess that's something everyone does at some point. After a few minutes, I showed him how to 'bookmark' a site so he could come back to it.

Then we went in search of other information. Kathy had some suggestions as well, as suddenly her book became less interesting than the site of Ben Franklin looking up stuff on the Internet. We spent a good part of the afternoon using search engines to look up all kinds of information from history to fashions to geography. Thankfully, he stayed away from more salacious subjects, but I knew we'd have to cross that bridge later.

Once he had a good handle on using the browser, I showed him some other functions. He was particularly fascinated with both Google Maps, and particularly Google Earth. I even showed him how to pull up his new house from space. He spent a lot of time tooling around Philadelphia and the surrounding area, so I let him play with that for several minutes, then gave him an overview of some of the other programs.

"Ben, there's one program I know you'll be interested in. It's called a 'Word Processor'. This one is what we use here in the office and what I use at home. Let me show you how it works."

For the next several minutes I showed him the basic operation of the word processor program – writing, formatting, saving, retrieving, and gave him a short course in how to organize files. I showed him how to create a folder and how to navigate between folders, and what to do if you get 'lost', then let him go through the whole thing himself.

Finally, I gave Ben a quick course in Internet security, which brought on a whole other conversation. I didn't get into defining terms like 'hacker', but I did warn him that there was a whole culture of people out there, particularly in third world countries, who spent their time trying to steal information and money from those online who they might find vulnerable, and that some nation-states had entire divisions set up just for that purpose. I even showed him the Nigerian prince spam that still to this day made its way around the Internet, and even got a pretty good laugh out of him when I showed him a cartoon of a Nigerian prince's supposed mattress full of money he'd been trying to give away for decades.

Finally, the afternoon waning, and lots to do on the following day, I brought it all to a close.

"Once you get moved into your house and get settled, I'll arrange for a more in-depth instruction on using the resources available on your computer so you can access information at your leisure."

"Wonderful!" said Ben

"Great. So why don't you grab what you need for an overnight stay. You're staying at our house tonight, and we'll get started in the morning moving you into your new house. It'll be good to relax for an evening before we begin the move."

Kathy spoke up, "And I'll have us a light dinner tonight, and we'll all sit down and watch something on TV."

"O-K." grinned Ben. "I should be only a few moments."

"Whenever you're ready," I said.

Ben got his stuff and we left. Just before going, Ben asked, "What shall I do during my days, once I am situated in my new abode?"

"Well," I said, "it's up to you, but if you'd like, you can come down here as often as you'd like. As soon as you get moved out, we're going to turn your apartment back into an office, and it'll be yours to use as you like. As I said, though, it's up to you, but we need to get prepared for your meeting with the President!"

"Excellent point," he said. Then he paused for a moment, got a bit serious, and said, "Tom, I must thank you for all your work and kind way in which I have been treated, not only by you and your staff, but by your lovely wife as well. For a while I was unsure as to how I should feel about this 'transference' you had performed on me, but particularly in the last several days, I have taken the advice of both you and your friend, Dr. Ken, and embraced this experience. Once I realized that I was the first person in history to experience this phenomenon, it occurred to me that maybe your 'Almighty' had His finger in this process as well."

"Oh, I can assure you He did," I said. "Otherwise, there would be only one Ben Franklin, and he'd be the one in 1787. I am so glad you feel that way, and it is our pleasure to be in your company."

"Yes," said Kathy. "The only sad part is that I am an acquaintance of Dr. Benjamin Franklin, and I can never brag about it to my friends."

"Madam," he said, "you can brag to me, if you wish. Am I not one of your friends?"

Kathy's eyes teared up and I thought she was going to cry. "Yes, Ben. You most certainly are. Thank you!"

Chapter 46

Monday – Week 3

Moving Day!

Bright and early we all rose, ate breakfast, and headed down to the office. Kathy was thrilled when Ben offered to ride with her and they appeared to be having a jolly time when they arrived. I promised myself to ask what that was all about later on, but for now, there was work to do.

Miriam had commissioned a moving company to fetch Ben's stuff, as well as the furnishings we had bought that had not already been delivered, so while they were packing up the apartment, we had a quick staff meeting to set the day's agenda, then got to work. Miriam and Kathy went on over to the house to supervise the unloading and begin the process of making a house into a home. Ben was in the conference room when I walked in.

"Want to go shopping, Ben?" I asked.

"Shopping?" he asked. "What are we shopping for?"

"Well, you're moving into a new house today, plus you need to see what merchandising looks like after 200 years."

"Oh! Most certainly!" he said.

"Fine!" I said. "Bill, let's take Ben to Lowe's."

"Sounds like a plan!" said Bill, and we headed out to the parking lot, loaded up in my SUV, and headed down to the shopping center. As we pulled in the parking lot, Ben was all eyes.

"My!" he said. "These buildings certainly are large. Is this much room required?"

I smiled as I looked back at Bill. "Just wait until you get inside," I said.

We exited and walked into the store and I grabbed a shopping cart. Unlike what would normally happen to me in the grocery store, this cart actually had good wheels and didn't try to slide sideways everywhere we went.

Ben was aghast at the selections available. He simply couldn't believe there were so many types of home products. His eyes really got big, though, when I took him over to the tool section.

"Precisely how many hammers does one require?" he asked at one point.

"Usually one more than you already have," I said. "Wait until you see the screwdrivers!"

We spent over an hour looking up and down the aisles, selecting things Ben might need for his new abode. When it was finished, we checked out – another experience Ben handled quietly, though I could see the wonder in his face. Then, back out to the SUV where we loaded everything and got ready to go.

"OK, now to Walmart."

"What is a 'Wall Mart'? Ben asked. "Is that where one purchases walls?"

That got a laugh from both Bill and me.

"No, It's like Lowes, except there's more stuff."

"Are Americans this prosperous?" he asked.

"Pretty much," I said. "We're the envy of the world – both in a good and bad way. We do tend, though, to overdo some things. Not that I'm complaining, you understand."

"I expect it has always been that way for those who have, as opposed to those who have not," he said.

"Well, Ben," I said. "We have!", and about that time we pulled up in the Walmart parking lot.

"Another huge building!" said Ben.

"Yep," said Bill. "Wait until we go to the grocery store!"

The Walmart experience was just like the Lowes, and it was particularly funny when I saw Ben looking through the underwear section! I rescued him before it go too weird, but Bill and I both got several smiles watching him gawking at all the selections. I took him to the electronics section and showed him all the available TVs. We picked out a nice fifty-five inch flat screen, as well as a small nineteen inch table model he could keep in his office, and we loaded them into our carts along with the other selections. When we checked out, Ben was once again enthralled with the checkout process, particularly, I found out later, when I paid for the whole shooting match with a credit card.

"You say I am going to receive one of these magic cards?" he asked when we got to the SUV.

"Yep!" I said. "But they're not magic. The bill still has to be paid with real money. It feels good when you check out, but not so good when the bill comes due."

"Isn't that always the case?" chuckled Ben.

Then it was time for the grocery store. This one was more involved. We went down each aisle, trying to determine what Ben needed to get started. I wasn't going to do the full supply at this time, since that needed Kathy's touch probably, but I wanted to use the occasion to acquaint Ben with how these types of stores were laid out. In particular, he again was fascinated with the frozen food section.

"So many selections!" he said. "Why are so many types required?"

"Because people come in all types," I said. "The free market system works wonderfully. If someone can think of something they might like to have, someone else will figure out a way to produce it and make money in the process. Two hundred years of supply and demand have brought us this far."

"Simply astounding!" said Ben. "It seems the common people now live much better than kings in my time!"

"Yes," I said, "so just imagine how kings live now!"

Ben shot me a look, then a smirk. "I suppose that's to be expected as well," he said.

The shopping cart was about half full – and yes, it had a broken wheel – when we went to check out and, again, I paid with the credit card.

When we got back out to the SUV, Ben had another question I had been waiting for.

"Tom, who pays for all these supplies?"

"Today, the bill is being picked up by the Federal Government," I said. "We were given a budget, assuming we were successful, that was to be used specifically to settle whomever we brought here. There's still a sizable amount, even after today's purchases, but we'll eventually use all of that up. There are certain things that still must be done to get you fully settled."

"I see," said Ben. "After which I shall be responsible, correct?"

"Correct," I said. "But, we will make sure you're fully aware of all the options, and you can always call on any of us whenever you have questions or needs and we'll point you in the right direction."

"Excellent!" said Ben. "I shall need much 'pointing', I suspect."

That got a laugh all around.

Finally, our shopping done, we went over to the house where everyone else had gathered, and Bill and I walked the grounds for a last minute security audit, as Ben and the ladies put the house together. We had just finished when the security detachment commissioned by the NSF showed up. There were six of them – three on a rotating daily stint, two for the weekend, and a floater who would relieve one of the others whenever needed. Every two weeks, the entire day shift would shift one position, so that the floater would become the day shift, the day shift would become the evening shift, and so on. Bill took them on a tour of the grounds and they spent much of the rest of the morning discussing logistics and notification procedures. The garage apartment would serve as their permanent headquarters on site, so that's where they ended up when the tour was finished. There was some work to do there – equipment to be installed, as well as the creature comforts needed for someone doing full duty – but they would handle that. When they were ready, I went in to fetch Ben, and accompanied him over to what would be the security office.

"Ben," I began as we assembled, "These gentlemen will be your on site security. They will also serve as your drivers when you wish to go somewhere. Gentlemen, I'd like to introduce you to Mr. Ben Folger."

They all shook hands and introduced themselves to Ben, and when the round was finished, Ben said, "Gentlemen, I shall try to not be a burden on you, as I am too old to be much trouble. Accordingly, do not expect me to move very fast!" and that got a laugh. They spent the next several minutes with some personal details – families, education, etc.

"Gents," I said, "Ben is your primary concern from here on. Do as he asks, objecting only if there is a security issue that he might not be aware of. If there are any problems, call Bill immediately. He will be your primary contact off site, and will arrange anything you need to perform your functions. Since Ben is new in town, he may want to do some looking around – that's entirely up to him. Does anyone have any questions?"

Nobody did, so I said, "Great! I assume the first shift starts immediately, right?"

Rick Swanson, the Team leader answered. "Yes, I'll take the rest of the day, then Dano here will relieve me at four."

Danny Myers nodded.

Rick continued, "Brad will do third shift, Frank and Pete will handle weekends, and Javier here will be this cycle's floater. That should take care of the next two weeks, then we'll swap things around."

"Sounds great," I said. "How about we let you guys get the office together and we'll get back to the house. I took the liberty of putting some menus from local restaurants on the table over there as well as the number for a couple of delivery services. Let us know if you need anything." They agreed, and we went back to putting the house together.

Several others showed up over the course of the day. The alarm company showed up and gave us the tour of the alarm system they'd installed last week. The cleaning service sent a rep over for the initial setup – they would come twice a week. The security team had an officer from the local police come over for a briefing – they handled that without our intervention, save for Bill's attendance. An IT rep from NSF came over and got the secure DSL system running. Without getting into the details with Ben, he was on a secure network through NSF's facilities so we wouldn't really have to worry as much about Internet security. Finally, the movers finished and left, so we ordered dinner that evening as we put the finishing touches on the house.

When all was said and done, Ben had a nice place to live. An office with everything Ben would need – desk, shelf full of classics and a few historical novels I thought he might like, laptop computer, a small TV, and all the paraphernalia one would need in a working home office. The living area was roomy with plenty of room to entertain, flat screen mounted on the wall, and the dining room/kitchen area was fully stocked and ready to go. His bedroom was just as we had it at the office, so he would still feel somewhat at home. All in all, Ben was ready to go.

Finally, with all the stuff in place, everything cleaned up, Danny on duty, we said good night to Ben and went home. Ben had decided he would show up at the office on a regular basis, unless he was working on something in his home office, so tomorrow we would begin in earnest the preparations for the Oval Office visit, and we set up a staff meeting for nine a.m.

Chapter 47

Tuesday – Week 3

We convened promptly at nine a.m. for an all encompassing staff meeting. Rick was fully briefed on who Ben really was, as were the other three rotating weekday detail team members, so he sat in on the meeting. I had asked Phillip to attend as well, and of course, Bill was there. I had even asked Kathy to attend, so there was a full contingent around the table. With everyone's consent, I opened the meeting with prayer, then got down to business.

"As you all know, a week from Friday we will be traveling to D.C. for Ben's meeting with the President of the United States. Everyone here at the table will be going, as well as whomever Rick decides he wants from his team. Bill, you and Phillip coordinate with Rick as to how much you'll be involved in the detail."

They all nodded.

"This will be one of the most historic meetings that has ever taken place in the Oval Office, and the general public may never know about it. As a matter of fact, most of the people in the White House won't know the details, and nobody outside our group and the President's confidants will know. Treat this like a military secret and you'll be fine. Miriam, you'll be contacted by a member of the President's staff and you will work out a cover story for the inevitable questions that will come up. It needs to be something that won't put anything in danger if Joe American finds out about it, and that includes our friends and family. We'll not broadcast in any manner where we're going and who we're seeing, other than that it's a meeting at the NSF in Washington. As you know, your spouses have been vetted, so you can tell them the meeting is at the White House, but don't divulge the President's involvement, since none of you will actually be meeting with the President. All other information concerning Ben's true identity will stay with the current protocol."

Ben spoke up. "My, this all sounds like much intrigue. Tell me, what are the dangers if other individuals find out?"

"Ben," I said, "this is one of the downsides of a free press. Any hint of who you really are and who you're going to see will bring hoards of reporters down on us instantly, and I do mean instantly. If, for example, the cable news networks find out, their ongoing programs will be interrupted immediately and everyone on earth will know within five minutes that Benjamin Franklin – THAT Benjamin Franklin – is alive and living in America and meeting with the President – and there'll be nothing we can do about that. So, our only option is to treat this with the utmost security. You can, of course, be as candid as you need to be with us and, of course, with the President when you get there, but for everyone else, you are Ben Folger, special consultant to the NSF, at a meeting with the rest of the staff at our D.C. office."

"I still do not understand this ability to do things globally in an instant," he said. "But from all the things you've revealed to me in the last several days, I have no choice but to accept exactly what you say. I suppose I shall understand more the longer I am here. Continue, sir!"

I smiled. "Oh, Ben, I believe you'll figure this out much sooner than you let on, but thank you."

I went around the table clarifying everyone's assumed function at this point in time, and asked for any questions. There were several, and a couple of hours later we were done.

"One more thing." I finished up. "Some people from the office supply company will be here right after lunch to put Ben's office together, so everyone be aware they are not in the loop. For them, it's just another office they're putting together for just another generic facility."

That done, they all went their way to begin the process. Ben came into my office and we had a long discussion about how he would approach his meeting with the President.

"I know there is much I still have to ascertain," he said. "But I already have some issues I wish to bring up with him. After I meet with the President, what shall be the next steps for me?"

"That's a good question, Ben. A lot hinges on this first meeting. You can try to drive the discussion as much as possible, but if he wants to go in a different direction, there's little we can do about it. From what I know, he's a really smart man, and his beliefs about the Constitution are similar to mine, so there's a real opportunity here for a major impact on the future of the country."

"Yes," said Ben, "I seem to have some experience in that matter".

I laughed. "Indeed you do, Ben, indeed you do. So, as your studies progress, let's keep a running list of possible things to bring up with the President, and just see where that takes us."

"Agreed," he said. "That said, then sir, I shall take my leave and return to the books!"

"Sounds good," I said. "When they have your office together, you'll have the entire world of online resources at your fingertips. That should open up some avenues for you as well".

"I very much anticipate those 'avenues'," he said as he stood up and left.

Lunch came and went and the installers from the office supply store came and unloaded all the furnishings for Ben's office. It took them most of the afternoon, and by four they were done. Ben and I went into his office and put together his computer system and made sure he was able to surf the web. There was one thing left to do for Ben to be able to do whatever he needed.

"Ben, here's a security card for the office. You've now seen us use these. It will allow you entry into the building any time you need to get in. We generally want to know when you're coming in after hours, so have your security team give me a call in those cases, though you should be able to do anything you need to after hours from your home office."

"I understand," said Ben. "Before we leave, please allow me to use this...device...so I can be certain of its use when I need it."

"Of course. Also, be aware that when you do enter and exit the building, that event is logged into our security system. Also, there is a phrase I need you to memorize. If you enter after hours, or you're here past a certain time after office hours, our security office will call and ask for this phrase. It lets them know that nothing untoward is going on. The phrase is "Gray Van". Just give them that phrase. They may ask for your name and how long you intend to be in the building, so just answer their questions and they'll go away."

"'Gray Van', you say?" asked Ben. I nodded. "I understand your need to maintain 'security', as you have indicated . Is this a widespread practice?"

"Yes," I said, "in practically every company of any size in the nation. With the fast pace of life these days, and the large amounts of expensive equipment and other items, it just makes sense to keep a close watch on things. It really serves as much as a deterrent as anything else. If people know you've secured your facilities, they're less likely to try something. It just keeps everyone honest."

"I see, I think," he said. We talked for a few more minutes, and finished putting the touches on his office, then it was time to get out and go home. As we left, I let Ben use his card to re-enter the building and the inner office, which of course went off without a hitch, so we left – me in my Tahoe, and he in the Suburban driven by Danny, who had come on duty at four.

When I arrived at home, Kathy had dinner ready. "How nervous are you about this meeting?" she asked.

"Very!" I said. "I have no idea how this will go, what the President's attitude will be, or for that matter, what Ben's will be. This whole thing could go sideways really quick. But, I have faith that we're on this path for a reason, so we'll just prepare the best we can and leave the rest in God's hands."

"Yeah," she said, "I think He can handle it."

I smiled. "Yep, me too. How nervous are you to meet the First Lady?"

"Pretty nervous!" she said with a crooked smile. "I have no idea what to say to her. How much does she know about what's going on?"

"I have no idea," I said. "Let's put that on the list of questions to ask the White House before we go. She seems nice on TV, though, and I've read some things about her that are very complimentary, so just get the rules straight, and enjoy yourself."

"What I really hate is that I won't be able to tell anyone," she said with a grimace.

"I know, sweetheart, I know. Me either!!"

"Yeah," she said nodding her head, "I guess your secret is somewhat bigger than mine."

"Yep," I said, "and there's every possibility that major historical changes can come from this and nobody will ever know I had anything to do with it."

She thought about that for a minute, and said, "Oh, Tom, the people that matter will know. Besides that, God already has this planned out. So, just give all that to Him, and do your best."

"Probably the best advice I've received today," I said.

Suddenly she sat straight up and said, "Oh, my! I have some shopping to do! I need a new dress!"

Chapter 48

Wednesday – Friday – Week 3

Ben showed up for the full day each day for the rest of the week. He was like a sponge as he brought himself up to date on U.S. and world history. I could see the thinker and the diplomat come out in him as he put together the relationships, causes, effects, accidents, and yes, even Providential events that had occurred down through the years. He had more of a problem with the societal changes than he did with the historical events that shaped the World powers. He had a real problem understanding how Communism and Socialism had come to the forefront in American politics.

"How can Americans, who have been blessed with Liberty, consider fleeing liberty for the shackles of totalitarianism?" he finally asked one afternoon.

I thought about that for a moment, then pulled up something on my phone. "Let me read you something the fortieth President of the United States said in a speech a decade and a half before he became President. It is one of the most famous speeches of the twentieth century. In that speech he said..." and I read from my phone:

"Freedom is never more than one generation away from extinction. We didn't pass it to our children in the bloodstream. It must be fought for, protected and handed on to them to do the same, or one day we will spend our sunset years telling our children and our children's children what it was once like to live in the United States where men were free."

Ben thought about that for a minute. "Are you telling me freedom is being lost through apathy?"

"Yes, Ben. I suppose you could say that. Look, it has been nearly a century in the making. We first began to, little by little, fail passing on the First Principles that established this country. Then we lost the sense of what government was for in the first place. Now, a sizable portion of the country is so invested in everyday life that they've become apathetic on matters of government, particularly with twenty-four hour news coverage. It's like trying to drink from a fire hose. At some point you just give up. It takes major tragedies to wake us up sometimes. Have you read about the attack in New York on nine-eleven 2001 yet?"

"I've seen some articles about that, but I have not delved into it fully as yet. Is that one of those wake-up tragedies you speak of?"

"It was, for a very short period of time," I said. "But, power has its advantages, and when you attack the most powerful country on earth, it doesn't take that power long to gain the upper hand. Soon, everyone was right back to fighting everyday issues again. We just lived through another 'emergency' where the government took extraordinary measures, but in the end not much changed."

"So," said Ben, "what do you think it will take?"

"Well, Ben. I often say that perhaps the best thing that could happen to America is probably also the worst thing that could happen to America. It may take a real tragedy to wake us up. You, on the other hand, may be able to bypass that event if you can get people at the top to take action against the very beast they've created."

"From what I have seen thus far," said Ben, "*beast* is a most appropriate word. As I believe I made clear to you in the last few days, this is not the government we envisioned when we signed the Constitution. How do I impress that on your – sorry, our – President in just one meeting?"

"Well, Dr. Franklin," I said in my most dignified voice, "you have a stature that no one else on earth, including the present President of the United States has. You were there when it all was written, and you know what the rest of the Founders were thinking. I'd suggest you make that the subject of your talk with the President."

Ben nodded and said, "I think you are correct, sir. I shall endeavor to do exactly that!"

He went back to work. There were several questions along the way the rest of the week about the causes, effects, and whys of how things got to where they are. Sometimes I had an answer, but I must say that much of the time I needed to do some research as well. Miriam was very helpful, since she'd been a history major, and had helped prepare the materials for Ben's study. By the end of the week, Ben was pretty much up to date on the major historical events since his time in the eighteenth century, but was still fuzzy on the sociological changes, particularly when it came to attitudes in the present day. We made it Saturday's task to tackle all those changes, particularly since the Second World War. This was another of those sessions I was not looking forward to. There was also the part I dreaded when the subject of the sexual revolution would come up. I was pretty certain Ben wasn't ready for the changes in morals since his day. It was one reason I had his Internet access filtered to make sure those issues didn't come up until we were ready to expose him to it. The last thing I needed was for a porn site to pop up right in the middle of one of his searches. So far so good.

Finally, Friday afternoon came and we had a quick sit-down for a quick status check just before going home for the day.

"Ben, I'd like to make tomorrow just another work day, but we'll focus on societal issues as they were affected by, and how they have affected history. I'm afraid it will be eye opening and likely unsettling on some levels, but it is necessary for the context of some of the historical events you have already studied. Miriam, Bill, Phillip, and Kathy will be here. We'll begin at nine sharp and take whatever time we need. That will give you all of next week to put all the pieces together. Is that acceptable to you?"

Ben nodded. "Yes. I must understand why some of these events occurred the way they did, and why some adjustments have as yet not been made."

"Good," I said. "Then let's get a good night's sleep, and I'll see everyone in the morning."

Five minutes later, the place was empty, and I was going to have a hard time sleeping tonight. But, it is what it is, and it was all going to be laid on the table tomorrow. While Ben was known for having somewhat liberal views on human interactions, this was going to be way out of his wheelhouse. But, so far, he had handled everything we'd thrown at him, and this was the last real hill to climb with him, so in the end, Kathy's advice was right on the mark. So, I followed her suggestion and left it all on the prayer alter and went to bed.

Chapter 49

Saturday – Week 3

Kathy and I went in early the next morning to find the building empty save for Phillip, who was waiting on the weekend crew. Since we were all going to participate in the discussions today, I wanted Phillip to be unconcerned with anything else. Not too long after we arrived, Bill came in, followed shortly by Miriam. They both had excuses along the line of 'I had some things I wanted to do first' for being there, but it was obvious they were anxious to see where this discussion would go.

I actually did have some setting up to do, so I went into the lounge and set up the computer interface for the big screen TV, and laid out some DVDs I had prepared for this session. I also had a number of books that I laid out near where I would be sitting. I arranged the chairs so Ben would be directly opposite the TV, and I and the rest would be sitting in a u-formation along either side of his chair. Everyone would be able to see the TV, but we would also be able to talk to Ben without too much head-craning. When I finished I went back into the conference room where the rest were basically lounging and drinking coffee and juice, waiting on Ben's arrival. The weekend security had showed up and he was parked outside at the entrance, so Phillip and Bill were also just waiting. At two minutes before nine, Ben came in with his driver, Frank. Since Frank wasn't cleared for Ben's true identity, I had him park himself in the security office so he could also keep an eye on the outside security cameras. Since he had access to the break room, he should be set for the day.

The rest of us adjourned to the lounge where I locked the door and had everyone seated. After exchanging some morning pleasantries, I got us down to business.

"Ben, as you may have already determined, cultural issues have many times been the driving force in political changes down through the years. What we want to do today is go through those changes that have happened since your time, and discuss how that has, and in a major way still does, affect the political climates through our history. I must confess, I have been dreading this day."

Ben interrupted. "Dreading? Why so?"

I hung my head a bit, and said, "Many of these changes are not things I am proud of our country for, and there have been some moments where many of us shook our heads and wondered where all this was going. Also, today's climate is, as I indicated earlier, affected in a major way by cultural changes that many of us still shake our heads over. I know that in the past things have also been culturally affected, so your perspective on the relative effect these have had on our present history as compared to such changes and their effect on the history of your time will be interesting, and possibly relevant. We will take whatever time we need, within reason, if all this sounds acceptable to you."

Ben sat back in his chair, and said, "I feel as though I'm facing an inquisition, but I wish to know these changes and their relevance. Proceed sir!"

"Well, if it's an inquisition, I'm afraid we're the ones in the hot seat, but be that as it may, here we go."

The first stop was the geographic cultural differences that Ben was already aware of, and how they continued to affect politics right up to the Civil War. Since we had already touched on this subject, I didn't spend much time on it. Then on to the Second Great Awakening of the early nineteenth century and the rise of Protestantism and denominationalism. Then, the expansion of America in the nineteenth Century and the regional tensions, particularly between the North and South that all came to a climax in the Civil War, and how those tensions continued even well into the twentieth Century. Then I went back to the nineteenth Century, and talked about social changes, especially in light of the Victorian era and attitudes on gender and sexual issues. From there we talked about the suffragette movement and the Nineteenth Amendment to the Constitution giving women the right to vote. Everyone contributed to the discussion, and I had encouraged them to give personal viewpoints on each of these issues.

Then, we covered the industrial revolution and the explosion in technological changes, many of which Ben had already been exposed to.

"Ben, as you might have already surmised, the change in the speed and methods of communication had a lot to do with the changes, both in culture and in government, and two primary inventions accelerated these changes: The invention of radio and of motion pictures. Let me give you some examples of what Americans could, beginning right after the turn of the twentieth century, listen to in their homes."

I played some snippets from some old radio programs. Some dramas, some news reports, some comedies, and some sports. This small presentation lasted about thirty minutes during which we discussed how each of these would have been received in their time frames.

"But, it was motion pictures that really began to change things," I said. "Suddenly, there were stories of events that most people would never be exposed to in their lifetimes that they could see for a very small fee. My own Mom told me she and my Dad would go to the movies most nights because the movie

246

theater had air conditioning and it was much more comfortable than their home. A night at the movies was not uncommon for most people on at least a weekly basis. Here are some of the stories they would have been exposed to."

I showed a slide from my computer with movie titles and short descriptions. Then I played some movie clips, just like I'd done with the radio programs.

"These were accelerated in the mid-twentieth century when television made its debut. Now, suddenly, all these movies, along with a new form of short story series of not more than an hour each, were streamed into every home with a television. Not only that, news that happened across the world would be available in a very short period of time. The world suddenly got much smaller, and we all became very aware of how the rest of the world lived."

Ben had absorbed all this with few comments.

"Ben, when I was small, I did not know we were poor. Everyone in our small town was poor – some poorer than others – but we were all relatively in the same economic strata. But, when we were able to afford a television, I began to see how others with more money lived, and the possessions they had, and suddenly I realized we were not very well off. I wanted some of that stuff for myself!"

Everyone else nodded in a 'me-too' agreement.

"Are you with me so far?" I asked.

Ben said, "Oh certainly. I can see how these influences would alter your perception of your life. Tell me, Tom, did it make you jealous of those others?"

"Not really," I said. "But it did make me want some of those same things. I don't know that I ever was angry that someone else had things I didn't have, I wasn't raised that way. But I did want some of those things, which meant I had to find a way to get them. I was not always successful in that endeavor, so I guess sometimes frustration set in."

"That, sir, is a problem we each have had at some time," said Ben. "As I have traveled abroad I have seen much in the way others in the world lived and I must confess there were times I wished for some of those amenities and possessions as well. I expect is has always been that way."

"It has." I agreed. "Now, let me go back and tie some of these events together and describe how that has affected our country from a governmental perspective."

Back to the Civil War. Defeat. Reconstruction. Jim Crow. Regional jealousy. Then women's rights. The battle of the sexes. The Roaring Twenties. Greed, and then ruin. I played some footage of the run on the banks at the beginning of the Great Depression, and the hungry living on the streets. As I did, the rest of the group chimed in with stories of their parents and grandparents and how they'd coped with economic ruin and depression. We all talked about how that single event affected three generations of Americans, and still hangs in the minds of many people, particularly the elderly who went through the remnants of those days.

Bill, in particular, had a story of how his great grandfather had lost all he had and taken his own life when he realized all he'd worked for was gone. His father had to take over for both his and his father's family. Even Ben agreed, once he'd realized the extent of the Depression, that this was probably the single worst event that had happened to the country – even considering the three wars that had been fought on our shores.

But, the worst was yet to come. So, I took a breath and dove in.

"Ben, the things we've talked about so far begin to pale in comparison to the period in our history that, aside from the Second World War, has had the greatest affect on our country, both culturally and governmentally. If you mention this to anyone today, they'll know exactly what you're talking about. It's called the sixties."

Everyone else nodded their heads.

I began with the first generation born after World War II. "We call these folks the 'Baby Boomers'. I was born at the very end of that era. Those born just prior to me were brought up in a time when the economy was exploding, and suddenly, if you wanted something, there was a way to obtain it – from cars and TVs, to homes and wealth. I had a friend who once stated that there was never a time in history where practically everyone had the ability to, if they wanted something badly enough, find a way to obtain it. The poorest in our land are wealthy compared to most of the rest of the world."

Ben nodded. "I am guessing this wealth all came at a cost."

"Yes," I said, "and it's a high one."

As I brought up each subject, the entire group became animated, since we'd all been through much of what we were now talking about.

I started with the Beatniks of the fifties. Then the musical revolution.

"Actually," Phillip said, "the music was great! Still is!"

"Yes," said Miriam, "I really like listening to radio stations that play those older songs".

We all nodded.

"But," I said. "These lyrics had an edge to them, and that edge was a sharp one".

I put up the lyrics to some of the songs. There was much to pick from, and I didn't have to cherry-pick the words. Almost the entire collection had overtones of rebellion of one sort of another. Either against authority, or traditional mores, and many were outright rejection of their parents' values.

"The truth is," I said, "that when I was listening to these songs myself, I was more interested in the music than I was in the lyrics. But once those words crept into your mind, there was no way it was not going to change your thinking at some point. And many of the people who wrote these songs and performed them were not what you, as a parent, would want to be, shall we say, role models."

"Yeah," said Kathy, "some of these I didn't even realize what they were saying until years later, and now I'm embarrassed to admit I used to sing some of these."

"Exactly," I said. "But, even having said that, I have to agree with Phillip and Miriam. The music itself was great."

"Well," said Ben, "let me hear some of this music".

"I will," I said. "Let's save that to do over lunch. I want to get all this in perspective first."

"Fine," said Ben, "I can wait for that. Please proceed."

"OK. This next point, and something we've struggled with ever since the sixties, can be summed up in one word. Vietnam."

Again, everyone's head around the group bobbed.

Chapter 50

Saturday – Week 3

The subject of Vietnam required some setting up. In the history segments we had talked about the effect of Communism in the last seventy years or so of history, so we revisited that for a moment. Then I explained how we got there in the first place. Next, time to pause and introduce another subject.

"In 1963," I began, "The United States had a relatively young President at forty-six years old. He was campaigning in Texas when some shots rang out and within the hour, the thirty-fifth President was dead. He was succeeded by the Vice President, who coincidentally was from Texas, Lyndon Johnson. Johnson had different ideas about our involvement in Asia, and on his watch, the American contingent in the tiny country of Vietnam was massively increased. Suddenly, young men from cities, towns, and villages all across the country found themselves called up for military service and sent to a place they'd scarcely heard of, all in the name of stopping the spread of Communism."

"I understand the fear of tyranny," said Ben, "but, why the interest in such a small country so far from our shores?"

"Well, Ben. That's the same question many were asking. Part of it, I suppose, came from the memory of the spread of Nazism years before, but there was also the fear that since Russia and her allies, collectively known as the Soviet Union, was a nuclear power and not only diametrically opposed to the U.S., but aggressive in causing problems around the globe. There was this 'domino theory' that suggested that if Vietnam fell to Communism, it would just be the first in a number of countries in the region that would eventually become Communist, and stopping them now might be easier than trying to stop them later."

Ben nodded, then said, "I have read of this conflict, and I don't know that I agree with their assumptions. I assume there was a cultural effect related to this event, since that's what we're discussing?"

"Exactly," I said. "Let me show you some videos."

I then played a series of newscasts and archived photos of the protests and riots that occurred as a result of our involvement there. When it was finished, I continued…

"The government did a poor job of explaining to the American People why we were there, and the story is more complicated than I have shown you so far, but there is much written about this, so you can do a deeper look at your leisure. The point is that the country was literally torn apart by our involvement in the Vietnam conflict, and it is important to remember that it never was a declared war. It was characterized as a 'police action'."

"Police action!" Ben exclaimed. "That's ridiculous! The Constitution has no such provision!"

"Which is why," I said, "that many people thought we shouldn't be involved there in the first place. The government's thinking was that a formal declaration of war would likely draw the Soviets into another larger war, and with nuclear weapons involved, they didn't want to take that chance. Like I said, the story is complicated."

Ben thought about that for a moment. "I suppose I do need to do further research to understand the reasons for these actions. So, for the moment, continue..."

"The controversy about the war," I continued, "was a major, major, issue in the 1964 Presidential campaign when Johnson ran and won re-election. Even after the campaign, the riots and protests just got worse, so much so that Johnson decided not to seek another term. In the 1968 campaign, a Republican, Richard Nixon, was elected and initially escalated the war in an attempt to drive the opposition to the negotiation table, which actually worked at first. However, they kept stalling and it didn't take long for him to realize there would never be enough support to prosecute the war properly, so he made the decision to pull out completely and bring the troops home."

"I suppose they were welcomed after having been gone so far away," said Ben.

"They were spat upon in the airports when they returned," Bill said.

The look on Ben's face was incredulous. "Why were our own troops disrespected? They weren't responsible for the conflict!"

"That's another story that's more complicated," I said, "but a lot of it had to do with how the conflict was portrayed in the press. Then there were some stories about some atrocities committed by some individual troops while there. The point is that this was a very unpopular war, and many of those, particularly of college age, wanted nothing to do with the war, or anyone who had anything to do with it. To this day, Vietnam veterans still suffer from the trauma of those days, and things that happened both in and out of military service."

"Let me give you an idea," I said. "There was a very popular television show in the 1970s that was set in the Korean Conflict, but was really about what was going on in Southeast Asia. It was about a group of Army doctors in a medical unit known as a Mobile Army Surgical Hospital, or 'MASH' unit. In fact, the name of the program was 'MASH'. Let me play you one episode that aired during that time."

I took a few minutes to tell Ben who the players were (I had a set of still shots for this), then told him, "Remember, while this episode is set in the Korean War, they are really talking about Vietnam here," and for the next twenty minutes we watched one of the more serious M*A*S*H episodes with very little humor.

When the episode ended, it was time for lunch, so I told Ben we would continue the discussion after lunch.

"Remember, we have some music to play while we eat!" I said, so we adjourned to the conference room.

When we did, Frank came in from the security office, so I told him to go ahead and take a couple of hours or so and go get lunch for himself and take a break, and when he came back we would continue for the afternoon. Kathy and I had stopped on the way home last night and collected a number of subs that she had put in the refrigerator when we came in the office that morning, so she retrieved them and some beverages while I set up some music on my Android. I connected it to the bluetooth sound system and while we ate, I played a number of songs from the 1930s forward, touching each of the genres that had been popular during each time period from then until now. Ben picked out a number of songs he liked, and he was fascinated with the development of instruments, particularly guitars and electronic keyboards, not to mention the methods of recording. Turns out he was a Beatles fan, as well!

Phillip was watching the external security cameras on his tablet and told us when Frank showed back up, so we wound up our conference room session and headed back to the lounge.

"So what is our afternoon subject?" asked Ben.

"You're not going to like it," I said. "But, you need to know some of the reasons our country is in debt."

"How much debt are we in?" he asked.

When I told him, he turned white, then red.

Chapter 51

Saturday – Week 3

As soon as everyone was settled in, I carried Ben back to the Depression and the reason for the establishment of Social Security. Since we had already talked about this the previous week, we didn't dwell on it but for a few minutes, but from there we went back to the 1960s and the Johnson Administration.

"Once the government began sending checks to individuals," I said, "it wasn't a big leap to go from distributing retirement checks to distributing money for other reasons. It was really accelerated with a program pushed through by President Johnson called the 'Great Society'. This was a program built on compassion for those having trouble making ends meet economically, and was supposedly started with the best of intentions. But, years later, it became clear this was just a slush fund used by politicians to garner votes."

"Wait a moment," he said. "Why are individuals entitled to funds from other citizens that they have not earned?"

"Well," I said, "that's the rub. Many believe that any payments made should be earned, or at least have some prospect of a return for those from whom the funds were taken in the first place."

"Absolutely!" agreed Franklin. "I have often said that those who are in poverty should be uncomfortable in that condition as an incentive to work their way out. Is this not a goal of this 'Great Society'?"

"No," said Phillip. "As a matter of fact, it's a trap. The economics of the program are structured in such a way that getting a job may actually bring in much less money than just continuing receiving payments from the government."

"And this is on purpose?" asked Ben.

"Yes," said Phillip. "I have family on welfare, and they just don't want a job. Why should they work when they can get paid for doing nothing. Believe me, there have been many arguments between those in our family who have jobs and those would could work, but won't."

"Just to be clear," I said, "there are government-sponsored efforts at employment, and they are somewhat effective, but if you're on government subsistence for any period of time, you are actually better off in some cases than if you had a job. Efforts have been made in recent years to reform the system, but the success has been small."

Ben shook his head. "How much money has been spent on these programs?"

"Trillions," said Miriam. "And it's getting worse. These programs are the primary reason we are in such debt, and there are millions of Americans on these programs with little hope of changing that trend."

Kathy spoke up next. "Ben, there is a whole culture of those on government assistance, and they really do feel entitled."

"Why are not Churches and other similar organizations caring for these individuals?" Ben asked.

"Well," said Kathy, "there are many programs offered by religions and civic organizations to help those in need – soup kitchens, food banks, job fairs, and the like, but they really end up in many cases being in competition with the free money the government distributes. Over time, those receiving this assistance have learned how to leverage all these programs and sometimes live better than those with full time jobs. During this last 'emergency', when a contagious virus was spreading across the country, Congress and the President spent over four trillion dollars to counteract the actions they'd taken to try to contain this disease, and much of that money went directly to taxpayers to replace lost wages as a result."

"Astounding!" exclaimed Ben. "This is the very reason many of us opposed using public funds for benevolent purposes."

The room got quiet for a moment as we let all that sink in. Then Ben said, "I still fail to see why the government is not using public organizations – particularly Churches – to address these issues."

'Well," I said. "I think that would be a better idea, but there's a problem. It stems from several Supreme Court decisions beginning with a case named 'Everson Versus the Board of Education' in 1947. That case was the genesis of the doctrine of the Separation of Church and State."

"But," said Ben. "as I understand the First Amendment to the Constitution, Congress cannot interfere in one's religion or the free exercise thereof. So what would that have to do with benevolent enterprises?"

"Let me tell you what the term 'Separation of Church and State' legally means in today's terms," I said, and for the next several minutes I, and the rest in the room, gave Ben the history that eventually disallowed any interactions whatsoever between the government and religion.

The furrow in Ben's brow said everything without his having to say a word, and once we reached a break in the history and our collective anecdotes, he had a serious question.

"Have the citizens of this country gone mad?" he asked. "Why would they allow their representatives, and especially the judiciary, to tell them that the Providence that provided for the establishment of this country is not allowed to have influence in its operation?"

I leaned towards Ben and asked, "Are you familiar with the story of the frog in the water pot?"

Ben screwed up his face. "The frog in the water pot? What has that to do with this subject?"

I told him the story of the frog in boiling water. "You see, Ben, most of these changes we've talked about that have given you pause happened in small pieces at a time over a period of two or three generations. What one generation allows, the next simply accepts. Add to that the general lack of understanding of the details of the Constitution, the nature of government, and the intent of the Founders, plus a general lack of knowledge of history, and you can see how we find ourselves in boiling water without realizing we actually put ourselves here in the first place."

Ben sat back in his chair. The room got quiet again. Then, Kathy spoke up. "You know, Dr. Franklin. In a few days you will be sitting across from the one individual in the nation with the most influence to change the path of where we're headed. I know Tom wants to give you all the information you need to give him your best advice, should he ask, but keep in mind it has taken us over 200 years to get to where we are."

"Yes," Ben said softly, "but it appears to be accelerating. How does one stop a bolder from rolling down a hill?"

"That's a good question," I said. "Believe me, there are many over the years who have asked similar questions, but yet here we are, still going in the wrong direction. The fact that we're sitting here talking to you about this just days before you have a meeting with the President of the United States is nothing short of miraculous – even Providential, or as my Pastor likes to quip: 'Do you think God had anything to do with that'? In your case, I'd have to answer 'yes'!"

"Tom," Ben said, "You are placing quite a burden on me. Are you sure I'm here by design?"

"Not necessarily," I said. "But if you are, it wasn't my design!"

For the rest of the afternoon we had a free-for-all discussion of how all this came to be and tried to fill in some of the blanks for Ben. It was sometimes a spirited and, yes loud, discussion, but by five p.m., we were all spent. It was time to bring it all to a close.

"Well," I said finally. "We've pretty much beat this horse to death, so let's knock off for the day. There is one more thing I want to make Ben aware of, and for this piece of cultural information, I need for it to be just Ben and me in the room. Miriam, if you don't mind, take Kathy home and I'll be on in a couple of hours. Bill, please get Ben's security detail set for the rest of the afternoon and tell them it'll be a bit longer, and I'll see the rest of you Monday."

They all agreed and left. When the door was closed, I told Ben. "There's one more part of culture that you need to be aware of, particularly with the increase in communications and the ability of any individual, regardless of age, sex, or location, to access virtually any kind of information. I wanted to do this with no others in the room because of its content, and I think you'll agree with that in a few minutes. It's a sensitive subject, but one I know you've already had some small exposure to."

"Oh?" asked Ben. "And what might that be."

"I know you spent some time in France."

"Yes," he said. "I was our first Ambassador to His Majesty in Paris."

"Yes," I said, "and I know the lifestyles in France at the time were somewhat, shall we say, a bit looser than here in the states." Then I pulled up an image of some of the more scantily clad women in Eighteenth Century France."

Ben smiled a wicked smile and said, "Yes. Your term 'looser' is very accurate."

"Well," I said, "since then, practices along these lines have become completely unhinged and global. You need to be warned how the word 'loose' is not a strong enough word these days. I am going to demonstrate just this once by showing you some images and a couple of video clips that anyone in the world can now access on the Internet."

I pulled up a couple of images from some "men's magazine" sites, then a couple of short videos from some of the seedier sites on the Internet. When they were finished, Ben looked at me with the same expression he had on his face that first evening initially viewed the first television. For the first time, Ben Franklin was embarrassed. So was I.

Then, as if planned, we were both looking at the floor!

Chapter 52

Saturday – Week 3

Finally, I said, "OK. One last major piece of the cultural puzzle, and it's one that affects a major argument within the government right now. Addiction."

"Addiction? To what?" asked Ben.

"Drugs, primarily."

"What manner of drugs?"

"Ben, with the increase in science, particularly chemistry, many new compounds over the years have been developed which have greatly enhanced our ability to treat and cure diseases. Those pills you take every day are good examples."

Ben nodded. "Yes," he said, "and I must say they appear to be remarkable. I feel better now than I have in years!"

"Exactly," I said. "But, there's a down side. Each of these compounds has side effects that must be managed. In your case, you probably don't even feel any side effects, but some, particularly those for pain and for treating mental disorders and/or the side effects of other compounds, can be misused. And they are! Additionally, some less than honest individuals with chemistry skills have created compounds whose only function is to affect an individual's mind and emotional responses."

"Explain some of these, if you please," Ben said.

"Well," I said. "Let me give you one that was prevalent when I was younger. I can't remember the exact chemical name, but its initials are LSD. It is an hallucinogenic drug that completely alters your perception of reality. Some of my generation simply killed themselves believing they were doing something they could not actually do, like jumping off of a cliff, or walking in the path of vehicles. Others simply took so much they overdosed to the point the body just shut down and they died. In other cases, individuals did things they would never have done in their right minds. It destroyed many promising young people."

"How many of these compounds are there?"

"Hundreds," I said. "Today's problem centers around something called 'opioids'. These chemicals are designed to manage pain. But taken improperly, or worse, modified to be stronger than intended, they produce a false sense of euphoria that is highly addictive, and dangerous when not monitored. Thousands die each month from opioid addiction."

"I see," said Ben. "I suppose each generation down through history has had its means of dealing with life's issues. How is this an argument inside our government?"

"It relates to where many of these drugs come from, primarily drugs like cocaine and opioids. Many of these come from across our southern border with Mexico, and originate there and in other countries in South America. But the argument is not about the drugs themselves, but about our failure to stem the tide of foreigners streaming across our border, some with nefarious intentions."

Ben thought for a moment, then said, "When presented with these documents required for my citizenship, I paid attention to some of the historical articles, and listened to the explanations for their purpose. I also understand there are requirements for anyone wishing to set foot our our shores, and I understand the reasons for these restrictions, particularly with the large population now."

"Yes," I said. "With the turmoil in the world, if we didn't control our borders, we'd have no country in short order."

"I agree," said Ben. "But I assume the Congress has laws in place for just this purpose?"

"They do," I said, "but that turmoil I just mentioned has greatly increased the number of people attempting to come here and bypass those laws. Congress simply has not kept up with the reality, and it's been a big argument for a while now."

"But why?" asked Ben. "Do we not now have the capability to simply close the border?"

"Yes," I said. "We have the ability, but not the will."

"Why in Heaven's name not?"

"Politics," I said flatly. "One side of the political debate believes in more or less open borders and many on that side see these individuals as potential voters for candidates they favor. The other side says they're wrong on both counts, and both sides play political games with this issue."

"You know," said Ben. "I've had conversations with General Washington about political factions, and he expressed his fear of them. It appears he was right."

"Doesn't matter," I said. "They're a reality, and were almost from the start. When you have three people in a room, you have at least two factions."

"Are you trying to enter my philosophical arena?" Ben asked with a smirk.

"Absolutely!" I said with a grin.

"All this is because of drugs?"

"Not really," I said. "And we just went the long way around to explain how drug addiction, and the availability of addictive substances, affects not only the culture, but many areas of government. For example, it is illegal to manufacture, sell, and even possess many of these substances, and our jails and penitentiaries are full of offenders. This, of course, clogs our court dockets, ties up our law enforcement personnel, and overloads our hospital emergency rooms. Government is forced to deal across the board with all these issues, and our citizens have, in many cases, just accepted this new reality. In many of the inner city areas it is not a pretty picture."

"This is a widespread problem, then?" asked Ben.

"Yes, and that's the point of this discussion," I agreed. "This problem touches almost every facet of our society, even though the number of people abusing these substances is a small minority. But, the effects, as we just discussed, have to be dealt with. What's worse, is that it is rampant in our schools so it's something that Americans have to deal with from their youth through their retirement."

Ben sat for a moment, trying to decide how to respond. "I should like to say that I am disappointed that our citizens would allow these abuses, but I wish to study this subject a bit further, especially in light of the size and scope of the country that, to me only a few days ago, was only thirteen colonies and a fraction of the population."

"Well," I said. "Do not put this at the top of items to be studied in detail, because the problems we face in this country are many and varied, but you cannot understand our government's policies entirely without factoring in this problem, as well as all the others we've discussed."

Ben shifted in his seat as he said, "I can understand why you had trepidation about today's subjects. They are somewhat depressing."

"I know," I said. "But, I am an optimistic individual, as I know you are, so let's leave this subject for the weekend. We can take any of these back up as necessary as we prepare next week for your trip."

Ben thought about that for a second, then slapped his legs as he stood. "Excellent idea! Shall we adjourn, then. I do believe I shall sleep well tonight despite these troubling subjects!"

I laughed and said, "Well, I certainly hope so! By the way, would you like to attend Church with us in the morning?"

Ben thought, and said, "I do believe I would like to hear your Pastor's sermon again this week. I very much enjoyed his last one. Shall I meet you at the same entrance tomorrow morning?"

"That'll be a good plan," I said. "If you'll be there around ten forty-five, either Kathy or I will meet you. It'll probably be Kathy since I'll be teaching my Sunday School class."

"Oh yes, I had forgotten. What is your lesson tomorrow?"

"We are studying the Book of Daniel. We are in the middle of a lesson about his prophecies. This week we're discussing his 'Seventy Weeks' prophecy."

"Would it meet with your approval for me to sit in on your class?"

I was a bit surprised. "Well, of course! If you want to do that, then be at that same entrance at nine forty-five and I'll meet you there."

"Excellent!" said Ben, "assuming I do not let the morning get away from me, I shall see you then."

"Great!" I said.

We went to collect Frank, and we all left for the night. I told Frank the schedule and how to get to the Church, which Frank was already familiar with, so I just told him where and when to drop Ben off. I also invited him to join us, but he said he'd just remain outside to provide additional security if that was OK. Since our Church had a rotating security team, I promised to introduce him to the team leader.

That done, we all left and I headed home.

When I arrived, Kathy had dinner waiting. I sat down at the table, she said the blessing and we began to dig in.

"So, how did tonight's session go?"

"Well, it's all done. He's been given all the major highlights of life in twenty-first Century America, so next week we try to put a cohesive picture together for his meeting with the President."

"Just what exactly did you discuss with him tonight", she asked?

"The big three," I said. "Sex, politics, and religion."

Chapter 53

Sunday – Week 4

I usually arrive a few minutes early for my class, so I went extra early this morning, because I wanted to have time to get Ben settled before we started. One thing you learn about Ben Franklin, though, is that even as Ben Folger, consultant, he's still a commanding presence in a room. His new clothing and eyewear made him look more like a "Folger" than a "Franklin", but I wasn't sure if anyone else would see the difference, so I was a bit concerned that I'd be telling people 'No, he doesn't look like Ben Franklin!' As it turns out, that wasn't the case. My class pretty much accepted him as presented, and ten minutes into the class, he was just another visitor to Tom's Class at Northside Baptist. He was charming, but he kept things low key. When we went into the service, some of the folks who'd seen him the last time, including the Pastor, welcomed him back, but other than that, he was, again, Ben Folger, visitor to Northside.

After the service, we went back to our house, and I grilled out burgers for all of us and we had a great lunch, as we discussed all that had happened in the last several days.

"So, Ben," asked Kathy, "you've been here a little over two weeks now. How do you like the twenty-first century so far?"

Ben smiled as he began. "I must say, there is much of what I see that could never have been predicted. But one thing I am gratified to observe is the spirit of the people. I immensely enjoyed the interactions I witnessed today in your Church service, and the way you, Tom, and your staff work together, not to mention the relationship I see between the two of you here. I believe my friends back in my time would feel the same way."

"Well," she said smiling, "you have certainly adapted to the time well!"

"I thank you madam, but there is much left for me to see. The conversations I had with you, Tom, and the rest yesterday afternoon, particularly the private talk Tom and I had last afternoon, lead me to believe there are factions of the population I have yet to be exposed to, but there have always been areas of society that present themselves as less than ideal. Still, I am encouraged to see the spirit of those I've met thus far."

"Are you beginning to get enough of a picture of today's America that can translate into your first meeting with the President?" she asked.

Ben chuckled a bit and said, "I am far from ready for that meeting as yet, but I feel there is sufficient time for me to present myself satisfactorily when I travel to this 'Oval Office' I've heard about. I certainly wish to present myself well when I do go, so there is some work still left for me."

"Well, Ben," I said, "you need to remember that while you'll be in the presence of the President of the United States, he'll be in the presence of Dr. Benjamin Franklin, who was not only instrumental in the production of the Constitution he has sworn to protect, but you personally knew all the other Founders. I doubt he'll be able to compare that with any other meeting he's had in his life!"

Ben smiled. "We shall see, sir. But one thing I can tell you. Once someone is in a present position of power and authority, others who have been, tend to fall from grace somewhat!"

"Yes," I said. "Good point. I doubt either of you will feel you have the upper hand, so I predict a meeting of two giants – one from now, and one from then."

Ben and Kathy both nodded. "We shall see, sir. We shall see," he said.

"If it is agreeable with you, I have something I'd like you to do with me this afternoon."

"And what might that be?", he asked.

"It is called 'America's Pastime', and you've already seen a bit of it that first night you were here. You recall the first images you saw on television?"

"Yes!" exclaimed Ben. "I have wanted to ask you to explain that event. It seemed that a great multitude of people were excited about what was happening, and I should like for you to explain that to me."

"Let's adjourn to the living room, then, and we'll explain it to you."

You know, it takes a while to explain baseball to someone who's never heard of it or seen a game. While we didn't only talk about the rules of the game, we went into the living room at one fifteen, and when the game began at two-thirty, there were still explanations to be made. Kathy and I tag-teamed the explanation, and hopefully it wasn't too discombobulated.

"This game is between the Atlanta Braves baseball team and the Arizona Diamondbacks. It's played in Phoenix, Arizona in a stadium that has a motorized roof that can be closed when the heat is too intense, and they have an artificial grass on the field that requires little maintenance."

When the pre-game program started and they showed a picture of the field, Ben said, "Are you saying, sir, that all that grass is not really grass?"

"Correct," I said. "Yesterday we talked about all the chemical compounds developed over the years. This grass is one of those developments. I don't know exactly how it's made, but this stuff doesn't grow, so each blade had to be placed individually, and the entire surface assembled into sections and woven together.

I read somewhere the other day they spent over two and a half million dollars to replace the grass that took so much maintenance out there in the desert."

"All for a game?"

"Yes," I said. "But when you realize that over eighty games will be played there this summer, and that they could average as many as 30,000 people at each of those games, there's lots of money being spent just for admission, not to mention all the money spent while there on food and souvenirs. Two million dollars is not that much money in the grand scheme of things."

"Careful, Mr. Reed. You sound like a Congressman!"

Well, that was actually funny.

As the game began and progressed, there were several times I paused the game to explain what was happening. After about the tenth time, Ben shook his head and said, "Sir, I shall never master this game! It seems there are so many rules!"

"Oh, there are, Ben. There are!" said Kathy. "Not only that, if you listen to the announcers, you'll hear a lot of statistics about different players and situations. But, don't give up. They don't call this America's Pastime for nothing. There are children that can spit out explanations of even the most obscure rules. When you watch this all the time, it all begins to sink in."

"If you say," said Ben. "But it appears to move so slowly!"

"At first, it does," I said. "But let me show you what's happening behind the scenes."

For the next several minutes I explained the subtleties of the game and how each action had a purpose, even the seemingly long pause between pitches, the looks between players, and even how the catcher crouched down. By the fifth inning, Ben was beginning to get into the game. The Braves won five to four with a double in the top of the ninth, and they held the score even with the bases loaded at the bottom of the inning. When the game was over, we discussed the game for a few minutes, and Ben was beginning to understand why so many people watched so many games over the course of a summer.

Finally, he said, "You must show me how to watch these games. It does seem something I might enjoy."

"Well, Ben, I don't want to get you too hooked on television. It can become quite a time waster, but on those nights when you just want to sit and do nothing after a long day, it does come in handy. Nevertheless, I'll be glad to show you how to find and watch these games, and I guarantee you your security guys will be aware of who's playing and when."

"Excellent!" said Ben. He patted his sides and rose. "I should get home. I have some reading to do before I retire tonight."

"No problem," I said. "We'll take you home to save your driver the trouble."

We all piled in the Navigator and took Ben home. On the way back Kathy and I discussed how Ben was doing.

"I think he'll be ready for the President," I said. "He seems to be getting quite a handle on how things work in modern day America."

"I hope you're right," said Kathy.

"Why? Are you worried?"

"I don't know," she said. "I'm afraid of a scene where here's Ben Franklin, Founding Father, in his first meeting with the current President of the United States, and all they end up talking about is whether it'll be the Braves or the Nationals who win the pennant."

Chapter 54

Monday and Tuesday – Week 4

At Monday's staff meeting, we had a long discussion laying out the week's work and schedule leading up to the trip to D.C. on Thursday afternoon in preparation for the Friday morning meeting with the President. While Ben had been exposed to a lot in the past three weeks, he was still having some difficulty putting all the pieces together to give him a picture of life, culture, and their effect on government, and more importantly, government's effect on life and culture. I had known this would be a daunting task from the get-go, but I doubt anyone other than Franklin could have pulled it off in this short amount of time.

Much of what we would do would be an all-hands-on-deck discussion helping Ben fill in the blanks. In the middle of all this was Ben's complete physical with Dr. Ken. It had been two weeks since his initial examination, and Ken wanted to do a full assessment prior to Ben's trip out of town. We had much to do between now and Thursday. We had the lunch and dinner meals delivered for the week, so no one had to worry about fetching meals, and we could maximize our time preparing not only Ben, but the rest of us as well. Wednesday would bring a briefing from the Secret Service and a video call from the White House protocol office in order to make sure there were no surprises. The plan was to fly out on the NSF Gulfstream at lunch on Thursday, checking into a nice, but affordable Hotel, followed by a motor tour of the Capitol from someone in the NSF Washington office.

So, the work began. We rewound all the way back to 1789, and marched forward through all the changes in America and Americans, and had discussions on why things were decided the way they were, not pulling any punches, and not making excuses. Needless to say it was an animated discussion, and on some points Ben had a really hard time understanding why 'anyone would make such a decision'. A good example was the Income Tax. He really had a hard time with that one, particularly with the concept of pre-pay confiscation of funds in the form or withholding taxes. He thought the Eighteenth and Twenty-First Amendments on Prohibition were a foolish waste of time, and he had a real problem with business licenses, calling them 'a form of government tyranny'.

But, it was the IRS that really gave him heartburn. I told him he was not alone in that feeling.

"Then, sir, why does the electorate not expel those who will not abolish this obvious theft?" he had asked in desperation.

"Ben," I said, "remember my analogy of the frog in boiling water?" Ben nodded. "Well, this is how we got here. The First World War had to be paid for. Then, it was World War Two, and Korea. Then, the so-called War on Poverty. Then the Cold War. The latest expenditure had to do with a nationwide health scare that essentially shut down the country for several weeks, and Congress voted to spend over four trillion dollars to help prop up the economy until we could all get back to work. In between all these were economic incentives to help other countries with various threats that could have propelled them into belligerency. Politicians are very adept at spending other people's money and making it look like it was someone else's fault. Besides, Congress has no appetite for cutting off their own power."

"Then why do not the States rise up and compel them to?"

"You mean, with the Convention of States?" I asked.

"Indeed! That was one of the last discussions we had just before completing the Constitution. Mr. Mason was very correct, and is it turns out prophetic, in pointing out the danger of leaving Congress alone in charge of the Amendment process."

"I realize that," I said, "but getting thirty four state legislatures to agree on a reason for a Convention of States is a very high bar, and when some of these states foresee a reduction in funds being funneled to them from Washington, they find reasons not to."

Ben's disappointment with the tax issue was great, but there were others as well. The increase in revenues had fed a massive growth in the size and scope of the government, and when he discovered an organizational chart of the Federal Government he was aghast. It was going to be a long week.

We met throughout the day, not even breaking in the conversation as we ate lunch and dinner, so by six-thirty, we were exhausted, and still had much to cover. Tuesday morning didn't go much better, though we were making progress. I could see we were going to burn ourselves out if we didn't have a break in the action somewhere. Luckily, that afternoon we had the exam at Dr. Ken's office, and I had an idea for something to take our minds off of things for a couple of hours. I hit up Kathy with it just before we left for Ken's office, and she agreed, so I told her to clue the rest of the group in. On the way over to Ken's office, I pitched the idea to Ben.

"Ben, you remember the movie we showed you the first week about the Revolution?"

"Yes. Very entertaining!" he said.

"Well, I think we all need a diversion. You saw that movie on the television set at the office. But, originally these movies were shown in theaters with a huge screen, and they're much more impressive when seen there. Would you like to see a movie tonight?"

Ben thought about that and said, "That might be interesting. What kind of a movie did you have in mind?"

"Well, my wife and I have a favorite movie that we've seen in theaters a number of times, and we never tire of it. It came out in the early 1980s. The local cineplex – another name for a movie theater – has something periodically they call 'Retro Night' where they play an old movie, and tonight's feature is that movie Kathy and I both like. Would you care to join us?"

"Certainly!" said Ben. "Tell me about this movie. What is it called?"

"Well," I said, "Kathy and I have seen this a ridiculous thirty-two times – in theaters! It's called 'Raiders of the Lost Ark', and it's a story that has a similar plot to your circumstance. Something from long ago is found to exist in the present day. An explorer called 'Indiana Jones' discovers the hidden Ark of the Covenant built by Moses and the Israelites. The movie starts at six-thirty, so we should be out by eight-thirty or so. What do you say?"

"I say fine, sir. Will Kathy be joining us for a thirty-third time?"

I chuckled and said, "Of course! In fact, I have asked her to invite the entire crew. It's all on me, and I'll even buy the popcorn and drinks. Just don't tell Dr. Ken about the refreshments."

Ben laughed and said, "Your secret is safe with me, sir!"

The exam went well, and Ken checked Ben out from stem to stern and pronounced him "in good shape for his vintage," which amused Ben. He adjusted his meds a bit, warned me about Ben's diet (Ben didn't rat me out), and afterwards I asked Ken if he had time for lunch with Ben and me. He immediately had his nurse juggle his appointments for the rest of the afternoon, and he, Ben and I went to a local restaurant where I'm guessing we made Ken's day.

Afterward we headed back to the office to finish out the day and collect the crew. We arrived in our own vehicles at the theater at six, grabbed the popcorn and drinks, and found some good seats in the theater. While we were waiting for the previews to start, I filled Ben in on what he was about see, and promptly at six-thirty the previews started. Then the movie, and I enjoyed it all over again. When it was over, we all headed out the front and prepared to leave.

We said goodnight to everyone, but just before she walked off, Miriam asked, "Thirty-two times, huh?"

Kathy nodded with a smile.

"You guys are nuts," and she turned around an walked to her vehicle and left.

Chapter 55

Wednesday and Thursday – Week 4

Frivolities out of the way, we were back to work on Wednesday morning, trying to put together the rest of the information Ben would need for his first meeting in the Oval Office. Like the previous two days, the conversations were brisk and Miriam's input was especially helpful, and some of the back and forth between Ben and her was interesting to watch.

At eleven we took the video call from the Protocol Office in the White House on the projection screen. The arrival plans were discussed, since we'd have to enter in stealth, and they told us the Secret Service would contact us with specific instructions on where to go and how to get through security. I had explained metal detectors and basic security protocols to Ben, but the Secret Service agents would give us specific details. Once there, we would be escorted to a holding room just off the Oval Office from where we would be led into the President's Office. Ben asked good questions about how to interact with the President. Kathy was also led through her meeting with the First Lady, which I found out later still thrilled her to no end.

Then the rest of us were addressed. I would be going in with Ben, and Miriam would be accompanying Kathy to the First Lady's meeting. She had not anticipated that, and had a big smile on her face when the call was over. Bill, Rick, and Phillip would avail themselves of a courtesy tour of the White House, then return to the holding room with the Secret Service handlers. Finally, they went over the exit procedures and the aftermath. We were told to expect an hour with the President, after which he would leave to go to Camp David. All this was followed up with a document dump in my secure email with all these details, as well as a timeline for the entire visit.

By then it was lunch, which we again had delivered, after which the Secret Service agents from Philadelphia came in and went through their security concerns – what to bring and/or not bring, how the White House security check would go. specifics of the covert entry, and finally a Q&A with the group until everyone was satisfied with what was expected. The last thing they admonished us to do was maintain secrecy about where we were going, and especially the details of the visit. Nothing we would see or hear could be divulged without their specific permission. No one had any problem with this. Our cover story was that we were at an NSF meeting.

They left, and we discussed the flight out of Philly to D. C. This would be Ben's first ride in any type of aircraft, and in this case it would be a pretty nice Gulfstream. I'd been on one before!

The rest of the day was basically cleanup on the historical information, and a quick check to see if we'd forgotten anything. We were to meet at the office and a van rented for the occasion would take us to the airport, and pick us up when we got back.

That night everyone went their separate ways, and the next morning we all rose early to prepare for our great adventure. At eleven, the van showed up and we all loaded up and headed for the airport. Since it was a private jet, we met it at a government-run terminal rather than the general terminal, so the check in was quick and easy, and they loaded all our luggage on the plane. Then we boarded, and I watched Ben carefully to see if he was navigating the process. He was only a bit shaky going up the stairs, but once inside, he had a nice wide seat to sit in, so we weren't jammed up against one another as we would be on a commercial airliner. While we were waiting I told Ben how the takeoff and flight would go, and to let us know if he had any problems. Since he was the reason for this trip, we would take whatever measures were necessary to make him comfortable.

"Ben," I said, "Here's what we call a 'barf bag'. If you feel queasy at any point, don't be embarrassed to use this. There might be a bit of turbulence while in the air, though the pilots will take care to avoid anything like that."

"You forget, sir," Ben said, "I have crossed the Atlantic on more than one occasion on a ship tossed to and fro, so I doubt this trip shall be any worse!"

"Yes," I said, "I had forgotten. Well, the flight will be less than an hour, and the worst part will be the landing. You'll feel like we're going to hit the ground, but we won't. You should do fine, but let me know if you have any problems. Otherwise, enjoy the view. We'll be several thousand feet off the ground, so there'll be lots of see, since it's a clear day all the way to D. C."

"Oh, yes," said Ben. "I am very much looking forward to that view!"

In a few minutes we took off and had a very uneventful flight, except for watching Ben's eyes as he stayed glued to the window the entire time.

We were met at Reagan National with another van belonging to the NSF and taken from there to our hotel. I checked us all in and got our room assignments, and we headed upstairs.

"Please tell me I'm not in the Nixon suite," said Bill when we got in the elevator.

"Oh, I don't think they have one of those anymore," laughed Kathy. I found out later they actually did! Everyone but Ben got the joke, but he was too busy watching the floors go by. Upstairs, we all went to our individual rooms, with Ben next door to us with a connecting door. We all gathered in our room to get the schedule straight, have one last discussion on the next day's business, and around eight everyone went to their own rooms and hit the sack. Friday was to be a monumental day for everyone – including the President of the United States, I suspected.

Chapter 56

Friday – Week 4

D. C.

The meeting with the President was at four p.m., the end of the week and the tail of the news week, just before the President would leave for the weekend. By 'sneaking' in through a covert entrance, the hope was that nobody would notice. The more under wraps we could keep the existence of Ben and his new role, the more he could do beyond politics and under the radar. Ben was totally on board with this approach, since he'd been a diplomat before and understood that while politics could be an ally, it could also be a powerful enemy. The fix was in!

We all arose early Friday morning and met again in our suite to set out the day's schedule. One of the things I wanted to do was take Ben on a tour of the Capitol to give him a sense of the history that was celebrated in the town. So, as soon as we could we all got in the van and headed out. Miriam had arranged for a tour guide to take us to the different historical sites with the understanding that we had to be back by lunch.

We saw all the historical sites from the Smithsonian (which I promised him we would visit), to the Washington Monument (which he thought exactly appropriate), to the Jefferson Memorial.

"Mr. Jefferson was a somewhat vain man, but quite brilliant with the quill," said Ben as he read some of the writings displayed at the memorial. "His expansion of the country I had read was seen with much more disdain in his time than it should have. Perhaps he had a vision many did not see. Still, like most men, he had his limitations. History has judged him well, though, I think."

The tour finished, we returned to the hotel where we had lunch and adjourned back to our suite to prepare for our trip to the White House. We left the hotel at one-thirty. We entered a nondescript entrance of a building not far from the White House where we were met by someone from the Protocol office. She accompanied us to an elevator that carried us to an underground passageway where the Secret Service had a security station and we underwent our first security scan for entrance into the White House. There was a vehicle very similar to a golf cart that carried us through the tunnel to the White House, and there was another security station where our credentials were again checked, and we passed through the metal detectors.

Finally through security, we were carried on a quick tour of the less public areas of the White House on the way to the Protocol Office, where we would receive last minute instructions for the Oval Office visit. I was nervous as a cat on a hot tin roof, as was Kathy, but Ben seemed to be unusually at ease, even anticipatory, of the event to happen within the next few hours.

Finally, an aide came to collect Kathy and Miriam for their visit to the First Lady, followed by another aide to fetch the rest of us and carry us to an anteroom. Once there, the Secret Service agents showed Ben and me the door to the Oval Office, and we waited for the word to enter while the remaining three went on their tour of the White House. Shortly afterward, the word came over their comm devices, and we arose and headed to the door. When it opened, Benjamin Franklin entered the oval office, me following behind, and history was again to be made.

When we entered, on the inside was the President's Chief of Staff who welcomed us and escorted us to two chairs opposite the famous Resolute Desk. A couple of minutes later, the President of the United States entered and we stood. He came directly over to us and I said, "Mr. President, I am Thomas Reed of the National Science Foundation, and it is my pleasure to introduce you to Dr. Benjamin Franklin."

Chapter 57

Friday – Week 4

The President of the United States

As I had introduced myself, the President gave me the perfunctory handshake, which was about what I expected since I was here as merely the escort for Ben. When I introduced Ben, the President turned his way, looked him square in the eye, grabbed his right hand, and overlaid his left hand on the handshake.

"Dr. Benjamin Franklin," he began. "This is a moment I will always remember as something that has never before occurred in history! It is a distinct pleasure to meet you."

Ben shook his hand and replied, "Sir, the pleasure is most assuredly mine. As you may imagine, I still find myself adjusting to my current situation, and this event shall certainly endure in the memories I take to my grave, and they shall occupy an honored place in those memories. I thank you, sir, for your kind invitation."

They concluded the handshake and the President said, "Please, have a seat. There is so much I wish to ask you, and I assume there are some observations you might have for me."

"Oh, I have my opinions, sir, but I wish for a fruitful exchange, so I expect we shall have a meeting of the minds, as it were."

The President smiled and said, "Well first, tell me about your experience your first day here. I understand from the reports I've read you took this massive change in your status very much in stride."

"To be honest, Mr. President," Ben said, "I was as much bewildered as I was perturbed. Once I realized that the information Tom here was giving me was accurate, I must admit my curiosity ascended. There were a few moments..." and he paused for a second, "...a few moments when my anger wanted to surge, but when I was assured that my – how do we put it, duplicate? - yes, that my 'duplicate' was still intact and unaware of my condition in this time and place, I allowed my curiosity to resurge. But, to answer your question specifically, that first day was one of the most amazing surprises. That, Mr. President, has yet to cease. I find more amazing surprises each day."

"I suppose so," said the President. "I cannot imagine being in such a position, and I'm afraid I would not take things so well. I appreciate your candor, and I know Tom here has issued his apologies for our putting you in this position. Even so let me add, on behalf of the United States government, my apologies as well. But, I assure you, your presence here has the possibility of having great effect on this government that you were instrumental in establishing."

"That, sir," said Ben, "might actually make all this worthwhile."

The President then turned to me. "Mr. Reed, I understand you and your staff have given Dr. Franklin an overview of how history has changed things since his time. How do you feel about the process thus far."

"Well, Mr. President," I said, "I can imagine no other individual in history who would so quickly assimilate information as has Dr. Franklin here. My wife and I have commented many times to each other how amazed we are at his ability to adjust to circumstances that any other individual might find daunting." I looked over at Ben and said, "But this man is no ordinary individual."

The President said, "Well, Mr. Reed, I do believe we already knew that from history," and he chuckled a bit. Then he turned to Ben.

"Dr. Franklin. I would like to say, first of all, that I had not even considered the fact that you might speak with what we consider to be a British accent. But, at the time you arrived here, you had only been truly separated from England for a short period of time. Have you had any difficulties understanding current day vernacular?"

Ben smiled, "Some. But, these folks," and he motioned to me, "were very adept at acquainting me with certain idioms that one might encounter. They even went so far as to arrange an excursion to a movie theater for a viewing of something called 'Raiders of the Lost Ark'. I tell you sir, there was plenty of vernacular to be heard that night."

We all laughed – the President the loudest.

"Very good, Dr. Franklin, very good!" said the President. "Well, let's get down to business, shall we?"

"Indeed, sir, and please, my name is Ben."

"OK, Ben," said the President with a smile. "Give me your frank opinion of what you see, first in American culture. We'll talk about the government separately."

"Well, sir," Ben began, "I would first say that I am not surprised at the resilience of our citizenry. The accomplishments and inventiveness excel beyond anything I could have imagined, and the interactions I have had, limited though they may be at this point, give me some evidence of the great hope we had sought as we labored to establish a new nation. With that I am very pleased."

The President smiled and nodded.

"However," said Ben, "there is also much to be concerned for. While I am no saint, as I assume history has thus spoken, some things that I see occurring, and behaviors I have discovered, give me great pause. To say that the same was not felt in my time would be inaccurate, but I fear things are not getting better. We placed so much faith in the People when we created the Constitution, but as I said earlier, my interactions have been limited. My hope is that these troubling activities are in the minority where they should be."

"I see," said the President. "Is there any one activity that troubles you the most?"

Ben paused before continuing. "Yes, Mr. President. I would say this practice of curing sexual sins by the death of babies in the womb would have to eclipse other activities that might give me concern. I fail, sir, to understand how a civil society could accept such an atrocity, and frankly, why the elimination of this practice would not be among the chief concerns of the citizenry."

"I agree with you," said the President. "I hope you're aware that this is something that started out as one thing and gradually grew into something else."

"Oh, I understand, sir," said Ben. "However, now that we are here, I am troubled at the lack of outcry, and even more troubling are those who celebrate this act. I read earlier this week that this atrocity has occurred some sixty million times since it was made legal? There is a word I've discovered for this, Mr. President," Ben said softly. Then he leaned forward and said, "Our country is guilty of Infanticide! And, for the ones who are born, we are stealing their livelihood in unrelenting spending. We, sir, are guilty of both murder and theft!"

Now, get the picture. Here's the current sitting President of the United States with one of the Founding Fathers of the country sitting before him accusing the United States of heinous crimes. You gotta give Franklin credit. He did not shrink from giving his opinion. Just shows you should be careful what you ask for.

Ben sat back, as did the President. "Ben," he said, "there are not many people that I would allow to come in to this office and accuse my citizens of such as this, but your stature certainly allows you that. Having said that, I cannot say I entirely disagree with you. I fear I may make things even worse with this question. Do you realize that your government has given funds to the largest abortion provider in the country?"

Ben sat up. "Sir. I was aware of no such arrangement. Public funds used to kill innocents in the womb??" He sat back, exhaled, and said, "Maybe we were not so clever as we thought a few days ago."

The President furrowed his brow and asked, "What do you mean, 'a few days ago'?"

Ben looked at me, then back at the President. "Perhaps this little piece of information was not in your reports." he said. "When I was nabbed off the street in Philadelphia, I was coming out of Independence Hall where we had just finished signing the Constitution."

Now the President was shocked. "What?" he asked, then looked over at me. "Is he serious?"

"Yes, Mr. President." I said. "It was one of the first of many surprises Ben sprung on me. Not only that, a few days after his arrival, we took a drive through Philadelphia and passed by Independence Hall, and that's when Ben dropped another little nugget on me. You may be aware of the event where Dr. Franklin was leaving Independence Hall and was stopped by a lady who asked what kind of government they had given us, and Ben's reply was 'A republic, if you can keep it'?"

"Yes," said the President, "I am very aware of that event."

"Well, Sir," I said, "he was forming that very reply when we plucked him out and brought him to present day."

The President was still in shock. "What you're saying is that, literally, just a few days ago, you and the other Founders were putting finishing touches on our Constitution?"

"Indeed," said Ben. "The last major addition was that of the ability of the States to call a Convention for the purpose of bypassing Congress and offering amendments to the several states."

"Yes," said the President. "I am very aware of the Convention of States provisions, but it has never been used."

"Well, sir," said Ben, "if our Congress is unable to take corrective actions, perhaps it is time for it to be used."

The President's eyebrows raised and he said, "Perhaps you're right. There actually are a couple of groups attempting that as we speak. And, I guess that brings us to the subject of the current government. Might I assume you never envisioned a government so large as our current one?"

Ben smiled a wry smile and said, "That, Mr. President, would be an understatement. In fact, were my contemporaries aware of what has transpired, our Constitutional arguments would have been much more vociferous. I am aware of something called the 'Annotated Constitution' that is nearly 3,000 pages long. I have seen this monstrosity and I can tell you, sir, that I am saddened by my countrymen in their inability to read their own language!"

The President gave his own wry smile and said, "I would expect no less a reaction from any other of our Founders. I know Tom here has explained, in the limited time between your arrival and now, that many forces over the years brought these changes. But, you must be aware that reversing any government program is exceedingly more difficult than enacting it in the first place."

"Yes," said Ben, "I concede that. Our purpose was to make enacting laws decidedly more difficult than in a monarchy, but we also knew that sword had a double edge. Again, we hoped the People would put representatives in place to resist such changes."

"Well," said the President, "in a political environment where the re-election rate is over ninety percent, many in Congress serve for several decades before retiring. Also, many times the two political parties spend as much time pounding each other as they do looking out for the nation's best interest. Unfortunately it is a political reality in my time."

Ben nodded. "Yes. General Washington – sorry, President Washington – was very outspoken in the dangers of factions, and was very much opposed to political parties, but we saw no way to prevent them without further limitations on liberty. Again, much hope was placed on the People."

"Well, Ben," said the President, "the People have managed to last over 230 years, so I don't think your hope was misplaced. But, now, with the government so large, and in so much debt, plus the divisions we have in our society of how to cure these ills, I feel we find ourselves at a crossroads. Have you any ideas you might bring to the table?"

Ben thought for a moment, then said with a smile, "Well, as we have just discussed, I have only been here a few days. I should be happy to offer any thoughts I might have once I am able to better understand all the forces that got us here, and all the forces keeping us here. Might you give me that opportunity?"

The President smiled. "You know, Ben. I had already decided how to accomplish that very thing. Let me outline something I have in mind, if you're willing."

"Certainly, Sir!"

For the next twenty minutes the President outlined a plan for Ben to become a special advisor to the President of the United States on the subject of government and its proper role in American life. There was some back and forth on how to accomplish this, and in the end Ben accepted his proposal.

Finally, the President announced, "Then, Dr. Benjamin Franklin. Consider yourself the special advisor to the President of the United States. I expect good things to come from this relationship."

The President then addressed me. "Mr. Reed, I know this is not exactly what you signed up for, but I understand Dr. Franklin now has his own residence not far from your office, and that he has an office in your facility?"

"Yes, sir. He's pretty well situated."

"Fine. Then I would like you to continue to serve as his primary liaison and serve as a primary resource for him for the foreseeable future."

Then he looked at Ben. "Dr. Franklin, you would work along side Tom and his staff, but you will have a direct contact here on my staff with the ability to arrange a meeting any time you feel the need to come in person. We will make sure all the resources of the Federal Government are available for your research, and make available any department where you might wish to make direct inquiries. Funding will be added to the NSF's budget from a discretionary fund the Congress has authorized for any additional expenses you may incur, and any facility or agency of the Federal Government will be open to you as you require. Would that suit you both?"

"Very much, Mr. President!" said Ben.

"Yes. I completely agree, sir," I said.

"Good. Then its decided!" said the President. "Tom, I understand you are here with your staff, and that your wife is visiting mine."

"That's correct, sir," I said. "She was very excited to do so."

"Give me a minute," said the President. He went over to the door, opened it and said a few words to his Chief of Staff, then returned to his desk. We both rose as he did.

"In the few moments we have left," he said, "I again want to say what a monumental pleasure it is to be in this moment with you Dr. Franklin – Ben." and he smiled. "I thank you for the service you have given to your country, both in the eighteenth century, and hopefully now in the twenty-first. I fear that it may be years, maybe even decades, before this truth can be told, but my hope is that the work you and I may be able to do will be the stuff of legend by the time we're finished."

"Well, Mr. President," said Ben with a grin, "according to some reports I have seen, some think I am already a legend. Perhaps now I may be able to add some truth to those rumors."

The President let out a great laugh, and we were laughing with him when the door opened. In came Bill, Rick, Phillip, and finally Kathy, Miriam and the First Lady. Kathy was practically on cloud nine.

I may have banked up several thousand points with her right then and there.

Part 3

Ben Franklin – Special Assistant to the President

Chapter 58

After we left the Oval Office, the Chief of Staff took us into his office and gave Ben and me some contact information, as well as communication protocols for documents and emails. Then he asked if we'd like to see some of the more private areas of the White House, which was a no-brainer for us! He took us upstairs to the residence and, while we were not allowed into the sleeping areas, we got a pretty good idea how the President might relax after a day 'in the office'. Then he took us to some places I didn't even know existed. Since he was aware of Ben's true identity, he showed us some of the areas that dated back to the eighteenth and early nineteenth centuries, including some places still charred by the fire during the War of 1812. Then, he took us on a quick tour of some of the Presidential portraits in the White House.

One of the places we went just before exiting the same way we came in was the first floor of the residence, where the formal receptions are held. He took us into the Green Room. Hanging there was a portrait painted in 1767 by an artist named David Martin. It was a fifty by forty inch portrait of a young Benjamin Franklin. I noticed it immediately, but it took Ben a few moments, and he was taken aback when he saw it. We all got another of those now-patented Ben Franklin looks as the realization set in.

He looked at me and said, "I remember sitting for that portrait! That document I'm holding is actually a deed belonging to my friend Robert Alexander who commissioned this portrait." He looked at the Chief of Staff and said, "I am humbled, sir, that this portrait, in this fine condition, is now hanging in the residence of the President!" He shook his head. "I would never have believed it!"

The Chief of Staff laughed and said, "Well, I thought you might enjoy this. I can't wait to tell the President your reaction."

"Oh, of course. Again, I'm humbled," he said.

We looked around the first floor for a few more minutes until the Chief of Staff said, "Well, gentlemen and ladies, if you would follow me, we need to release this floor before someone starts asking questions as to why we have it closed off."

"Oh!" I said. "It didn't occur to me you would close off portions we would be visiting. By all means, let us get out of the way."

"Oh, you're not in the way!" he said. "I just want to maintain the secrecy. If you'll follow me, we'll head to the exit.

A few minutes later we were coming out the same way we'd entered and into the waiting van. By now it was after six and we were beginning to get a bit hungry, not to mention a bit tired from the day's activities, though I was sure getting to sleep tonight would be a bit tough after all we'd been through.

As we left, Ben had a question. "Tom, we went over several of the wars our country has been through since Independence, and that one of those wars this century was very costly both in many ways. This war in Vietnam – I understand there is a remarkable memorial here. Would it be possible to visit that before we retire for the day?"

"Of course!"

I told the driver to take us the to the memorial, and upon our arrival he let us off at the curb and we walked the remaining short distance. Bill served as our guide as he'd been there and I hadn't, and as we made our way down the walkway the memorial came into view and just seemed to go on and on. It didn't take long for the enormity of not just the memorial itself, but of all the names on it set in, we suddenly got real quiet.

"I have heard of this for years," I finally said, "but I had no idea of the effect it would have on me."

Ben walked up to the wall and rubbed his fingers over some of the names. Then he stood back and did a long end to end take of the entire wall. He hung his head and shook it, then came back over to where I was standing.

"We ask so much of our young," he said. "It is one thing to shed young blood in defense of our own shores, but...so...many...lives in a land of such seemingly insignificance! This will be difficult for me to understand."

Miriam agreed and said, "Now you get some idea of why there was so much turmoil when this war was going on. I still don't understand it myself."

We just stood there and looked at it for a few minutes, until Kathy said, "I don't know about everyone else, but I'm not sure I can stand here much longer. All these lives....."

"Yeah," I said. "Let's go", and we all headed back to the access road in silence. When the van came back around we all got in with no one saying a word until were were on the way back to the Hotel.

Finally, Ben said, "I apologize. I had not expected to put such a gloomy end to such an enormous day."

"Not at all your fault, Ben," I said. "Tell you what. Let's find a good restaurant, have a great meal, and celebrate today. I don't know if the rest of you realize it, but we made history today – again!"

"Yes!" said Ben. "And I have a rather large task to begin. I shall need the help of each of you."

"And," I said, "You shall have it!"

The driver recommended a local restaurant and soon we were in the middle of a delicious meal talking about the White House and all the sights we'd seen that day. A couple of hours later we were back at the hotel, again in our suite where we set out the schedule for the next day. Rise at nine, have breakfast, then pack up and head for Reagan National for the short hop home. That done, everyone headed for their rooms.

The next day in the plane headed back to Philly, Ben was again enthralled with the sights passing beneath us. I had already thought about what to do next.

"Everyone take the weekend off," I said, "and let's not get started until one p.m. Monday. We'll take Monday easy and simply to an aftermath meeting then, and probably get an idea on the path forward. Don't think about this during the weekend. Rest up and take it easy. And, in case I haven't said it yet, great job, everyone!!"

That got an applause.

Chapter 59

Friday Week 4 Through Monday Week 5

Everyone did as ordered. I didn't hear a peep out of anyone all weekend long. Kathy and I had a serious prayer of thanks Saturday morning and we relaxed the rest of the day. Ben didn't come to Church, and after the service we went back home and just watched the game on TV. We slept in Monday, did a couple of errands that we'd both been putting off, then after lunch Kathy and I went into the office to look at our next steps.

I got there a few minutes early to check emails and sure enough, there was one from the White House encrypted with the key the Chief of Staff had given me. The document that was attached contained a list of preliminary contacts in the White House, the Pentagon, at the Library of Congress, and at the National Archives. These individuals had been given instructions on behalf of the President of the United States to provide us with whatever materials requested, no questions asked. They also had secure emails set up for them, so I emailed each one just to introduce myself. For the time being, I would be the one requesting materials, simply because that would expedite things. But, I told each of them there might be others from our office who would be authorized to make requests, and that I'd provide that contact information when necessary.

Finally, everyone else showed up, and we sat down. It was all smiles around the table. After the pleasantries, I started things off.

"OK, people, we have a new mandate. Up until now we were involved in a highly experimental scientific enterprise, but last Friday that all changed. The focus for the foreseeable future is to support Ben in his new position as Special Advisor to the President on Government and its Proper Role in American Life. Let's see, 'SAPOGAIPRIAL'. No, that's just too hard. How about just 'SAP'?"

They all laughed.

"No," I said, "to keep things under wraps, let's just refer to Ben as The Consultant. That'll be fuzzy enough. If anyone asks what he's consulting on, just tell them 'Government History'. That'll sound boring enough they should just go away."

The group nodded, so I continued. "Ben, I'm not sure where to start. We covered so much in a couple of weeks that we might have overloaded you. What do you think?"

"I have been considering that very question, Tom," said Ben. "There's a term I ran across this weekend. 'Connect the dots'. I think that may be where to start."

"Yes," I said. "I think that's exactly it. Connecting the dots. How about this: Ben, get us a list, starting with the day after your leaving the eighteenth Century, of things you don't fully understand. I know that this will all take quite a while, but we will use that as a map, as it were, on how to proceed."

"I agree," said Ben. "That is a lengthy list."

"I know," I said. "But, we can turn that into something more manageable. Next, you need something more efficient for note-taking, correspondence, research, et cetera, so I have an idea. I know you don't have any keyboard skills, so I'd like to attack that in three ways. First, we'll teach you how to use a computer keyboard and type more efficiently. Second, you need a more in depth abilities in using the word processing software, so I'll get you some instruction in that. Finally, there is some software that will take your speech and turn into words on the screen, so we'll set you up with that and show you how to use it."

Miriam spoke up. "I can help with all of those."

"Great!" I said. "The job's yours. Secondly, you need a research assistant. Someone who will request and manage your materials, help organize your notes, do proofreading, those kinds of things. I know you already know how to do some of that since, surprise, you're a newspaperman, but it never hurts to have someone to help out and free you up for actual research."

Miriam again. "I can do that as well".

Kathy said, "Can I help, too? I was pretty good at research in college."

"Done!" I said, "With your permission, Ben."

"Of course!" he said. "Delighted to have your assistance, both of you."

Next, I said, "When it comes to military matters, Bill and Phillip both are ex-military – Bill was in the Navy, and Phillip was in the Marines – so they can help you out with military-related issues. Miriam's expertise in history will also help put things in context. On things World War 2 and the subsequent decades, that's a bit of a forté for me, so I can help out there. But, we all know American history pretty well, so don't be afraid to get multiple viewpoints. I promise we won't be offended. Kathy can serve as your administrative assistant for anything you might require in your preparations. She's really good at that! Finally, the President has opened up the entire government for you, so let's think of ways we might be able to use that resource."

"Agreed, and thank you all," said Ben. "I should have hoped for such a well rounded group of individuals in my former life. This should be exciting."

"I hope so," I said, and everyone around the table agreed.

We took a few more minutes to set the schedule for the rest of the week, then I broke up the meeting.

"I have some things to do, including getting that software you need for your transcription, so Miriam, how about Ben's first keyboard lesson. Be sure to get him further along in word processing use and get him started learning qwerty keyboards."

"Kwerty?" asked Ben.

"You'll see," I said with a chuckle. "Kathy, how about seeing what supplies Ben might need to begin this process and get his office set up, and lets get that in here so he can hit the ground running. Bill, for right now, you and Phillip are back to normal duty, with the proviso that you'll serve as military and history consultants whenever Ben needs you."

"Check," said Bill.

"Copy that!" said Phillip.

"Great. Let's get to it then!" and everyone scattered.

I had some paperwork to do in my office, so I got to that. Kathy did an inventory of Ben's office and left to go get some supplies. Miriam and Ben adjourned to his office where they began Ben's first lesson in keyboards. After I'd been in the office a few minutes, I got a bit thirsty, so I headed to the break room to get something to drink. As I turned into the break room, Ben's office door across the hall was open, and I heard him say, "Whatever possessed them to arrange the alphabet in this order?"

Qwerty lessons were going strong.

Chapter 60

Week 5

By the end of the week, we had settled into a pretty good rhythm. Mornings were spent in discussion on how and why things are the way they are, with the afternoons spent looking at new material, and looking at what materials we might still need. Miriam schooled Ben in keyboard and mouse operation, a refresher on to booting up and shutting down his computer, and what to do if something came up, how to start up Apps on the desktop, a more extensive course in use of the word processor, and finally instructions on browser use, and in particular, how to use search engines and bookmarking pages, as well as organizing bookmarks. I got several chuckles listening to the back and forth between Miriam and Ben, particularly when she'd use a term that either had yet to be defined for Ben, or more often, was still misunderstood by him.

Kathy got his office set up, then moved back into her original office adjacent to Ben's, and settled back into her administrative assistant role. It was great having her back on the staff!

I took it upon myself to give him a course in files and the arrangement of the filing system on the drive. I likened it to entering a room by the front door and going room to room storing stuff. By thinking of the filesystem in physical terms rather than digital terms, he was able to pick up the concept pretty quickly. I also talked about the computer as if it were a person. 'He's doing this', or 'He's doing that', or 'He's still booting up – give him a minute', which also helped. Since we were using Linux, we went ahead and named his computer Linus, and he got a kick out of my showing him the 'Peanuts' cartoon character. I hope Linus Torvalds didn't mind.

By Friday, he could do pretty much everything he needed to do, and do basic searches using search engines. He could create documents and save them and print them, and he could download information from the Net and put it on the hard disk. Then, he could go back cold turkey and find things he'd stored previously without doing too much searching around.

While all this was going on, Kathy was working on all the materials Ben would need to perform his Presidential task. She made several trips to the office supply store, and to discount stores to gather the needed supplies. Someone delivered a file cabinet and installed it in Ben's office. She even purchased a thirty-two inch flat screen TV so Ben could keep up with the twenty-four hour news cycle whenever he needed. I wasn't sure that was a good idea, but I also remembered he had one at home, so if he hadn't already turned into a news junkie, it wouldn't take long.

Friday afternoon, we sat down and reviewed the week. With everything in place, and a list of topics to be focused on, we called it a week and went home.

Saturday Kathy and I went over to Ben's house just to see how he was getting along and, sure enough, he was ensconced in his chair in the home office he'd set up surfing the Net and watching a replay of the British Parliament on C-Span.

"Ben!" I said. "You've turned into an information junkie!"

Ben laughed, then said, "Maybe so, Tom, but watching the House and the Senate is disheartening. Their debates are more about how to spear the opposition than to do anything constructive, and when they do get to something of substance, it takes them forever to get through vote after vote, though I suppose that was one of our desires – to make it difficult as a bulwark against tyranny."

"Well, Ben," I said. "You did tell them to devise their own rules."

"Yes," said Ben, "but do they even understand them?"

"Oh yes they do, Ben, and they use them to bludgeon their opponents, or to outmaneuver them. When that doesn't work, they simply change the rules. And the longer you've been there, the more you become adept at manipulating the process. But, don't let it get to you. When push comes to shove, they will generally step up."

"I would like to see that just once," said Ben, "but I suppose they are helping me make the case for repairing the ship."

"Don't worry about it. Just keep learning, but don't obsess. It's been over 200 years in the making, and it's not going to get fixed overnight. It's best to take your time and get it right."

Ben agreed to go to Church with us Sunday, so we ordered dinner, watched a bit of TV, then Kathy and I went home. Sunday, true to his word, Ben showed up for Sunday School, and after the service we all went out to eat again. The weekend done, we all retired and awaited the new week, which would begin in earnest the job of Benjamin Franklin, Presidential Advisor.

I just wasn't sure what my title was now....

Chapter 61

Week 6

Everything was in place. The staff meeting Monday morning lasted nearly three hours, as we went over point by point all the things Ben would need, and how we would support him. As the meeting wound down, I took the opportunity to reset our operation.

"I know we signed up to prove a physics theory and we knew that if we were successful it would change how we did our jobs. But none of us expected to be put in the support and advise position as we now find ourselves. The President could have just ordered a complete reorganization, or moved the entire initiative to D. C., but he chose, for whatever reason, to leave things as they are. That puts a big target on us. If we don't perform, we'll all be circulating résumés. But, if we are successful, there is no telling where this can go. So, to that end, our only focus is on helping Ben in his advisory role. Now, I don't want to say Ben is the boss here, at least not at this point, but whatever he needs within reason, he gets."

Heads nodded on each of the staff members, including Kathy, whom I had reinstated as an official staff member for the foreseeable future. Then I turned to Ben.

"Ben, I know there is still much you are not as yet aware of, and for the next weeks and months we will answer any question, bring to bear any resource, take any field trip, or arrange any interview required for you to become an expert on America in the twenty-first century. We have been promised the complete support of the White House, and the resources of the entire government at our disposal, so I intend to use them."

Ben nodded. "I thank each of you," he said as he looked around the table. "I shall do my finest, but you must remember, I am an old man with limitations on my physical frame, so while I shall not shirk any responsibility, I do intend to do a thorough job. I shall depend upon each of you to guide me as we progress."

Everyone nodded, and the meeting broke up as everyone scattered to perform their first tasks on the list of things to be done. The first order of business was to get a complete library of the U.S. Government code of regulations. I made a call to one of the attorneys on the list I'd been given by the President's Chief of Staff. He gave me another number to call, and within the hour I had a complete library of brand new bound law books on the way. I knew we could get all this digitally, so my next call was to get a copy of that as well. We had outfitted Ben's office with plenty of shelving, so I was about to fill them up.

In the middle of all this I called Ben into my office where I presented him with his new cellphone. It was not a smartphone, not wishing to further complicate his already-technology-overloaded life, but an easy to use flip phone. I showed him how to make and receive calls, and how to access and store phone numbers in its memory. I warned him about unknown numbers, since I had preloaded it with all the numbers he would need, so if anything showed up not on his list, to just let it ring. Then I showed him how to access voicemail and told him that if he got a call he was unsure of, to let me know and I'd handle it for him. The last thing we needed was for Ben Franklin to be the victim of a phone scam.

There were a couple of unused offices, one on each side of Ben's office, so Miriam's was moved into one of those offices, and Kathy set up shop in the other one. In between getting their offices put together, they were both in and out of Ben's office as they began putting the process together. By the end of the day Monday, we had actually accomplished a lot.

The rest of the week began in earnest the lengthy detail work. Tuesday afternoon Ben had a follow up exam with Dr. Ken, so his driver got him there and back. Ken told him to take it easy, since we'd had a pretty hectic schedule for an eighty-two year old man, so Ben took his advice and worked from home Wednesday. That gave the rest of us the time to put the finishing touches on the offices.

I also took that opportunity to touch base with the Chief of Staff. I left a callback message and he returned the call within a few minutes. I gave him a quick status report, and told him to expect a weekly report to be emailed via our secure email we'd established, and also that at some point we would be making another trip to D.C. to get a better tour of the city, as well as give an in-person update.

The legal books arrived Thursday afternoon, so we all put Ben's library together and I showed him the digital version of the U.S. Code, so he could make quick references if he desired. I knew Ben would be more of a book person, at least starting off, but it never hurts to have more efficient methods of accessing information and I suspected he would warm up to the digital version once he'd used it a few times and became acclimated to its use.

Friday we spent all day reviewing the Supreme Court over the years, since Ben had correctly surmised that rulings by the Court had been pivotal in shaping the legal landscape and affected both other branches of government. Ben's take was the same as mine.

"The Courts were never supposed to be this powerful," he exclaimed. "They were to be the weakest of the three branches, and merely serve as a deciding factor when the other two branches disagreed. But it appears they almost immediately overstepped their bounds. What puzzles me is why the other branches allowed them to usurp their power?"

"That is the question," I said. "Starting with Marbury Versus Madison, the Court established its right to outright invalidate laws. I'm not a legal scholar, but while it seems to me unconstitutional laws should not be allowed to stand, over time they've actually started issuing their own laws. I'm guessing you never intended that."

"Precisely," said Franklin. "If I were President, I'd simply refuse their new laws as unconstitutional as well! Perhaps that is why I was never President!" he said as he laughed.

We went through many of the Supreme Court decisions down through the years, and we identified several that Ben wanted to dive into further. Before we left for the weekend, he made a statement that I believed would end up as one of his suggested remedies.

"Had we known this were a possible outcome for the Courts," he said, "we might have limited the time justices could serve. I am also beginning to believe we may have erred in not limiting terms of other positions as well."

"Well, you're in good company there, Ben," I said. "Upwards of eighty percent of the American people agree with that idea. As a matter of fact, there is a move to call an Article Five Convention of States with one of the goals to amend the Constitution to impose term limits on both Congress and the Courts."

"Perhaps we got that part of the Constitution right!" said Ben.

"Oh, you got a lot of it right, Ben. You just underestimated the ability of men to compromise."

Finally, the day finished, we went home. On the way out the door I asked Ben if he was coming to Church Sunday.

"Possibly," he said. "I believe I shall take this weekend a bit easy, following your good doctor's orders. Besides, I understand there is a baseball contest tomorrow, and I want to learn more about this team called the Yankees. I am a Yankee, you know!"

"Yes, I know! Perhaps you should learn about the game of football as well. There's a football team named the New England Patriots you might be interested in."

Chapter 62

Research

Ben came into the office one Monday to announce he had discovered something called the Smithsonian Channel, and he'd spent the weekend viewing documentaries on aircraft carriers, and their use in the Middle East fighting terrorist forces, as well as one documentary on the history of aircraft carriers.

"I wish to see one of these!" he announced during our staff meeting. "If these ships are the primary response to threats against our country, I wish to see how they are built and used."

"Way ahead of you, Ben," I said. "I have already made contacts at various military bases and manufacturers. With the help of the office of the President, all we need to do is arrange the dates and transport."

"Excellent!" said Ben. "I leave it to your staff to make those arrangements as soon as you can!"

Over the next several weeks we took Ben on visits to shipyards, naval bases, Army bases, and Marine detachments. He was most impressed with the construction techniques and the scale of building aircraft carriers, as well as the aircraft that flew off them. He had many good questions of those with whom he met, though sometimes it was obvious he'd not seen some of the technology before. At one point I told a Navy admiral that he'd been coached to ask those questions that way as part of his confidential research into military techniques.

"But don't worry, sir," I said. "Everyone here performed admirably, Admiral." For some reason he didn't find that as hilarious as I did. Oh well.

Then, we took him to other facilities. NASA's facilities in Florida, Alabama, Mississippi, and Texas. The NORAD facility in Cheyenne Mountain. Then a quick trip back to D.C. where he first went to the NSA and was given an insight into how the U.S. gathered intelligence from around the world, and then to the Pentagon. There he met with the Chairman of the Joint Chiefs, who was confused as to why he was meeting a gentlemen he'd never heard of or met before. The following day we met again with the President's Chief of Staff in a spare office in the Pentagon, where we stitched together a picture for him of all we'd done so far, much of which he'd seen in individual reports I'd been sending for the last several weeks.

The idea was for Ben to get a picture of the threats that faced our country, and how the military was prepared to address them.

"I must understand this," said Ben, "before I can begin to understand the reasons behind many of these departments and agencies. Defense of the Republic is the government's primary reason for existence, and apparently, with the situations this country has faced over the intervening years, this has precipitated an increase in the size of government agencies and responsibilities. How this relates to the public and how and what government should be responsible for, will take some time. I am, however, impressed with, and appreciative of the information that has thus far been provided me. With your permission, I shall continue this course until all becomes clear in my mind. In the intervening period, I expect Tom here is keeping you well informed."

"Oh, he is," said the Chief of Staff. "Do you have any idea as to how long it will be before you have some preliminary findings"?

"Oh, I shouldn't like to proffer any opinions," said Ben, "until I fully understand all the issues. I will, however, offer this preliminary critique. I find it troubling that so much of what is being done in the name of freedom is done at the expense of liberty. I hope to find valid reasons for this, but some of what I have observed gives me pause, and strikes me as frighteningly similar to policies of a certain king with which I am well acquainted. I pray, sir, that we have not turned into the Britain of my time."

The Chief of Staff paused for a few moments, then said, "I do believe, Dr. Frank....sorry, Mr. Folger, that this is what we are becoming afraid of ourselves. Please, take whatever time you need. However, please be aware that we are in the middle of an election cycle now that won't end until late next year, so you have plenty of time before then. I believe the President will want to wait until after the Presidential and Congressional elections to present any findings you may have to the Congress, or at least to select members of Congress. But do present your findings as soon as you have them so we may prepare for those next steps."

Ben smiled and rose. "I shall, sir. I shall. Please pass my greetings to the President, and perhaps we can arrange a meeting with him at a future time."

"He is out of the country now, but I will pass your message to him in our next conversation."

Ben smiled again and shook his head. "I am still amazed at the ease with which one traverses the seas now. Thank you, sir, and good day to you."

Handshakes were exchanged all around and we exited right out the front door with the rest of the tourists. Nobody was the wiser. We finished out the trip with a detailed tour of the Capitol City, and when we returned to Philly, Ben decided to take a couple of days off. We had kept him quite busy and he was beginning to tire more easily.

A few days later I was informed to expect a call from the President that afternoon, and that I should have Ben with me at the time. I took the liberty of asking Miriam and Kathy to attend as well, since they were both assistants to Ben. At two forty-five the call came in and I put it on the speaker.

"Gentlemen." he began. "First of all thank you for your efforts thus far."

"Thank you, Mr. President!" said Ben.

The President continued. "I have been given a compendium of the reports of your efforts, and I see that you have indeed been very busy. My Chief of Staff tells me he's informed you that not much action will probably be taken until after the election, but I would urge you to submit as much as you can between now and then. While I fully expect to be re-elected, in the case I am not, I want to have compelling information to give to the next President. I am sure you understand."

"Indeed, sir," said Ben. "We are working diligently, but I wish to take sufficient time to provide a 'compelling report', as you ask. I thank you for opening up access to me and the staff here, and I want to personally thank them for all their efforts as well."

"As do I," said the President. "As you know, this effort is unprecedented in the annals of history, so it is my hope to get this right. To that end, let me know if there is anything we can do here to assist you. I am sorry I wasn't able to meet with you on your recent visit, but hopefully we can arrange a meeting in the near future when you have some opinions formed."

"Yes," said Ben, "I shall very much look forward to that."

"Well, then," said the President, "I will let you get back to your work. Thank you. Thank you all."

"Thank you, Mr. President," we both said, and the call terminated.

I smiled at Ben and said, "You know, it's not every day you get a pat on the back from the President of the United States."

"I know," said Ben with a sly grin. "Remember, though. He is the first one I've ever met!"

Chapter 63

Development

We had to slow down the trips for two reasons. First, the need for more information was dwindling, but primarily everyone, especially Ben, was getting weary of all the travel. In reality it was only a period of about six months that we visited the places Ben thought he needed to see, but it seemed like a lifetime, and eventually we just wanted to be able to come to work and go home. Some weeks the only time we had been at home was during the weekends.

One of the last trips Ben and I took was to Wright-Patterson Air Force Base in Dayton, Ohio. It's the home of the USAF Museum, and I wanted him to see in person some of the advances in military aviation over the years. Actually, that was just an excuse, though a good one. Dayton is the home of one of the largest gatherings of amateur radio operators in the world. Each May, 30,000 or so of us hams would gather just outside Dayton for the annual Dayton Hamvention. In addition to the forums and commercial displays in the convention center, there was the flea market. Every type of electronic contraption you could imagine could be found at someone's table at Dayton. As we went through the flea market, I would explain to Ben what various pieces of equipment were and how they were used.

One guy in particular had several World War II German Enigma machines, and I was fascinated. Some were replicas, but this guy had two actual machines which had been used by the Germans in combat that he'd come across somehow. He wouldn't even talk about selling them, and by now I'm guessing they are priceless, since many were destroyed in the waning days of the war. As you might suspect, this trip with Ben was a big deal to me, and he found it very useful putting the pieces together about how communications evolved through the years and how that translated into the culture, and specifically into government policies.

Another area that gave Ben heartburn was all the policies that came from the Supreme Court decisions from the 1940s forward, and in particular their use of the phrase "separation of church and state".

"There are no such words in the Constitution!" said Ben. "As I understand it, the First Amendment was placed there to protect the free exercise of one's religious beliefs, not to curtail them. The intent was, as was ours, to keep government out of religion, and when you read the language, it applies specifically to Congress. We were afraid of what had happened in Britain with the Church of England and its tyranny over those of other beliefs. We did not want an officially sanctioned Church. But, that Amendment contains this phrase: 'or prohibiting the free exercise thereof'. Those words are in English, Tom. The Court changed that. That is tyranny!"

"How do you repair that?" I asked.

"Excellent question, Tom. I shall work on that."

Over the remaining months of the year, we sorted through all the information Ben had collected, and Miriam and Kathy helped him organize the history timeline with the notes that had been taken by everyone on the excursions. Once all that was done, the real work began on how to address issues he would present to the President. For that, we had many sessions in conference where no holds were barred. We ended up breaking all the issues down into four major areas: The Congress, The Courts, The Presidency, and The States. In each of these areas, the overriding theme was their ultimate effects on The People. In other words, how does anything done by the government, including the States, affect the individual who just wants to live his or her life free of interference, including interference from their own government. As we did, it became obvious that whatever changes Ben would recommend would face serious opposition from sources already entrenched in decades and decades of precedence, practice, and tradition.

Once there was a plan in place, Ben wrote his first preliminary report to the President. In it he outlined how the Founders had envisioned the country's government, how history had presented challenges since the establishment of the Constitution and the Bill of Rights, how government had responded to those challenges, and finally how the result had differed from what the Founders envisioned. The paper offered no conclusions, only areas to be studied in more detail. Since this was a report directly to the President, the only input besides Ben's came from our staff. We were careful not to guide Ben's conclusions – only to ensure the accuracy of the information on which Ben was depending. That was an arduous process, and not immune from some controversy. But, even that controversy added to Ben's report, with the understanding that if we had controversies among our group, it was sure to be magnified when more people were brought into the process.

During all this process I had, with Ben's knowledge, been sending regular reports to the President's Chief of Staff as to where we were in the process, what sources we were drawing from, and an updated timeline. Additionally, I included a personal assessment of how Ben's health was, including his mental state. I was careful each time to stress that I was not trained in psychology, but simply an observer who had been with Ben since the beginning. This assessment was something the Chief of Staff had ordered, and this part of my reporting was done without Ben's knowledge. The goal was to identify any issues that might require an actual psychologist. Included in my comments were comments made by Dr. Ken, who would drop in every so often to check up on Ben and with whom I kept a regular update. After all, Ben had already been through a lot and, particularly during our travels, a fair amount of stress had been endured, so this constant analysis helped us keep from going too far.

Nine months after our visit to the President, Ben's preliminary report was done and sent by encrypted email to the Chief of Staff. We took a week off while we waited to see if there was any input from the White House. It gave everyone a chance to decompress and get prepared mentally for the next phase – getting specific.

During this time, Ben became acclimated to his local community, and to those at our Church. He was careful not to stand out too much, and what opinions he did offer were carefully worded, even in my Sunday School class. He particularly enjoyed the frequent social events at the Church, as well as some events in the local community, and he especially enjoyed the holiday celebrations we attended in Philadelphia. The irony was not lost on me or any of the rest of the staff that the Fourth of July celebration was at Independence Hall. On our first excursion inside the Hall, Ben was careful to surreptitiously point out the differences between today's Hall and the one he was familiar with. That was a surreal trip.

One of the highlights of my time with Ben was taking him to a baseball game at Citizen's Bank Park. Of course, I waited until the Braves were playing them, and of course I had to take Bill along so we could rib each other when our team scored. Unfortunately, the Braves were having a bad day and just couldn't keep the Phillies from taking the game in an eight to four contest. Ben found out he liked hot dogs. Who doesn't?

The following Monday the work began, with the goal of helping Ben provide some specific areas that needed to be addressed, and his opinion, as one of the Founding Fathers, as to how they might have felt. This was really the hard part, and while we were nervous as to how the President and others might receive such suggestions, Ben was adamant that he was not the least bit concerned. In a conversation with him, he explained his point.

"Tom, I was there when the king was forcing our hand. I know what to live under tyranny is like, and many of my friends and acquaintances perished in the fight to free ourselves from an invasive and tyrannical government. We established these United States in the hope that we wouldn't revert to that same condition. What I have seen is a country that has excelled beyond anything we could have imagined. The power of the individual, free to pursue his dreams, was unleashed upon the world, and look what has been done with it. But, what I also see are the seeds and, yes, the actuality, of those same forces that we so diligently fought against. I do not wish to see, and I would be abdicating my destiny were it to occur without my opposition, another descent into tyranny, regardless of the intentions of those involved. I shall not shrink from my destiny!"

How could anyone argue with that? Given who was sitting in front of me, I certainly wasn't going to!

That Thursday, the call came from the White House. To put things bluntly, his message was 'go for it'. So, we did.

Chapter 64

Reunion

Early on I had mentioned to Ben that there were probably some descendants of his living in the area, and I'd never really chased that possibility, but in the paper today was a short article that caused me to sit up in my chair. The headline read:

"Descendants of Benjamin Franklin to Gather"

The article described how a couple of years ago there had been a push by some of the ancestry sites on the Internet to find out how many descendants of the Founders might be alive, so they issued an invitation for people to submit DNA and consent to have them look for that possibility. Well, lo and behold, someone who'd been identified as a descendant of Franklin had taken it upon herself to contact other descendants and set up a *meet and greet*. It was the following weekend in, you guessed it, Philadelphia. My first thought was '*I hope Ben didn't see this article. I want to be the one to tell him.*'

I called Ben's cell.

"Ben, do you have any plans for Saturday?"

"None, sir. What do you have in mind?"

"I want to take you to a family reunion in Philly."

"Oh?" he said. "You want me to meet your family?"

"No," I said with a small chuckle. "Yours!"

"Mine??"

I explained for a few minutes how technology allowed us to trace ancestry with a blood test (I didn't get into DNA), and that is how they had identified Ben's descendants.

"They are meeting Saturday," I explained, "and I thought you might want to be there. Since Abiah Folger was your mother's maiden name, I believe we can get you in as a descendant of your mother's brother, without having to explain your lineage as though you were one of your own descendants."

I heard a soft chuckle on the other end. "General Washington could have used your subterfuge during the Revolution, my dear man. Yes. I think it would be interesting to see how much of me is left on this earth."

"Great," I said. "I'll pick you up at eight-thirty and we'll head there."

Saturday morning I went, collected Ben, and we headed for Philadelphia. Fittingly, the reunion was at Independence Hall! When we got there a couple of people were standing at the door welcoming those who were coming to the meeting. It had taken a bit of bluffing to get Ben on the list the previous day, but the fact that the picture of Ben I had emailed the organizer had a striking family resemblance didn't hurt!

On the inside were about a dozen people who were milling around and the organizer of the group came up to us as we walked in.

"You must be Mr. Folger!" she said as she offered her hand.

"Yes," said Ben. "I am," as he shot me a quick look. "It's a pleasure to be here. I see there are others who share a common ancestor."

"Yes!" she said. "Let me introduce you!"

She took Ben around to each member of the group and introduced him. Ben was in his element. It wasn't long before they were referring to him as "Uncle Ben". Now, that was funny. If these people had any idea who they were talking to we would have had to call the paramedics.

We stayed until mid-afternoon, and what was really funny was to hear stories about 'ancestor Ben' some of the others were telling while watching the expression on Ben's face. More than once he gave me a knowing smile that either indicated they were right about a certain story, or more often, that they'd completely missed the mark. Someone asked Ben if he had any stories told him by his parents.

"Well, very few, and yours are most entertaining. However, there are a couple that were handed down from our matriarch about my 'brother'."

He launched into a couple of stories about when he was a boy in Boston, but he told it from his cousin's perspective, the whole time giving me the twinkle-eye, and the only thing I could think of was '*I hope he doesn't get too specific. I don't want to have to explain details he shouldn't know*', but Ben, ever the diplomat who had interacted with everyone from paupers to royalty, didn't miss a beat and he played them all like a fiddle. All I could do was laugh.

After we left Independence Hall on the ride home I asked Ben if he'd had a good time.

"Why yes!" he said. "Thank you for arranging my attendance."

"Did you see anybody you knew?"

Ben laughed. "No, I don't think so. I am, after all, much older than these youngsters."

I laughed, and said, "Well, I didn't want to say anything at the time, but the lady who put all this together and introduced you to everyone...?"

"Yes," said Ben.

"She is your fifth great granddaughter."

I just love putting shocked faces on Ben Franklin. Nobody was ever going to believe this, so I decided to leave this little event out of my next report to the White House!

Chapter 65

Presidential Report

We were getting closer to the first finished product – the initial document for the President. In addition to sending regular reports to the Chief of Staff, I had been sending, with the Chief of Staff's permission, copies to Lawrence Freeland at NSF, so I was not too surprised to see him walk in the door early one Monday morning.

"Hi, Lawrence!" I said. "I didn't know you were coming today. How are you?"

"Fine, Tom, and I decided literally this morning to fly up. I see from your reports you're about to produce the first recommendations to send to the President."

"Yes, we're planning to assemble all that this week."

"Good," he said. "I would like to get a briefing as to where you're headed."

"Sure. The rest will be here within the half hour and we'll start our regular Monday staff meeting. We can take whatever time necessary to not only get our business done, but to bring you up to date, if that's OK."

"Yes, thank you. But, can I talk to you in your office for a few minutes first?"

I nodded and we went into my office and Larry shut the door.

"What's on your mind, sir?"

"Tom, you've done a great job here, even though this was not what you had envisioned when this process started."

"Thank you, Larry. We have tried to adapt to the situation, and I'm proud of how the staff has performed."

"As am I," he said, then paused for a moment. "I have concerns, though."

"Alright. What are your concerns."

"Well, Tom, as you might suspect, the information you've given the President, and the recommendations and comments that will be in your report have possible deep ramifications, not only for you and your staff, but for the rest of us at the NSF as well."

I nodded. "Yes, I have thought about that, and while we've tried to provide Ben with all the information he needed to get a picture of why things are as they are, we have avoided putting ideas in his head, or guiding his recommendations, so whatever is in the report will be a product of his mind alone."

"I realize that, but what if Ben recommends that operations like the NSF be curtailed, or worse, eliminated?"

Truth be told, I was amazed the politics hadn't entered the picture before now. But, I was prepared for this one.

"Well, Larry, from my conversations with Ben, one thing has always been apparent. He knows that there are some things that are appropriately performed by government, and one of those is scientific experimentation for the purpose of furthering science itself. In fact, Article I, Section 8, of the Constitution specifically tasks Congress with those purposes. Plus, this is Ben Franklin. He will not turn his back on scientific development."

Larry nodded. "I hope you're right, Tom. But, there are those, few that they are, in the know at NSF who are very nervous about this. While there is nothing we can do to thwart any negative recommendations that might affect us, we certainly hope this won't provoke the higher-ups at NSF into a defensive posture. In fact, that is why I am here. To determine what, if anything, and how much we need to be prepared for."

"Well, sir. I hope you will leave here with your mind at ease. I don't want to introduce politics into our deliberations, at least not at this stage, so if it's OK with you, sit in on the meeting this morning, and afterwards let me know if you still have concerns, and we'll go from there."

Larry nodded. "Fair enough. Let's go, then."

We headed into the conference room where everyone was there except Ben, but it wasn't quite time to start, so I wasn't worried. As Larry greeted everyone there, Ben walked in with his driver.

"Dr. Freeland!" he said as he crossed the room to shake Larry's hand. "We are honored to have your presence here today."

"Hello, Ben. How have you been?"

"I am well, sir, and you?"

"I am as well. I am sorry to spring this on you all, but I just wanted to get an update in person to see how things are going and find out if there is anything we need to do to make this process easier. I am also interested to hear your impressions, Dr. Franklin. So, please. Start your meeting."

With that, we began. Because Larry was there, and nervous about the possible ramifications of Ben's report, I decided to go ahead and give him the full show. We did a top to bottom review. I told everyone to be frank, especially Ben, and we spent all morning discussing where we'd been, where we were, and more importantly, where Ben was going with all this, and the list was extensive.

We literally took each of the departments headed by the Cabinet members and discussed how they fit into the Founders' vision, and where there might be some adjustments needed. I already knew some departments such as Education and

EPA were problematic for Ben and sure enough, he just flat came out and said they needed to be eliminated.

"I understand issues with clean water and so forth," said Ben, "but those should be standards set by another department, or possibly a new agency created by combining other agencies, possibly including the Department of the Interior, whose task would be to resolve any issues between the States. However, the States should primarily be in charge of their own environments. They are the ones closest to these issues and you cannot depend on someone in a far away capitol on the other side of the country ruling on matters inside a single state."

On education, Ben was adamant that education should be a much more localized issue. As he saw it, the current method was much too intrusive and inefficient. There were several other agencies and departments that Ben had issues with, but none greater than the Internal Revenue Service.

"I cannot accept," he said, "a system that would steal citizens' money directly out of their employer's coffers, then prosecute them for not telling the government what they did with their own money. That is the very definition of a tyrannical government. No, the Sixteenth Amendment was an egregious error, and should be repealed with prejudice. There are other ways to raise the revenues necessary to fund a proper government."

Ben insisted he did not want to singlehandedly rearrange the government, so his recommendations would mostly be general in nature and he'd leave it up to the President and Congress to determine if and how to enact any changes. He was adamant about one thing though.

"Gentlemen, and Ladies, I have a somewhat firm grasp on why and how the government of these United States devolved into its current state. My fellow Founders, to a man sir, would stand in opposition to this government just as they did to a similar government in 1776. Much of what I see occurring in the District of Columbia – I refuse to associate General Washington's name with it – is what we fought to liberate ourselves from, so the position in which I find myself compels me to speak for them."

I glanced at Larry and while he remained mostly passive at this statement, I knew he was churning on the inside. The one saving grace was, when the subject of departments and agencies came up, Franklin singled out scientific endeavors for exactly the same reason I had pointed out to Larry in my office. There were other areas that fit that mold as well – Defense, for instance – but nothing was to escape the scalpel of revision. At any rate, the die was cast.

Larry did, however, take us all to lunch, and he again thanked us for the job we'd done. After lunch the rest of the crew went back to the office, but Larry asked me to accompany him to the airport and he'd have his driver return me to the office after he was gone. It didn't take a psychic to predict why.

"Tom, I have to say I am very nervous about this report. This thing is going to have political hair all over it, even if the NSF, DARPA, and the Pentagon comes out relatively unscathed. You need to remember this is Ben Franklin's report, not NSF's, and not yours. Your job, and you have done it well, was to provide him information and facilitate his research. I have met the President, and he'll be sympathetic to most of what Ben will tell him, but Congress is where the problems will come from. If this gets widely distributed to any extent, the long knives will come out and you don't want to be anywhere in range when they do."

I nodded and said, "I know, sir. Once Ben's reaction to the current condition of the government became clear, I knew where this would go. Put yourself in his place. Do you think this is what the Founders envisioned?"

Larry stroked his chin for a moment and said, "I guess not. But, they are not here, and haven't gone through what this country has gone through over the last 200 plus years."

"They aren't, sir, but one of them is, and what they collectively went through has bought them the right, albeit through Ben Franklin, to take exception, even 230 years later. But, I get your point, and don't worry, I'll take care of myself, my crew, and look out for the interests of the NSF. Let's just hope the right people get their hands on this report, at least people with some measure of statesmanship."

"Tom, that's a word you just don't hear as much any more."

We pulled up to the hanger where the private plane was and the pilot started up the engines. We got out and headed for the stairs to the plane. Larry stopped, shook my hand, and said, "You're a good man, Tom. You've done a good job so far. You continue to do that, but take care you don't get caught up in what I fear is a coming storm."

"Thank you, sir. I'll be fine."

He nodded and said, "Keep me in the loop."

"I will, sir. Safe travels," and Larry was off.

I went back to the office, and assembled the staff.

"In case nobody realized it," I said, "this was a warning as much as it was a fact finding trip. Larry made this statement: 'This report will have political hair all over it'. Ben," I said as I turned to face him, "he is exactly right. There are political redoubts entrenched all over Washington, and if threatened, they will react, and react viciously. That's what Larry came to warn us about."

Ben laughed. "Oh, and you think I was unaware of this? I have been in this position before. I know I shall be the lightning rod when this arrives. But, what are they going to do to me? Firstly, I invented the lightning rod, so I am acutely aware of its properties. It is only the conduit. However, I shall ensure that any destruction is routed away from you and your fine staff and lands squarely where it should – on the shoulders of the other Founders."

"I appreciate that, Ben," I said, "but politics is vicious, as you may have seen in some of the news reports. They won't care that you're Ben Franklin – they'll come after you anyway."

"Again, sir," smiled Ben, "what are they going to do? Kill me? I've been dead for over 200 years!"

Chapter 66

Reaction

The President's report was submitted. That slowed things down significantly at the office, and we took advantage of it. I called a small catering company and had them fix us nice meals for the week, so each day at lunch, they came in with a different meal for all of us, which kept morale high as we waited for the reaction from D.C. We all had work we'd let go, so by the end of the week, we were as caught up as we'd ever been. I even had the opportunity to get on twenty meters and work some DX with Ben looking on. As I talked to Ham stations all over the world, Ben asked questions about the terms and signals we used, as well as how some of the gear worked. One contact was a station just outside Paris, and I asked Ben if he'd like to try out his French.

Now, get this picture: Here's me sitting off to one side while, mike in hand, Ben Franklin, just months from having come forward in time from 1787, is having a conversation over shortwave radio with a French politician in a local municipality outside Paris. They had a spirited conversation for a few minutes, then I signaled for Ben to wind it up. I kinda hated to, because he seemed to be having fun, but I didn't want too much information getting out over the airwaves, because you can never tell who's listening. When we signed off I asked the Frenchman to send a QSL card to Ben as a keepsake. Then I showed Ben some of the cards I'd received from hams over the years.

There was a Ham Radio contest on the airwaves this weekend requiring constant quick-fire contacts over a twenty-four hour period of time, so I told everyone to only call me if something came up, that I'd be busy until after Church Sunday. And I was. I worked the contest until time to go to Church, and finished up the last three hours when I got back, and when it was all over I had a decent score. Looking at last year's scores, I had a chance of placing pretty high in my section, though I was pretty sure I didn't have a shot at placing nationally, but I enjoyed it anyway. All in all, a great end to a not so hectic week. I went to bed early Sunday night to catch up on the sleep I lost in in the contest, and Monday came with great expectations.

Sure enough, about ten thirty I received a call from the White House Chief of Staff. He only wanted to talk to me initially, and I was in my office when he called, so I just shut the door.

"Tom, the President has reviewed Ben's report, and I must say, he was as impressed with the level of detail as he was shocked with Ben's impressions. While he expected some criticism on the size of government and on some Constitutional issues, we had not expected it to be so excoriating. It is clear that Dr. Franklin thinks we have strayed far from the Founders' intentions. We're not sure what to do with that."

"I understand," I said. "Let me help you with some context. Put yourself in his place. Imagine you were instrumental in establishing our nation – a small government, with the focus on the States and on individual liberty with no interference from a national government. No income tax, no federal regulations, no huge military, no surveillance, no requirements for licensing for anything. You can basically do whatever you want on your own land and nobody can say anything to you. Suddenly, you find yourself trying to figure out how that got transformed into what we have today. How would your opinion differ from his?"

"I understand that, Tom, but even though it was a very small interval for him, it was over 200 years for us. A myriad of events conspired to bring us to this point, so you can't just draw a straight line from there to here without understanding those events."

"You're absolutely right," I said. "Ben understands that as well. He struggled mightily to comprehend the decisions that went into the buildup of our government to where it is today. He also knows that any changes will not come overnight, and that it's a certainty that not all of his suggestions will be implemented. But, you asked for his opinion, and that's exactly what you got."

There was silence for a moment, and for a moment I thought I might be in trouble. Finally, he said, "I think another trip to the White House might be in order, and the sooner the better. We have an election next year, and that will be all consuming, so we'd like to take what time we do have before then to get a handle on the reasons and expectations for his recommendations."

"Oh, I agree," I said. "I think there needs to be a meeting of the minds, as it were, between Ben and the President. When do you suggest?"

"Well, we have a full week this week, but we need to keep this under the radar. How about an evening meeting Friday night, following up the next day, all at Camp David. If you can get there Friday morning before the Press descends on the area, we can let them know the President wants to take a private weekend with no press coverage – just a quiet time with him and the First Lady at the Camp. I would suggest you and Dr. Franklin be the only two attending. I realize you have some security, but keep it light, and we'll have the Secret Service provide protection for you here."

"We can do that," I said. "Do you want me to inform Ben, or do you want to."

"Oh, I have a better idea for that. He will receive a call from the President within the hour, so if you'd simply tell him the White House notified you to set up the call, we'll take it from there."

"Excellent idea," I said. "If you would send me any particulars about the travel and check-in information, as well as anything you wish us to bring, and I'll have him there at the appointed time Friday morning."

"Will do, Tom. We'll talk later."

We said our goodbyes and I went off to fetch the staff. We quickly assembled in the conference room.

"I just received a call from the White House. Ben, you will be receiving a call from the President within the hour, and you and I will be invited to a private meeting Friday and this weekend with the President at Camp David. The Chief of Staff will contact me with the particulars, but I expect the President will be inviting you personally."

"Good," said Ben. "I wish to gauge his reaction to my comments and proposals."

"Well," I said, "I assume that's what the meeting will be about, but we'll know shortly."

"What do the rest of us need to be doing?", asked Miriam.

"I don't know yet. The information I have is that just Ben and I will be going, but I'll let you know as soon as I know."

We talked about the possible reaction by the President and how we might have to prepare for the encounter and sure enough, in a few minutes, the phone rang. I answered and the operator informed me there was a call for Ben Folger from the President. So I handed the phone to Ben, and sat back as the conversation took place. It was a short call, and Ben gave us the gist when he hung up the phone.

"Well, you were correct, Tom," he said. "You and I are to travel to Camp David Friday morning where we will be met by the Secret Service who will escort us to the meeting place. The President will be there late Friday afternoon for our first meeting. This is a private meeting that no one outside our office can know about, and he wants to go over my report in detail."

"Well, that's what you'd hoped for," I said. "I expect we will have a long weekend. So, for the time being, everyone just relax until I get details from the Chief of Staff, and we'll see what that entails."

That done, everyone retreated to their cubbyholes – including Ben – and the rest of the morning was uneventful. At two forty-five or so, I received a call from the Deputy Chief of Staff informing me there would be an itinerary emailed to me via secure email shortly, and to contact her if I had any questions. Sure enough, about an hour later, it came in.

It was simple enough. It was about a three hour drive, and we were asked to drive rather than fly to keep the visibility low. Included were driving instructions, an access pass-phrase, the identity of the Secret Service personnel to meet us, and simple instructions on getting in without notice. Bring any research information we might wish, but other than copies of the report Ben had sent to the President, everything else would be provided. I got with Ben, Miriam, and Kathy, and we quickly decided to put all our research on a laptop as well as a secure thumb drive, and to take a couple of the copies of the printed report. Other than those, and clothing and personal care items, everything else would be provided, including office facilities if needed.

The ladies prepared all the documentation, put it on the laptop and thumb drive, printed out the reports, and by the time we went home, we were ready to leave. The problem was, it was only Monday!

Friday took an exceedingly long time to get here, and we were more than ready when it was time to leave. Rick Swanson would drive and would be provided accommodations while there. We were expected by ten thirty, so we left at seven on what turned out to be an uneventful trip. We arrived, our IDs were checked, and the Secret Service agent showed us to our lodging. We were informed we'd be told when the President arrived, but until then we were to remain in the guest area. About six-forty p.m., the agent came to collect Ben and me and we headed to an adjacent facility with a medium sized conference room. Shortly after we got there, the President and his Chief of Staff entered. We rose, shook hands all around, and we settled down at the table and the President began.

"Dr. Franklin, I appreciate all the work you've put into this report. I know there was a lot of information to assemble to understand the reasons and events that have brought us here over the last 230 years, and it is apparent from your comments in the report that you have a pretty firm grasp of the issues. I congratulate you on what must have been an extremely difficult process to bring you fully into the twenty-first century."

Ben smiled. "Thank you, Mr. President. I must give due credit to Tom and his staff, who retrieved any piece of information I needed, arranged and accompanied me on tours of important historical locations, as well as current installations, all of which helped in the understanding of our country in today's world."

"Well, I agree they did a good job. But, what I want to focus on is your conclusions, and particularly your recommendations."

"As do I," agreed Ben.

The President folded his hands, looked down for a moment, then back up and straight into Ben's eyes.

"I take it you don't think much of the way our government operates."

Ben looked him square in the eye, and without missing a beat, said, "You are correct, sir. I. Do. Not!"

The staring contest was only a few moments, but it seemed like an hour, and I was not comfortable.

Finally, the President said. "You know, Dr. Franklin. I understand why you don't. My Chief of Staff here was instrumental in my coming to that understanding. He asked me to put myself in your place."

Chapter 67

Negotiation

The President smiled a wry smile at Ben, and Ben sat back in his chair and gave the President a nod. Then he said, "Mr. President, I knew when I submitted these suggestions they would not receive immediate embrace. I also knew that the ones, if any, that were eventually given due consideration and possible action would only do so after much debate. You see, sir, I am more of a politician than you have given me credit for. Between you and me, I use that impression to my advantage in my negotiations. I shall not, however, do that with you. May I offer a suggestion?"

The President sat back in his chair and said, "Of course!"

"I would suggest, sir, if indeed you are amenable to changing the direction of our country, that we discuss which of the items I have proffered might be possible to receive a hearing in the Congress. I would then offer suggestions as to how you might present such proposals in light of the Founders' ideals."

The President smiled. "Dr. Franklin, you are indeed a better politician than you let on. Here you hit me with a number of proposals you knew would be overkill, intending all along to focus on the ones you felt would have the best chance, as well as the greatest effect. Am I right?"

Ben laughed. "I see why you are now the President. Of course that is true! I determined that if you were willing to discuss these proposals at all, that you would be willing to discuss at least some of these seriously. Might I renew my previous request, then sir?"

The President nodded. "Agreed, Dr. Franklin. That was actually my intent when I called this meeting."

The tension was now broken, so the President signaled for the stewards to bring in a light meal for us to consume while working. For the next three hours Ben and the President looked at each of the proposals Ben had offered in his report and sorted them into three basic categories: (1) Ain't gonna happen, (2) If it happens at all it'll be an ugly fight, and (3) We might be able to do something with these.

By ten p.m. the President was starting to fade. With the campaign coming, pressures from overseas from some of the usual suspects, as well as domestic issues that had flared up during the last few days, he'd had a long week, so he suggested we begin again tomorrow morning after a late breakfast and go through these last two categories.

I called Kathy to let her know all was well, and since I couldn't say anything about where we were, we just talked a few minutes about family and private things, then I said goodnight and went to bed. While the accommodations were nothing short of luxurious, I still had trouble getting to sleep. I was, after all, at Camp David with the President of the United States and Founding Father Ben Franklin where they were deciding on the possible future of the country.

When all this had started, I had begun a journal. Today's entry was a doozie. As I was finishing up just before I called Kathy, I thought to myself *'Why am I keeping this. I will never be able to tell anyone?'*, but I kept on typing anyway.

Regardless, I finally got to sleep and woke at seven a.m. when I received a wakeup call from the Camp David operator, so I dressed and went over to the dining area where Ben was halfway through his meal. We were told that the President had to make a couple of phone calls and receive his daily briefing, but would meet us in the conference room shortly. So, meal finished, we collected our materials and headed over.

As the President came in he apologized for being a bit late. There were some international issues he was working through, but nothing should interrupt us for the rest of the morning. With that we got down to business. My job was to keep notes for Ben and make sure any research info he needed would be at his fingertips. The Chief of Staff did basically the same thing for the President.

By lunch, some progress had been made, particularly on ideas that had been tossed around over the years – elimination and combination of some departments; changing the ways revenues were collected; spending reductions; simplifying the Federal Code, etc., but there was still much to be discussed.

At lunch the stewards again brought a meal, a bit more substantial this time than last night, and as one might imagine, it was very very good. While we were eating, the President had to take another call, and had a visit from his National Security advisor, and I began to wonder if something had flared up I was unaware of. We had not watched or read any news since we got there, so while he was out of the room, I did a quick look at the online news outlets, but nothing more out of the ordinary popped up. It occurred to me this might be a regular part of a President's day, so I gave it no more thought.

When he came back into the room, he again apologized. "Sorry, Gentlemen. Seems there's always something to attend to. Hopefully that'll be over for the day."

Back to work. By the end of the day, the President and Ben had agreed on the major areas to be addressed, and had drilled down to some specifics on a few, but one apparent thing was that Congress would have to be brought into the picture at an early stage, or none of these would go anywhere. In the end, that's where the discussion went.

"We have this election cycle coming up," said the President, "and as you know, all of the House and one third of the Senate are up for re-election, as well as my own position. While none of us has a crystal ball, we do have polling data that gives us a pretty accurate idea of who will win and who might have a race on their hands. So, whoever we do decide to let in will depend a great deal on their chances to be here in November."

"I understand," said Ben. "I leave that decision making process entirely up to you, sir, as that is a process in which I am not competent. I do have one question, though. How will you make an impression on these gentlemen to evoke a positive response?"

The President sat back and smiled. "Oh, I won't have to. You will do that for me."

Ben's eyebrows shot up. "In what way, sir?"

"I plan to bring in some key members of both the House and the Senate, one at at time, and have them briefed on 'Ben Franklin of the National Science Foundation, Special Advisor to the President'. That done, you will meet personally with these individuals, one at a time, and we will find out just how skilled a diplomat you really are – and for the record, I believe you are very skilled. You will certainly have the upper hand!"

Ben smiled. "Yes, I learned the 'dance' of diplomacy representing our new country in France, so I appreciate your confidence, sir."

The President leaned forward and said, "You don't seem surprised."

"Of course not!" said Ben. "My preparing a report of structural changes in the government would be of no effect without your using me as your tool – a process I am looking forward to with anticipation."

Now, the President smiled. "You had this figured out from the beginning, didn't you?"

"I merely let the common sense of the situation play itself out," he said. "I simply assumed you to be both an intelligent man, and a skilled tactician. The rest was obvious."

"Well," said the President. "Be careful. These men you will meet have been doing this every day for many years."

"So have I," said Ben, and we all laughed!

Chapter 68

The Plan

It took longer than had been planned. There was so much in Ben's report, but it would have taken longer had they not taken at least one third of his proposals completely off the table. There was no use in fighting battles they couldn't win, the President reminded Ben. Ben readily agreed, and I think that's the point where I realized how brilliantly Franklin had played this game. While reading about the Gulf War, Ben had come across the term 'shock and awe', and we'd had a short discussion of its meaning. It occurred to me he had taken this term and woven it into his report, though it only shared its name, rather than its meaning, with the military term. By proposing so many changes, Ben had used his personal stature to 'shock' the President, then 'awed' him by acceding to his request to pare down the number and scope of his proposals. In doing so, he let the President 'win'. But, the President was no dummy, and soon he realized what had happened, but instead of making him angry, he simply shook his head. He'd been 'Franklin-ed', and the way Ben had done it so adroitly was something to behold. In that, history had not been fair to Ben. He really was a much better diplomat than we'd thought.

Saturday night came, and we were not even half finished. We started bright and early Sunday morning. All had to be done before retiring Sunday night, because the President had to be back in the White House Monday morning, not only to keep up appearances, but because there were items he had to address, which was apparent by the number of interruptions we had during the day.

There was agreement on eliminating and dispersing some departments of questionable Constitutionality, and the President agreed that repealing the Sixteenth Amendment and replacing it with a consumption tax would be a worthy goal. The military was spared most of the knife, though the President volunteered that he had already been looking at ways to be more responsible in spending. Larry Freeland would be gratified to find that Ben not only thought the nations scientific endeavors should not be curtailed, but that they should be encouraged to engage in responsible research.

There was a long discussion, though, on the nation's law enforcement and intelligence agencies, particularly the latter. Ben was very dubious of entities

312

such as the CIA and NSA and stories he'd read of their surveillance on the nation's citizens, especially in light of the Fourth and Fifth Amendments.

"I must be able to trust," said Ben, "that my government will not be sticking its nose into my personal business and using that information to build a case against me without cause, and further using that information as though I would be testifying against myself. It was our fear that even a government conceived in liberty would become oppressive and think itself our master. No matter the intentions, men are not angels, and something put in motion for the best reasons at the time will become a cancer for succeeding generations."

"I understand that," said the President. "It is a fine line I have to walk every day. The technology we have available to us today allows us the opportunity to delve deep into people's lives, and I am acutely aware of the danger that poses. That is why we have special courts set up just for surveillance activities to keep these agencies in check."

"From what I understand," said Ben, "that is not working as well as expected. There have seemingly been some cases where such 'authorized' activities should have been better considered. My suggestion is that this so-called 'FISA' court either needs to be eliminated, or at best restructured. Additionally, citizens should be free from concern from their government unless evidence exists outside their castle, and even then it should be faced head on, rather than done in secret. Accuse and convict, or harbor no accusations. Are we, or are we not at liberty?"

"I understand where you're coming from, Dr. Franklin, but in our present situation, things are sometimes not so simple."

"Mr. President, things do not have to be simple. But they must be honest, and human beings, sir, are not honest beings, even if they do work for the government."

The President sat back in his seat. "Dr. Franklin, you don't seem to have much trust in the American people."

"Oh, I have faith in the People, sir. It was the People to whom we gave this government. What I have little faith in, though, are human beings with power. Remember, our Constitution was not written to create a powerful government. It was written to authorize a necessary government while at the same time keeping a leash on the lion. In my humble opinion, the leash needs to be tightened."

The President leaned forward. "I see your point. However, there are some things that just cannot be put into the light of day. For instance, sometimes the information our government receives comes from sources that, if found out, would be eliminated. Real lives, as well as methods we use to keep those who would harm us at bay, would be in peril if some of this information was publicly available."

"Then place stricter guidelines on these secret activities, and introduce an oversight on this court. It should not be allowed to stray."

The President considered that for a moment. "There may be a good middle ground in there, Dr. Franklin. Please go back and do an in depth study of this issue and return with a revised recommendation. I'll make sure you have the access you need to the inner workings of the FISA court."

By around ten forty-five p.m., the list of possible action items had been revised, and Ben was given more research and recommendations to work on, after which he would submit a revised report to the President. We were about to wrap up when the President had a question for me.

"I understand, Mr. Reed, that you teach Sunday School at your local church, is that correct?"

"It is, sir, though on occasions like this I have a substitute."

"How did you handle that?"

"Oh, I had told my sub that we had a series of meetings at the NSF, one of which would go too long for me to get back, so she had no problem taking my class today."

"I see," said the President. "Well, the reason I asked, is that we, Ben and I, are going down a road that has huge ramifications, particularly when some in our Congress are informed of his true identity. I am concerned about how this whole process will be received, and what the possible outcome might be. I won't speak for Dr. Franklin here, but I for one, do not possess all knowledge, however I think we all know Someone who does. Would you mind offering a prayer for our task, and particularly for Dr. Franklin's role?"

"I would be honored, sir".

Finally. Something concrete I knew how to do! So, we bowed in prayer and asked God's guidance on what we were attempting, that it would meet His goals rather than ours. When I finished, the President said, "I believe you have the right idea, Mr. Reed. If we get this right in God's eyes, it will BE right."

"Amen, sir," I said.

"Amen indeed!" said Ben.

Chapter 69

Revisions

Monday morning we started our staff meeting which, I assumed, would take a while since we had new marching orders, so I began to bring the staff up to date on our meeting with the President. I had just begun when Bill interrupted me to read an alert he'd just received on his phone.

"Turn on the TV," he said. I hit the remote to bring down the projection screen while at the same time turning on the projector and switching it over to the TV tuner. Then I punched up the twenty-four hour cable news station which was right in the middle of live coverage of a breaking news story. In a few minutes, the announcer did a quick summary:

"For those of you just joining us, here's what we know. Apparently the U.S. had intelligence of a pending attack on the aircraft carrier George H. W. Bush from insurgent forces inside Syria. Acting on this intelligence, the President authorized a strike from this same carrier on these forces destroying them before the attack could take place. Over the weekend, while at Camp David, the President was in contact with the Pentagon and his National Security Advisor, as well as intelligence services, and as a result of this intelligence, late last night he ordered the strike. As expected, Iran and other similarly aligned countries immediately condemned the strike, and at least one source is claiming civilian casualties. No word from the White House as yet, but we are awaiting a briefing to begin within the hour."

I muted the TV, told Bill to go in the lounge and have the news coverage recorded on the DVR, and called the meeting back to task. "Well, I guess we now know our meeting with the President will be kept secret. There were some phone calls and some quick asides with the National Security Advisor, but we had no idea this was all going on in the background. However, it does point out one theme we were discussing – the roll of intelligence assets and the need for doing things in secret. Ben, this might be a great case to study as you look at the proper Constitutional role for intelligence, and what adjustments might need to be made there."

"Yes," said Ben. "I suppose in one way it is fortunate this is happening just as we are addressing this need for intelligence. It seems the Almighty is reaching His hand into history for our benefit."

"Oh, Ben," I said, "I have felt that from the beginning. So, let's do the job right."

Everyone nodded, so we got back to work.

Over the next few weeks, Ben went over every one of the items on the to-do list we'd assembled based on the Camp David meetings, and developed a list of items he wished to study further. To dig deeper into these items, some questions had to be answered that were beyond our scope of knowledge. In those cases I emailed requests to the Chief of Staff who then arranged for the appropriate people with the knowledge and, in some cases the clearance, to discuss these matters personally with Ben and me. We were given temporary security clearances for some of these meetings, which came with very specific and somber warnings on sharing any of the classified information we might have become aware of. Since these meetings were for background purposes only, and any revelations would first be reviewed by the President and his Chief of Staff, we were careful to document any information we garnered from background briefings that made their way into Ben's reports.

We decided to break each recommendation down into separate sections which could then be assembled into a single report once all of the sections were completed. In the meantime, the President, and whomever he chose to do a review, could critique Ben's conclusions, or offer him further perspective, until both parties were satisfied that no further changes were possible. At that time, the report would become Ben's and Ben's only to the President. As one might expect, the ramifications would be far reaching, and quite impossible but for the stature of Ben Franklin.

All this took several weeks, and by the time Ben pronounced the report complete, the various campaigns had heated up. So I emailed the report using my White House encryption key, and we waited. The current polls indicated a close Presidential race, with a number of Senate and House seats up for grabs, but it was still a long time before the November election. Because of the pressures of the campaign and all the focus on the various races, it took several days for the President to react to Ben's recommendations. Finally, late one Thursday afternoon in July, I fielded a call from the Chief of Staff.

"Tom, we need you and Ben at the White House Friday. Can you be here at six p.m.?"

"Yes, sir." I said. What else was I going to say?

So, like last time, I received all the information on arrival, but since all the work had been done on the report, all we really took with us was the information we'd gathered along the way on a secure thumb drive, along with a virgin laptop on which we could access that information, and printed and bound copies of Ben's report – one for each of us, and a spare. Since this was a classified report, our security would be tasked with protecting both the reports and the thumb drive as well as our physical security. While we didn't expect anyone to actually threaten us, there was always the danger of accident or theft, so the extra security would be there as a check on anything like that.

Friday we left on the NSF jet headed for Washington, and in short order after landing we were entering the White House through the same passageway we'd used on our first visit. While we waited in the anteroom just off the President's area, I was nervous as a cat, but Ben was in good spirits.

"So, Ben. Are you ready for this?" I asked.

"Of course," said Ben. "Apparently I was born for this."

Shortly the Secret Service came to fetch us and ushered us into the Oval Office where the President was waiting. He crossed the room and shook hands with us and motioned us to the couch adjacent to a plush chair where he sat down and began.

"Thank you for coming on such short notice, but with the press focused on the coming primary and the last minute push this weekend, I thought this might be a good time to bring you in under the radar for another chat."

"Very enterprising, Mr. President," said Ben. "Keep the wolves at bay while the lambs make their plots. How would you like to begin?"

"I have read each section of your report," he said, "including the footnotes you provided with the rationale for your conclusions. While I agree with the thrust of what you recommend on most of these proposals, I fear you are still far too radical with some of these far reaching changes."

Ben chuckled a bit and said, "Oh, Mr. President. You forget – I am a radical!"

The President laughed at this one, then said, "Well, I guess that's right, but there are political realities that unfortunately cannot be ignored."

"I anticipated that," said Ben. "Believe me when I tell you that these 'realities' are no different than realities I have faced before. But you must understand, sir, that I firmly believe that by not enacting these changes at a minimum, our country will continue to stray from liberty, as have all governments throughout history."

"I am aware of history, Dr. Franklin," the President said as he nodded, "and I agree that some things need to change. But there are over 200 years of history behind these changes, and it will take nothing short of a miracle to get consideration on any of these."

"Our entire country is a miracle, Mr. President," Ben said. "I refuse to believe the Almighty has finished His work here. What kind of miracle do you think is needed?"

The President sat back and smiled. I actually saw this one coming. "Dr. Franklin. I already have my miracle, if you're willing."

"Oh, I am most certainly willing. What do you propose?"

"A joint committee of the House and Senate on the reorganization of government," the President said emphatically. "Beginning next week, as we discussed, we will bring in certain key members of Congress whose races are either safe or are not up for election this cycle, and brief them on Tom's project and its success. This initial briefing will take place strictly between the White House and these individual members. Depending on the success of those revelations, we will schedule introductions between you and each of these members. Your job will be to set them up for the contents of your report, which we will release to them at the proper moment. I will insist on this committee made up of these members, and that they convene a special joint committee, in secret, which you will work with to further your proposals. Are you up to this task?"

Ben immediately nodded and said, "Of course, Mr. President. I relish this task!"

For the next hour the President and Ben went over the names of the members he had in mind, and I made notes on each one so we could research them back at the office. Finally the President looked over at me.

"Tom, you will be in integral part of this process."

"In what way, sir?"

"There will be opposition, of course, so Ben's identity will have to be proven. I have to believe you have already addressed this issue, so I need you to be prepared to offer whatever evidence is necessary to convince these men from Congress that this Dr. Franklin is indeed the Dr. Franklin of 1787. Only if they truly believe he is who he is will his words carry any weight. There will necessarily be meetings between you and these members, so you'll need to be prepared for pointed questions and no small amount of skepticism."

"I understand, Mr. President. I will assemble some proposals and run it by your Chief of Staff. He has been very helpful thus far, so I feel confident we can put together a plan."

"Good. Use whatever resources you need. You'll be notified when the process is underway. Now, do either of you have any questions?"

"Just one," said Ben.

"Sure, go ahead," said the President.

"How hard are you willing to fight for this?"

Chapter 70

Congressional Preparation

Over the weekend I received an email from the Chief of Staff containing the names of the members of Congress the President had singled out for briefing on our project. The plan was to break this into two elements: The first would focus on proving the existence of the real Ben Franklin. The second would be his desire that Ben, as one of the Founders, would recommend governmental changes for Congress' consideration. The shock of the first revelation, it was hoped, would prepare the way for the second. In the meantime, our job was to look at these members in order to determine the best approach to them.

I assembled the crew, and passed out the names, instructing them to prepare information packets on each one. I tasked Kathy with personal bios on each one, Miriam with their congressional records, and I asked Bill to look into their political careers from obscurity through the present. This detail should help Bill determine the best approach when speaking with each of these leaders, and we wanted to give him the best shot possible.

It took the rest of the week to assemble all the information, so we had a final review Friday afternoon just before breaking for the week. Afterwards I felt we had a pretty good handle on each of the members, but I wanted Ben's opinion.

"Ben. How do you feel about meeting these gentlemen?"

"One thing I have learned," he said. "Men all down through history have done things for the same reasons. The methods may change, but the men and their motivations don't. With the proper appeal, most will do the right thing. However, the approach must be right." He smiled for a moment, then said, "I think, from what we have here, I shall find the right approach."

"Alright then. We're adjourned for the weekend. See everyone again on Monday."

I was watching the ballgame Saturday afternoon when there was a knock at the door. Kathy opened it to find Ben standing there.

"Hi, Ben," she said. "Please, come in."

"Come on in, Ben," I said. "Have a seat. What's on your mind?"

"I feel we are at a precipice," he began. "The Republic is in peril and I fear we have this one chance to put it back on course. I appreciate the work you and the rest have done, Tom, and I feel that we are prepared, but there is always a danger that events may intervene, and since no one can foresee the future, I feel we are lacking an important element."

"Oh, I don't know about that, Ben," I said. "I just happen to know Someone who knows the future, and I have not left Him out of this process."

"That is exactly what I was talking about. How can we know we have Providence on our side?"

"Well, Ben," I said, "there is a famous quote from President Abraham Lincoln, that was echoed by President Ronald Reagan about that. They said '*My concern is not whether God is on our side; my greatest concern is that we are on God's side*'. I believe that's exactly what the Bible tells us. If we seek His will, doors will open."

Ben nodded. "Well, my dear sir. We are facing an open door. I believe how we enter it will affect what's on the other side."

"I agree," I said. "Tell you what. Come to Church tomorrow. I know a way to enlist others to appeal to God without disclosing the reason. Afterwards, let me know how you feel. Whatever the outcome, I believe if we do our best and ask for His intervention, nothing will be impossible."

We talked for a while longer, and Ben stayed through the end of the game, and shared our evening meal with us. We had a nice relaxing time until Ben said he wanted to do some reading before bed. The next morning, just as I was preparing to start our Sunday School class, Ben walked in, to the greetings of the rest of the class. He had been a frequent attendee anyway, but I was still glad to see him there. Just before I opened in prayer, I made a quick request.

"We have been asked to pray for our country this week, and for those in positions of authority. This is a request for an unspoken reason, but like so many times before, we know God is always aware of the situations here. So, I ask you to, as we have before, to include this simple request in your daily prayers."

I then opened in prayer, and we conducted our class without any questions on the prayer reason. After the prayer, I caught the Pastor before we went into the sanctuary and made the same request of him. Just before beginning the service, the Pastor made a similar announcement from the pulpit and offered a special prayer for our nation. Our entire Church was, without knowing the specific purpose, offering prayers for our success. Additionally, the Pastor's sermon was on faith as the '*substance of things hoped for, and the evidence of things not seen*'. Again, I had no idea of the subject before the service.

After Church, we asked Ben to lunch at our house, but he declined, and his reason to me was one that really put me in my place.

"Thank you, Tom, for the invitation, but I shall spend the rest of this weekend fasting for the upcoming events. I thank you for your arranging these supplications before Providence this morning. Once your Pastor started his sermon, to me the way was clear. We shall do our utmost, and leave the rest to the Almighty."

"Well said, Ben!" I replied. "I believe we are on the right track, and that you are here for a purpose. I'm honored to be part of this process. I also believe that history may be made here that very few this side of eternity will ever be aware of."

We shook hands and Ben went his way. Monday morning, at the staff meeting, I opened by recounting the weekend's events, and we had prayer specifically for Ben and his mission, as well as for each of the members of Congress who would be involved. From that point on, we were on the mission with him, and we were ready for however it all turned out.

Chapter 71

Congress

The White House Chief of Staff called again to give me an update on the President's plan. Starting Tuesday he would be bringing in members of Congress from the list he'd provided and begin briefing them on our project. The first would be the Majority and Minority Leaders of the Senate, and the Speaker of the House, and the House Minority Leader along with the Vice President. Once these gentlemen were convinced, they would be instrumental in bringing the other members on board. But, to convince these leaders, our presence would be required. Back to D. C.

When we arrived via our now-familiar covert entrance, we were escorted back to the holding room off the Presidential offices. When it was time, the Secret Service brought me into the Oval Office where the President and his Chief of Staff were waiting along with the Vice President. After exchanging greetings, I was informed that the Vice President had been briefed and kept up to speed since our initial meeting and, indeed, was introduced to the project right after the President first became aware of it. After a few minutes the President was informed the four Congressional leaders were there, so he had them brought in.

As they entered and greeted the President, Vice President, and his Chief of Staff, the President brought them over to the seating area opposite his desk where I was parked.

"Gentlemen," the President began, "This is Tom Reed of the National Science Foundation, and he's the reason I've asked you here today."

We shook hands, and the President asked us all to have a seat, at which point he started with an introduction to the reason for their being here.

"I apologize for asking you to keep this meeting off the books, but what we are going to discuss here is highly classified, for the reasons you will shortly understand. As you all know, there are several initiatives I have discussed with you recently in a general way, and while we never turned it into anything concrete, today's briefing will begin a process to move these initiatives forward. But, before we get to that point, there is some background you must first understand, and secondly accept. This will take a while, so I'll ask you to be patient until Mr. Reed here has fully explained his part in all this. You may ask any question you like, and I expect you to be frank in both your questions and your concerns."

"Sounds ominous," said the Senate Minority Leader, and the Speaker nodded. "But, at your request, we've both blocked the afternoon for a conference on western government lands and crop rights that we ducked out of, so proceed and tell us what this is all about."

"With that, Tom, you're up," said the President.

I started with the Star Trek reference without mentioning Star Trek, the DARPA Project which, as it turns out they had been briefed on.

"Wait," said the Speaker. "That project was yours?"

"Yes," I said. "My team developed the project and turned it over to DARPA. That project was to be able to transfer inanimate objects from one place to another using a time portal to reassemble a molecular 'snapshot'."

"So, you're the guy who crashed CERN, huh?" asked the Senate Majority Leader.

"Yes, I'm afraid so. That was an accident, but we quickly learned from it, readjusted, and finally used it to transfer some objects. I haven't been kept briefed on that project since we turned it over to DARPA, but it was the genesis for our current project."

"Well, I certainly hope you don't crash the supercollider again." he said with a wry grin. "I was on the technology subcommittee at the time and had a rather embarrassing meeting with the Director over there. I'd rather not do that again!"

"Well, Senator, we've learned our lesson on that one. However, we have learned other lessons as well."

I proceeded to describe the issues with molecular transfer of biologics, and how we'd addressed them. I described the cockroach and the other initial transfers which led to the subject of having two of initially-identical organisms, and how that would be a problem. When I told them about transferring the chimpanzee, that really got their attention.

"Wait," said the Speaker. "Are you telling me you were able to make an exact duplicate of a live chimpanzee while keeping the original alive?"

"Yes," I said, "And he was completely unaware that anything had occurred."

"Amazing!" said the Senate Minority Leader, then he looked over at the President. "And all of this has been verified?"

"Absolutely," said the President. "I have a binder full of briefing material for you once we're done here. It is truly revolutionary!" and he shot me a knowing look. It was all I could do not to laugh.

"What are the plans for this technology?" asked the House Minority Leader.

"The original idea," I continued, "was when I was with DARPA. They saw it as a possible way of transporting covert operatives, maybe even troops, into trouble areas. But, the problems associated with that scenario caused the program to be shelved until the NSF became aware of the program. That led to the current project."

"Describe some of those problems," said the President.

I took the next few minutes to talk about what happens when you have two identical Joe Americans running around, and even offered the only real way to remedy those issues: One of the identities had to cease to exist.

"I see," said the Speaker. "So if those are the problems, and I assume you have not solved them, what are we here to talk about?"

Here we go. "Well, remember how we're opening portals into the recent past to 'freeze' the subject, then replicating them into the immediate present?"

"Yes," he said.

"Who said it had to be in the recent past?" and I just let that sit there for a moment.

The Senator Majority Leader spoke first. "Are you saying what I think you're saying?"

"Yes, Senator," I said. "If the original subject is no longer living, we don't have the problem of two of them running around. Now, sending someone back in time is problematic on several fronts, not the least of which is the highly unpredictable disastrous effects on history. But, bringing a figure from the past to the present is possible."

"Possible?" said the Speaker.

"Absolutely," I said.

"And how far back in history can you go?" he asked.

"Well, Mr. Speaker, that is unknown, since we've only done it once." The bomb had been dropped. It only took a couple of seconds to explode.

"What!? You've already done this!?" asked the Senate Minority Leader incredulously.

"Yes." I then went on to explain the problem of time and place back in history, then the creation of the list, and the command for the supercomputer to work with the supercollider to retrieve the highest person on the list it could find.

The Congressmen all exchanged looks. Then, they looked at the President.

"Mr. President," said the Senator Minority Leader, "are you seriously telling me we have succeeded in breaking the time barrier and brought someone from the past into present day?"

"Yes," said the President, "and I've met him on more than one occasion, and his identity has been verified. Mr. Vice-President?"

The Vice-President took over. "The day after he arrived, Mr. Reed here had some blood samples taken. These were forwarded by the ex-Navy physician to the Surgeon General. I was tasked by the President with verifying his identity. I had those samples taken to three labs – at the CIA, the NSA, and the FBI - where the DNA information was extracted without telling them where the sample came from. That DNA information was then taken to three different labs, including one used by the FBI, again without divulging any information. It was then compared to known samples in the present day and without exception there was a match. In addition, Mr. Reed here, separately, had the same tests performed. I

324

am as sure of this identity as I am of my own. In fact, I trust this man is who he appears to be more than I trust who you gentlemen are, since I've never verified your DNA," and he smiled.

I had been unaware of the NSA/CIA/FBI angle, but it didn't surprise me.

The Congressmen all looked at each other again.

"And you've seen him, too, Mr. Vice President?"

"The evidence, yes," he said, "but the person, no. The Chief of Staff here has, though, and has indeed verified the whole incredible story."

They looked at each other again, then the Majority Leader of the United States Senate asked the question I'd been waiting on.

"So. Who is it?"

The President pressed a button on his phone and said, simply, "Send him in."

The door opened and the President stood up, followed by everyone else in the room as Ben walked through the door wearing the clothes, including his spectacles, he was wearing that first day. He walked right up to the Speaker of the House of Representatives, bowed slightly, and offered his hand.

"Greetings, Gentlemen. My name is Ben. Benjamin Franklin of Philadelphia, Pennsylvania."

Chapter 72

Buildup

It was a thing to behold. Ben was in his element. All those years of dealing with politicians, and his time as America's diplomat, had all led to this moment. He charmed the socks off the best politicians in the land and when it was all over, they had no doubt this was the actual Ben Franklin, Founding Father, standing in front of them, and he had an agenda. So, if you're one of the leaders of the government, what are you going to do? You're not going to like what Ben has to say, but if word ever gets out that you snubbed one of our most revered Founders, you and your Party are done!

The President gave them their marching orders. Arrange meetings with the others on his list and give serious consideration to Ben's ideas. In the briefing package the President gave the Congressmen, was a copy of Ben's revised report, and a copy of his national security statement classifying the very existence of Benjamin Franklin as well as the entire project that brought him here. He was very cordial to them, but he left them no wiggle room. But, since all of this would be done in secret, he had hoped grandstanding would be minimized. Time would tell. Since both parties were represented in the meeting, and since Ben had no Party affiliation, everything had an initial feel of bi-partisanship to it, but none of us were under any illusion. That would quickly cease to be the case, particularly as these proposals encroached heavily on partisan agencies, policies, and pet projects. But, the President was behind Ben on these, so the game was on.

With the bringing on board the other members of Congress left to the leadership, and the Vice-President monitoring the process for the President, we went back to Philadelphia. We were told not to expect phone calls from any of the members, but face to face meetings in D. C. would certainly be required, so we resigned ourselves to the fact we'd be back. At the staff meeting we had after the meeting, we went back over every member on the President's list as we reviewed the reaction of the leadership we'd met with. After a couple of days we felt confident in Ben's ability to discuss the issues in the proper historical and, more importantly, political contexts. So we waited. It didn't take long.

A few days later I received a call from the President's Chief of Staff informing me there were a series of *meet and greet* meetings set up for the end of the week with the members who had been contacted by the Leadership, so back to D. C. we went. One by one we met with the individual Congressmen and Ben was just as impressive with them as he had been in the Oval Office. Each of these individuals, though, had problems with at least some of Ben's proposals, but he handled each objection firmly and with not only a Founder's perspective, but with well articulated arguments behind each one. A couple of times I would really like to have seen this televised, because Ben was just that impressive. In the end I, while not a political animal of any kind, would guess Ben had at least an even chance of getting most of his proposals through this group. The question was, where was all this going to go? We were talking to only a minority of the members of Congress, and the full House and Senate both had to agree on any changes, but these were the movers and shakers, and if this episode ever came to light, while the public reaction would be impossible to gauge, it would certainly be something to fear. So the pressure was on to figure out a way to make at least some of this work.

One powerful senator who represented a Southern state in particular, though, voiced doubts of the reality of what we'd done. I get that. Had I not been there and involved in the project as long as I had been, I would have had problems with it as well. But, this gentleman was a powerful committee chairman, and his support would be crucial. So, after a particularly difficult meeting with him where he expressed he still had doubts about the possibility of this technology, I offered a proposal of my own.

"Senator," I said, "would you like to see it work?"

"What do you mean 'see it work'? How?" he asked in his trademark Southern drawl.

"What if I could prove the technology works in a way that would be unmistakable?"

Ben gave me a 'where are you going with this look', but the Senator said, "I'm open to that possibility. How would you suggest we proceed?"

"Well, sir," I said, "I read you lost a family pet, a dog as I recall, a couple of years ago. He was hit by a car, as I remember."

"Yes, that's true," said the Congressman as he shook his head. "I loved that dog."

"Well, sir. It will take a few days, a couple of favors, and some Providential help, as well as help from some of our friends overseas, but I might be able to arrange a demonstration. Will you commit to traveling to our office as soon as I can set something up?"

He was trapped, and he knew it. "Yes, I suppose."

"Then, I need a couple of pieces of information from you. I will have a member of my staff contact you for that information while I work out the logistics."

327

He agreed, and we went on to finish out the rest of the meetings with no more major glitches. We went back to the office, and I had Miriam do a work up of the information we'd need. If we could pull this off, the Senator's doubts would vanish. She contacted the Senator's office, emailed him the requests, and we waited for his reply. Two days later, we got what we were looking for. I loaded all the particulars into the software, and made some phone calls – the most important one to my contact in Geneva. Some strings were pulled, and we ended up with time booked on both the supercomputer and on the LHC. All was set for this Saturday at 2200 Zulu time, which would be five p.m. in Philly. I called the Senator's office and left him a message. In a half hour he called back, and I asked him to be here at four Saturday. He reluctantly agreed.

Saturday, a bit after four, he came walking into our office. When it was almost time, I escorted him into the room where Ben had first appeared, asked him to have a seat on the the the bench I had sat on that first day. Then, I excused myself, went into the office and typed a couple of commands into the dedicated link to the supercomputer, and went back to join the Senator. At exactly five p.m. we heard the five beeps from the outer room, and a few seconds later, a beautiful German Shepherd appeared in front of us, paused for a second, then when he saw the Senator sitting there, immediately jumped into his arms and began licking him in the face. As the realization set in that this might actually be true, the Senator's eyes welled up with tears, and when he examined the dog's tag around his neck, they started streaming down his face.

"Is...can...how did you...." he stammered as he pet the dog. In a few moments he regained his composure. "My wife bought him for me for my birthday. She died last year. I....I can't believe you actually brought him back to me."

"Glad to," I said as he continued to pet the dog, who was obviously glad to see him. I reached over and gave the dog a good rub, then said, "So, Senator. What's your opinion of Dr. Franklin now?"

He stood up, shook my hand, and said, "I don't think you could have done anything any more than this to convince me. Is he here?"

"Yes. Just down the hall. Would you like to say hello?"

"Of course! Come on, boy," he said to the dog as we left the room and went down the hall. Ben was in his office reading when we knocked on the door and walked in. As the Senator walked over to him Ben rose and the Senator extended his hand. "Dr. Franklin," he said as he grasped Ben's hand in both of his, "I just wanted to say I apologize for doubting you, but this..." and he motioned, teary-eyed, to his newly-arrived companion, "...this is proof beyond all doubt for me. While I am still uncomfortable with your proposals, because of who you are, I will give them, and all the reasons you have supplied with them, all the consideration they deserve."

Ben smiled as he shook his hand. "That is all we ask, sir. If you ever have any questions, I shall be at your service."

The Senator looked over at me, then down to his pet, then back to Ben. "I will always remember this day. Thank you. Thank you both."

"It was our pleasure, Senator," said Ben.

"Well, I should be on my way. I have much to consider. I'll see my way out. Please come by my office the next time you're in Washington. I would like to see you again – both of you!"

"We will," I said. The Senator turned, and with his friend in step with him, walked down the hall, and out of the building for the trip back to D.C. "Well, Ben," I said. "I think we just gained at least part of a vote."

Ben laughed. "I would say, Tom, that Providence has once again smiled on us. But, the retrieving of his dog was genius."

"Well, I've always said God works out of left field, and I know you may not understand that baseball term, but in this case, He worked in the form of a German Shepard dog!"

Ben nodded and said with a grin, "Apparently, this time he worked out of the South!"

Chapter 73

Joint Committee

There was a bit of a lull after the episode with the Senator in our office, and I learned later that he had related that story to a number of the other members on the list of those read in on the project, and while we didn't know what the effect was, I suspected it couldn't have been anything but positive. It simply reinforced our insistence that the technology existed, had been used, and Ben Franklin was the result. I had a couple of email exchanges with the Chief of Staff's office that rendered the information that, basically, things were moving along, albeit slow. Actually, Ben was satisfied with that information.

"We never intended Congress to act swiftly," he said. "Our intent was for them to deliberate and justify every action, examining issues from every viewpoint, in the hope that any damage a government could inflict on the public would be minimal. It appears at least that part still works to some degree."

Well, I understood that, but I was still anxious. I was in the middle of a political windstorm that could turn into a cyclone at any minute, and here I was without a storm shelter. Ben, on the other hand, was very much enjoying the process. While he was adamant his suggested changes needed to be made, getting representatives of the People to deliberate these changes - their wisdom or lack thereof - and what the ramifications might be if enacted, this was the process they'd put in place, and he had an almost front row seat. Little did I know that's exactly what was going to happen.

The election took place, and the President was re-elected, along with all the members on the selection list with one exception, and that one apparently didn't throw a monkey wrench into things, but the process did, as a result of the elections, slow down to a crawl. We waited.

One of the things we did was watch a lot of C-Span. Ben had already been a convert, and any time the Congress was in session, you could go in his office and coverage of either the House or the Senate would be on his TV, and many conversations took place over lunch about his impressions of how the nation's business was conducted. It took Ben, and the rest of us for that matter, a long time to understand the complicated and sometimes arcane rules of both houses of Congress, but in the end Ben understood their rules better than most in the

Congress did. Because of our ongoing research, early on we received copies of the actual rules in place, and were kept updated on any changes that took place when Congress was in session. Additionally, Ben received a copy of the Congressional Record as soon as it was ready, so over time he became what people refer to as a 'policy wonk'. I'm still not sure where the term 'wonk' came from, but it sure sounded appropriate. I couldn't get into the minutia of all the posturing and maneuvering that was the daily currency in Congress. I suppose if you're the center of major proposals in Congress, you might want to be aware of the rules, so in that case I really didn't blame him.

The inauguration came. Congress had reconvened. There was a flurry of activity with the new Congress coming right out of an election cycle as promises made had to either be kept, or the lack of progress blamed on someone else so funds could be raised for the next election cycle. Either way, it was the middle of the year before Ben came back to the center of attention, at least in the minds of those who'd been selected.

I received a call from the White House operator informing me that the President would be calling at one-thirty p.m., and had asked that my entire staff be available to take the call. I had Ben, Miriam, Kathy, Bill, Phillip, and Rick, who happened to be on daytime duty as Ben's security, assembled in the conference room when the call came in.

"I want to tell you all," said the President, "that I appreciate the work you've done in preparing Dr. Franklin for this endeavor. I can tell from the reports we've been provided with that much research went into his preparation, and it certainly shows in the finished product."

"On behalf of the staff, I thank you, Mr. President," I said.

"Well, the next stage is upon us. I received a call from the Speaker of the House, and they have scheduled a series of highly confidential hearings on the reality of one of our Founding Father's being present in our time, and the proposal that Dr. Franklin has advanced, and that I have asked them to consider. As you may suspect, there is considerable controversy surrounding these proposals, and the only thing that kept them from being dead on arrival in Congress is who they came from. So, Dr. Franklin. Are you prepared to back up your conclusions?"

"Unquestionably, Mr. President!" Ben exclaimed.

"Well, then. That is exactly what you may be required to do. As I understand it, these hearings will take place in secret over the next two weeks, culminating in your personal testimony on Saturday, two weeks from now. You will be sworn in, and sit before a joint committee co-chaired by the Majority Leader of the Senate, and the Speaker of the House. You will make an opening statement, as lengthy as you deem appropriate, after which all the members of the select committee will be allowed time to ask you questions and to challenge your assumptions and conclusions. Are you sure you're prepared for this?"

"Of course, Mr. President. I have watched many hours of these types of hearings on C-Span, so I am quite aware of the process, and indeed I have already prepared an opening statement. I shall work with the staff here to ensure all my facts are accurate, and shall answer any questions the members may have for me."

I had been unaware of his opening statement preparation, but now that I thought about it, I should have anticipated this. Realizing this, though, I was glad Ben had already taken the initiative. My next goal would be to read that thing!

"Excellent," said the President. "Would it be too much to ask you to provide me an advanced copy?"

"Of course not!" said Ben. "As soon as I have a finished statement ready, I will have Tom forward you a copy."

"Thank You," said the President. "I will be provided a closed-circuit feed of the hearings here in the Oval Office, so I'll be watching with great interest the hearings. As always, let my staff know if there's anything you require."

"We shall," said Ben.

"I would like you to come up the day before and dine with me and the First Lady, if that's acceptable. I just want to make sure all the points are covered. I assure you, we have some of the best chefs in the world here in the White House, so I promise you a sumptuous meal. Tom, I would ask you and your entire staff to join us as well."

Wow! That was not expected.

"Of course, Mr. President," I said. "We'd all be delighted!"

Ben spoke up next. "Delightful, sir. I very much look forward to spending this time with you and the First Lady."

"Fine," said the President. "It's set, then. I'll have my office contact you with the usual details. Until then, gentlemen."

"Thank you, Mr. President," I said as he ended the call.

I looked around the table, and there were shocked faces, but beaming smiles all around. I hoped this would still be the case in two weeks after the hearings!

Chapter 74

The White House – Again

We decided to drive from Philly to Washington this time, so Miriam rented us a nice van and we headed out. Since we were going to be there for the duration of the hearings, it just seemed better to have our own vehicle that we could just turn back in when we came back home. Just over three hours later we pulled up in front of the hotel and checked in. It was time for lunch, but since we were having dinner at the White House, I ordered some sandwiches from room service and we ate in. The plan that came in from the White House had us arriving via the usual route at five p.m. wherein we were ushered into the Oval Office. Ben and I had been here several times already, but this was only the second trip for the rest of the crew, and I could tell the wonder had not diminished.

The President greeted each one of us, and had us sit in the mini-conference area where we had mostly small talk about the trip, but the President also gave us an overview of the weekend to come. A lot of work had gone into setting up mundane meetings designed to do anything but garner media attention. Once the subterfuge was in place, the appropriate Congressmen would leave and enter a secure conference room where the hearing would take place. There were backup stories in case someone in the media got a whiff of a covert meeting, but the fact that it was a Saturday went a long way towards keeping things behind the curtain. The leaders had decided to go into the night Saturday to keep the number of meetings down, but they also left open the option of meeting the following day if it was required. There was also a plan to have Ben on hand the following week for the members to spend additional time with him individually. But, this is what Ben had hoped for. I was going to be a long week.

After spending almost an hour in the Oval Office, the President invited us to the dining area, and when we walked in there I wasn't sure about anybody else, but I felt under-dressed. The room was beautiful and the table immaculate, and each plate had a menu in handwritten calligraphy. We were informed that the stewards were not in on who Ben was, so when they were in the room, we put all the focus on Miriam, as though she was the honored guest. This delighted her to no end, and at the end of the meal the President autographed a copy of the menu for her, which of course she would never be able to show anyone!

The President was charming, animated, and told some pretty good jokes. But the real fun came when he asked Ben to tell us some of the things from before we had grabbed him. Ben was once again in his element. He regaled us with stories of the Founders, including some anecdotes that should never appear in a history book! He had detailed information on the world of the time, foreign leaders, diplomatic endeavors he'd been involved in, including his famous dust-up with John Adams during their time in Paris.

"Don't misunderstand," he said. "Mr. Adams is a brilliant man, but he tends to be much too direct and that does not serve him well in his encounters with others with slightly differing opinions. His salvation, though, is Abigail, whom I believe to be the force behind the man. She truly also is brilliant."

It was strange to hear him speak of others of his colleagues in present tense, since they'd all been deceased for 200 years, but for him, it had only been around two and a half years. Still, it was surreal. I wish I had taken notes, but I did make a mental note to have Ben document as much of this as he could when we returned. This would be another document that would never make it to the public arena, but I could certainly see a briefing book for incoming Presidents and other select individuals.

The session continued until almost ten-thirty p.m., and we all had a long weekend ahead of us, so the President began to wrap things up.

"Well," he said, "I know you all have a lot ahead of you, but I swear Dr. Franklin, I could sit all night and talk with you. Promise me that after all this political turmoil is completed, you'll come to Camp David with me and continue relating your experiences."

"Of course, Mr. President! I would be honored!"

"No, Dr. Franklin," said the President. "The honor will, of course, be all mine."

We left the White House shortly afterward and headed for the Hotel. Reveille would be early, and I didn't want to tire Ben out any more than we already had. An hour later we were all tucked in and fighting the anticipation in hopes of a good night's sleep. I didn't have much luck, but I hoped more than anything that Ben did.

Chapter 75

Joint Special Congressional Committee

The hearing was scheduled to begin at ten, but we arrived at eight to be sure we were fully prepared and ready to start. The Speaker of the House had a waiting area for us and I had a special request.

"Is there a place where Ben can change clothes?", I asked. "The one's he's wearing were only for the trip over here."

The Speaker was a bit confused, but provided access to a restroom adjacent to the holding room we were to enter from. The rest of our staff went in through a different door, as they were among the few non-staffers to be seated behind Ben in the audience area. At ten, the Speaker, House Minority Leader, the Senate Majority and Minority leaders, as well as the other select members seated themselves, and a member of the Speaker's staff came in to collect Ben and myself. I would be sitting beside him at the table, but only in case there were additional questions on the process that brought him here. When the staff member came in, though, he had a shock. So did the rest of the Committee. As we walked in and sat down, every eye was on Ben Franklin, who once again was dressed in the exact clothing he was wearing the day he appeared in our offices, spectacles, trademark walking stick and all. He even had his Wagstaff in his watch pocket. He had every weapon in his arsenal ready for this encounter. The Speaker gaveled the hearing to order and welcomed the members, then welcomed us. There was a short period of instructions, laying out the procedures for the hearing, which would be much less stringent than those you'd see on TV. The only camera in the room was the closed circuit camera for the President. Next, he addressed Ben.

"Dr. Franklin, I must say, you are a sight to behold. Many of us had a problem coming to the conclusion that your existence here in our time was not only possible, but likely, but to see the vision we have before us, it is much less difficult to accept now. There have been a few occasions in my time in Congress where I could say I had been a part of a major historical event, and today's hearing certainly falls into that category, and eclipses anything else I have experienced. I expect that is the case for everyone else here on the Committee. Per the rules we have agreed on, and per the standard rules of both the House and the Senate, our first task is to swear you and Mr. Reed in, after which you can make your opening statements. Would you both please rise and raise your right hands."

We did, and he administered the oath to each of us and we resumed our seats. The Speaker then recognized me for an opening statement. I had vowed to keep mine simple, since this was Ben's hearing.

"Thank you, Mr. Speaker. Ladies and Gentlemen, first I am honored and humbled to be sitting here today. My role in all that has transpired has been that of a glorified transport agent. You are all now aware of the genesis of the project that began at DARPA, and that project is still ongoing. This part of the project was designed to supplement that previous project by transferring humans quickly and covertly, but there were problems with that plan, as I have outlined in my notes which you now have, so I won't go into that. However, those problems essentially disappeared when we considered the possibility of copying and replicating individuals from far enough in the past that their existence would no longer pose logistical problems. That project resulted in this distinguished gentleman sitting beside me today. My staff, seated behind me, has been instrumental in helping Dr. Franklin through this adjustment period, and when asked, helping him with the research he required for the proposals you will be considering."

"In all this preparation, we have limited ourselves to providing him with facts, and allowing him to form his own opinions, which he will no doubt express to you without hesitation. In that time, I have come to know one of the most unique individuals in history. We have spent a considerable amount of time together over the last two and a half years, and it strains obviousness to say he is an impressive individual. Imagine, if you will, that first day when I asked his name and he replied 'Ben Franklin of Philadelphia, Pennsylvania'. I was as shocked as he was, but there was a difference. I could go home that night. He couldn't. I have apologized to Dr. Franklin on a number of occasions for having done this to him, and each time his graciousness has been exceeded only by the stature of his person."

"I have learned much from him, but that knowledge has only scratched the surface as I learned anew last evening as he told stories of his contemporaries, stories that have been lost to history but that offer an even greater insight and respect for those who gave us this government. So, my presence here today serves only one purpose. To offer any insight into his process in getting here, his time while here, and to support him in his endeavors. Other than that, this hearing is for Dr. Franklin, and Dr. Franklin only. I am, however, at your disposal for any area where I may have expertise. Thank you."

My part done, the Chairman called on Ben for his opening statement.

"Thank you, Mr. Chairman, and thank you Ladies and Gentlemen of the United States Congress. This is not my first Congress. My previous Congressional experience resulted in a small document known as the

Constitution of the United States of America. In fact, when Mr. Reed acquired me from my time and replicated me here into this time, I had just exited Independence Hall after having signed our Constitution."

Ben then held up a large parchment, and continued.

"I have here a replica of that Constitution. As you'll see, as the senior member of the delegates from Pennsylvania, my signature is here just above my good friend Thomas Mifflin. The ink was barely dry when I was transported to an office just outside Philadelphia some thirty one months ago. In the days following that event, Tom here and his staff provided me with documentation from the government archives that detailed our history since that day in Philadelphia."

Ben dipped his head and paused for a moment, then looked back up to the assembled committee and continued in a soft somber tone.

"We had such hopes for our country, and in many ways we were not disappointed. When I see the enterprising nature of our people, the resiliency in the face of many adversities, the inventiveness – something I am somewhat known for – all these traits of our people down through the centuries, all of which brought the United States into prominence and thrust her into a position as the most powerful nation on earth, I can confirm that that part of our hopes came true. There is much to celebrate. But, there is much to be concerned with as well. Powerful nations have existed all down through history, and until the United States, power was their primary concern. We – myself and the other Founders – wanted to change that."

As he continued, his voice increased somewhat in volume, and he took on a stern look on his face.

"What we wished for was Liberty. As was written, '*We hold these truths to be self evident, that all men are created equal and endowed BY THEIR CREATOR with certain unalienable rights.*' Freedom. Rights. We have those! What was needed was Liberty! Man needs to be able to exist on his own terms without being shackled with the whims and ambitions of others. We created this Constitution for the purpose of guaranteeing that liberty."

Ben placed the replica on the table, then picked up a large book off the floor.

"Imagine my disappointment when I discovered this cursed monstrosity!" and he slammed down on the table his copy of the Annotated Constitution, "All 2,882 pages of it. Laws. Rulings. Outright usurpations. A mastery of explanations into the minds of my fellow contemporaries – patriots all – that COMPLETELY MISSED THE MARK!", and at that he slammed his fist down on top of the book. "I see in this heresy decisions, rulings, interpretations, and opinions that constitute changes to the very document I signed, but were arrived at without the permission of the States, who are the final arbiters of any changes to our Constitution. Further I discover that future generations as far as one can see are saddled with a debt that every generation continues to add to with no intent to reverse the trend. A government that has invaded every facet of our citizen's lives. We invade their homes. We invade their enterprises. We confiscate their earnings. We regulate the very land and homes they live in. I use the term 'We', because apparently, not having done our job sufficiently, I and every other Founder must now condemn ourselves as complicit in this distortion of a document and standard we had hoped would do exactly the opposite!!", and he again pounded the desk with his fist.

As he had been speaking his voice gradually rose in volume with each sentence until he was practically shouting at the end.

Ben paused, looked around the room, then looked down, finally continuing again in a somber voice.

"Ladies and Gentlemen, I have experienced first hand what happens when an all invasive, all powerful government dips its hands into private lives. It is very easy to do, once you reach that point where you forget the purpose of government in the first place. In my first meeting with our President, I expressed these same sentiments, and he asked me to provide suggestions that I felt would alter a course that cannot lead to anything apart from disaster. I provided him with those suggestions, and was told that they were politically impossible. I recall another such meeting where we were told things were politically impossible. But, in the end, what we achieved was this." and he picked up the replica of the Constitution.

"We all, in those deliberations in Philadelphia, believed that men of good will could set aside their differences, suspicions, passions, and ambitions to create a land where freedom and rights would exist in liberty. We were propitious at the time. Perhaps, based on what I've seen in the last two and half years, we were wrong. I took the President's advice, and pared down my original suggestions to the document you have in your hands. To me, this is a bare minimum. I have spoken with each of you, and to varying degrees, I believe you all to be individuals who love and want what is best for this land and for the people whom you serve. I pray that in this process, we will discover that is indeed true."

"To that end, I....."

I was watching the committee when Ben paused in his speech. It took a couple of seconds for me to react when I saw the looks on the faces of all those seated in front of me. I looked over to my left and the chair was empty! As I started looking around to see where Ben had gone, members began rising from their seats, and in short order pandemonium broke out. I looked and there were guards at each of the doors, my staff was behind me, the members of Congress were still in front of me, but Ben was nowhere to be found. He had simply disappeared into thin air!

Chapter 76

Aftermath

Someone shouted, "Guard the doors!". There were shufflings and security personnel came out of nowhere. I looked at Kathy, then Miriam, and finally at Bill and Rick, who all looked to be helpless. Finally, the Speaker gaveled the room silent and ordered everyone to take their seats.

"Will the security personnel begin an immediate sweep of the room and the outer offices please?" he said. "Everyone else remain seated until we know what just happened to Dr. Franklin."

To say everyone was in a state of shock would be an understatement. My first thought was '*is there another time travel device somewhere that snatched up Ben*'? I couldn't fathom that possibility knowing what I had learned about the states of matter and time itself, but if anything I had demonstrated beyond a doubt that anything was possible. Shortly one of the plain clothes security members came up and whispered something to the two co-chairmen and the Speaker gaveled the room silent again.

"Ladies and Gentlemen, it appears that Dr. Franklin has vanished. He was here before us in one moment, and the next he was not. I am not sure how to proceed."

"Mr. Speaker," said the Senate Majority leader.

"Senator." replied the Speaker.

"May I ask a couple of questions?"

"Certainly!"

"Thank you," the Senator replied. Then he looked at me. "Mr. Reed. Have you any explanation for what has just transpired?"

The way he said that took me back to that very question Ben had asked that very moment he appeared that first day two and a half years ago. Wait, what was that thought...

"Mr. Reed! Have you an explanation?"

I looked at the Senator, then the Speaker, then around the table. Suddenly, the though coalesced in my brain, and I asked, "Wh-what is the date? What is today?"

"Why is that important..."

"The twelfth, right?"

"Why yes, of course," said the Senator. "Why?"

"Just a second, Senator. Let me check something. Does anyone here have a calendar that would go back at least three years?"

Someone pulled out an appointment book and showed it to the Chairman. He handed it to an aide who brought it over to me.

"What do you have in mind, Mr. Reed?"

I flipped the calendar back to the date Ben arrived, then to today's date, and did some quick calculations. Then the blood drained from my face.

"Mr. Reed?" insisted the Senator.

"Senator, I may have an idea, but I must admit it's just a theory."

"Well, let's have it then, Mr. Reed!"

"Ben first showed up in my office exactly two years and seven months ago to the day." I began. "Now, I haven't looked at the historical timeline, but one thing I do remember from his life was that he passed away from pleurisy. We knew much about his health before he appeared and were prepared to treat that ailment before it developed. He also suffered from occasional kidney stones and gout, both of which were also treated. The physician, a former Navy doctor of high regard, had given him a clean bill of health, and his expectation was that, absent some new malady he might be exposed to, he should live longer than his original life."

"Wait, are you telling us he just died?"

"Actually, Senator. What I'm telling you is that he already died, 230 years ago. You see, one of the ethical issues I struggled with was how God fit into all of this. I am a born again Christian, so I have a strong belief in the immortality of the human soul, and one of the first questions I asked was '*does this Ben Franklin have a soul, or did the other, or did both? How does that work?*'. I had no clue. So I left that issue up to God Himself, with the belief that if I was infringing in His territory, He would stop me. Well, He just did."

"How do you mean?" asked the Speaker.

"Ladies and Gentlemen, Ben Franklin died exactly two years and seven months to the day from the date of the signing of the Constitution of the United States. In other words, two years and seven months from the day we transferred him from in front of Independence Hall into our offices. Two years and seven months ago today, Ben Franklin was transported into the twenty-first century. Today he may have reached his time limit here on earth. So, as I said, he didn't die. He had already died. He just was not going to live any longer."

That caused some murmurs among the members. There were several conversations that started up at once until the Chairman again gaveled the room quiet.

"So, Mr. Reed," he began. "You're telling me we are not going to hear from Dr. Franklin, that he's permanently gone, and that this hearing no longer has a purpose?"

340

I thought for a minute, then replied. "I....don't think that's the case, Mr. Chairman."

"How do you mean?"

I picked up Ben's prepared statement and the binder with his proposals and all the information he had prepared to answer every question he could conceive of, and held it up. "We have already heard from Dr. Benjamin Franklin. He has left us this. You have a summary of what Dr. Franklin has proposed, and digital copies of the full document are in your packets as well, and the video of this testimony. Dr. Franklin was so insistent that this document be his and his only that he initialed each page and signed the document using a quill and ink, just as he had signed the Constitution. This binder contains all his proposals and his reasons for them, as well as insights from his conversations with the other Founders. This was his purpose here today – to present this document to the Committee," and I then placed the binder in front of me on the table.

"So, no chance for us to hear directly the opinions of Dr. Franklin, his reasons for arriving at these conclusions, and more importantly, to ask questions of one of our Founding Fathers?"

"If I'm correct, Mr. Chairman, then no. Not beyond what you've already heard from him."

Again the members began talking among themselves. I looked back at Kathy and got a shrug. The same from Miriam. At this point, I was not sure what to do next, until I heard a familiar voice with a distinctive Southern drawl from behind me at the far end of the committee table.

"So, Mister Reed. Who else can you get for us?"

– End --

Acknowledgments

Writing a book turned out to be much more involved than I had anticipated, but the process was much easier with the help of several individuals along the way. First, my daughters, Carly McGee and Lindsay Clifton, were immensely helpful in spotting the many errors in my first draft. Dianne Formsma provided much needed editing in the final draft. Their eagle eyes corrected many otherwise embarrassing errors. My wife, Amy, of course, was my primary sounding board during the process, which is why I dedicated the book to her. It was her idea in the first place! My good friends Ruth and Perry Malone provided feedback and encouragement along the way. Finally, Keith Carroll, with many years in the publishing business, provided valuable context, guidance, and suggestions.

To these people I am indebted, and without them this work would probably have been just an unfinished idea.

Made in the USA
Columbia, SC
05 August 2023

21314132R00207